RABBIS AND WIVES

RABBIS
AND
WIVES

CHAIM GRADE

TRANSLATED FROM THE YIDDISH BY

HAROLD RABINOWITZ AND INNA HECKER GRADE

VINTAGE BOOKS

A DIVISION OF RANDOM HOUSE

NEW YORK

First Vintage Books Edition, October 1983
English language translation Copyright © 1982 by Inna Hecker Grade
All rights reserved under International and Pan-American
Copyright Conventions. Published in the United States by
Random House, Inc., New York, and simultaneously in Canada
by Random House of Canada Limited, Toronto.
Originally published by Alfred A. Knopf, Inc. in 1982.

These stories were originally published in *Di Kloyz un di Gas:
Dertseylungn* with the support of the American Academy for
Jewish Research and the Lucius N. Littaner Foundation,
and printed by Schulsinger Brothers, Inc., New York.
Copyright © 1974 by Chaim Grade.

Library of Congress Cataloging in Publication Data
Grade, Chaim, 1910-
Rabbis and wives.
Contents: Rebbitzin—The courtyard—The oath.
1. Grade, Chaim, 1910-   —Translations, English.
I. Title.
PJ5129.G68A2 1983   839'.0933   83-5855
ISBN 0-394-71647-7

Manufactured in the United States of America

I wish to thank Harold Rabinowitz for his painstaking work on this translation, and Melvin Rosenthal and Ashbel Green, editors at Knopf, for their help and good counsel both before and after the sudden passing of my dearest husband, Chaim Grade.

Inna Hecker Grade

CONTENTS

THE
REBBETZIN

1

THE GRAIPEWO RAV and his wife had reached their later years. Their children were all married and lived in Horadna. The Rav, Rabbi Uri-Zvi HaCohen Koenigsberg, was a huge, fleshy man, tall and wide, with wavy sidelocks flowing into a snow-white beard and large, innocent light-blue eyes. Though widely respected as a scholar and preacher, Rabbi Koenigsberg had never sought a more prestigious pulpit. He remained in Graipewo, never arguing with his congregants or ruling them with an iron hand—and never flattering the wealthier of them either. It was his wish to avoid contention at all cost.

When litigants came before him for a ruling, he was so persistent in urging them to settle the dispute themselves that only rarely did he have to render a verdict. When the townspeople urged him to rebuke the young men who were straying from the right path, he would never publicly chastise the impudent youths in his sermons. Instead, he would come down where they congregated and talk to them behind the bima; he would even seek them out in the marketplace. And there was a great deal to reproach these young men for: much desecration of the Sabbath, and cavorting with girls by the river, and just plain recklessness. But the Rav would simply ask them: "How long is one young?"—and continue plaintively, "You're all going to be older someday. And you'll be ashamed all your life for what you are doing now. Is this proper for children of such nice homes as yours?" He would say this with such anguish and sincerity that even the most brazen youths would not dare to answer back.

With the same solemnity and care with which he chanted the morning prayers he conducted classes in Mishnah every morning after services. And so clear and simple were his explanations that even a child could understand. With that same patience did he eat, study, write out his Talmudic insights, and prepare his sermons. And when he grew tired, he would stroll down the path behind his house. Calmly, with his hands clasped behind him, he would walk, half murmuring, half chanting to himself a song of praise to God for such a beautiful day.

If he met anyone on the way, he would nod amiably without waiting to be greeted first, and then continue his brisk stroll to a pleasant, barely audible melody. But should a man approach him looking worried and say, "Rabbi, I'd like to ask your advice," his entire demeanor would express concern and he would hear out the man's problem right there on the road. He would then take the troubled man into his home and, in private, continue to listen until the man had finished pouring out his heart and could leave consoled.

Even the more contentious among his congregants respected and admired the Rav's humility. Once the president of the congregation re-marked: "The Rav, may he live and be well, is beloved and esteemed by all of us, and Graipewo would not think for a moment of his leaving. But we wonder, why is it that the Rav has never sought a larger congregation, as so many of his colleagues have done?"

"I have nothing against Graipewo," he answered. "Except perhaps this: When our children were small, my Rebbetzin and I worried about their education. But now that our children are grown and have, thank God, married well, we are only two people. So do we really need a larger house or a city with half-a-dozen synagogues? We can only sleep in one room at a time and pray in one synagogue."

This reply endeared the Rav to the townspeople even more. Even so, the Jews of Graipewo knew that he was concealing from them the persis-tent urging of his wife that he seek a new pulpit.

The Rebbetzin Perele was the exact opposite of her husband in appearance as well as character: a slight woman with narrow shoulders and thin arms, with sharp, searching eyes and a tall rabbinic forehead inherited from her father, the great sage Rabbi Osherel Broido, the Gaon of Staropol. Perele suffered from headaches, extreme nervousness, and indigestion, and was given to fits of moodiness. She had a medicine chest bursting with bottles, and spent days on end lying on the sofa with a wet cloth on her forehead. She would suck valerian-soaked sugar cubes and take teaspoon after teaspoon of her medicines. The women of the town always insisted that there was nothing wrong with her. "Why, she's as strong as a hard, bitter radish," they declared. "All these illnesses she imagines she has, come from her wretched personality." It was a common saying among the people of Graipewo that, as nice as the Rav was, that's how nasty was his Rebbetzin.

Not that Perele minded what the townspeople said about her. She never befriended any of them anyway: if you let the ignorant get too close, they'll jump all over you. And she would tell her husband that when he spent hours listening to someone's problems, that person looked upon the Rav as a tzaddik, a saint, while he was unburdening himself. But if that same man should see him lavishing such attention on someone else, that first ignoramus would think, "What a fool the Rav is!"

In her father's house back in Staropol, and later in her own home, Perele had heard many snatches of Talmudic lore, which she could cite with fluency and ease. Yet she did not attend services, except on an occasional Sabbath when the New Moon was blessed, or on a holiday. No one could have accused the Graipewo Rebbetzin of being too religious. But that didn't stop her from complaining to her husband because they didn't fear him as if he were a hetman with a mace.

No woman in town had as many dresses, coats, or fancy hats as Perele. But her clothes were all made in the old classic style; she even ordered that her new dresses be made in that old-fashioned way. And she had a saying for this, too: "The difference between a sacred book and one of your little secular books is that one reads an ordinary book and then throws it away, but a sacred book one kisses after reading and places it on the shelf to come back to again and again throughout one's life. It's exactly the same, if you'll forgive the comparison, with clothes. The old styles you can wear and wear, but today's styles you wear just today and throw out tomorrow."

Emissaries from distant yeshivas and itinerant maggidim who spent the Sabbath with the Rav could not praise the Rebbetzin enough. Although it is not altogether proper for a pious scholar to talk about another man's wife, these guests could not help but make an exception in this case, declaring to the men of Graipewo that their Rebbetzin was as keen as Bruriah, the wife of the Talmudic sage Rabbi Meir. When the men would go home and tell this to their wives, the women would sneer, "That show-off! She only wants to show that she's smarter than her husband and that she's the real boss in that house."

Even in the early days of their marriage the Rebbetzin had nagged her husband to seek a new position. Reb Uri-Zvi had an answer ready for her. "In the first place," he would say, "how can you be sure that another town will be any better than Graipewo? In the second place, it rarely happens that a rabbi assumes a new position without causing a storm of controversy. So what's the use of moving?" Fed up as Perele was with the

mud of Graipewo, she had had to admit that her husband was not entirely
wrong. But now that the children were married and living in Horadna, she
pestered him incessantly about moving there.

Reb Uri-Zvi would shrug. "There's already a Chief Rabbi in Horadna,
with a whole Rabbinical Court."

"So who says you have to be a Rav all your life? We could just move
there and live with the children."

This Reb Uri-Zvi did not want to hear, and Perele understood why
even better than her husband: as long as parents have their health and are
able to get along on their own, they should not live with their children. So
she would drop this kind of talk as suddenly as she had begun.

The Graipewo Rebbetzin was, however, quite well aware that it was
not just to be near the children that she wanted to move to Horadna. There
was another reason, a very secret one, and no one, thank God, not even
her husband, knew the secret; she was ashamed to admit it even to herself. But to this day she often thought of the Rav of Horadna, Rabbi
Moshe-Mordecai HaLevi Eisenstadt, to whom she had once been engaged
—and against whom she still measured her husband, Rabbi Koenigsberg.

Perele was the only child of the Staropol Rav, Rabbi Osherel
Broido, a small man with a wizened, parchment-like face and a thin,
wispy gray beard. He wore a short fur overcoat in summer and winter
alike, for he felt constantly cold. The Jews of Staropol were aware that
their Rav was considered a gaon, a giant among scholars. Prominent
rabbis, awesome men with great white beards—they looked like gigantic
snow-covered oaks—traveled from afar to Staropol just to spend a Sabbath with the Rav and discuss the Talmud with him.

Reb Osherel never talked about the goings-on in the town and never
interested himself in communal matters. "A rabbi," he would say, "must
sit and study. There is no lack of those who can attend to the affairs of the
community, but there is a lack of scholars." The people listened quietly,
but were very much annoyed by this attitude. They could only console
themselves with the recognition that their Rav was indeed a renowned
scholar and that he really did study Talmud day and night.

The Talmud and his daughter—these were Reb Osherel's only con-
solations after his wife passed away. He had his daughter tutored in Hebrew, Russian, and even German literature, although her teachers had to
come to the Rav's house so he could be sure that his daughter was not,
along with the secular subjects, being taught anything heretical. Though
short and unattractive, Perele, even as a child, was thought to be very
bright and very learned.

The groom chosen for her was the renowned young scholar Moshe-Mordecai Eisenstadt—the "Zhetler Prodigy," as he was called in his youth. The young man was to study with his father-in-law, the Gaon of Staropol, after the wedding, and in time assume the position of Rav of Staropol.

The groom was even a houseguest in the bride's home several times. Shortly before the wedding day, however, he unexpectedly returned the betrothal agreement and all the presents he had received. He also sent a letter in which he described the leaders of the community as telling him plainly that they would not accept him as the new Rav of Staropol merely because he was the present Rav's son-in-law: Reb Osherel was, after all, Reb Osherel. They had cherished him all these years, they had told him, but the new Rav would have to be a good speaker and a worldly person as well; and as far as rabbinic learning was concerned, it would be no calamity if he was not an earth-shaking genius. "I, however," wrote the young man, "do not know Russian or Polish, certainly not enough to talk to government officials. And I am even less inclined to public speaking, so that this arrangement would not seem to be entered into in good faith on either side." It was thus that the groom explained to the old Rav his withdrawal from the marriage. But to his own family he told the truth: He did not want to marry Perele because he felt she was a shrew.

Perele understood this. The young scholar had often told her, "You may be intelligent, but you're not good-natured." At first he had said this in jest, but afterward she understood that her fiancé's doubts about her were no laughing matter.

"Do you know why the Zhetler Prodigy doesn't want me?" she said to her father, her lips taut. "Staropol is too small a town for him . . . and I'm too small a bride for him. He wants a big city and a big bride. A big, fat cow—a benign fool—is what he wants. But there is no such thing as a good-natured fool. A fool is a spiritual cripple," she said with stern Talmudic resolve, "and a cripple cannot be good-natured."

This was the tirade she would sing in her father's ears. The old sage would listen with troubled, watery eyes and then bury his head once again in his sacred volumes, thinking that when it came to judging his daughter's character, the Zhetler Prodigy did not err.

2

PERELE WAS ENGAGED a second time, to a student from Keidany, Uri-Zvi Koenigsberg, a strong and handsome young man with bright eyes that shone from a clear face, and a tranquil manner. When she compared him to her first betrothed, she thought she really ought to be thankful that the first one had changed his mind—he, after all, was shorter and thinner, with a nose as long and as bent as a ram's horn, and he spoke with a cloying, nasal twang. His only striking features were the clever, laughing eyes that sparkled like the silver brocade on a prayer shawl. Upon first meeting Perele, the Zhetler Prodigy had apologized for his lisp, telling her that although Moses had been a stammerer, he nevertheless had conquered the world with his teachings. But the young man from Keidany, besides being a scholar, could speak beautifully. The bride, trembling in fear lest this splendid groom be snatched from her, hurried the wedding plans along. After living for a few years in the house of his father-in-law, immersed in study, Reb Uri-Zvi became the Rav of Graipewo—not wanting to force himself on Staropol merely because he was the Rav's son-in-law, he assumed this smaller pulpit. And so, Perele became the Rebbetzin of Graipewo, and the mother of a girl and two boys.

From time to time, news of her first betrothed would reach her: Rabbi Moshe-Mordecai Eisenstadt had married the Horadna Rav's daughter, and soon attained his own eminence. He was not awarded any appointments, neither did he pursue any high position; yet he became head of the Rabbinical Court of Horadna during his father-in-law's life-time. In time, word reached Perele that Reb Moshe-Mordecai was deemed the outstanding scholar of the day; his responsa were sought by Jewish communities all over the world. He was invited to become the Chief Rabbi of Bialystok, even of Lodz. But the Jews of Horadna were ever watchful against any attempt to rob them of their jewel. When the Graipewo Rebbetzin heard such reports, her throat became parched. She could remember how young Moshe-Mordecai of Zhetler stood and how he walked, as clearly as if he were still her betrothed. His every movement and gesture spoke of brilliance; in his every answer there flashed the unmistakable mark of genius.

The more the world praised the Horadna Rav, the greater were the failings Perele found in her husband. To begin with, he was a simpleton —in every dispute that was brought before him, both sides were right. He was never firm in his opinions, so naturally his congregants had no cause to fear him. His sermons were adequate for a small town, but he was afraid to speak publicly in the large cities or to aspire to a pulpit there. Yet what a man truly knows, she declared, he is not afraid to display anywhere.

In matters of learning, needless to say, her husband could not compare to her father, of blessed memory. Perele found fault even with her husband's appearance and mannerisms: A rabbi should not be so tall and husky. How many times had she not pleaded with him to comb down his sidelocks, yet they were always curled up like a goat's. When he drank tea, he sweated and panted noisily, blowing in and out through thick, pursed lips as if he had burned himself.

Still, it was really only when her ears rang with praises of the Horadna Rav that Perele was disposed to deprecate her husband. On any ordinary day Reb Uri-Zvi was a crown on her head. She basked in his kindly gaze and fretted about his health. And yet, if some time passed without word of the Horadna Rav, she felt an emptiness. This was not a matter she wished to discuss with her husband, and certainly not with the women of the town—women can have long memories, and she feared that they would recall how the Horadna Rav had once been her intended, but had rejected her. And Perele did not, in any case, care to waste her time with the town women. But when a rabbi was a guest in her home and her husband had not yet returned from the synagogue, she would remark casually, "We hear that the Horadna Rav is the outstanding rabbinical authority today. Tell me, is he really as great as they say? In what does his greatness lie?"

"A gaon!" the guest would declare ecstatically, stroking his beard for emphasis. "A Rabbi Moshe-Mordecai Eisenstadt appears only once in a generation."

"And worldly-wise, too—everyone says he's very worldly-wise," the Rebbetzin would add sadly, as she went back to the kitchen to get another glass of tea for her guest. Half the water in the kettle would already have boiled out, yet Perele stood lost in thought, staring blankly at the flame, a cold gleam in her wide eyes.

The Graipewo Rav's daughter, eldest of his three children, married into a merchant family of Horadna, which invited the rabbis of the town to the wedding—and foremost among them, Rabbi Moshe-Mordecai Eisenstadt. Even before she could see his face, Perele recognized his gait—those same brisk movements as of old. But when she saw his face, she could hardly believe her eyes: she was certain that Reb Moshe-

Mordecai was no more than fifty, yet he looked much older, with stooped shoulders and a great gray beard. After the ceremony the Graipewo Rebbetzin sat next to her daughter at the women's table and observed the Horadna Rav's friendliness toward her husband at the men's table.

Reb Moshe-Mordecai stayed for a short time and then rose to leave, and Perele watched as all the rabbis and important guests rose to accompany him to the door. He was evidently in a jocular and convivial mood, because those around him were smiling and laughing. And yet, although the Rav was to all appearances at ease and did not look in her direction, it seemed to Perele that her presence in that great, crowded wedding hall had made him uneasy and that that was why he was so quick to leave.

The Graipewo Rav's two sons, both yeshiva students at that time, later married into Horadna families as well, with their mother's eager encouragement. Of all the matches proposed for her sons, Perele approved only of the girls of Horadna. In the frequent and long arguments between husband and wife, the ordinarily patient and soft-spoken Reb Uri-Zvi lost his temper and shouted, "What is this infatuation you have with Horadna?" Perele would reply very calmly that if he had greater understanding, he would not be so perplexed. Since their daughter lived in Horadna, it was only logical that their sons should settle there. First, the children would not feel like strangers if all of them were living in the same city. Second, their parents would not have to travel to three different cities to visit them. Besides, the girls of Horadna were all of fine families. And since the sons had been trained since childhood to obey their mother, they each took a Horadna bride.

Perele had heard that Rabbi Moshe-Mordecai Eisenstadt's wife became pregnant a year after they were married and that she miscarried. She became very ill after that, and the doctors advised her not to have any children. But she did not listen to them, again became pregnant, and gave birth to a girl. Perele heard that the only daughter of the Horadna Rebbetzin had a weak heart and suffered from asthma. She was pale and fretful, and often cried for days at a time. Ashamed of her sickly, wan appearance, she did not attend the girls' school and had no friends. She was continually sipping something from a bottle through a glass straw to ease her breathing. Her father would take her for walks or to the doctors, and her mother constantly gave charity in her behalf. Whenever her mother met a pious Jew, she would ask him for a blessing for her one and only child. Sometimes when the Graipewo Rebbetzin heard all this, she would sigh deeply, first in sympathy and then with relief that her children were, thank God, healthy. After a while the young girl's health improved and it was reported that her parents were interested in arranging a marriage.

In winter Graipewo sank in a sea of snow that lapped onto the sealed double windows of the houses. The gray daylight and the early nightfall cast a lethargy over the town, a deep gloom. After these long nights the people of Graipewo would arise with cold aches in their bones, as if they had been sleeping all night in a swamp. The only bright and cheerful times of the week were Friday night, with the golden flames of Sabbath candles in the houses, and the Sabbath day in the beth midrash—the cantor's melodies in the morning services, the Rabbi's sermon in the afternoon after services, and the chanting of Psalms by the congregation in the dim twilight. But then, on the Friday before Hanukah, one man disturbed the serenity of the Sabbath.

He had spent the week in Horadna and returned to Graipewo in time for the Friday morning services. As he removed his hood and his snow-covered coat, he announced the tragic news that the Horadna Rav's daughter had suddenly died—there had not been time even to call a doctor. The man told how all Horadna had grieved at the funeral, looking pityingly on the broken and weeping father, and the mother standing beside him frozen as a stone. For an entire week the city had been shrouded in mourning and darkness, as if the sun had been eclipsed.

The men in the Graipewo synagogue that morning were stunned by this news. Although they murmured "Blessed is the Righteous Judge," they gazed questioningly at the Holy Ark all during the service. Why had such sorrow been meted out to the Gaon, Rabbi Moshe-Mordecai Eisenstadt? The worshippers hurried home afterward and told their wives of the tragedy; the women wrung their hands and carried the dark tidings into the marketplace. So that by the time Reb Uri-Zvi came home from the synagogue his wife knew everything.

Perele's face was painfully drawn and ashen pale, and her eyes betrayed secret, troubled thoughts. The tragedy that had befallen the Horadna Rav gave her more cause to shudder than any other woman in Graipewo. She had the eerie feeling that she and her children had been spared from her onetime fiancé's evil fate. Yet, at the same time, she seethed with anger to hear the women of the town say that this would indeed be a joyless Sabbath—they were talking as if the Rav of Horadna were also the Rav of Graipewo.

Reb Uri-Zvi, with characteristic sensitivity and delicacy, had always refrained from mentioning the Horadna Rav to his wife, not wishing to remind her of the embarrassment of her broken engagement. This time, however, he felt no need to be careful of her feelings. He sighed and moaned and wrung his hands: "Such a terrible edict from Heaven! Such a sorrow! The entire rabbinical world will be shaken!" Perele could not stand her husband's old-womanish hand-wringing, his foolish prattling about "the entire rabbinical world"—what, nothing less than the whole rabbinical world? The Rebbetzin felt a sharp pain in her chest and started coughing. She lay on the couch for a long time, her silent lips parched.

The Graipewo Rebbetzin was suffering deeply, partly out of pity for the Horadna Rav, partly from an anger that she herself did not understand. Still and all, there remained much for her to do, to prepare for the Sabbath. And so, rising painfully from the couch, she turned to her husband, who was reciting the Grace After Meals with his eyes closed, still groaning, and said: "Even so, after services tonight tell the men, and tell them to tell their wives, that mourning is not permitted on the Sabbath, especially since they are not relatives of Rabbi Moshe-Mordecai Eisenstadt and he isn't their Rav either."

Reb Uri-Zvi's eyes widened. Although his dear wife spoke in a dry and sober tone, she seemed to him as if possessed. And the Rebbetzin, notwithstanding her concern that others avoid gloom on the Sabbath, herself spent the entire day lying on the sofa, grim and sullen. That Saturday night, when Reb Uri-Zvi returned from the synagogue, she was still lying there, and spoke to him through the darkness. Rabbi Moshe-Mordecai Eisenstadt, she told him, had as a young man deluded himself, like every smart one who tries to be too smart. The girl he married had been sickly as a child, but this had not mattered to him. He had taken a sickly, cheerless bride because he was eager to become the Rav of Horadna.

"I feel very sorry for him," she said finally. Then, with great effort, she rose from the sofa, walked toward her husband, and stood motionless while he recited the Havdalah.

3

FOR THE REST OF THE WINTER, Perele relentlessly nagged her husband to move to Horadna. Reb Uri-Zvi interpreted this to mean that his wife had been terrified by the tragic death of the Horadna Rav's daughter, and that she now simply wanted to be near her own children. He tried to reassure her: "What are you worried about, silly one? Our children, thank

God, are strong and healthy. A Jew must believe in God's will. The Talmud says that a man cannot hurt a finger in this world if it is not decreed in Heaven."

Perele retorted that she had had her fill of Talmudic sayings. Had he forgotten, or was he just making believe he'd forgotten, that their daughter Serel was about to become a mother again? And while Serel was giving birth, who would be taking care of her twins? Their son-in-law was a busy man.

"So you'll go there for a while, then. And when there will be a brith or a party for a baby girl, then I'll come, too," the Rabbi said. He pleaded with her to let him study, prepare his sermons, and answer letters. But the Rebbetzin only mocked him sardonically: "How wonderful that you'll be able to come to our grandson's brith! And just who is going to help Serel when she has a nursing baby at her breast and the twins tugging at her apron?"

The Rebbetzin spoke calmly, with the dry, exact measure of a loud-ticking wall clock. The discussion did not prevent her from serving dinner, or interfere with her housework. But the Rav could not concentrate on his work and talk to her at the same time. When Perele had, for the time being, exhausted her concern for her daughter, she would start fretting about her sons. They, too, had children, thank God, and she was not being much of a grandmother to them—she saw her grandchildren once in a blue moon. She might have been proud of her sons had they not been so much like their father, a man with no ambition. Yankel-Dovid and Gedaliah did not care to be rabbis, and they weren't even good businessmen. They just took things as they came and never really accomplished anything—just like their father. Now, if she were living near her children, she could prod them not to fritter away their youth. Seeking to prove that her children had inherited their weak character from their father and not from herself, she never let him forget that he had not even tried to become the Rav of Staropol, where her father had been Rav all his life and where she had been born. His reply—that he did not want to start any arguments—was really no answer. Her father, may his soul rest in peace, used to say a rabbi should not look for a fight, but he shouldn't be afraid of one either.

"And I say," shouted the Rav, "a Torah scholar should run to the ends of the earth to avoid an argument!"

He felt as if his brains were glowing in the heat of his wife's incessant complaints, like a teakettle that is left on the fire until all the water has boiled away. But to any visitor whom the Rebbetzin greeted in the

foyer of the Rav's house she spoke about her husband with so much
respect and admiration that one would think she was his humble servant.
"You would like to see the Rav? Let me see if he isn't taking a nap."
Perele also made sure the visitor's business was important enough. She
didn't want to hear any details or confidences and she didn't care to get
involved in other people's problems, but one must understand that she
could not allow the Rav to be barraged with trivialities. He mustn't be de-
prived of his time for study or rest. After these preliminaries she would
usher the visitor into the inner chamber and promptly leave. Reb Uri-Zvi
would heave a sigh of relief at being free of his wife for a few moments.
He was so upset by the way she dealt with people that he found it difficult
to concentrate on his guest. Even old friends were made to feel as if they
were being granted a formal audience.

The Rav found a way around this predicament: He simply stayed in
the synagogue more than at home. Yet, his wife warned him, it is not fitting
for the Rav of a town to stay all day in the synagogue like an indigent
scholar who has no home to go to. He didn't want to hear any more
complaints? Very well, so be it. And Perele stopped talking to her husband, leaving all the housework undone. It seemed that she could arrange
to be sick whenever she pleased. Once again she suffered from headaches
and lay for days on the sofa with a wet compress on her forehead. She
washed down teaspoons of medicine with sweet, lukewarm tea as she
sighed and stared out the window.

Outside, even the days were darkened by the thick gray snow which
fell without end, whirling and rearranging every street, every porch, step,
and threshold. And whenever the snow abated briefly, Perele would watch
the lowering clouds and feel them closing in on her heart, nearly smother-
ing it. She broke into stubborn fits of dry, angry, rasping coughing. Then
she would resume taking spoonful after spoonful of concoctions and spend
the day in silence again. Her silence and coughing tormented her husband more than her nagging. So he approached the sofa and begged her:
If she was so lonely for the children and grandchildren, then let her go to
Horadna for a few weeks. He'd manage somehow without her. She listened quietly and then turned her head toward the window, as if to reproach him for wanting her to travel in a blizzard when it would be a sin
to send a dog out into the street.

Reb Uri-Zvi returned to his study and Perele looked after him as he
walked away with stooped shoulders, clad in a long knitted housecoat of
green wool and wearing a worn, tall black-velvet yarmulka atop unkempt
white hair. It hurt her to have to torment him so, but she couldn't forgive

him for getting stuck in Graipewo, in its dusty summers, its muddy autumns and the mountainous snows of its winters. He never attended rabbinical gatherings, and he wasn't even interested in seeing the children. Perele remembered that she had to prepare supper for her husband; he must be hungry, though he wasn't saying anything. So she went into the kitchen and warmed some porridge, boiled a kettle of tea, and cooked two eggs. Afterward she went to him in the study. His head was bowed over an open book, but he wasn't reading. "Go and wash and eat," he heard her say.

Reb Uri-Zvi lifted his pleading eyes. "Perele, I don't understand you. I often don't know if I should take you seriously. Tell me, why should we leave a place where we're earning a dignified livelihood and move somewhere where we'll have to rely on our children for support?"

The Rebbetzin smiled like one who patronizes someone speaking nonsense. "And living in Graipewo at the whim of the congregation is more honorable than being supported by one's own children?" And she again argued, this time lovingly, sufferingly, and with a quiet insistence. Instead of having a pulpit in a town no bigger than a fig, it would be more dignified to sit in the synagogue of Horadna and study for oneself. At least, then, people would say, "That man could have been the Rav of a large city!" Perele pointed to the long sheets of paper covered with an elaborately twisted script that lay in a large pile on the table. For years he had been working on his treatise, and it still wasn't finished. With no scholars in Graipewo to converse with, he often lost his enthusiasm for committing his insights and reflections to paper. In Horadna, though, there was no lack of scholars; there he'd have many with whom to discuss the intricacies of the Talmud and he'd be spurred on to complete his work and have it published.

"And as long as we're talking about this wonderful living we're supposed to be making here, tell your congregants that we can't manage on your salary anymore. The cost of everything has tripled and we're still getting the same forty-seven zlotys and fifty groschen a week."

At this, the Rav was elated: when he received a raise and his dear wife saw how he was valued by the town, she'd certainly stop nagging him to move. But when, after morning services, Rabbi Koenigsberg broached the subject of a raise with the president of the congregation, he was startled by the response: "The people feel quite to the contrary. They feel that since the Rav has successfully married off his children and now he and the Rebbetzin are but two people living alone, they should be getting less than they received when they were supporting a whole family. The town treasury doesn't even have enough funds to heat the synagogue all day. The teachers in the school are getting a third of what they need to live, and the orphans are walking around literally in rags and hungry."

Reb Uri-Zvi grasped anxiously at his silver beard, fearful, it seemed, lest it fall off.

"The rabbis of other towns no bigger than Graipewo are getting seventy-five or even a hundred zlotys a week. I get barely fifty. In American money that's less than ten dollars a week! And you're telling me that it's too much?"

To this the president replied, as cold and grim as the wintry day outside, that the shopkeepers of Graipewo were not making even thirty zlotys a week.

With a downcast heart and a chastened look the Rav related this conversation to his wife. To his amazement, she was not a bit perturbed. But the next day, while shopping, she was telling people that, God willing, they'd be leaving Graipewo after Passover. The Rav found out about this the following day in the synagogue when the president complained harshly: "For over twenty-five years, Rabbi, you have been our Rav. Suddenly you've decided to abandon us because you haven't gotten a raise? And you didn't even think it proper to inform the congregation of this—we had to find out from your wife in the marketplace!"

The anger Reb Uri-Zvi felt toward his wife he vented on the congregation. For all this time he had served as their Rav and never had he haggled with them about money. So if this one time he asked for a raise, was it right to answer that the shopkeepers made less? If that was the case, perhaps he really ought to consider leaving Graipewo.

At home, however, the Rav could not muster the strength to start an argument with his wife. "How could you do such a thing without telling me?" was all he could manage to say with a resigned sigh. But Perele answered him excitedly, fairly singing, as if she had become twenty years younger. "There was no doubt in my mind that they'd refuse to give you a raise. I just wanted you to see for yourself what kind of respect they have for your learning. They're ready to do anything for you—as long as it doesn't cost them an extra groschen."

A dispute over the question now festered in the community. One side argued that if the Rav had no sympathy for the townspeople's economic situation, then let him leave. The other side, the majority, felt that some settlement should be made. Finally the officers came to a decision, which they presented to the Rav one day in the synagogue. The community, they declared, simply couldn't afford to give him a raise, but they were willing to grant the Rebbetzin the sole right to sell yeast, and this would bring them a sizable additional income.

Rabbi Koenigsberg could not tell them that his wife would never agree to this. It was perfectly true, he knew, that in years past every small-town rebbetzin had sold yeast; but Perele's face blanched at the very idea, and for a minute she looked at her husband in trembling disbelief, as if he had asked her to remove her wig and shoes and go out prancing in the snow barefoot. Her next reaction was to laugh herself to tears. Why only yeast? Rebbetzins also used to sell candles, salt, and kerosene. But her mother, the Staropol Rebbetzin, had never sold yeast, and when her mother died and she, Perele, had been left alone with her father, she, too, had not sold yeast. So now, after decades of being a rebbetzin, was she to become a yeast merchant? She had always kept aloof from the women of the town; now they'd become her bosses: "Rebbetzin, you're not giving me full weight," she could hear one yente saying; "Rebbetzin, you're charging too much," from another yente.

"Now you see what their respect for your learning is worth, and here you've been a friend to everyone and served the town like a soldier. They couldn't even show you the courtesy of coming to talk to me here in the house. They threw me this bone through you."

The Rav became even more irritated. Perele's every word stung him like a thorn. He quickly secluded himself in the study. When he returned to the dining room, the Rebbetzin said not a word about the raise or about leaving. She knew that the words she had sown were warming themselves in her husband's mind under his snowy white hair and would in time yield the blossoms she wanted.

4

As the winter passed, the rift between the Rav and his congregation developed into a serious quarrel. To the congregants it seemed that the Rav harbored real hostility toward them, "and all because we wouldn't give him a few extra zlotys." To the Rav it seemed that the congregants were no longer interested in his sermons and were not even greeting him with a warm "Good Sabbath." "And all because I asked them for a little raise. If that's the case, then Perele is right!" So Reb Uri-Zvi told his wife to make preparations to move right after Passover.

The Rav and the congregation parted amicably, if somewhat stiffly. He had managed to put aside some money, and he owned the house in which he lived. The synagogue trustees assured him that the new Rav would have to buy the house and pay him in cash.

In his last moments in Graipewo, Reb Uri-Zvi felt a sharp pang in his heart at leaving the place where for twenty-five years he had lived in peace and with dignity. Nor did the couple find any joy upon their arrival in Horadna. Instead of welcoming them, the children reproached their mother for uprooting their father in his old age. Perele replied that when they had grandchildren of their own, they would understand a grandparent's longing to be near grandchildren. Besides, they had nothing to worry about: So far, their parents did not have to depend on them and were not going to live with them.

The two sons, Yankel-Dovid and Gedaliah, both the image of their father with their curly hair and thick, full faces, were like him in character as well: calm, gentle, none too talkative, they were men who valued their peace of mind. After their marriages, they had opened a shoe store together, glad to be living in Horadna, far from their mother's meddling. They were not at all pleased about her arrival in town, knowing as they did that she would once again try to run their lives as she had right up to their wedding days. They realized all too well that she was fed up with being the rebbetzin in a small town. Was she going to be satisfied, then, with being just her grandchildren's nanny? But the brothers did not discuss their feelings with anyone—not with their wives, not even with their sister.

The daughter, in contrast to the sons, had never listened to Perele, and when the Rebbetzin wanted anything of her, she had to appeal to her husband to remind Serel of the respect due a mother. Serel was the very image of her mother in appearance, perhaps a little taller and broader; but, unlike her mother, she had particularly sought to marry a man whom she could obey. Her husband had a pock-marked face, happy eyes, broad shoulders, and large hands. His name was Ezra Edelman, though *edelman* —"gentleman"—was not exactly the proper word for him. He owned a yard-goods store and conducted himself like a God-fearing, though not fanatically observant, Jew. By nature he was too lazy for subtleties, so that when his wife asked him, "Don't you realize what my mother's purpose is in moving to Horadna?" he answered, "What are you worried about?" He knew that, whatever it was his mother-in-law wanted, she'd get nowhere with him.

Rabbi Koenigsberg expected they would rent a two-room dwelling and planned to give his children those volumes of his library he would not be needing. "Meanwhile we're still alive," Perele said and she rented an apartment of five rooms. In addition to the old furniture she brought with them from Graipewo, she bought a new sofa, a cupboard, a long table with leaves for the dining room, a linen chest, and half a dozen chairs, and had new shelves built for all her husband's books. She had the faded wallpaper in the new home peeled off and hired painters to paint the walls dark blue and the ceilings white. When the house was painted and the furniture was arranged, Perele and a maid hired for the occasion washed the windows and hung the drapes and curtains. Reb Uri-Zvi beheld all this in glazed astonishment and said in a trembling voice, "Who ever heard of a rabbi who has given up his pulpit, and retired in his old age to have a little peace and quiet, who would ever imagine him moving into such a home?" His wife replied, "God is like a Father; He will provide." All his life, she said, he had urged everyone to have faith in God, yet he himself had no faith at all.

His wife even chose the synagogue in which he was to pray and study. Reb Uri-Zvi would have preferred to settle into a small wooden synagogue with a doorway so low he would have to duck his head to enter; with a bima right in front of the ark in a simple, homey atmosphere; with a large stove against the western wall to warm one's back against in winter; and with long, bare tables where the old men could pore over their texts beneath the pale glow of a kerosene lamp. But Perele chose a big stone synagogue with a high ceiling. The small-town Rav was always uncomfortably aware of the heavy bronze chandelier swaying over his head. Broad beams of sunlight streamed through the large windows, blinding anyone who tried to look outside. To ascend the bima or the ark, one had to climb stairs with wrought-iron handrails that made one think of a prison, God forbid. But since this was the synagogue his two sons attended, Perele insisted that he should pray and study there as well. On a holiday she could stand near the curtains of the women's section and peer out at her husband and sons standing in front of the ark with the other cohanim, blessing the congregation. "Grant me this joy," she implored, and Reb Uri-Zvi thought: "So be it, why should I deny her this modest request?"

The Jews of Horadna spoke with excitement about the Graipewo Rav—how he had resigned his pulpit to devote himself to study and prayer. The congregants of the Stone Synagogue were particularly pleased that a new scholar had come to their sanctuary to illumine them with his Torah and his piety.

The first trustee of the Stone Synagogue, David Ganz, a man whose head constantly bobbed, was also the synagogue's Torah reader. He was as thin as a needle, but his beard was thick, flowing in rings and curls, and his eyes were large, dark, and expressionless, as if he were frozen or had drowned. The second trustee, Meir-Michael Jaffe, loved to lead the congregation when the cantor did not officiate; his mouth was filled with gold teeth, and both his beard and his belly were smooth and round. On a holiday he wore a top hat and a dress coat.

The third trustee, by far the synagogue's biggest noisemaker, was Moshe Moskowitz, a short, sprightly man with a prickly white beard and warts on his nose. How he earned his living depended on the time of year. Before Passover he took orders for matzos, and before Sukkoth he sold citrons. In his home one could purchase a Hanukah lamp, a new prayer shawl, or a used set of Talmud. If a town was looking for a rabbi, or a rabbi was looking for a son-in-law, Moshe Moskowitz could be relied on to provide a worthy candidate. On the High Holy Days it was he who blew the shofar, and on Simchat Torah he was the one who called out the names of those chosen for the honor of carrying the Torah scrolls. And the rest of the year it was a firmly established tradition that he would recite the Havdalah at the close of the Sabbath day.

The former Graipewo Rav, Rabbi Uri-Zvi HaCohen Koenigsberg, had not yet managed to introduce himself properly to his fellow congregants when, on a bleak afternoon a week or so before Shavuoth, the three trustees surrounded him in the synagogue and addressed him in a manner at once friendly and respectful.

"We have decided, Rabbi, that this coming Shavuoth you must deliver a discourse on the giving of the Torah," announced Moshe Moskowitz.

"The congregation is looking forward to it. We can assure you that the synagogue will be packed from wall to wall. There will be no room to breathe," sang Meir-Michael Jaffe.

" 'Ho, everyone that thirsteth, come ye to the waters,' says the prophet, and water everywhere is the symbol of Torah. Our town longs to hear a good sermon at least once every Jubilee year, as a dry desert thirsts for water." This from the Torah reader David Ganz, as he fixed his melancholy eyes on the Rabbi.

Moshe Moskowitz, however, not being given to such florid sentiments, and much preferring a direct approach, interrupted his colleague: "Please understand that the rabbis of Horadna are fine rabbis. And the Rav, Rabbi Moshe-Mordecai HaLevi Eisenstadt, is a world-famous scholar. People come to him from every corner of the world. It's just that not one of our rabbis can deliver an inspiring sermon. So could we prevail upon you, Rabbi, to favor us in honor of the holiday that commemorates our receiving the Torah?"

When the Rebbetzin learned from her husband of this invitation, her cheeks blazed with a rosy cheerfulness—and with anger at her simpleton's reluctance. Of course he would deliver a sermon in the great Stone Synagogue, why shouldn't he? she sang out. The Rabbinical Court of Horadna should have had the decency to invite him to speak in the city's main synagogue just as he had honored visiting rabbis in Graipewo by inviting them to speak, even though as scholars they didn't come up to his ankles. Since no one at the Rabbinical Court had thought of it, all the more, then, were the trustees of the other synagogue to be commended for their invitation. Besides, it was an honor for the children. A fine thing it would be for the family if the Graipewo Rav were to settle in Horadna without so much as being noticed by the townspeople.

For Perele it was the fulfillment of her fondest dreams. During services on Shavuoth morning she peered through the curtains in front of the women's section at her husband and sons standing on the bima chanting the priestly blessing before the congregation. The other cohanim who stood there seemed to muffle their chants as if to allow the congregation better to hear the voices of the Graipewo Rav and his sons. And in the balcony the women showed the utmost respect for Perele. Nearest to her sat the wealthy elderly women, bedecked in broad-brimmed hats, some with ribbons, others with ostrich feathers. The middle-aged and less prominent women wore less elaborate hats and coats with deep pockets. The very young wives were wearing small hats with gay decorations and short veils. The richly attired matrons prayed from Redelsheimer mahzorim, prayer books with glossy covers of brown leather on which shone embossed gold lettering. The poorer women, with shawls covering their heads and necks, prayed from large mahzorim with simple dark-cloth covers, which had the Hebrew text on the top half of the page and the Yiddish translation on the bottom. But Perele, like a scholar, prayed from a delicate little siddur, printed in Jerusalem and bound in intricately carved wooden covers that depicted a palm tree hovering over Rachel's Tomb. Though she murmured the prayers steadily, her thoughtful whisper just barely audible, she was very much aware that all eyes were trained on her and on her attire.

Another woman in such an outfit might have provoked derisive smirks, but on Perele these old-fashioned clothes only enhanced her noble bearing. The women in the balcony could not help but think that this really was the way a rebbetzin should dress. Her dark-red dress had long, tight sleeves, a tightly drawn waist, and padding on the hips—a style that had long since seen its day. The sleeves barely revealed the tips of her fingers, and the skirt only the tips of her high-heeled shoes. Around her neck she wore a dark-gray fur collar, and on her wig was perched a hat no bigger than a little bird with fluttering wings. The wealthy women around her sparkled with strings of pearls, large rings, and heavy brooches. Yet somehow Perele appeared much more stately than they, even though she wore no jewelry except for simple gold earrings. Her cheeks were so smooth and free of wrinkles that to look at her one could not believe she was a grandmother. Her slight build and peculiar attire made her appear like a porcelain figurine or a carved figure that springs out of a wooden music box. But when Perele raised her huge, clear eyes and wrinkled her tall forehead, one felt that this little Rebbetzin was the embodiment of wisdom itself. There was about her an aura of noble breeding and gentle ways. Her pricked-up ears caught the whispers of the women around her. And who is to say they weren't talking just loud enough for her to hear?

"Her father was a great rabbi and her husband is a great rabbi. The Divine Spirit shines from his face. Her sons could have been rabbis, too, but they preferred being businessmen. And not only that—her husband even gave up his rabbinical position so he would not be dependent on people. Truly a blessed family."

"A difference of night and day, really, between her and the Horadna Rebbetzin. She shines like the sun, and the other is a pathetic, broken shard. On the other hand, you can understand her, a heartbroken mother who has lost her only child."

Perele understood that they meant the wife of Rabbi Moshe-Mordecai Eisenstadt. In the synagogue the services were over, and the women rushed to wish Perele "Good Yom Tov." "Tomorrow we say Yizkor, and after lunch, God willing, we expect to come to hear your husband. In fact, the whole town is looking forward to hearing him."

The Rebbetzin closed her prayer book, gently kissed it, and told the women that her husband, may he live and be well, didn't really want to deliver a sermon. That was why he had stayed in such a small town . . . and he'd even left there so he wouldn't have to speak so often before a large audience. Even so, she had managed to persuade him to favor the people of Horadna with a sermon just this once.

On the second day of Shavuoth the Rebbetzin once again stationed herself right behind the curtains of the women's section, surrounded by her entourage and surveying a packed synagogue listening to her husband's sermon. She could not see him, she could only hear his voice and see some of the men, including both her sons. Yankel-Dovid and Gedaliah stood leaning on their lecterns at the front of the synagogue, listening to their father and staring intently at their fingernails. Their mother knew that this had been their habit from their yeshiva days: the harder they thought or concentrated on the discourse, the more glazed and intent was their stare at their fingernails. But today they should have had enough sense to look directly at their father so that the others could see how they hung on his every word.

Rabbi Koenigsberg did not deliver an intricate legal discourse; he spoke about the weekly Torah portion and its Midrashic interpretation in a manner which all could understand: "When the Israelites departed from Egypt, they knew that fifty days later they would stand at the foot of Mount Sinai and accept the Torah, as it is written, 'When thou hast brought forth the people out of Egypt, *ta'avdun*—you shall serve—God upon this mountain.' The proper word for 'you shall serve' is *ta'avdu*; the addition of the letter *nun*, numerically equivalent to the number fifty, teaches that the period of fifty days from the Exodus from Egypt to the Revelation at Sinai was decreed by God. It is for this reason that the days between Passover and Shavuoth are counted. To what may it be compared? A king riding in his carriage passed by a ditch in which lay a prisoner. He told the man that upon his return trip he would rescue him from the ditch. So the prisoner began counting the days to the king's return."

He then told the story of Count Potocki of Vilna, who was burned at the stake on Shavuoth for converting to Judaism. "Because of this, the main synagogue of Vilna to this day says a special memorial prayer on the second day of Shavuoth for the martyr Abraham, the convert, son of Abraham the Patriarch. A poignant word comes to us from this righteous convert: Our sages tell us that at first the Almighty offered the Torah to other nations—to Edom and to Ishmael, to Ammon and to Moab. Not one of them, however, wanted to take upon themselves the yoke of the six hundred and thirteen precepts. Yet it stands to reason that there must have been a select few in each of these nations who did stand ready to accept the precepts of Torah. It is from their descendants that the converts to Judaism come in each generation. For this reason we read the

Book of Ruth on the day of the Revelation of Torah. The convert Ruth must have been a descendant of those children of Moab who wanted to receive the Torah."

The majority of the listeners, simple people, enjoyed the sermon immensely, if only because they understood it all. Perele, though, watched her sons. It was obvious from their stolid reaction that they were less than overwhelmed by their father's address. There were others, especially the more learned men, who sat twitching their beards and wrinkling their brows. They had been expecting, it seemed, deeper thoughts or perhaps a word on some complex Talmudic text. Perele bit her lip. Her husband, she was thinking, had become dried up and foolish in his old age. The sermon was for yentes.

Suddenly, from the rear of the synagogue a murmur could be heard that swept across the throng and grew into a commotion. The thickly occupied pews began to move. The people rose one after another like an onrushing wave. The crush of people in the aisles split to make a path for an old man with a white beard and stooped shoulders. Those closest to him bowed and quietly greeted him with great respect: "Good Yom Tov, Rabbi," to which he responded with a slight, friendly nod. He walked to the very front of the synagogue and remained standing next to the Koenigsberg brothers. Someone soon brought over a lectern for the Rabbi to lean on with his elbows. When Perele spied him from the balcony, she gasped to catch her breath: It was he, her first betrothed, Rabbi Moshe-Mordecai Eisenstadt. Her eyes widened and her heart shrank out of pity for him. She could see how gray he had become, gray as a dove, and hunched. His arm, like a tree's half-broken branch, hung down from the lectern. His daughter's death had dealt him a great blow. But Perele's pity for him turned quickly into anger. She saw that every gaze continued to be fixed on him. Even her own sons could not take their eyes off him, as if they were anxious lest he disapprove of their father's sermon. Perele felt her lips parch: Was it possible that the Horadna Rav had come to display his authority over the townspeople? Now she was looking daggers at him, and as for her husband, she nearly hissed at him: "Just look at him! He's so terrified he's practically lost his tongue."

As everyone knew, Rabbi Moshe-Mordecai Eisenstadt never delivered sermons and never came to listen to sermons. His sudden appearance at the synagogue was therefore nothing short of extraordinary, and even Rabbi Uri-Zvi Koenigsberg became flustered. After a moment he managed to recover his composure, and left his popular theme abruptly to discourse on a matter of Jewish law in honor of the esteemed guest: "We find a dispute in the Talmud about just when the Torah was given: Was it the sixth day of the month of Sivan or the seventh? The dispute revolves around the interpretation of the verse 'And you shall sanctify yourselves today and tomorrow,' and is relevant in practical Halachic matters pertaining to seminal discharges. . . ."

Perele could see that Rabbi Eisenstadt was listening with only half an ear. His wrinkled face had been consumed by his overwhelming grief. A matronly woman two heads taller than Perele leaned over and blurted out, "It's quite an honor, Rebbetzin, that our Rav has come to hear your husband. Since his only daughter died, God help us, he never goes out."

The woman had a square face that seemed to be made of kneaded clay. Wafting from her mouth came the essence of chopped liver and onions. Perele was nauseated by this tall, fat woman, but she managed to don a piteous face and sighed loudly, "Yes, yes, we heard about the sorrow, may every mother be spared."

She remembered how her father had talked about young Moshe-Mordecai Eisenstadt, her betrothed: "He is so great a genius that there is no way to keep pace with his brilliance." Now Perele looked at her two sons and tried to imagine what kind of children she and the Horadna Rav would have had if they had married. She could not see her husband standing in front of the ark, but she could surmise from his unsteady voice that he was not for a moment unmindful of having in his audience none other than Rabbi Moshe-Mordecai Eisenstadt. The Horadna Rav finally grew tired and sat down on the bench. Then Perele could see only a snatch of his silver beard and his aged profile with his eye closed.

When Rabbi Koenigsberg had begun, a blue sky had been shining in through the windows. A golden holiday glow had announced the first strains of summer. Now, the sky grew darker; the glow had fallen from the synagogue's high windows. A green light looked through the window-panes as if wondering why there were still so many people in the synagogue when the holiday was obviously over and the streets were already deserted. From everywhere the shadows crept out, wending their way through the crowd until they found a place to rest. But the speaker's voice found no place to hide; it hovered momentarily over everyone's head and then made its way out of the door.

5

THE CONGREGATION LEFT the synagogue very pleased after the Graipewo Rav's sermon. But this did not prevent his Rebbetzin from scolding him for speaking like an old woman or for having stood there dazed like a schoolboy when the Horadna Rav walked into the synagogue. Neither did Perele particularly care for her husband's habit of praising the Horadna Rav to the skies. "Let him praise you first," she would say, "and then you praise him." Reb Uri-Zvi couldn't understand what she wanted of him—the Horadna Rav had, after all, come to hear his sermon, which was most unusual for him. But, answered his wife, she was not at all certain whether Reb Moshe-Mordecai had really come to honor him or to show he was not afraid of competition. At this Reb Uri-Zvi could only shrug his shoulders in exasperation: A scholar as great as Rabbi Moshe-Mordecai Eisenstadt need have no fear of any competition.

"Is he so great a scholar?" she retorted mockingly. "Perhaps in comparison with you. But my father, may he rest in peace, was a greater scholar than he. And more famous, even though he was the Rav of a much smaller place than Horadna."

Perele insisted he prepare new sermons; the people wanted to hear more. Why not discourse on Talmudic topics from the book he'd been writing all these years? And he should be sure to include some profound thoughts for the more sophisticated, not the fairy tales about the Vilna Convert he had used in the first sermon. If he must tell stories for the common people, then at least let them be stories about the Maccabees from Josippon. She had read Josippon, and knew there were interesting stories in his works. "The Horadna Rav may be a greater scholar in your eyes, but a public speaker he is not."

Reb Uri-Zvi became incensed. "And what if I can speak? Is this why we came to Horadna? So I could become a maggid?" Perele answered this with silence. She lay down on the sofa and simmered quietly, just as she had always done in Graipewo.

Like many other things in their Horadna apartment, the sofa was brand-new, with a neat brown cover and firm springs. Gone was the soft, low sofa, frayed but comfortable, of their home in Graipewo. Their windows here did not look out on a sleepy town at which one could while away hours gazing, dreaming, thinking of the past. When Perele gazed out at the big-city scenes of Horadna, she saw three- and four-storied white houses that reflected the sun blindingly. The windows of the buildings across the way looked foreign and indifferent, covered with curtains and drapes so that neither the sun nor the neighbors could look in. On the balconies, hidden by flower pots and shrubbery, people moved about half-clad in slippers and housecoats.

People continually walked into and out of the stores on the ground floors of buildings, like ants at the entrance of an ant hill. Large wagons laden with goods were hauled over the cobblestones, drawn by teams of huge horses. There were carts and wheelbarrows pushed by workers, and horse-drawn buggies filled with passengers. Outside the window of the room with the sofa was a square park enclosed by a metal fence. From that height, the leafy trees had a silvery gray veneer and looked as if they had been powdered with dust. The summer had already set in with its dry, hot days, and when the wind picked up, a swirl of blackened, discarded newspaper pages rose from the park.

As she lay on the sofa, it seemed to the Graipewo Rebbetzin that her headaches were more agonizing than ever before. Here in Horadna, however, she could no longer lie about with a wet rag on her head taking spoonfuls of medicine without end, as she had in Graipewo. Their daughter, Serel, well into her ninth month of pregnancy, stormed into their home, shouting, "If you're sick, we'll call a doctor!"

Perele replied with restraint, lest their daughter suffer harsh punishment for the grave sin of disrespect toward her mother. She raised her head from the cushion and measured her words like drops of medicine. "Don't worry about me," she said. But at this Serel shrieked, "It's not you I'm worrying about. You're perfectly well. I'm worrying about my father; you're wearing him out!" Serel would never talk like this when her father was home. She knew how it pained him to see her in any way disrespectful to her mother.

After her daughter left, Perele lay motionless like a cut-down, withered tree. Could any wife be more devoted to her husband than she? She doted on him even more than on her children. She knew very well that a husband of straw is better than children of gold. He was the crown upon her head, the apple of her eye. She never forgot for an instant how her father, of blessed memory, had admired his son-in-law's clear-headed approach to study and his warm human qualities. But just because of her devotion to him she had suffered time and again from his lack of ambition and blindness to his own worth. "Some people are just like that," she thought, "they crawl into a corner at every opportunity." The Horadna Rav, by contrast, was not content to rely on the fact that the world

hung on his every word; wherever he went, he sat in front to make sure
he was seen. Her husband always joked that she liked being the center of
attention because she was so short. She managed to turn this around,
though, saying that because he was so tall and broad, he declined to sit in
his rightful place so as not to eclipse anyone else.

Serel gave birth to a son, her third. There wasn't even time to take
her to the hospital when she suddenly went into labor, so the doctor had
to rush to the house. She delivered with an angry, strident cry. Ezra
Edelman remembered all too well how during Serel's first delivery, when
she had given birth to the twins, he had stood outside the door of the
delivery room and torn at his thick shock of hair while the time seemed to
stretch into hours and his wife's cries became louder and more violent.
Ezra tore at his hair this time, too, but from joy; he practically burst out
laughing. "Finished already? All done, one, two, three? Thank God!"
And by the third day the mother felt perfectly fine. Only her face had a
faint yellowish hue, the same color as her long fingernails, and she shivered a bit.

Now she lay in bed while her husband and her mother stood beside
her talking about the forthcoming brith. They were discussing how many
guests to invite and which persons should receive the various honors.

"The sandak really ought to be the Horadna Rav, Rabbi Moshe-
Mordecai Eisenstadt," Perele said faintly, as though conversing with her
own thoughts.

"What do you mean?" Serel cried angrily, turning so violently as to
make herself grimace with pain. "The sandak will be my father, the
child's grandfather. As far as I'm concerned, my father is the greatest
rabbi there is."

"Your mother also believes your father is the greatest rabbi. Why
are you getting so excited?" Ezra calmed his wife, and then turned to
his mother-in-law. "Why the Horadna Rav? Since when is he part of our
family?"

The Graipewo Rebbetzin would have given her right arm to have
those words back—she, who would have fought tooth and nail against the
notion that anyone other than her husband, the father of their daughter
and the newborn's grandfather, should have the honor of holding the
child during the ceremony. Perele couldn't understand what had gotten
into her to make such a foolish suggestion. She mumbled something about
having really meant . . . well, she really hadn't meant anything at all. It
was just that, after all, the Horadna Rav was still in mourning for his only
daughter, yet he had come to hear Serel's father's sermon out of respect. It

seemed to her that they ought to repay him in some way—that was all she had meant.

"For coming to hear Father's sermon, Father will pay him back with a visit. He doesn't owe him anything else," Serel retorted, still angry; then she turned away and said nothing more. Her mother, she suspected, wanted to parade her children and grandchildren before her former betrothed. And yet, although the hot-tempered Serel was accustomed to speaking freely to her husband about all her arguments with her mother, she refrained from telling him of this particular suspicion, even after her mother left.

Whereas Perele was a quite fastidious housekeeper—not a thing left out of place or untidy—her daughter's home was always strewn about with clothing and linens. Serel never had a moment to herself—the twins were always tugging at her apron. So the beds remained unmade until late afternoon, the dishes were left unwashed, and the broom stood vigil in the middle of the room. Whenever she needed a dress or a hat, she had no idea in which closet to look. Perele could not stomach this disorder, but she was afraid to say anything to her daughter—she could only console herself with the thought that Serel's messiness, begun as just another way of aggravating her mother, had become second nature to her after her wedding.

Serel's husband, by contrast, was not in the least bothered by the disorder. Ezra, in fact, liked a home in constant commotion and with an open door to people coming and going all day. Naturally, then, he prepared for an expansive and tumultuous celebration of the brith, and invited a big crowd. Perele helped with the preparations, suffering in silence because such plain, ordinary food was being cooked: spleen, chicken giblets, stewed meat. Bowl after bowl was being filled with sauerkraut and pickled cucumber, and the platters overflowing with herring slices seemed endless. For whom were all these loaves of bread, all these bottles of whiskey, intended? Tables and benches were arranged haphazardly, with no sense of propriety. They were preparing for the brith of a rabbi's grandson as if it were a peasant's wedding in a village tavern.

On the morning of the brith, the guests crushed into every room of the house. People sat wherever they could, on chairs, benches, stools, even on the beds. The grandmother herself, the Graipewo Rebbetzin Perele, elaborately dressed, could barely squeeze into the room where her children were and where her husband, in his prayer shawl, sat in a deep chair, waiting for his grandchild to be placed on his lap. But the grandmother quickly pushed her way back out of the room; she couldn't stand the sweaty stench of the crowd. In the house of her father, the Staropol Rav, and even in her own house back in Graipewo, no such unruly rabble would ever have been allowed to enter.

Suddenly she heard an outburst of "Mazel tov! Mazel tov!" as the infant's father lumbered around the rooms with a bottle of whiskey in each hand, pouring into all the glasses stretched out toward him from every side. An army of hands grabbed every morsel of cold food from the plates on the tables, while others rushed to the kitchen for the hot food still in the pots. In the midst of all this, Perele stood stunned. Her son-in-law, drunk and sweating, stumbled toward her shouting boisterously, "Come on, Mother-in-law, give us a hand. My guests are also your guests. Here you're no rebbetzin and no princess."

The grandmother of rabbinical descent had enough sense to know when to answer and when to act as if she had heard nothing. Without meaning to, Perele turned her thoughts to the Horadna Rav: Thank God he had not been invited to be the sandak and would not see into what company the Staropol Rav's daughter had fallen, and what sort of treatment she received from her son-in-law. She looked over at her sheepish husband; to him everything was just fine, he was enjoying himself even among this riffraff.

Not until late afternoon, when the hordes of strangers attending the brith at last thinned out, was Perele noticed by the guests. With delicate and nimble fingers she arranged platters of food and carried them to the table in the large living room, around which sat the three trustees of the large stone synagogue, engrossed in conversation with her husband. Her two sons were also there, as silent as ever. Behind the two brothers stood her son-in-law, hands in his pockets, listening intently to the discussion.

Meir-Michael Jaffe, gold teeth flashing from his full, rounded beard, had already offered many toasts, and now raised yet another glass of whiskey. "LeChayim, Rabbi. It's settled, then. You will be the permanent Rabbi of our synagogue. You'll conduct a Gemara class every weekday evening and deliver a sermon every Sabbath and on holidays." David Ganz, the frozen-eyed Torah reader, chewed slowly on a dry kichel that crumbled onto his broad gray beard. Even more slowly did he chew on his words. "We'll pay you a salary every week or every month, whichever you prefer. Not that we're going to make a case of it," he joked. And the third trustee, the bantam Moshe Moskowitz, licking a piece of challah he had soaked in fish jelly, laughed: "And if you wanted to make a case of it, is there a rabbi to take it to? The Horadna Rav is busy with more earth-shaking affairs, he has no time for trivial local matters."

Rabbi Koenigsberg sat at the head of the table in a broad, tall velvet yarmulka and his Sabbath coat, a bit tired from talking all day with guests, his cheeks rosy and flushed from the many tots of whiskey he had downed in honor of his grandchild's brith. The lights in the room stung his eyes, and drops of perspiration welled from behind his ears, from his forehead, from under his beard. He wiped off the perspiration with a white towel and listened attentively to the trustees.

"The head of the Rabbinical Court, Rabbi Moshe-Mordecai Eisenstadt, and the other rabbis, won't they object?" he finally asked.

"Why should Reb Moshe-Mordecai and the other rabbis object to our having a rabbi and paying him out of our own pockets?" Meir-Michael Jaffe wondered aloud. And Moshe Moskowitz added quickly that, logically, the Horadna rabbis should be very pleased—as long as it wasn't at their expense, they ought to say, "Fine, the more Torah the better."

Reb Uri-Zvi looked questioningly at his two sons and his son-in-law, but all three maintained a conspiratorial silence, as if they had met together beforehand and agreed not to get involved. Reb Uri-Zvi was afraid to look at his wife; he was certain she would want him to accept. So he was stunned to hear her argue against the trustees.

"If my husband will not be able to finish his treatise, then what was the whole point of our leaving Graipewo?" The Rebbetzin fidgeted nervously with the lace collar of her blouse. "The world awaits my husband's work, and that's why we came here—so he could have time for study and for work."

Her son-in-law smiled at her knowingly. "My mother-in-law can really sell the goods," he thought. Her husband looked at her dumbfounded, and her sons stared down at the table, avoiding the mocking gaze of anyone who saw through their mother.

"Who's going to disturb the Rabbi in his research and prevent him from completing his work?" one trustee exclaimed. "No one is going to bother the Rabbi with communal matters as in Graipewo," added a second trustee. And the third sprang up in righteous indignation and waved his hands: How could the Rebbetzin compare a little nothing of a town like Graipewo to Horadna's big Stone Synagogue? More than one rabbi would give up his pulpit just to serve in one of the side rooms of the Stone Synagogue of Horadna. Besides, hadn't the Rabbi and Rebbetzin moved to Horadna to be near their children?

Reb Uri-Zvi listened to the conversation and calmly stroked his thick silver beard, as if to reassure it that conducting a Talmud class with the men and delivering sermons would definitely not delay the completion of his book. Perele could hardly contain her joy at her husband's ascension to the pulpit of a synagogue more prestigious than the entire town of Graipewo. "And that simpleton," she thought, "he's still worried whether the Horadna Rav is going to have any objections."

6

RABBI KOENIGSBERG BEGAN delivering his Sabbath sermons at a time of the year that was near to his heart—just after Tishah B'Av. " 'Comfort ye, comfort ye, my people, saith the Lord,' as the prophet declares," he chanted in the cantillation of the Haphtorah. "The great sage, the Malbim, interprets the prophet Isaiah as saying: 'Comfort ye! once, should the Lord hasten the Redemption before its time, and once again, should the Redemption not come until its appointed time.' " The most important members of the congregation—well-to-do shopkeepers, small manufacturers, and landlords—were all supporters of Mizrahi; this was not a synagogue in which the Agudah people had much of a say. Understandably, then, Rabbi Koenigsberg's sermon was very successful: He held that it was permissible to cooperate with Zionists who were not all that observant. And he enjoyed even greater success the next week, when once again he poured out in chant his thoughts on exile and redemption and the return to Zion.

"But Zion said, 'The Lord hath forsaken me, and my Lord hath forgotten me . . .' Zion weeps that not only has the Lord abandoned her, but He has also forgotten her!" This time even young people came to hear the Graipewo Rav, youths who would otherwise have been riding the steamer on the Sabbath up the Neman River to a soft, sandy shore where they could bathe or frolic with girls in the bushes or play cards. Yet while in town they would not smoke in the street on a Sabbath; after all, they came from good homes. So this one Saturday they gave in to their fathers and stayed to hear the new Rabbi, who, it was said, didn't preach down to them but talked of the Land of Israel. True, until half-past four they could only loiter around the town, dying of boredom. When the day was hot and all the stores were closed, the hours wore on like thick tar. Time itself seemed to have come to a dead stop. Even the sun appeared to have fallen asleep in the sky, unaware that yellow molten brass was pouring out of it. The drooping branches, fainting from the heat, looked like thirsty animals stretching their necks into the dried riverbed. So these well-bred young men stood in the empty streets, dreaming of the soft, deep green grassy meadows and the tall cornfields where one could lie down with a girl, and they thought, "One has to be an idiot to pass that up in order to hear an old preacher with a beard." But when they were seated in the crowded synagogue and listened to the Rabbi, they no longer regretted giving in to their fathers. The chant of the Rabbi awakened within them the memories of their schooldays, when they had studied the weekly portion of the Torah. A golden thread was drawn out of their childhood and entwined them with the silver-haired men sitting around them. The synagogue grew dark and the Rabbi's white head, high up on the pulpit, before the dark curtains of the ark, seemed like the moon drifting out from among the clouds.

On the third Sabbath after Tishah B'Av, Rabbi Koenigsberg again interpreted the prophetic reading according to the great sage, the Malbim: " 'O thou afflicted, tossed with tempest, and not comforted' . . . the poor, tempest-tossed daughter of Zion, expound the rabbis, is yet unconsoled. Though her children have returned, she has not yet been rebuilt."

The Rabbi's two sons, Yankel-Dovid and Gedaliah, came every Sabbath to hear these sermons, as a demonstration of respect for their father. But the truth was, they were a little embarrassed that he was not delivering learned Talmudic discourses on problems of Jewish law, as befitted a scholar of his stature; instead, he was speaking like a common preacher, a maggid. The synagogue's leading members, however, were not bothered by this at all. "If there be among the listeners a scholar who doubts the depth of the Graipewo Rav's erudition," they said, "let him take the trouble to come down to the synagogue any weekday evening and he'll hear the Rabbi deliver a profound and brilliant lecture on the Gemara. But when you speak to an audience, people must be able to understand. Now, the Chief Rabbi of Horadna is a great genius, but do we have anything to show for it? When he speaks, he mutters about some esoteric point intelligible only to a few select scholars, while the rest of us sit as wide-eyed and open-mouthed as a kapporoth chicken about to be slaughtered on the eve of Yom Kippur."

Toward the end of summer an early autumn wind shook the tree branches, rustling leaves that had been dried and curled by the intense summer heat. The clouds fled in silent panic one over another, but no rain fell. It did not take long for the winds to pick up, chasing away all the clouds, until nothing stood between heaven and earth except a deep empty sky that gradually filled with darkness. In the back rows of the synagogues sat the laborers with worried faces and, with them, thin shop-keepers with pointed beards, wearing long cloth coats. They wanted the Rabbi to speak still longer, to soothe their hearts with yet another word of consolation. The gloom in their eyes shone back at him like a silent mirror, reflecting a dark night sky.

After such a comforting sermon a new spirit infused the traditional recitation of Psalms before the Saturday evening service. A shadowy fig-ure on the bima sang out a verse and the crowded pews replied by repeat-ing the verse with a special sweetness and intensity. The words came from the depths, struggling against despair like the Patriarch Jacob, who wres-tled with the angel in the dark on the other side of the River Jabbok. The trees outside became a congregation unto themselves and recited the Psalms in their leafy, windswept tongue. The rustling of the leaves on the twisted branches drifted out to the shores of the Neman, where the wind-whipped waves and swaying treetops lamented together with the syna-gogue: "Lord be merciful unto us, and bless us; and cause His face to shine upon us, Selah."

Perele stopped going to hear her husband's sermons. She knew, however, that he was becoming very popular. The audience grew from week to week, although the other rabbis and some of the more learned men still hadn't come to hear him. And this was his own fault, she re-buked him. He should have paid each of the other rabbis a visit after he arrived in Horadna—then they would have attended. Reb Uri-Zvi replied that he was pleased the learned men didn't come: he would have to inject rabbinic material for them, but the trustees wanted him to talk as simply as possible about the Torah and Prophets and Midrash. The Rebbetzin laughed at her simpleton of a husband who had been a rabbi for three decades and still hadn't learned that when the people understand the entire sermon from beginning to end, they lose respect for the Rabbi. And when the common people saw that scholars didn't come to hear the Rabbi, he would be lowered in their eyes. The masses are asses.

"Have you already forgotten how your audience watched the Horadna Rav's every move to see if he was pleased with your sermon? And why haven't you paid the Chief Rabbi a visit, especially since he came to hear you?"

"I don't know," said a baffled Reb Uri-Zvi with disquietude in his large eyes. "You and Reb Moshe-Mordecai, after all, were once be-trothed. I feel I ought to keep my distance from him. And he seems to feel the same way. That's the way it's been between us all these years, except when we had no choice."

"So what does that have to do with you, that we were betrothed before I knew you?" Perele answered with even wider eyes, filled with amazement. "Things happen in life, so because of such a trifle you're not paying him a visit? What's more, he's in mourning for his daughter, so you certainly ought to go and pay your respects."

Reb Uri-Zvi had to admit that his dear wife was right again, and he promised her that on Saturday night, right after services, he would go directly from the synagogue to see the Chief Rabbi. Perele herself planned to invite the wives of the town's other rabbis to tea on Sabbath afternoon. During the week she went to each of the wives, and they all promised to come. They wanted to get to know the Rebbetzin who had talked her husband into retiring from the rabbinate.

On Sabbath afternoon, while Rabbi Koenigsberg delivered his sermon in the Stone Synagogue, analyzing the Haphtorah portion—"I, even I, am he that comforteth you"—the wives of the rabbinical judges of Horadna sat in his living room partaking of the delicacies Perele had prepared: a cake filled with cherries and lavishly sprinkled with powdered sugar and grated lemon peel; fluffy white meringues and dry sugar cookies. There were plates laden with fruit, and a large glass bowl of walnuts and filberts. The hostess took a kettle from the oven and filled the cups with clear, wine-colored tea.

The wife of the Wolkowysk Street Rabbi grasped two hard walnuts in her masculine hand and crushed them with one motion, as if with an iron nutcracker. A broad, stocky woman with a plain kerchief on her head, she had the steaming face of someone just emerging from the ritual baths. In her husky voice she shouted: "If only God would be so good to me, my husband could give up his post in Horadna. Better to be a woodchopper than like a public rag everyone uses to dry their hands when they leave the baths. If the rabbi declares the chicken not kosher, the housewife says he has a cruel heart; if he declares it kosher, the woman's husband suddenly becomes pious and doesn't trust the rabbi anymore. He tells everyone that the rabbi is putty in the hands of the women. And it hasn't happened yet that one side in a litigation doesn't become the rabbi's bitter enemy. If he doesn't talk enough to people, they say he's arrogant; and if he does talk to people, they say he's a gossip. They all watch him to see if he's wearing a new hat, and they watch his wife to make sure she isn't buying too good a piece of meat for Sabbath.

A rabbi has to be a confirmed pauper for his congregation not to begrudge him the rabbinate. I tell you, we all can be envious of the Graipewo Rebbetzin for having rid herself of all this."

"Please, don't call me the Graipewo Rebbetzin. I am not that anymore." Perele smiled sweetly as she moved the plates closer to her guests.

"My husband and I are not complaining about the Jews of Horadna," sang out the wife of the Schloss Street Rabbi. "They're all very fine Jews."

"Well, your husband is chummy with everyone and you carry on with every woman as if she were your dearest sister," burst out the husky Wolkowysk Street Rebbetzin as she cracked open another pair of nuts in her hands. "So naturally your husband has more income than just his salary. He's the permanent officiant at a hall that caters expensive weddings, and the businessmen all come to him to settle their arguments."

Bashka, the Schloss Street Rebbetzin, did indeed get along very well with people. She was by nature a gentle person with a happy disposition and not fanatically religious. Whole locks of chestnut hair winked attractively from under her hat. She had no qualms about wearing the latest styles: a white blouse with an embroidered neckline and a suit of black and gray stripes, with sharp, angular shoulders and neatly tailored lapels. She had placed her large black handbag and her long black gloves on the table. It was plain to anyone that she was very pleased with her appearance, as she constantly gazed approvingly at herself in a small hand mirror. When Bashka spoke, she cocked her head charmingly, like some innocent, slender, peaceful creature lapping water at a forest stream. One glance from her husband was enough for her wise and alert eyes to see all that was going on among the rabbis, but she never discussed anything except children, clothing, and food. So, instead of getting into an argument with the embittered Wolkowysk Street Rebbetzin, Bashka calmly chewed a small piece of cake and sipped tea. The hot tea had made the faintest beads of sweat appear on her radiant face.

"This cake melts in your mouth," she declared with the assurance of a connoisseur. "It has sugar, crushed almonds, cinnamon, and cloves—am I right, Graipewo Rebbetzin?"

"True, but please don't call me Graipewo Rebbetzin. I'm not the Graipewo Rebbetzin anymore." Perele smiled sweetly once again.

"Our Rav's wife, Sarah-Rivkah, also does not want to be called Rebbetzin," said the wife of the Old Marketplace Rabbi, nodding under a huge Sabbath headdress adorned in false pearls, with silver-plated beads that covered her ears. An elderly woman with a shriveled, wizened face, the Old Marketplace Rebbetzin had reached that stage in life when the head constantly shakes and the hands tremble. Not one of her teeth was left in her mouth. Yet, old and hunched as she was, she loved to dress up in brightly colored kerchiefs, layered one after another, and scarfs on top of scarves, shawls on top of shawls. Everything on her was pleated, a blend of colors, and, though faded and worn, her clothes gave her the exotic aura of ancient Oriental nobility.

"Since the Rebbetzin Sarah-Rivkah lost her only child, she completely shuns people," sighed Bashka goodheartedly.

"Please, I have nothing against the Horadna Rebbetzin. She has always been a kindly and outgoing woman, even if her husband is none other than Rabbi Moshe-Mordecai Eisenstadt," the burly Wolkowysk Street Rebbetzin said in as gentle a tone as she could manage. "Her husband, our town's Rav, is, after all, the Jewish Pope."

"What do you mean, the Jewish Pope?" Perele asked.

"Well, if you'll forgive the comparison, as great as the Pope is to the Gentiles so is our Rav to the Jews. People come to see him from all over the world."

Thick praise for the Horadna Rav oozed from the woman as if she were talking about an older brother. "Rabbi Moshe-Mordecai Eisenstadt receives questions from every corner of the globe and he answers each one of them, the great and small alike. The rabbis and the organizations in America who collect money for yeshivas and charities here in Europe send all of it to him to dole out. They say the great Chofetz Chaim of Radun doesn't make a move without consulting him. At the rabbinical conferences in Vilna and Warsaw, the Horadna Rav's word carries as much weight as that of all the other rabbis put together. Even the Hassidic Rabbis of Poland pay deference to him, though he's a Lithuanian and a Misnaged. And in spite of all this, his Rebbetzin, Sarah-Rivkah, is his queen. The house may be packed with rabbis and the most important Jews of the town, but he'll leave everyone the instant he hears his Rebbetzin call him to her room. Since the death of their only daughter, may God have mercy on us, Sarah-Rivkah has been acting quite strangely. She calls him just when he's overwhelmed with important business and keeps him for hours. But the Rabbi never loses patience with her. On the contrary, he talks to her understandingly until she has calmed herself. He has even stopped traveling to rabbinical gatherings, so as not to leave his wife alone."

"But he has no talent for delivering a sermon, and the people of Horadna are very displeased about this," Perele unthinkingly blurted out.

She would have given anything to call back these hastily uttered words, but the Wolkowysk Street Rebbetzin lost no time in pouncing on her, bellowing, "It's a sorry state we've come to when Rabbi Moshe-Mordecai Eisenstadt has to depend for his living on being able to please the Jews of Horadna. The whole world regards him as the greatest Talmudic scholar of our time. Rabbis come from everywhere to hear words of Torah from him. But the boors of Horadna would like him to stand in front of the ark and give them fairy tales, clever interpretations, and cute parables. Is there any justice in this world?" And the old woman from the Old Marketplace chimed in, her voice rasping through her toothless gums: "We have plenty of preachers, thank God, but the Horadna Rav is in a class by himself."

Bashka alone felt pity for the Graipewo Rebbetzin, whose face was changing colors. "Don't say that," Bashka said sharply to the other two women. "Speaking before people is a difficult skill. My husband also speaks sometimes to the people in his synagogue, but he's nowhere near as brilliant an orator as the Graipewo Rav. All of Horadna runs to the Stone Synagogue to hear him. They say he is a master of his craft."

The Graipewo Rebbetzin wanted to shout that her husband was also a brilliant scholar, not just a preacher. But she realized that there was no way to salvage any dignity here, so she kept still. Her suppressed anger brought on needle-like pains in her chest and spasms in her knee. Desperate not to reveal her suffering, she intently peered out the window and reckoned aloud: "Let's see, candle-lighting was five minutes to six, so when will we be able to make Havdalah and turn on the lights?" Pleased that the room was dark and no one could see her face, Perele bit her lip and heaved a heavy sigh to clear the choking feeling in her throat.

7

IT HAD BEEN the custom for the Horadna Rav's inner circle to visit him every Sabbath afternoon to discuss matters of Jewish learning and converse about affairs of the day. But for the first few weeks of Rabbi Eisenstadt's mourning for his only daughter these Sabbath get-togethers had ceased. His intimates came only for services in the morning and evening so that he would not have to go out to the synagogue. The young men in this group noticed how the Rav rushed through the prayers; he would be the first to finish the Silent Prayer, and would recite the mourner's Kaddish in a rapid murmur. The group would leave in silence. Not until the young men were outside did they voice their observation that, whereas the Rav had cried bitterly at his daughter's funeral while his wife stood frozen, now it was she who spent the entire day in the bedroom sobbing while he struggled to get back to his normal routine.

Eventually, the Rav asked them to resume their Sabbath afternoon visits. They came, but they noticed immediately that his scintillating observations on life and Torah were no more. He had become more hunched; his white beard was even whiter and had split into two pointy wisps. His mourning lay on his face, more in his silence than in his speech.

On a Saturday night in the middle of the Hebrew month of Elul, about mid-September, after the Havdalah ceremony, Rabbi Eisenstadt's house was filled with people. He sat in his court chamber at a desk piled high with books and, as usual, was engaged in several activities at once. From time to time he looked into an open book that lay at his left on the table and copied from it onto a large white sheet of paper—a responsum to an intricate rabbinical problem. At one side of the desk stood a short woman wrapped in a shawl, pouring out the details of her hard life since her husband, a poor dedicated scholar, had died; on the other side hovered a rabbi from a small town, a man with sparkling light-blue eyes and a red beard, who had been expounding a point in rabbinics until his discourse was brought to a halt by the plaintive tale of the poor widow. "Speak, speak, I hear every word." Reb Moshe-Mordecai smiled at the rabbi as he reached into a drawer and withdrew a blank piece of paper with his name printed at the top. In a neat, flowing script, the letters nestling and winding into each other, he wrote a few lines on the paper as straight as a ruler, addressed to the town's charity committee. He folded the letter and handed it to the widow. The small-town rabbi, pleased to be rid of this talkative woman, moved closer to Rabbi Eisenstadt and whispered to him of his eagerness to assume the Graipewo pulpit now that it had become vacant, and his hope that he would have in this the support of the head of the Horadna Rabbinical Court.

"I don't know if I should get involved and thereby spoil the chances of the other candidates," murmured Reb Moshe-Mordecai as he reached for the narrow red notebook in which he recorded the charity funds he had distributed each Friday. This did not perturb the red-bearded guest, who drew himself up and resumed delivery of his full-blown discourse, in hopes of demonstrating to the Rav that he was more worthy of the

Graipewo pulpit than other candidates. Engrossed in recording his disbursement of charity, Reb Moshe-Mordecai listened with only half an ear. Suddenly he interjected, in a casual nasal tone, an objection to the rabbi's reasoning which left the latter frozen, open-mouthed, his woven beard lying as still as a sculpture and his thumb suspended in mid-air.

At that moment a restaurant proprietor approached to request the Rav's endorsement of the kashruth of his establishment. He was a tall man with many rings on his fingers and a full face, with smooth red cheeks and a round, thick black goatee that flowed from under an upturned black mustache. The beard and mustache gave the impression of having been donned specifically for this occasion. The Rav darted a quick glance at the restaurateur and laughed a quiet laugh.

"Tell me, my good man, are the people who eat in your restaurant so pious that they will not eat there unless there is supervision of the kashruth?"

"Such pious people don't eat in my restaurant," the restaurateur answered loudly with a cheerful, boisterous laugh. "I had heard, Rabbi, that, besides being learned, you're also very sharp. Now I see they were right."

Seeing that he had no chance of getting his endorsement, the man promptly left. Right behind him came two trustees of the Talmud Torah, wearing small Polish caps with visors, wrinkled boots, and long coats. They blew smoke from rolled cigarettes into the air like chimneys, and spoke angrily: "Those bratty orphans are turning the place upside down and breaking the furniture. Everything, from the mattresses to the Bibles, is in tatters, and they themselves walk around in filthy rags. The townspeople aren't paying their weekly tax, and from the Kehillah allocations there's not enough for a bowl of kasha, and now the teachers are threatening to go out on strike if they don't get a raise, just like the teachers in the public schools. That's how they're talking!" The trustees shouted, and pointed to two teachers who had come as a delegation.

One teacher—with a broad snow-white beard and a thick mustache that completely netted his lips as if to conceal any desire to imbibe of the pleasures of this world—stood calm and unruffled. The second teacher was a thin, dark-eyed young man, beardless, intense, and still wearing the student's cap of a Polish university. Speaking with the melodious accent of Warsaw, he heatedly declared that he was under no obligation to starve. He was teaching in the Talmud Torah only because he was an observant Jew, but if he was not paid, he'd have to teach in a gymnasium school. The teacher with the dignified mustache suggested similarly that he could, if he wished, become a teacher in a fine religious school for higher-class children.

The trustees, in reply, accused them of acting like Bolsheviks: "We have to worry about orphans and care for them, but you don't?" The Rav, by this time totally exhausted, raised his hands and pleaded with both sides to stop arguing. A meeting of the Kehillah would have to be called, and he would be there as well. A solution would be found, they could be sure of that, but, please, let the teachers not interrupt the poor children's schooling.

In the next room sat the men of the Rav's inner circle. He had asked them to visit him in the afternoon and to remain after Sabbath ended at nightfall. But after Havdalah, when the townspeople besieged the Rav with problems, the disciples moved to another room.

Rabbi Eisenstadt's circle consisted of young men native to Horadna who had studied in yeshivas all over Lithuania, and were now being supported by their fathers-in-law. They were all favorite sons, with rosy cheeks, moist lips, soft, youthful beards, blond or black, piercing gazes, and quick, abrupt movements. Some had already started a business, others had entered the rabbinate, and still others had not yet decided whether to become businessmen or assume pulpits. For the time being, they were living with their parents or in-laws and busying themselves with Agudah politics. They looked upon Rabbi Eisenstadt, who was chairman of the Rabbinical Association of Poland, as their leader. Although he never came into open conflict with the Mizrahi, it was well known that he stood behind these fiery zealots of the Agudah.

Two young men, wearing their fine Sabbath frock coats with silken lapels, sat on a bench. Another lifted the bottom of his coat about his waist and perched on the edge of the table. Two others stood near the bookcase, engrossed in conversation as they leafed through Talmudic commentaries. And two others gazed out the window at a couple strolling by. The main topic of conversation was the Graipewo Rav; they were all seething over him.

"Since he's been speaking in the Stone Synagogue every Sabbath about returning to the Land of Israel, the Mizrahi have come into their own."

"We ought to talk to his sons, the Koenigsberg brothers. They may be only shoe merchants, but they are, after all, yeshiva graduates. Let *them* explain to their simpleton of a father that he's playing with fire."

"The sons weren't happy about his becoming a maggid in the first place. They say their mother, the Graipewo Rebbetzin, is behind all this.

She maneuvered him into becoming the maggid in a synagogue crawling with Mizrahi."

One of them opened the door to the court chamber and peered in to see if the visitors had left yet. He quickly closed the door and turned suddenly to the others with his finger on his lips. "Shh! Speak of the Devil, and he appears! The Graipewo Rav!" The young Agudahniks looked at one another, surprised and pleased: Divine Providence had guided him into their hands to be given the lesson of his life.

One by one, they entered the other room with careful, quiet steps and took their places along the wall behind the Horadna Rav's chair, like a king's retinue.

All the townspeople who had come to see Rabbi Eisenstadt had left. Seated now at the table were only himself and his guest. The reddish glow of the lamp cast shadows into the corners of the room as the two Rabbis talked in friendly, hushed voices. The Horadna Rav asked about the people of Graipewo and the Rav's salary there: several rabbis from smaller towns were interested in assuming the post, and had inquired about some details. Rabbi Koenigsberg answered guardedly that, though the salary was modest, the congregants of Graipewo were very fine people.

Since he had come to console the Horadna Rav, Reb Uri-Zvi now uttered a deep sigh and said he had heard even in Graipewo about the tragedy . . . Reb Moshe-Mordecai shuddered and hastily interrupted to ask his guest about his grandchildren—were they going to school yet? Reb Uri-Zvi replied about his grandchildren and then sighed again as he continued: He had left Graipewo in order to get the peace and quiet he needed for his study and writing; but now too much of his time had to be devoted to preparing sermons for the Stone Synagogue. But Reb Moshe-Mordecai did not want to hear about this either, so he made another inquiry, this time with a broad smile on his face: Hadn't he heard that the Graipewo Rav's daughter had made him a grandfather again? He owed him a "Mazel tov!"

"The Stone Synagogue had no right to install a maggid without the permission of the Horadna Court," a young man standing behind Rabbi Eisenstadt said sharply. "It seems the Graipewo Rav is unaware that the congregants of the Stone Synagogue are the ringleaders of the Mizrahi and that they're using his sermons about the Return to Zion to further their cause."

Reb Uri-Zvi looked up, his eyes filled with surprise and apprehension; till then, he had not even noticed the young men standing in the shadowy corners of the room.

Reb Moshe-Mordecai turned and spoke harshly to the angry young man: "The Graipewo Rav does well to be talking to Jews about returning to the Land of Israel. Is there, then, a God-fearing Jew who wouldn't like to see the Holy Land rebuilt?" He turned quickly back to his guest and, in a soft voice, excused his rash disciple: "When we were young, scholars never meddled in party politics. But these days the danger of heresy is much greater and the forces of doubt are much more cunning. The rabbis of the older generation often cannot recognize where this heresy lies, or its many guises. So the young scholars are forced to become embroiled in politics."

The young men looked knowingly and smiled at one another through the dimness: They understood very well that Rabbi Eisenstadt was in full agreement with them, and was simply phrasing it more politely.

Just then a maid came into the room and said to the Rav in a low, weary voice, "The Rebbetzin is crying again. She's calling you." Instantly a look of sadness passed over Reb Moshe-Mordecai's face; he rose abruptly and, muttering some words of apology to his guest—"I don't know how long I'll be gone. You're welcome to stay, if you care to wait"—he hurried from the room.

The moment Rabbi Eisenstadt left, the young men descended on Rabbi Koenigsberg. They shouted at him with such vehemence that he sat flustered, open-mouthed, unable to say a word, his eyes wide with astonishment at the way these youngsters were berating a rabbi many years their senior. Finally the scholar in him became enraged and he rose, his face aflame with indignation. He grabbed his overcoat from the hook near the door and went out into the street without a word.

At first he walked quickly, panting as if he were being chased. Then he stood still, wiping the sweat from under his collar, straining his face toward the heavens as if asking the Almighty what heresy he had been espousing in his sermons that he deserved such abuse? "A Mizrahi rabbi is as bad as a heretic!" one young man had screamed at him. Overhead a pale light seeped through the thick clouds as they flew across the sky. A sudden gust of wind blew his broad, flat hat off his head. He just managed to grab it by the brim with one hand as he held onto his yarmulka with the other. For an anxious moment he feared they would both blow away and he would have to walk through the streets of Horadna bareheaded. His ears still rang with a sarcastic remark by one of Reb Moshe-Mordecai's young followers: that he should thank God he hadn't another daughter to marry off—"a Mizrahi rabbi can't get a son-in-law in the yeshivas."

As if that weren't enough, when he arrived home he found his wife lying on the sofa with a damp cloth on her forehead. All the lights in the house were on, as if she had awakened from a bad dream and was afraid of the shadows. Strewn over the fine linen tablecloth were the nearly empty platters from the rebbetzins' tea. Perele's full afternoon of conversation with her guests had made her ill.

This one time, however, her husband was unmindful of her frayed nerves, and he let all his anger out on her: To shame and humiliate him, that was why she had taken him out of Graipewo and made him a maggid in Horadna. And to shame and humiliate him, that was why she had sent him to Rabbi Moshe-Mordecai Eisenstadt. He proceeded to give a full account of his visit to the Rav, in the course of which he remembered something else an Agudahnik had yelled at him: that he and his entire Stone Synagogue weren't worth an onion compared to the Chief Rabbi of Horadna, the Rav of all Jewry.

"Do you hear? An onion! That's what I am, compared to the Horadna Rav, and to them he is no less than the Rav of all Jewry. And not only that, one of his followers insulted me in front of him just before he was called away to his wife, and he didn't appear to me to be much disturbed by this, even if he did pretend to speak harshly to them."

"My guests today, the rebbetzins, also prattled on about how he is the Jewish Pope, how he is in a class by himself, while of maggidim there are plenty." Perele spoke very quietly and pointed weakly to a chair near the sofa, motioning him to sit down near her. "When I saw how angry you were when you came in, I thought it was because of something the Rav had said about me."

His heavy hands resting on his knees, a perplexed Reb Uri-Zvi sat down beside his wife. Why on earth should the Horadna Rav speak ill of her? Because they had once been engaged to be married? He hadn't seemed to remember at all that Perele had once been his betrothed. Reb Uri-Zvi went on to say that no matter what he had tried to talk about, the Rav had interrupted him abruptly and inquired about their grandchildren, as if it was beneath him to discuss serious matters with the former Graipewo Rav.

Perele looked at her husband with eyes that seemed made of molten glass as she dampened her dry lips with the tip of her tongue. She was lying on her back with her hands stiffly at her side, as if unable to move. "He's forgotten already that I was once to be his bride? Never mind, he'll remind himself yet!" she whispered to herself. She asked her husband why he hadn't taken their sons with him to the Rav. After all, Yankel-Dovid and Gedaliah had attended his sermon as usual that afternoon in the synagogue. He should have taken them along.

"And if I had taken them along, would they have made me more important in the Rav's eyes? Do you think his followers would have been afraid to insult me before my own sons? I don't know." He shrugged as he turned on his chair. "Today you're talking sheer nonsense. Did you hear what I said? To his followers I am a nothing; in their eyes he is nothing less than the Chief Rabbi of all the Jews in the world!"

Perele wanted to say that Yankel-Dovid and Gedaliah also had a higher regard for the Horadna Rav than for their own father, but instead she said in a choking, sickly voice, "The wives of the Horadna rabbis are right, and that gang of Reb Moshe-Mordecai's followers, that band of underlings, they're also right. A maggid in a synagogue is one thing and the Rav of a city is quite another. A maggid doesn't command the respect of a Rav." From now on, he would not be speaking in the Stone Synagogue. If he was so dear to the trustees as they claimed, then let them arrange, by hook or by crook, for him to become a member of the Horadna Rabbinical Court and be paid from the treasury like all the other rabbis. Only then would he deliver sermons in their synagogue. And if he wouldn't listen and continued to speak before becoming a rabbinical judge, then he might as well start preparing a eulogy for her.

Rabbi Koenigsberg had been about to make an angry retort when her talk of dying startled him. And in truth, he was quite pleased that Perele was so concerned to fight for his honor. The Horadna Rav might indeed be the Horadna Rav, but he, Reb Uri-Zvi, had also dedicated himself to the study of Torah for many years, and as a rabbi he was not allowed to demean his own standing as a scholar or to accept any diminution of the respect that was his due.

8

AFTER THE SUMMER DRYNESS, the wind had by early autumn already shaken many of the scorched leaves from the trees. Then came the rainy days, and the remaining clusters of leaves hung here and there, soaked and swollen. A cold, lazy mustiness stung the nostrils. Dampness seeped into the bones and stiffened the joints. Not until late in the fall did the weather suddenly clear and the last remaining leaves on the bared branches shine delicately with a transparent golden hue. The townspeople took off their galoshes and raincoats and left their umbrellas home. Faces were smiling once more at the cleansed blue sky as they basked in the fall's last rays of sunshine. But the pious and learned Jews of Horadna were not soothed by the healing wings of the sun; their beards and eyes were ablaze with dissension.

At the head of the table in his court chamber sat Rabbi Moshe-Mordecai Eisenstadt. On one side of the table sat the other judges of the Rabbinical Court, and opposite them sat the trustees of the Stone Synagogue. This session had already dragged on for quite a long time. There had been ample opportunity for both sides to argue in anger and then apologize several times. The rabbi from the Old Marketplace, a kindly old man with a small beard and spectacles, was forever warding off evil eyes and bestowing blessings on everyone; but now his anger caused him to sputter in a deep, rusty giggle: "Heh, heh, heh, just because some maggid from some small town can explain a simple verse of the Bible, does that mean we have to make him a judge on the Horadna Court?"

The Schloss Street Rabbi, a man with a soft beard and broad shoulders and wise, quick eyes, was known to be soft-hearted by nature, yet thoroughly adept in business matters and in dealing with people, as was his good-natured and fashionable wife, Bashka. But now he stroked his long, downy beard into two neat parts and nervously rocked to and fro in great agitation. "We mustn't belittle the Graipewo Rav by calling him just a small-town maggid. He is really a fine scholar and a decent human being. The question, however, is: How can we afford to share the meager salary of the Court with yet another judge?"

"Impossible!" shouted the Wolkowysk Street Rabbi, a fastidious man with a stooped back, a long gray beard, and thick black eyebrows like bundles of wire. "Even if the Graipewo Rav were as great as Rabbi Akiva Eiger and even if the court treasury were brimming with gold, we cannot permit ourselves to seat another judge just because the Stone Synagogue requests it. Tomorrow the trustees of every other synagogue will come to demand that we seat *their* rabbis on the Court. Impossible!"

"Even a rabbi of Horadna cannot bring his son or son-in-law onto the Court unless he is of equal stature in scholarship, and even then only with the consent of the entire Court," Rabbi Eisenstadt declared in support of the other judges, though he spoke calmly and softly.

But the committee of trustees was not to be silenced. Meir-Michael Jaffe, his gold teeth shining, was first to answer the judges: "But if the

Graipewo Rav were to denigrate the Mizrahi people and call them 'worse than Karaites,' instead of talking about building the Land of Israel, you wouldn't be arguing against him!"

"And how *are* the Mizrahi any better than Karaites?" retorted the Wolkowysk Rabbi in sharp, mocking tones. "Neither of them has any respect for the words of the rabbis."

David Ganz fixed his melancholy eyes on the judge. "Are we supposed to have respect for the rabbis? In our synagogue we have ordinary worshippers who are greater scholars than the judges on the Horadna Court!"

Moshe Moskowitz no longer cared to argue with the other judges; he addressed himself directly to the Rav: "Two of our members are on the Town Council, and they can arrange matters with the other councilmen at any time. So, if the Court will not seat the Graipewo Rav, then we'll have the council appoint him to the bench."

"Well, if that's the case, we have nothing further to discuss," an incensed Reb Moshe-Mordecai said curtly as he rose from his seat; he particularly disliked Moshe Moskowitz for his impudence. But Moshe Moskowitz, not the least bit fazed, answered, "Indeed, there is nothing more to discuss. If the Court is looking for an argument, so be it. Come, gentlemen!" he said to the others.

As they stood at the doorway, Moshe Moskowitz turned and said to the Rav, "None of this is our fault. The Chief Rabbi's supporters, they're the ones to blame—if they hadn't insulted the Graipewo Rav in this very house about his sermons, his Rebbetzin would not have forbidden him to preach in our synagogue and we would not have to defend his honor."

Instantly, Rabbi Eisenstadt saw to the bottom of the whole affair. Aha! So this was the work of the Staropol Rav's daughter! Not wanting the others to see the angry light of understanding that flashed in his eyes, he cast them down on his beard, murmuring to himself, "Yes, even as a young girl she was a shrew."

After the committee had left the court chamber, the long table, with the judges sitting all on one side and the other side empty, seemed like a man with only half a beard. The judges fidgeted in their places, like the rattling covers of pots of boiling water. "Such gall! Such hutzpah!" But Reb Moshe-Mordecai, addressing himself wearily to the white tips of his beard, observed that their enemies would now have something to use against them: The Horadna rabbinate refuses to allow anyone else to join them.

His colleagues looked at their Chief Rabbi in bewilderment. True,

he was a compassionate man, but he was also known as one who stood his
ground and would not budge unless there was no other way out. And the
Graipewo Rav did not, after all, have such a strong case for being seated
on the Horadna Court. "We have got to think this over carefully," repeated the Rav, and long after the others had left, he sat lost in thought.

Reb Moshe-Mordecai had always tried to be very friendly to the
Graipewo Rav's sons, thinking that the sedate and dignified young
Koenigsberg brothers must surely take after their father. And it just might
have been that their mother was not the shrew he had thought her to be
when, as a young man, he had broken off their engagement. Now he felt
certain that his first impressions of her were not at all mistaken. No doubt
about it, she was the one fanning the flames of this controversy. And yet,
he felt it would be unseemly of him to contend with the husband of his
former betrothed.

"Why did you allow them to argue so? And what harm is there in
having another rabbi on the Court?"

These words came from behind his chair, where Sarah-Rivkah stood.
She was ten years younger than her husband, not yet fifty. Her thin frame,
her gaunt, clear face, the pitch-black hair under her kerchief, and her
coal-black eyes made her appear even younger. But her long, bony chin
and the flat chest under her clothes robbed her of womanly appeal. Outside, the fall day was dry and warm, but Sarah-Rivkah shivered and
rubbed her arms as if she had just gotten out of a bed with frozen covers.

"The new Rabbi will not take your place or overshadow you in the
eyes of the Horadna Jews, nor in the eyes of the Jews who come to you
from elsewhere."

Reb Moshe-Mordecai could see in the smile in his wife's eyes that
she, too, felt it would be best for him to avoid any dispute with the
husband of the Staropol Rav's daughter.

"I'm not afraid, and I'm not at all worried that he will overshadow
me," he answered, opening and peering into one of the volumes that lay
on the table. He wanted to avoid discussing his old fiancée with his wife,
especially while they were both still in mourning for their only child. But
Sarah-Rivkah was not reluctant to discuss this openly: Since he had once
shamed the Staropol's daughter by calling off their engagement, he ought
to take special pains not to shame her again by refusing to allow her husband to sit on the Court.

"You talk as if everything depended upon me," Reb Moshe-
Mordecai said curtly, closing the volume and rising from the table. "In
seating another rabbi on the Court, the other judges have just as much of

a say as I. And they simply don't want him! They don't! If this happened in another town and I were asked to rule on the case, I would rule against the Graipewo Rav, and find him in the wrong to try and force his way onto the Court by creating a public outcry."

At that moment two young men, well dressed and reserved in manner, entered the Rav's house. Sarah-Rivkah watched as her husband went to greet them with great warmth, while his face betrayed a greater anxiety. "Sholem Aleychem! These are the Koenigsberg brothers," Rabbi Eisenstadt introduced the guests to his wife. "The sons of the Graipewo Rav, both married into Horadna families." Sarah-Rivkah understood by her husband's wink that he wanted her to leave. She looked at the young men first with surprise, then with curiosity and warmth, and finally with a confused stare . . . and then quietly left the chamber.

The Koenigsberg brothers politely answered the Rav's friendly queries about their families and business, but they could not muster the courage to tell him the reason for their visit. Rabbi Eisenstadt tried to help them: No doubt they had come to say that they had no part in their father's quarrel with the Horadna Court. Well, they could rest assured that he was aware of this. Elated that the Rav laid none of the blame on them, the younger brother said that he, as well as his brother and sister, did not feel that their father's leaving the Graipewo pulpit had been the best thing for him.

"Your father probably didn't want to bear the burden of a congregation any longer," the Rav said in an innocently probing tone. "Yes, our father no longer cared to remain in Graipewo," the older brother replied, heaving a long sigh. And at the same moment the thought flashed through Reb Moshe-Mordecai's mind: "More likely, their mother no longer cared to remain in such a small town."

Silence flooded the room. Bands of light played on the leather spines on the bookshelves. A large, buzzing fly was crashing rhythmically against a windowpane with heavy thuds. The two brothers shot glances at each other, each urging the other to speak—they shouldn't be wasting the Rav's time like this. Finally, the elder brother coughed, loudly cleared his throat, and asked if there wasn't something they could do to help end the controversy. This feigned innocence annoyed the Rav, who answered sharply that indeed there was a great deal they could do: they could prevail upon their father to drop his demand for that which was neither legally nor morally his due.

"It's not our father," replied the younger brother. "It's the trustees of the synagogue that are behind all this."

The Rav dismissed this argument with an impatient wave of his hand. He rose and walked to the window: "Don't tell that to me. You have learned Talmud, haven't you? 'It is not the mouse that is the thief, but the hole!'"

Again the brothers looked at each other. The Rav's standing at the window with his back toward them, they decided, meant the conversation was over and they must depart.

As they were leaving, Gedaliah, the younger brother, screwed up his courage and resolutely told the Rav that if his father was not seated on the Court, the dispute would get hotter. The Rav acknowledged with a nod that he had heard, and as soon as the two brothers left, he went into the bedroom excited and upset.

"First they tell me they have nothing to do with this," he said to his wife, who was sitting on the edge of the bed, "and then they threaten that if their father isn't made a member of the Court, the dispute will get worse."

Sarah-Rivkah had quickly hidden their daughter's photograph under the pillow when she heard her husband's approaching footsteps—she did not want him to be aggrieved over her inability to let go of their little Blumele's picture. When Reb Moshe-Mordecai entered the room, Sarah-Rivkah was sitting stiffly, staring at a large portrait photograph of her mother on the wall. A heavy wig framed her long face and sharp-angled jaw; a pained, taut smile played on her lips. Sarah-Rivkah remembered that her father had never wanted to be photographed—"idolized," he would call it. "What am I, a sacred inscription, the name of the Almighty engraved on the cover of the ark, that the living have to look at me?" He hadn't wanted to leave any remembrance of himself for the children. That was why, Sarah-Rivkah thought, her mother's smile had been so pained when she had had her picture taken without her husband.

Engrossed in his own thoughts, Reb Moshe-Mordecai at last declared loudly that the Graipewo Rav's sons were, at least, not nearly so brazen as the trustees of the Stone Synagogue. The brothers had stammered and stuttered a long time before they could come out with what their father had forced upon them as obedient sons. "And how do you know it was their father who forced them?" Sarah-Rivkah said, her dim eyes suddenly coming to life. "Perhaps they were pushed into this by their mother. The Graipewo Rebbetzin imagines that you will soften when you see her sons."

Her husband looked at her quizzically for a moment and then remembered the passage in the Talmud: "A wife knows her guests better than her husband." With his hands clasped behind him, he turned abruptly and walked about the bedroom muttering to himself that it really didn't matter to him who had sent them. The Graipewo Rav was a new-comer to Horadna, he had no standing here and no basis for any claim.

Sarah-Rivkah again gazed on her mother's elaborately formal por-trait and said, as if she were reading the answer from it, "The Graipewo Rav has every right. His children live in Horadna and a Horadna syna-gogue wants him as a rabbi." She then turned from her mother's portrait and smiled at her husband. "And, besides, you mustn't stand in the way. Don't let people say that you're jealous of him because his wife was once your bride-to-be and you are still upset that the engagement was broken."

Reb Moshe-Mordecai, alarmed and angry, shouted at her, "What nonsense!"

Sarah-Rivkah laughed anxiously, but her face became even paler and her long, bony chin quivered. "I'm not saying you really feel that way; only that the townspeople will say that." She was silent a moment and then laughed even more sadly. "Really, Moshe-Mordecai, why didn't you marry the Staropol Rav's daughter? I think you would have fared much better with her. You would have had beautiful children with her, just like her two handsome sons. I understand she has a daughter, too, and from all her children she has grandchildren! Maybe God has pun-ished us because you shamed her as a young girl." Large, cold tears ran from Sarah-Rivkah's eyes.

Reb Moshe-Mordecai's anger left him. He lovingly stroked her head, and in a trembling voice he pleaded with her not to cry. Why should they be punished because of the Staropol Rav's daughter? She hadn't been shamed, after all, or left an old maid. She had a husband and children and grandchildren.

Sarah-Rivkah clung to her husband, breathing heavily into his warm beard. "You mustn't stand in the way of the Graipewo Rav's becoming a judge here," and her husband promised her he would not oppose it. But how was he going to get the other rabbis to agree?

9

The Horadna Rebbetzin, Sarah-Rivkah, was named after her great-great-grandmother, the mother of the sage Rabbi Alexander Ziskind, author of *The Foundations and Principles of Prayer*. In it he examined the holy thoughts that must flow through one's mind during prayer, and how one must reach the point where at any moment one is prepared to lay down his life in the name of God. When Rabbi Ziskind passed away, he left two testaments to his children which came to be called the major and minor testaments, and a separate set of instructions for the burial society. He directed those who prepared his body for burial to place a stone on his heart, then to throw his body onto the earth from a high place, then to singe his beard with a candle's flame, and then to place a blade at his throat—symbolically administering to his corpse the four kinds of capital punishment that could be meted out by a Jewish court, as outlined in the Talmud. If he had ever sinned in his thoughts at any time while in this world, he hoped this would expiate his transgressions before he came to be judged before the Heavenly Court. In addition, he instructed that two monuments be placed on his grave, one at the head and the other at the foot, both inscribed on the inner side so that the inscriptions would be facing each other. And these inscriptions, he warned, should not extol his righteousness, but simply say that he was the son of Reb Moshe, born of the woman Rivkah, and that he was a servant of God.

This servant of God and holy man of the two monuments had never wanted to become the Rav of Horadna, and he told his children that both they and their children should avoid high clerical office. In time this proved impossible, however, and before long these admonitions against high office were interpreted by his descendants as not including the rabbinate. His son, Aryeh, and his grandsons were already members of the Rabbinical Court of Horadna, and the position passed on to Alexander Ziskind's great-grandson Reb Yitzhak-Isaac, son of Reb Shmuel Sender. With the passing generations, the family married into the most eminent rabbinical families of Lithuanian Jewry and even wove their way into the Hassidic dynasties of Wolyn and Karlin. Only Sarah-Rivkah's mother, the old Horadna Rebbetzin, had come from humble beginnings. Her father, a wealthy village merchant, had married off his daughter to the great-grandson of the venerated author of *The Foundations and Principles of Prayer* by offering a huge dowry.

For as long as Sarah-Rivkah could remember, her father's house had always bustled with her rabbinical uncles, who traveled to Horadna to buy books or to have their own books published, or with her rebbetzin aunts, who came to see doctors or to have new clothes made by the big-city dressmakers. Her father often traveled to attend the funerals of relatives who had been rabbis or famous scholars, and Sarah-Rivkah and her mother went with her father to weddings. The Rav of Suprasl might be marrying off a son. Another time the Rav of Tykocin, a distant cousin through Reb Shmuel Sender, married off a daughter. At each wedding the bride and groom were cousins on both their fathers' and their mothers' sides.

Blumele, the old Horadna Rebbetzin of humble origins, now trapped within this aristocratic rabbinical family, complained to her daughter, Sarah-Rivkah: "For heaven's sake, why can't one find in your father's family at least one ordinary Jew, a common laborer or shopkeeper? They're all rabbis and rabbis, like a dynasty of kings. So where are the plain soldiers, the simple, honest Jews? Being always surrounded by such aristocrats, one can become very conceited."

The old Rebbetzin was not alone—even her husband, Reb Yitzhak-Isaac, harbored a grievance against his father and grandfather for having made their livelihoods as rabbis and for preparing him only for the rabbinate. "Our Patriarchs, Abraham, Isaac, and Jacob, were shepherds, and our own great-grandfather, the saintly Rabbi Alexander Ziskind, wouldn't hear of becoming the head of the Rabbinical Court. Why was it decreed that I should have to deal with an entire city of congregants when all I really wanted was to be a carpenter, just a simple carpenter?" he sufferingly lamented to his wife and daughter. When he said this, he looked like a child, a schoolboy whining that he just can't manage to carry a huge log on his weak shoulders. Reb Yitzhak-Isaac was a small man with thick sidelocks and clean, smooth cheeks where no beard grew. Only on his chin did a small, stark beard barely hang. He had kind, tearful eyes and a pair of delicately pious hands fit for leafing through books, for writing complex responsa, or for feeling the gizzard of a chicken in which a housewife had found a splinter, to determine if it was still kosher.

"But, Father, how could you have lifted those heavy boards, or driven nails with a heavy hammer, or carried a heavy chest on your shoulders?" Sarah-Rivkah laughed, as her mother, Blumele, the old Horadna Rebbetzin with her high cheekbones, smiled sadly.

"And why couldn't I? I certainly could," Reb Yitzhak-Isaac said, vexatiously tugging at his narrow gray beard. He told his wife and daughter of the men of the Talmud who were cobblers and blacksmiths, and about Reb Mordcale of Pokrow, who was a Rav as well as a carpenter. "Now, there was an extraordinary man, that Reb Mordcale! He was the greatest saint of all the countless humble saints in Zamut. He lived during the time of the Vilna Gaon, who delighted in him. Reb Mordcale surely lived by the words of the sages: 'Love work and eschew the pulpit.' And what about our own Rabbi Akiva Eiger? The whole world lives off his brilliance, yet here he is, the Poznan Rav, asking one of his students in a small town if there is perhaps an opening there for a sexton in a small synagogue. So why couldn't I be a worker?" Yitzhak-Isaac asked his wife and daughter. These words never left the innermost chambers of the Rav's house; no carpenter in Horadna could have imagined that he was the object of the Rav's envy. To all appearances, Reb Yitzhak-Isaac was quite satisfied with his lot, and his family realized full well that outsiders must not know anything about the Rav's dreams.

The sprawling family of the venerable Horadna Sage, the author of *The Principles*, had become a dense primordial forest. With the passage of generations and the inevitable bolts of lightning, the great oaks are broken, the tall pines are twisted, and pieces of bark lie beside the smoothed trunks that look like forlorn, ragged, old people. Instead of fresh green grass, a silvery moss spreads out and blankets the dried creeping vines. At the same time, at the forest's edge the fresh saplings of nut trees, alders, and birches are already rustling. Their bark sparkles with a dark silver luster as they whisper confidences to the centuries-old trees, their stately ancestors in the impenetrable thicket. Yet even the sun never reaches the inner sanctum of this wood. A tranquillity reigns there, a hush and a darkness even at noonday. So did the family of Rabbi Alexander Ziskind grow and proliferate while the main trunk, his children and grandchildren, shriveled. Sarah-Rivkah was an only daughter of Reb Yitzhak-Isaac, just as he was the only son of Reb Shmuel Sender. Sarah-Rivkah grew up pale and sickly, as if she were paying the price for her saintly great-grandfather's fasting and asceticism. An anemic girl, this Rabbi's daughter was fatigued by her formidable ancestry, which burdened her like a train of night shadows. In her quiet smile one saw the last faint glimmer of a faded, ancient tapestry. Just as her father complained to her that he should have become a carpenter, her mother constantly grumbled to her as well.

"At my wedding I dreamed of having a half-dozen healthy, bouncing children like my country brothers and sisters, and like myself as a young girl. Even your father hoped you would take after my family instead of his. But your great-grandfather, the Tzaddik of the two monuments, looked down from the heavens and decreed that you should look like one of his own, who consider even laughing out loud a transgression."

Nevertheless, the old Rebbetzin, Blumele, agreed with her husband that their only daughter must marry a great Torah scholar. And Sarah-Rivkah's groom was indeed a flaming genius, descended from generations of brilliant scholars who turned the pages of the Talmud as easily as the wind turns the leaves in the forest. The rabbis of the Eisenstadt family had steadily ascended to higher and higher positions, like the High Priest who would use progressively bigger vessels during the Temple Service on the Day of Atonement. A Hassid could no more be found among them than could a piece of leavened bread in their homes during Passover. Plain, pious Jews and all sorts of miracle-workers they would dismiss with a wave of the hand, and they looked down upon preachers for the common people. They would rush through prayers, the sooner to sit down and study. The Eisenstadts knew nothing of retreat or compromise. When they issued a decree or even just expressed an opinion, everyone had to bow down to their wishes.

"Your Moshe-Mordecai will conduct the Horadna rabbinate with an iron hand," Reb Yitzhak-Isaac said prophetically to his daughter. "He has inherited from his fathers the strength and the authority to govern a city, a state, even the whole world. Anyway, you won't find him wasting away with a yearning to become a carpenter."

Reb Moshe-Mordecai Eisenstadt was in fact a gentle person, and one could have even called him witty. "It's because your husband is very bright, and because the times are different, that he knows how to conceal the arrogance for which his family is famous," Reb Yitzhak-Isaac told his daughter.

While yet a young wife Sarah-Rivkah asked her husband why he had broken off his engagement with the Staropol Rav's daughter. "Was it because you wanted a lamb for a wife?" she would ask teasingly. "You're cleverer than she," he answered, adding that in his family the women were women, not men. A Rav's wife has to know how to get along with people and be friendly to guests and not mix in communal matters. But the Staropol Rav's daughter would have been the kind who hides under the Rav's prayer shawl and prompts his every move. In the end, the people lose all respect for such a Rav and call him "our worthy Rebbetzin's husband."

Reb Yitzhak-Isaac had lived to see Sarah-Rivkah's first miscarriage before joining his sainted ancestors. Her mother suffered through a few years more with her daughter yearning for a child in the face of the doctor's warning that another pregnancy would be dangerous. When Sarah-Rivkah at last gave birth to a baby girl, they named her Blumele after the old Rebbetzin, who had died just before the baby was born, as if Heaven had called her away in order to spare her the grief of seeing how sickly was her only grandchild.

Throughout all her seventeen years of life, Blumele was almost always either crying or suddenly screaming because of her asthma, until even her father was utterly broken. In his own mind, Reb Moshe-Mordecai made peace with his lot, resigning himself to a life very different from that of his ancestors. True, he had become the outstanding scholar of his day, famous the world over, but he seemed to merit no personal joy or peace from the Almighty.

As for Sarah-Rivkah, her unending anxiety over her daughter utterly exhausted her; and she would constantly plead with her husband to be lenient in his decisions, even when the very authority of the Torah was being challenged. Even after their daughter had been torn away from them, she would beg him to give way to his opponents, as in the case of the Graipewo Rav. At long last, she succeeded in extracting from Moshe-Mordecai a promise that not only would he not object, but would do his utmost to persuade the other rabbis to accept the Graipewo Rav on the Horadna Rabbinical Court.

10

THE RAINS FELL steadily until late in the fall, and then the ground became icy with the first frosts. In his rabbinic winter attire, a long fur coat and a tall fur hat, Rabbi Koenigsberg presented a splendid and stately appearance, radiating dignity and confidence over the town.

It was only in the chambers of the Rabbinical Court that he sat on pins and needles. There his colleagues either suffocated him with their hostile silence or addressed him in tones of anger. When the Court adjudicated minor cases or ruled on matters of ritual law, it convened without the town's Rav, in a small room maintained by the Kehillah. When an important case arose, however, the judges gathered in the Rav's home. Although Rabbi Eisenstadt was less obvious about it than the others, it was clear that he, too, was keeping his distance from the Court's new member.

One Thursday, around noon, the Court was in session and the rabbis were seated with the Rav. Rabbi Koenigsberg gazed through the window at the darkening gray sky and watched a flurry of snowflakes dancing gaily through the air, trying to decide where to alight. The snow grew thicker every minute, transforming before his very eyes from thin, wispy ribbons into white sheets and swirling linen canvases. Reb Uri-Zvi recalled how on such winter mornings in Graipewo he would walk to the early morning services, met by every passer-by's warm good-morning. After the services the men would sit with him around a table and learn mishnayot, eager to hear some profound insight of Torah. Afterwards he went home and had his breakfast, then sat down in his study to read, and later lay down to rest. When he arose, a man would come for some advice or a housewife for a ruling in some ritual matter. They all showed him the greatest respect and love—he was the Rav, the shepherd watching over his flock. But what was he now?

The case now before them would at any other time have been considered trivial; but the other members of the Court were apparently prepared to seize every opportunity to embarrass the Graipewo Rav. The trustees of the Stone Synagogue were planning a Hanukkah concert. Besides the town's cantor and his choir leading the services for the lighting of the menorah, an orchestra was to perform, followed by a sermon on the Hasmoneans to be delivered by Rabbi Koenigsberg. The plan called for selling tickets, which would bring in a great deal of money, half of which was to go to the synagogue and the other half to the Land of Israel.

"I know from experience that at the lighting of Hanukkah candles with musicians, men and women will be crowded together. Such anarchy should not be permitted. We must declare it forbidden!" the Wolkowysk Street Rabbi argued vehemently.

"They can't fool me. The money will fall into Mizrahi's coffers," the Schloss Street Rabbi declared with great assurance. "None of it will go to the synagogue or to the Land of Israel."

"Musicians, like at a peasant wedding? That's an abomination of the Gentiles!" cried the Old Marketplace Rabbi, boiling over in outrage.

Rabbi Moshe-Mordecai Eisenstadt sat at the head of the table, half stooped over, his fingers fidgeting with his beard as if he were looking for some clever way out. "Perhaps the trustees could be made to understand how important it is that men and women not sit together. The musicians and choir really ought not to concern us very much. Our main concern should be that people not forget the miracle of Hanukkah and think that Judah the Maccabee was victorious through his own strength."

By this Rabbi Eisenstadt meant to hint strongly to Rabbi Koenigsberg that he feared the Graipewo Rav was planning to speak on a Zionist theme instead of emphasizing the Providential aspects of the miracle. The other rabbis, however, found this much too tame a rebuke, and this time they told the Rav that, with all due respect, he was making a big mistake. The trustees of the Stone Synagogue would never be able to ensure separate seating for men and women, especially since they really wanted the opposite: mixed seating would guarantee a bigger crowd. Thereupon the Wolkowysk Street Rabbi turned to Rabbi Koenigsberg and pointed a finger menacingly at him. "Your congregants have placed you in charge in order to get permission for something clearly prohibited and which they never before had the nerve to do."

Dazed by this open display of hostility, Rabbi Koenigsberg mumbled something that no one could make out. Just at that moment, Rabbi Eisenstadt's wife entered the court chamber. Her gaunt, pale face looked even paler against the snow that was falling outside. With both hands she was carrying a tray laden with glasses of tea, sweet, dry cookies, ground sugar in a porcelain bowl, and slices of lemon on saucers. Sarah-Rivkah placed the refreshments on the table and said to the Graipewo Rav—a bit too loudly, it seemed—"Have some tea." And then, turning to the others, "And you, too, please. Your mouths must be dry from all that screaming and shouting."

The rabbis gaped at the Rav and he at his wife. This was the first time since her daughter's death that Sarah-Rivkah had set foot in the court chamber when the rabbis were there—and she was even bringing refreshments. The Rav quickly surmised that she wished to silence the tirade being launched against Rabbi Koenigsberg.

"Drink, Rabbis. Please have some tea. Let's all have some tea, and don't forget the cake," the Rav said cheerfully to his guests.

The rabbis muttered a blessing, spread apart their mustaches with their fingers, and sipped tea as they chewed the hard, crumbling cookies. Sarah-Rivkah remained standing beside the table and spoke in an excessively loud voice about Hanka Lapidus, the wife of Reb Chaim-Yonah, the ritual slaughterer in Graipewo. Hanka, she said, had been her friend since childhood, and on a visit a couple of days earlier had told her that Graipewo really missed their former Rav: No matter who applied for the position, they couldn't seem to find a satisfactory replacement. They said they would like a Rav just like Rabbi Uri-Zvi HaCohen Koenigsberg.

"I would really like to meet your Rebbetzin," Sarah-Rivkah said and looked innocently at her husband, as if unaware of his motioning for her to leave. Not until some people entered the court chamber on other business, and she could be certain that the rabbis would not return to their previous argument in the presence of laymen, did Sarah-Rivkah leave the room.

At dusk the Horadna Rebbetzin looked from her bedroom window at the thick snow falling outside, and with a frozen smile listened to her enraged husband's complaint: What was the meaning of this—coming in and purposely disrupting the deliberations of the rabbis? She'd never done that before!

Sarah-Rivkah sat motionless, her pale hands on her lap, her gaze fixed on the scene outside the window. "You must see to it," she replied, "that your colleagues don't embarrass the Graipewo Rav. To me, he's a much finer man than any of them."

This vexed the Rav even more. "How could you tell him you'd be happy to meet his wife? It's not nice, it's not proper."

Sarah-Rivkah just smiled and answered in a weary voice, "I'm not all that eager to meet her. But what's not proper about it? Rabbi Koenigsberg was never engaged to me as his wife was once to you."

This quiet answer addled Reb Moshe-Mordecai completely, and he could only murmur into his beard that he hadn't the time to stand guard and protect the Graipewo Rav from insult. He had much studying to do and hundreds of letters to answer. Since they had lost their Blumele, he hadn't written a single word of Talmudic analysis and had made no progress at all in completing his book.

Sarah-Rivkah angrily turned her head toward her husband, and her eyes shone with eerie derision and cold melancholy. "It's really a wonder that because of your one and only daughter's death you haven't finished your sixth book—or is it your seventh?"

Reb Moshe-Mordecai, still hunched over, was dumbfounded and regarded his wife fearfully. Sarah-Rivkah's high cheekbones quivered violently, but she steeled herself to speak calmly. Her father had managed not to write any books at all. Of course, Rabbi Eisenstadt was certainly a more famous scholar than her father—so what of it? Books were not children. . . . At that Sarah-Rivkah also fell silent. She peered out through the window and thought that this was the first snow to fall on Blumele's grave—Blumele's wedding veil.

"DON'T GO TO THE COURT ANYMORE, or to the Rav's house!" Perele shouted at her husband that same night after he told her what he had to put up with from the other rabbis, and that only the Horadna Rebbetzin was friendly toward him. "Don't you dare set foot in the Rav's house, do you hear? The Horadna Rebbetzin is polite to him, and this fool repeats it yet."

Reb Uri-Zvi stood lamely before his wife, his hands hanging heavily at his sides, his beard disheveled. He was totally bewildered by his wife's fury; Perele seemed to be standing on her toes so she could yell louder. Reb Uri-Zvi pleaded with her: What did she want of him? She had schemed and plotted to make him a member of the Horadna Rabbinical Court. Now, how could he continue to accept a salary for sitting on the Court if he refused to go there, especially when they met in the Rav's house? His critics were already complaining that he was getting a double salary, first as a rabbinical judge and then as rabbi at the Stone Synagogue.

Perele's face blanched from anger and her lips became parched as if she were in a desert. She scoffed at her foolish husband's worries about what people were saying, especially since everyone knew that the other rabbis on the Court were making two and three times as much as he at their other positions—even ten times as much. The other judges would be more than happy to send him his salary at home if only he'd promise not to come to the Court. They had seated him, after all, gritting their teeth because they'd had no choice but to accept him. True, she had wanted him to have the title of judge so that the other rabbis' wives could not flaunt their husbands' positions at her. But she had never intended that he should go running to the Horadna Rav's house where the Rav would lord it over him and the Horadna Rebbetzin could do him a favor and be friendly to him. She deserved a pinch on her cheek for that, didn't she?

Reb Uri-Zvi reminded his unpredictable wife that it had been her idea that he visit Rabbi Eisenstadt in the first place. And why was she so furious with Reb Moshe-Mordecai's wife? "After all, she specifically said she'd like to meet you."

Perele bristled anew and sarcastically replied, "Oh, really? She would like to meet me, would she? Perhaps she thinks that just as you don't know how to thank her enough for being friendly, she's also doing me a favor." Reb Uri-Zvi listened, mesmerized, for a long time, until he suddenly waved his hand and went away to his books. He had never come across a single passage of the Talmud with as much confusion or as many contradictions as the words and deeds of his wife.

Perele now went about her housework in the same manner as once in Graipewo, when she had succeeded in convincing her husband to move out of that town. She cooked supper and set the table, all the while talking to herself aloud: "He wants to have it all. He has grabbed everything, that Rabbi Moshe-Mordecai Eisenstadt. He's the Rav of Horadna and sits at the head of the Rabbinical Court. He's the leader of the Agudahniks and yeshivas in Lithuania. When they send money from America for the yeshivas or for the poor of Horadna, it's up to him alone to decide who gets what. When rabbis and solicitors come to Horadna, they have to pay him the first visit, that 'Jewish Pope,' as the women call him. He writes books, has them published immediately, and is already selling them, while my husband has been writing all his life, struggles to get his one and only book ready to be published—and still isn't close to finishing it."

II

I T ALL HAPPENED exactly as Perele had predicted. Although Rabbi Koenigsberg no longer showed his face in the Rabbinical Court, they sent him his salary with the sexton, yet breathed not a word about his returning. At first he was greatly distressed, but then came to see this as a fortunate development—it would give him more time to study and to prepare his sermons. Perele, however, twisted her mouth bitterly as she realized that her words had come to pass and that the Horadna Court could get along very well without her husband. She relieved her anger in heaving long sighs and finally seized upon the consolation that she had, after all, moved to Horadna to be near the children, God bless them. So she began visiting her daughter more often.

It was simply not in Perele's character, however, to play the role of the kindly old grandma bringing treats for the grandchildren; she wanted to help her Serel run the house. By nature a meticulous and orderly woman, it pained Perele to see the house become even more of a dump after her daughter had yet one more child. Everything was thrown about, rumpled and overturned; underwear hung out of dresser drawers, clothes were stuffed into the closets, the linens were strewn all over the beds, and rubbers lay in confusion near the front door. The foyer floor was muddied by the slush trodden in from outside. Serel, an infant at her breast, went about in a loose housecoat, her hair disheveled and uncovered. The twins either wandered aimlessly from room to room getting filthier and hungrier, or else would wrestle, tweaking each other's nose and whimpering. At the last moment before her husband was due to come home from work, she would pause to decide what to start cooking for his supper.

Perele could hardly believe her eyes as she sat at the table. The twins were so identical that even she, their own grandmother, would get them confused. Yet each one did all he could to spite the other. If one wanted to eat dairy, the other demanded only meat. Serel screamed at them while her husband sat at the table either laughing at it all or reading a newspaper, hearing and seeing nothing of what was going on around him. Perele asked her daughter why she didn't hire a maid, and although her mother had asked quietly and sweetly, Serel shouted her reply.

"I can't stand being helped by strangers—or by my own family either! I hate it when someone does me a favor and then becomes my boss."

The Rebbetzin kept still. In her rabbinical family a mother and daughter would never argue in front of the son-in-law. But another time, when they were alone in the house, Perele rebuked her daughter for her slovenly appearance. "Today's women dress up for strange men," she said, "but for their own husbands they'll walk around in housecoats until the husbands come to detest them. You are a rabbi's daughter; did you ever see such things in your father's house? How can a man love his wife if he comes home for dinner and finds the children squirming on the floor like piglets in the mud?" The mother had much more to say, but the daughter interrupted her with a screech.

"Listen, you've already gnawed my father clean to the bone! Did you come here to gnaw at me, too?"

And when her husband came home at last, she greeted him, too, with a screech.

"Are you listening, Ezra? My mother was here today and she told me you don't love me."

Ezra Edelman knew that nothing could quiet his wife faster than telling her she was just like her mother. So this time, too, he sternly raised his finger and said, half seriously, half jokingly, "The more you argue with your mother, the more you prove that the two of you are alike—two sides of the very same coin." And to his mother-in-law he had once said, "Come on the Sabbath. Everything will look just the way you want it. Meanwhile, during the week we're busy people."

Perele was by now accustomed to hearing her son-in-law—with the sweet name of Edelman—speak to her in such a churlish manner. She knew that if she answered him as he deserved, he would tell her that she could play the boss in her husband's home but not in his, and Serel would surely side with him. So Perele bit her lip and decided that she would not set foot in her daughter's house again. Serel was already teaching the twins to have no respect for their grandmother. Her sons would remain her only comfort in life; both Yankel-Dovid and Gedaliah had always shown great respect for their mother.

The winter set in with a thick, dry snow that fell so steadily it seemed as if a heavenly mill were pouring flour down on the city. On the third morning a gray light seeped through the thinning cover of clouds. Around midday a pale blue patch could be seen in the sky out of which stared a brassy, wall-eyed sun. In the evening a frost struck the land and covered the pure white snow with a frozen gleam. The next day the people in the street had to walk in small, careful steps so as not to slip on the ice. Days like these were the very busiest part of the winter season in the Koenigsberg brothers' shoe store. The two proprietors, with their exquisite silken beards and delicate white hands, waited on customers along with their salesmen. They hadn't even time to go home for lunch. Just at that time an unexpected guest appeared: their mother. She strolled in, bedecked like an in-law at a lavish old-fashioned wedding, wearing a worn, fitted sealskin coat with a stiff, upturned collar and broad, flat lapels, over a long, flowing dress with many pleats. Her hands were concealed in a muff, also of black sealskin. She went directly behind the cashier's counter and stood next to the safe, contemplating her sons' business.

The salesmen bounded like demons up to the high shelves, seized the white cardboard shoe boxes, leaped to the floor, and then knelt down to fit the shoes on the customers sitting before them on chairs and benches. There were fat old women in thick fur coats buying overshoes; young women, looking like stretched and twisted springs, were trying on tall, narrow, fashionable boots. The owners, the Koenigsberg brothers, didn't rest for a moment; both were attending male customers. The older men were purchasing high rubber galoshes, while the young men were fitting low-cut half-rubbers with a red lining that came all the way from Riga. The elder brother, Yankel-Dovid, was bustling about two small boys who were holding up their feet stiffly in knitted socks of heavy red wool. Nearby sat their mother, a thin, freckled woman with a sour face that bespoke a morning spent arguing with her husband. No matter which shoes Yankel-Dovid put on their feet, she would reject them in disgust.

"So it's for this that Yankel-Dovid spent years studying in the yeshiva?" Perele said to herself. Then she turned to watch her younger son.

Gedaliah had earlier attended to a wizened old man, beardless and without a tooth in his mouth. He had wanted a pair of heavy, warm slippers in which he could step outside for a moment. A little later Gedaliah had tried to satisfy a tall, burly young man who sat in a waist-length coat, his hands as big as shovels resting on his knees, and his head, sporting a thick shock of hair, hatless even now in the dead of winter. The fellow wanted some sport shoes with double soles. The shopkeeper knelt before the customer's huge feet, but whatever he was shown he tossed aside. He rejected one pair because they were tied with leather laces; he wanted sport shoes with clasps and straps. Another pair was waved away because the chap didn't care for the pattern of the soles, and besides, the edges were too smooth and the soles didn't have grooves for ice-skates. "And it is this village boor with a horse's mane who must be waited on by my Gedaliah, son of the Graipewo Rav and grandson of the Staropol Rav?"

Finally, both brothers managed to free themselves from their customers for a while and came over to their mother, exhausted but with faces beaming over their brisk business. They spoke quietly and respectfully, as always: Did Mother have anything particular on her mind, or was she just paying them a visit? Perele replied that she had come to take pride in her sons. "Some pride! Both of you crawling on all fours before such riffraff, who yet have the nerve to complain." The brothers moved closer to their mother and spoke more quietly so no one else could hear: "And would it be better, Mother, for the shoe leather to dry up on the shelf?" They were happy that customers came in and let themselves be waited on.

Perele did not want to turn against her daughters-in-law, but she just couldn't let a flaw go unmentioned. "And why don't your wives come down to help you in the business? Seems to me they think it beneath them. They must feel they come from finer families than the two of you."

The brothers answered in barely restrained anger that their wives had more than enough work in the house and in taking care of the children—and there was nothing shameful about selling shoes. "A Rav is at the mercy of his congregants, but we tremble before no customer, even if we do kneel at his feet to try on his shoes." Yankel-Dovid and Gedaliah went back to their customers and did not return to their mother. She stood there like a surly old woman who had come in so often to haggle over a pair of slippers that the salesmen had learned to ignore her. Not until she went toward the door did the brothers suddenly appear at her side to see her out respectfully. But she said nothing. She walked out in a huff, her head tilted back.

The Rebbetzin returned home with her face drawn and determined, and found her husband at his desk, swaying over an open Talmud. Rabbi Koenigsberg was sitting in his old, long green knitted robe, his flat velvet yarmulka atop disheveled tufts of white hair, looking just as he always had in Graipewo. He didn't ask Perele where she had been, nor did he get up from his chair to help her take off her coat. This was how he had always been, Perele thought, and when children had seen this since their early days, was it any wonder they had no respect for their mother? She looked about the room and suddenly noticed that not one piece of furniture was in the best place.

"Help me move the sofa between those two windows and the chest to where the sofa is now," she ordered her husband.

"Why, all of a sudden?" he asked, bewildered.

His wife shouted back at him: "Regards from your daughter. Her house is also the town dump and she doesn't even know it."

Perele was seething, but she still insisted on doing things in the proper order. She went to the bedroom, took off her fancy clothes, and put on a housedress. Reb Uri-Zvi crouched down to grab hold of the sofa while Perele pushed it from behind. He had taken off his robe and stood panting in his tallith katan. Then he tried to pry the chest, its drawers filled with clothes, away from the wall. "This is a job for movers, not for old people like us," he said as he wiped the sweat from his forehead.

"If we'll just use our heads it won't be difficult," Perele snapped back. " 'Where there's Torah, there's wisdom,' " as though she didn't deem her husband to be a Torah scholar either. With teeth-clenched stubbornness, she single-handedly pushed the chest from against the wall until it stood in the middle of the room and she was out of breath.

"In Graipewo the furniture stood for twenty-five years in the same place and looked fine, as if it had grown there. Here everything looks like wooden counters thrown about a marketplace after a fair; the furniture sticks out like logs," Perele said, casting disgusted looks about the room. "And how do things look in the Horadna Rebbetzin's home? What kind of furniture does she have?"

"I don't know, I really didn't notice," Reb Uri-Zvi panted, sitting down exhausted. "We're going to have to get someone to finish arranging the furniture the way you want."

Perele, beside herself, yelled at her husband. He'd been to meetings at the Horadna Rav's home countless times and come back with a beard full of barbs and insults from the other judges. He'd drunk tea and eaten kichel there until he was overcome by the Rebbetzin's hospitality. Had he really not noticed what kind of furniture she had? "What are you? Are you blind, are you deaf . . . or both?"

"I'm just no expert on such things," Reb Uri-Zvi stammered.

His lame answer only enraged Perele more. Standing amid the displaced furniture, she pointed an accusing finger at her husband, blaming him for their children's lack of respect for her. It was his fault that they cared as much for her wishes as for last week's leftovers. And if he ever did warn Serel that she must mind her mother, he did it so halfheartedly that the daughter understood her father secretly sided with her. He had never encouraged his sons to aspire to a position in life befitting a Rav's children. He cared not a whit that Yankel-Dovid and Gedaliah had become shoe salesmen, any more than he had been troubled about wasting his life as the Rav in a town no bigger than a fig . . . or any more than he was bothered now that he was nothing more than a maggid. The more his wife berated him, the lower Reb Uri-Zvi's head fell and the deeper was his silence. He had long known that no one is more brazen to a rabbi than his own rebbetzin. But as he listened, he wondered about something else: Perele had always been wise and always so very logical. Then what on earth, he asked himself, did moving the furniture have to do with their children or his position?

12

IN THE MAJOR JEWISH DAILIES in Warsaw it was reported that a delegation of Orthodox professors, rabieners, and community leaders from Hamburg, Frankfurt am Main, Amsterdam, and Brussels had come to Poland. Some time later these same Warsaw papers reported that, having visited several Hassidic enclaves and Lithuanian yeshivas, this delegation from distant Orthodox communities planned to visit the great Rav of Horadna, Rabbi Moshe-Mordecai Eisenstadt. The newspaper that published a Sabbath supplement sent reporters to Horadna on the nine o'clock train Friday morning, and it was no more than a few hours before the entire town was abuzz with the news. People talked of nothing else Friday night in their homes or Saturday in the synagogues. "So Rabbi Eisenstadt is the 'Jewish Pope' after all, just as they say." The people felt proud and important because the leader of world Jewry, to whom such learned dignitaries came for an audience, was also their Rav. Word had gotten out that when the guests were to meet Rabbi Eisenstadt, only his closest associates and the Rabbinical Court would be invited to attend.

They talked about this in the Stone Synagogue as well, but Rabbi Uri-Zvi Koenigsberg, the preacher of the synagogue, was not the least bit enthralled by it all. Though he was still officially a member of the Rabbinical Court, he in fact no longer met with the other rabbis and so knew full well that he would not be invited to the reception for the visiting dignitaries. On that particular Sabbath morning—the Sabbath of the Blessing of the New Moon for the month of Shevat—Perele had come to services. The women around her in the balcony could not stop chattering about the pious foreign professors coming to visit the Horadna Rav, and Perele listened with a stiff smile on her face. "It is an honor to the Torah. I'd like to see the Warsaw papers that have written about it," she said loudly, and several women promised to bring her a copy when they were finished with it. Later at dinner, while a distracted and despondent Rabbi Koenigsberg forced down his bowl of tcholent, an enraged Perele, her food getting cold on the plate, turned the pages of the newspaper so violently that she seemed to have forgotten it was Sabbath, and nearly tore it all up. She finally took a bit of food in her mouth and almost choked on it, coughing and rasping. "The Evil One must have talked me into moving to Horadna to be with the children. I have as much joy from my children as I have respect and honor from my husband."

On the first two days of the following week a hard snow fell, thick as hail. On Tuesday the grainy snow settled on the ground, squeaking underfoot and sparkling like crystal. By Thursday a blinding sun emerged, igniting the icicles dangling from the eaves of roofs, and the frost-covered windows sparkled with tears and diamonds. The townspeople stopped to gape at the evergreens in front of the church; they seemed even greener under a mantle of snow than they did in the middle of summer. Somewhere, someone laughed and the laughter drifted out over this frozen world of snow like the ring of silver chimes. Perele went to the butcher to buy meat for the Sabbath. The butcher's wife was telling a group of women that even the weather was trying to improve in honor of the pious scholars that were coming to Horadna for Sabbath. It was as if the Almighty wanted to do something to console the Rav and his Rebbetzin for the loss of their daughter, so he sent them these exalted guests.

The women encircled Perele and spoke to her as if she were the mother of the bride at a grand wedding. "Rebbetzin, is it true that the Horadna Rebbetzin Sarah-Rivkah hired a caterer to serve the meals to the pious professors and rabieners?" "It's true," Perele answered, though this was the first she had heard of it. "Rebbetzin, is it true that the younger men of the foreign delegation kiss our Rav's hand because that is their custom back home?" "True," answered Perele in a voice as dry as pepper. The butcher's wife had a question, too: Was it true that on Sabbath after the afternoon prayer one of the rabieners was going to speak in the Grand Synagogue? The Graipewo Rebbetzin ought to know; her husband was, after all, the maggid in the Stone Synagogue.

"I couldn't say, my husband said nothing to me about it. And how would the people of Horadna be able to understand the rabiener anyway? He speaks only German," Perele wondered aloud and then asked the butcher's wife to weigh her order of meat. The odor of the butcher shop was making her sick; she was beginning to feel nausea. "And my husband is not just the maggid in the Stone Synagogue; my husband is the Rav of that synagogue. A butcher who sells kosher meat that is supervised by rabbis ought to know the difference between a maggid and a rav."

The butcher's wife, holding her meat cleaver over the side of beef before her, said she knew only that the Rebbetzin's husband had been the Rav in Graipewo, but in Horadna the Rav was Rabbi Moshe-Mordecai Eisenstadt. On the way home, her basket in hand, Perele let her anger break out in a sharp, quiet, bitter laugh that sputtered out like pebbles cast aside by footfalls. What a fine turn of events! In Graipewo they had sent the best cuts of meat right to her home, but here she had to wait in line in the butcher shop with all those yentes. When she arrived home, she immediately reported the news to her husband: "Did you hear? The Horadna Rebbetzin, Sarah-Rivkah, has hired a caterer to serve her guests marzipan. Why, it's barely a year since their daughter passed away and she's already throwing parties." Perele tugged at her clothes and placed her hands on her hips, as if she were even uncertain whether her underwear stayed in place. "Seems like the Horadna Rav really does think he's the Jewish Pope—he even lets those German professors kiss his hand."

She turned suddenly toward her husband and yelled at him. "But you . . . they didn't invite you to the reception, did they?"

"How could Reb Moshe-Mordecai have invited me after you turned over heaven and earth so I wouldn't go to the court sessions or to his home anymore?" Reb Uri-Zvi yelled back at her, and Perele could hear in the yelling his anguish at being an outcast to the rabbis of Horadna. "There'll be no sermon this Sabbath. Everyone's going to the Grand Synagogue to hear the Rabiener, and I'm going too."

The little Rebbetzin didn't yell anymore; she drew herself up to her full height, stood motionless, her hands clenched in fists at her side, and spoke through gnashing teeth in a voice that was barely audible: "Don't you dare go! Now, if you don't go, people will think that you were not invited because you are too important a member of the opposition. If you do go and crowd yourself into the Grand Synagogue to hear the sermon, you'll be making a nothing of yourself." Rabbi Koenigsberg heaved a heavy sigh and did not reply. He still believed his wife was shrewder than he and knew better how to protect his dignity. On that Saturday night he realized that by not going he had avoided shame and humiliation.

He had not yet had a chance to say Havdalah that evening when his door flew open and in burst his synagogue's three trustees, in an uproar. "A good week to you, Rabbi! Rabbi, it's an outrage! We must not keep silent!" They turned on the lights and sat down around the table as Meir-Michael Jaffe, his gold teeth flashing, began to relate what they had just seen in the mobbed Grand Synagogue. "Up front sat the Horadna Rav, Rabbi Moshe-Mordecai Eisenstadt, his colleagues, and the delegation, while their Rabiener stood in front of the ark and spoke. He stood as stiff as a statue, and he didn't speak in German, but in a thick, garbled Yiddish—he's probably from Galicia, or he may even be a fanatic from Hungary. Fire and brimstone spewed out of his mouth—against believing Jews who throw in their lot with the settlers, the halutzim, who are rebuilding the Land of Israel. 'The Jews of our congregation, Adath Yeshurun,' he said, 'will have nothing to do with the reformers in the temples. Even though the reformers claim to believe in God, they have shortened the prayerbook, and men and women sit together. But imagine, even in Horadna, where the Rav is also the leader of the religious Jews of the world'—those were his exact words—'in Horadna, where the Rav is also the leader of the religious Jews of the world, in the very town of the gaon Rabbi Moshe-Mordecai HaLevi Eisenstadt, there are Jews who want to rebuild the Land of Israel together with those Zionist atheists. But we know from the Torah that the Holy Land spits out sinners.' And then this preacher started talking about this week's reading from the Prophets—how much Jeremiah was tormented by the people, by the king and the princes, because he told the Jews of Jerusalem not to resist Nebuchadnezzar, the Babylonian king, and because he wrote to the Jews of Babylon that they should build houses, plant vineyards, and wait until the God of their fathers would lead them back to their land. For that they beat Jeremiah, imprisoned him, spat on him, and called him a traitor. 'And who was right?' he said, and he raised his voice and drew himself up. 'And who was right, Jeremiah or the false prophets?'

"You, Rabbi—it was you the Rabiener meant by 'false prophets,'" said Meir-Michael Jaffe, sternly pointing a finger at Reb Uri-Zvi. "He must have heard from the Rav's lackeys, or maybe even from the Rav himself, that you're always citing the Prophets to praise the Land of Israel. So he cited the Prophets to speak against you and against rebuilding the Land of Israel."

"Not only their Rabiener but that whole crowd of Germans are clean-shaven. They say there is a kind of paste that takes out the hair, and a Jew is permitted to use it," blurted out David Ganz with the long white beard, his eyes dark and bulging.

The third trustee, Moshe Moskowitz, a merchant of religious articles and seasoned matchmaker to rabbinical families, impatiently invoked silence with a quick wave of his hand. "All right, let's talk business! Rabbi, we've deliberated and we have decided: Next week, on Sabbath afternoon, you are not going to speak in our synagogue; you're going to speak in the Grand Synagogue. And we want your words to cut like a knife. Tell them that rebuilding the Land of Israel is the greatest precept in the entire Torah and that those halutzim who are rebuilding Israel are our own flesh and blood, even if they are not observant Jews. That's what you should tell them! If the rabbis or those young freeloaders who run the Agudah are going to talk against the halutzim, there's going to be fire."

"I've always said that Rabbi Moshe-Mordecai Eisenstadt is the Rav only of the local Agudahniks and not the Rav of all the Jews of Horadna," David Ganz stammered slowly, as if his mouth had suddenly been paralyzed.

"I said it even before you," declared little Moshe Moskowitz, cutting him off. "Those are my words exactly: Rabbi Moshe-Mordecai Eisenstadt should come right out with it and admit that he supports the Agudah completely. So he can be the Horadna Rav of the Agudah and Rabbi Uri-Zvi Koenigsberg, the former Rav of Graipewo, can be the Rav of the Mizrahi of Horadna."

"We'll wage a holy war, Rabbi, to make you the Horadna Rav of the Mizrahi, just as Rabbi Moshe-Mordecai Eisenstadt is the Rav of the Agudah," Meir-Michael Jaffe added loudly and then spoke to no one in particular. "My God, how does anyone have the hutzpah to stand before the ark of the Grand Synagogue and insult an entire city of Jews for not wanting to while away the exile rotting in Horadna, waiting for the Messiah? And his German bunch, those yeckies, nodding their heads like sheep . . ."

"I don't understand why this comes as such a big surprise," Perele interposed liltingly, her face bright and cheerful. "The way I hear it, the Rabiener is from Brussels and the Jews there are all diamond merchants and aren't plagued with Jew-haters as we are here. They can very easily wait for Messiah. . . . You must be hungry, gentlemen—come wash and have something to eat."

The men replied boisterously: Of course they were hungry. They had, after all, been in the synagogue since early that afternoon. Perele brought some cold fish to the table, along with jellied calf's feet, noodle pudding, and prune compote, and then went back to the kitchen to make some tea. Their mouths full and vigorously chewing, the trustees said that the Germans, those yeckies, would be leaving tomorrow morning. And during the coming week the Graipewo Rav's sermon in the Grand Synagogue next Sabbath—the Sabbath when the Song at the Sea is read from the Torah—would be the talk of Horadna. The synagogue would undoubtedly be packed, the trustees said triumphantly, and that would make the Agudahniks jump out of their skins. The trustees ground their teeth over this battle as one sharpens a knife on a fork, and mumbled again that by "false prophet" the Rabiener meant their Rabbi Uri-Zvi Koenigsberg. From time to time they complimented the Rebbetzin for her hospitality and praised her wisdom as they gulped down the food and sipped the hot tea. Then they rose in unison and stormed out as abruptly as they had arrived.

Not until then did Reb Uri-Zvi cast a pair of anxious eyes at his wife and sigh. How could he stand before the ark and say that settling the Land of Israel was the great precept of the Torah?

"You can say it and you must say it," Perele replied, standing challengingly in front of her husband with her hands on her hips. "Wait just a second! Which is mentioned more often in the Torah, phylacteries or the Land of Israel? As great a precept as phylacteries is, it's mentioned only a few times, but Israel is mentioned on every page of the Bible! Why do you look at me with your mouth open? I'm not saying anything out of my own head. I remember hearing a maggid tell my father this when I was a little girl. And if my father had no answer to this, then the Horadna Rav's lackeys will surely have nothing to say."

With that she went back into the kitchen to wash the dishes, muttering to herself: it would have never occurred to her simpleton of a husband to dare to preach a sermon in the Grand Synagogue and get supporters so that Rabbi Moshe-Mordecai HaLevi Eisenstadt should not be the only Rav in Horadna.

13

NEXT SABBATH, following the afternoon service, in the middle of Rabbi Koenigsberg's sermon before a packed audience in the Grand Synagogue, a voice rang out from the back: "The Graipewo Rav should be ashamed of himself even to suggest that Dr. Herzl and his gang of Zionists are sanctioned by the Torah!" The Rabbi stopped speaking and stood stunned as the crowd turned to see who had interrupted the sermon. Then another voice called out: "The Talmud talks about a High Priest who in his old age became a Sadducee." And then a third voice: "It's an outrage that a Torah scholar should speak out against the Supreme Rabbinical Council." These outcries all came from a group of young men who had come to the synagogue for the sole purpose of heckling Rabbi Koenigsberg. The Mizrahi's insistence that Rabbi Koenigsberg speak in the Grand Synagogue, the very next Sabbath after the German Rabiener had spoken against the Zionists, had been taken by the Agudah people as a declaration of war.

The Mizrahi people were not about to take this quietly. "Cutthroats! Rabble-rousers!" stormed Meir-Michael Jaffe. "They should be thrown out like rotten herring!" roared David Ganz in such boisterous tones that only his shaking head betrayed his age. "The leaders of the Agudah instigated these rabble-rousers—they and the town's Rav, who thinks he is the Jewish Pope!" shouted Moshe Moskowitz. Upon hearing such insults thrown at their Rav, the great Rabbi Moshe-Mordecai HaLevi Eisenstadt, his supporters shook their fists at Moshe Moskowitz shrieking, "Heretic! You Jeroboam, you! Do you realize you are talking about the Rav of the whole Diaspora? Trample him! Squash him like a worm! I don't care if it is the Sabbath!" The two sides screamed at each other from opposite ends of the synagogue, with the throng separating them like the rapids of a wide, deep river.

For a time the crowd, perplexed and curious, looked on passively, not siding with either faction. But then, gradually, they began to lose patience with the hecklers. Their hearts went out to the Graipewo Rav as he stood dumbfounded before the ark curtain, his white beard disheveled, his yellowed face aglow with a deathly pallor. Compassion for him now fueled the crowd's anger against the zealots, these gluttonous, impudent, freeloading sons-in-law with their fat, bloated cheeks. Men on both sides of the ark, old men with silken beards and stiff-brimmed hats sitting with their backs against the eastern wall, cried out in great indignation that they would not permit strangers to take over the synagogue. Peddlers and poor merchants who sat in the center pews in their tall fur hats and warm half-coats, their faces notched like stone from the winter frosts, seethed even more—they had enough arguing the rest of the week; on the Sabbath all they wanted was a little peace and a good sermon. From the back rows the voices of a hundred burly laborers shouting and waving their crooked, work-hewn fingers rose above the tumult: "Is this what they taught you in the yeshiva? That's what you call respect for an old rabbi? And you're supposed to be religious people! You should live so long!"

Raging most fiercely among the Agudahniks was one young man wearing a dandy's hat like a dandy, cocked to the side. With his brown fur-trimmed gloves and a white scarf beneath a black fur collar, he looked like a bridegroom on his honeymoon. His thick, parted lips revealed a full set of pointed teeth that flashed as he became more and more boisterous, and from his eyes, pointed as his teeth, darted a mischievous laugh. The people despised him instantly and yelled at him from all sides, "Just look at that fanatic, with his fur gloves! Throw him out, head first! Drag him out by his ears!" The people closest to the dandy started jostling him, pushing him toward the door, while his friends elbowed a path for themselves through the crowd. When the Agudahniks reached the door and were about to force their way out, they turned to the congregation and shouted in chorus: "Horadna is a condemned city!"

Some of the people hadn't heard and others hadn't understood, but those who had both heard and understood squared their shoulders and smacked their lips in outrage: "What a disgrace! A disgrace! To proclaim a Jewish city like Horadna condemned." The crowd turned to the dazed Rabbi standing in front of the ark and jarred him back to his senses: "Continue, Rabbi. Speak. Go on, we hear you. You are our maggid."

It was all Reb Uri-Zvi could do to keep from weeping before the entire crowd: He had no intention of uttering a single critical word against the Torah or the Sages. Why did he deserve to be publicly shamed like this, to be denounced as a Sadducee? He wanted desperately to end the sermon then and there; but abruptly he remembered Perele and realized that she would never forgive him if he didn't forge ahead—and this time she'd be right. Who could tell, perhaps the rabbinical judges had sent that wild mob of fanatics to heckle him, perhaps even with the knowledge of the Rav, Rabbi Eisenstadt himself. If that was the case, then he must stand his ground and prove that he, too, was a worthy rabbi. He pulled himself together and dived back into his sermon. But his speech was garbled and the people weren't listening anyway, they were talking heatedly among themselves and reviling the other rabbis: "Last week the town Rav and his whole Rabbinical Court came to hear the rabiener from abroad, but they couldn't come to hear the Graipewo Rav because he's a thorn in their side."

THE CONTROVERSY SPILLED OVER into the deliberations of the Kehillah and became the central issue at a meeting originally called for a totally different purpose.

For a long time the Kehillah had grappled with the matter of setting up orphanages. Some Kehillah members preferred to house both boys and girls in one building. The Orthodox members, however, wouldn't hear of it, insisting on separate buildings for males and females; and the Rav, Rabbi Eisenstadt, and his Rabbinical Court threatened to issue a ban on housing the children together under one roof.

At the meeting of the Kehillah, the first to speak was the leader of the Horadna Zionists, a young halutz with a thick black shock of hair, his face sunburned as if already baked by the sun of the Promised Land. His deep voice carried a faint hint of song, the melody perhaps of a halutz folk dance: "On a Kibbutz in the Land of Israel, boys and girls live together. Only Horadna is still medieval. The ministry of darkness still rules here. We should be getting the young people used to living together in a friendly atmosphere so they'll be ready to settle in the Land. . . . By all means," he concluded, "let the orphans all live in one house."

Although the curly-haired halutz leader cooed melodiously as he spoke, his bearded colleagues glared at him as if he were Satan incarnate spitting forth venom with every word. These venerable elders could not even speak the Yiddish of the day, let alone converse with those impudent young political people who prattled on about left wings and right wings, coalitions, fronts, and tactical maneuvers. The elders would sit and listen with half-embarrassed, half-mocking smiles as they thought back to a time when they had built orphanages with their own hands. They had actually brought the straw for the mattresses themselves, and gone round to all the housewives begging for Sabbath fish and hallah for the orphans, hired teachers to teach boys Hebrew and later sent them to artisans to learn a trade. Now here came these thugs, these politicians, demanding that the orphanages be combined and boys and girls be housed together. What was this world coming to?

Meir-Michael Jaffe, the trustee of the Stone Synagogue and a member of the Kehillah, rose and asked for the floor. He spoke with assurance, buoyed by an awareness of the members of his synagogue and his party who had come to hear and support him. "Is it any wonder," he said emphatically, "that there isn't enough money to support separate orphanages when the Horadna Rav is unaware of the needs of the community? He's always busy with rabbis from all over Poland and with foreign rabieners. He's simply too busy to find out what is going on in Horadna and get involved. Therefore, gentlemen, on behalf of the membership of Mizrahi and on behalf of all the unaffiliated Jews of Horadna who believe in the importance of harmony, I move that the former Graipewo Rav, Rabbi Uri-Zvi HaCohen Koenigsberg, be made the Rav of Mizrahi and that Rabbi Moshe-Mordecai HaLevi Eisenstadt remain as Rav of the Agudah of Horadna."

"Stick to the issue!" came angry shouts from every corner of the room. "We're talking about the orphanages. Should we combine them or shouldn't we?"

"Mizrahi is opposed to combining the orphanages, but Mizrahi *is* in favor of dividing up the Horadna Rabbinate," replied Meir-Michael Jaffe resolutely.

"And what if we do have a combined orphanage? Will you, Mr. Jaffe, not be able to spend your nights playing cards?" A member of the socialist Bund rose in protest. He had gray ringlets of hair on his head, stooped shoulders, and deep-set, dark eyes that flashed angrily. His hoarse voice reverberated like the growl of a lion. "The reactionaries," he proclaimed, "have taken over the Jewish community." And he described how the citizens of Horadna had supposedly cared for the orphans, over the years: Each Thursday two orphans would accompany the sexton to the butcher shops, where they would have to beg for some discarded lungs or calves' feet for their Sabbath meals. At every funeral of some blood-sucking tycoon, orphans had to precede the coffin, crying out: "Righteousness shall precede the righteous!" All the orphans had to wear a uniform—a dark-brown coat and a hat with a little green band—so as to set them apart from other children. And if, God forbid, any orphan made a mistake or missed a service, he was beaten within an inch of his life. The craftsmen who took them on as apprentices made them do all the dirty housework and kept them toiling eighteen hours at a stretch.

The Bundist thundered long against those fine Jews of Horadna who required two rabbis and two orphanages. Finally, he made a motion:

"The Bund is the only party in the community that cares enough to provide the poor with firewood for the winter. In the name of the socialists of Horadna, I offer the following resolution, consisting of two points: First, fire all the rabbis of Horadna and abolish their paid positions. Let those lazy freeloaders go to work! Second, the orphanages should be combined, and let's give the children a proper secular-Yiddish education and a Bundist, socialist upbringing."

The religious councilmen had heard quite enough. They leaped to their feet and bellowed, "Blood will mix in the streets if the orphans are mixed together!" One enraged elderly member, in a small Polish Hassidic hat and a black frock coat with a silver chain across his vest, waved his walking stick threateningly at the Bundist and cried out: "You brazen boor! Just to spite you, the orphans will wear fringes and not your red ties!"

The Bundist laughed in his face. He was a man who had had no fear of Cossack whips or Siberian hard labor under the czar. So was he going to tremble before a Hassid? The Orthodox Kehillah members argued among themselves even more bitterly and heatedly. The Agudah people accused the Mizrahi of responsibility for this sacrilege: if one could speak against the Horadna Rav, the head of the council of great Talmudic scholars, they argued, then why not worship idols! The Mizrahi people shouted back that however great a scholar the Horadna Rav was, he didn't have a monopoly on the Torah. The Torah belongs to all Jews!

The meeting broke up with the business at hand unresolved, and the dispute spilled out into the streets. It was dark, the snow whipped at inflamed faces, a sharp wind blew into open mouths. People continued arguing till the overlapping clusters of shadows thinned out, but gradually they disappeared each into his alley, ducking to enter their low houses. Only the whirling snowstorm continued to howl in the darkness outside.

14

Tʜᴇ ᴄᴏɴᴛʀᴏᴠᴇʀꜱʏ ᴛʜᴀᴛ ᴘᴀꜱꜱᴇᴅ from the Grand Synagogue to the Kehillah snowballed through the other synagogues of Horadna. It became a subject of sharp wrangling even in homes and shops.

The owner of a hardware store, finding himself without customers, felt his very body rusting away as he contemplated his piles of unsold merchandise: rolls of sheet metal, boxes of nails, keys and locks and door bolts. He ducked his head into the collar of his lambskin coat as he struggled through the snowstorm to Ezra Edelman's yard-goods store across the street. Here, too, there were no customers—no one came out in such weather to buy fabric. The only people present were all neighborhood shopkeepers, who had gathered together to discuss the Horadna rabbinate. Ezra himself, despite his being the Graipewo Rav's son-in-law, did not care—or pretended not to care—about what they were saying. The men argued good-naturedly, expressing themselves in half-parables.

"Our Rav is like a beacon to the entire world," observed one, "they come to him from everywhere; but what does Horadna get out of it? Nothing."

"To compare anyone to the Horadna Rav," retorted another man, "is like comparing an old bag of sticks to the moon."

To which the first speaker rejoined: "Our Rav is like a daughter-in-law with the face of a doll. It's a joy to look at her and to be seen with her in public, but at home she can't tie a ribbon on a cat's tail."

Just then the hardware merchant walked in, and promptly interjected: "And what would you do if God sent you a daughter-in-law who was good for nothing and looked like a monkey?" At this, Ezra Edelman burst out laughing, to show he had no concern about his father-in-law's problems and that he knew they didn't mean his wife.

When, however, he returned home for the midday meal, Serel was standing in the middle of the room with the twins clutching her apron and the baby at her breast, and she greeted her husband with a screech:

"I don't want my mother to become the Horadna Rebbetzin. Do you hear? I don't want it!"

Ezra had always been pleased by the pattern: the more Serel argued with her mother, the more she listened to him. It was just that this time she hadn't prepared his dinner, and to him all this rabbinical talk was as appetizing as a bitter onion, he was really fed up with it. Furrowing his narrow forehead in frustration, he stuck his stubby hands into his pockets and grumbled, as he struggled to keep himself from raising a hand to a woman with a child at her breast:

"Listen to me, Serel, how many times have I told you that the more you fight with your mother, the more you show that the two of you are out of the same mold? And I hate a shrew. Why should you worry if your mother becomes the Horadna Rebbetzin?"

Just like her mother, Serel could keep quiet when she had to. With her baby in her arms, she turned abruptly and rushed to put him into his crib, then back into the kitchen to fix some dinner for her husband, leaving the twins to crawl on the floor at their father's feet. Ezra eased himself into an armchair, leafed through a newspaper, and let out a deep sigh. "My neighbor, the hardware man, hit the nail on the head with his example of the good-for-nothing wife."

Serel could hardly wait for her husband to finish eating and return to the shop. Leaving the dishes on the table, she called her neighbor's thin, pale daughter to keep an eye on the children. Then she threw on her long overcoat, set a beret over her disheveled hair, burst out of the house, her overshoes unfastened, and ran to her brothers' shoe store.

As usual, the storm had driven many customers into the store for rubbers, half-boots, warm overshoes, and sport shoes. The salesmen could barely handle all the business. Yet the Koenigsberg brothers refused to come out from behind the counter. Every time the door opened, they would tremble and then heave a sigh of relief, thanking God if the man who walked in was not one of the Horadna Rav's followers. Their Agudah friends were berating them at every turn—at services in the morning, all day in the store, and even at night in their homes, always with the same complaint: How could they allow their father to be dragged into this attack on the gaon Rabbi Moshe-Mordecai HaLevi Eisenstadt? For heaven's sake! Had they not also been yeshiva students? They should know what ordinary people didn't know: that these rabble-rousers didn't care a bit about the glory of the Torah, and that when they insulted one rabbi, they were insulting all rabbis. So why didn't they sit down and talk to their father? But Yankel-Dovid and Gedaliah both knew that it was their mother that they would have to talk to. So they stayed in the store, ruefully anticipating the inevitable confrontation. Then the door burst open and the snowstorm blew in their sister, her mouth open and ready to shout at them, but the din of the crowded store startled her. In a moment she was standing next to her brothers, half hidden from the customers by the counter.

"Our father married very badly . . . Why do you look at me like that? Don't you know why Mother is pushing Father to become the Rav of Horadna? She wants revenge on the Horadna Rav for breaking their engagement before Father married her."

Serel had always complained to her husband that her brothers were such sheep, such dishrags, such big lummoxes—their mother ruled them completely, and they let her. So she was not prepared for the two furious faces that confronted her now. Both men were beside themselves with anger, and before they spoke, they turned to make sure no one could hear them.

"Shut up! Your big mouth will be the end of all of us. Don't we have enough trouble as it is? All we need is for everyone to know what the Graipewo Rav's daughter is saying about her mother!"

Serel was petrified by her brothers' outburst even more than she had been by her husband's. In a low voice she answered, "But I haven't told a soul, not even Ezra." Yet Yankel-Dovid breathed heavily and Gedaliah anxiously wiped the sweat under his beard with a handkerchief. "Don't even let it come to your lips!" they warned, and did not mention to her that they were going to see their mother that very night.

Perele could hardly recognize her sons. They said nothing about her grandchildren and they even refused to have a glass of tea. They had come while their father was conducting a class in the synagogue so that they could tell her the harsh truth, recalling all her sins ever since she had brought their father to Horadna and made him become a member of the Rabbinical Court. Now she was pushing him again, into something he had never dreamed of—becoming the Rav of the Mizrahi of Horadna.

Meanwhile, their father was being held up to ridicule and hated by his adversaries, while his so-called supporters were using him as an excuse to abuse a great gaon and a grieving father who had just lost his only daughter. And this after the Horadna Rav had supported their father for a seat on the Rabbinical Court, against the opposition of all the other rabbis. So what did Mother want of her family, what was she after?

Perele sat near a small table, her right hand leaning on a huge prayerbook, a harried smile on her lips. The longer her sons berated her, the more nervously her fingers tapped on the cover of the prayerbook. But she let her sons vent their anger on her before she answered. It was not she, she said quietly, who had started this war between the Agudah and the Mizrahi; it was not she who had instigated the riot last Sabbath in the Grand Synagogue; and it was not she who had aroused the people to challenge the Horadna Rav and his followers. Besides, Yankel-Dovid and

Gedaliah should remember how, when she had visited their shoe store and watched them crawl about on their knees attending to customers and asked them why their wives didn't come down and help, her own two sons had told her, as gruffly as one speaks to a stepmother, not to interfere in their lives. But now they were meddling in her life and even had the nerve to come and scold her.

Grimacing as if she had a sharp pain in her back, Perele got up from her chair and hobbled to the sofa. The sons wanted to help their mother, but she warded them off with her elbows, and her entire body shrank away from them as if they were two evil spirits who had come for her soul. Perele stretched herself out on the sofa, with her sons standing by as if already accused, tried, and convicted. Lying on her back, her face became even more drawn and her wide-open eyes shone with a tearful gleam. When she spoke, her voice was hoarse, saturated with grief and bitterness. She looked intently at the ceiling, as if her sons weren't there and she was talking to herself.

Every sage prays that his sons will grow up to be just like him or even greater. Every rabbi wants his son-in-law to be a Talmudic scholar. That was exactly what the Graipewo Rav's sons and the Staropol Rav's grandsons should have become—prominent rabbis in big cities. Yet they preferred to sell shoes and to think less of themselves than the whole world thought of them. As for her son-in-law, why even talk about him? Serel's husband was a vulgar ignoramus. So, instead of wanting some dignity for their old father, his children would like him to be a nobody like them, respected by no one. Still, Yankel-Dovid and Gedaliah were upstanding members of the community, their support of their father would mean something. They could inspire their friends to stand behind the Graipewo Rav. But why should strangers get involved when his own sons seemed to have more respect for other rabbis than for their own father? It didn't even bother them when their father was not permitted to finish a sermon in the Grand Synagogue. And now they came to their mother with complaints against her for holding their father's honor dear.

The Rebbetzin was still gazing straight up at the ceiling as tears ran from her eyes. The sons knew it was not like their mother to cry—she hated tears and sentimentality. Yet they also knew that, when brought to tears, she got very angry and it was best not to console her. So both sons stood silent near the sofa till their mother finally turned her face to them and told them to go home to their wives and children. She didn't want their father to find them here when he returned from synagogue and see how ill they'd made her. He would never forgive them, she said, but they could rest assured that she would never tell him of the great respect they had come to show their mother.

15

THE OVERCAST SKY of Purim eve seemed to be wrapped in a smoky fog. The frost had settled and the snow had turned gray on the ground. A tree was rustling its crown of last year's shriveled leaves. The wind plucked the leaves as if mocking the tree for still wearing last season's ashen crown even though an entire winter had passed and it was nearly spring again. The quarrels surrounding the Graipewo Rav had not abated over the winter, but had indeed grown more heated. On Purim eve the rabbinical judges, the Agudahniks, and all the Horadna Rav's followers came to the Rav's home and spoke to him openly, accusingly:

"With all due respect to the Rav, may the Rav forgive us—he alone is to blame! If the Rav had not allowed the Graipewo Rav to join the Horadna Court in the first place, his followers wouldn't have had the nerve to mount this scandalous campaign to make him the Town Maggid and Rav of the Mizrahi. If we give in to them on this, they'll have more to say later on religious matters...."

"But if," they urged the Rav, "we hold our ground, the dispute will eventually fade away. The anger has already boiled itself out. Even the man in the street isn't sympathetic to the Graipewo's claims anymore."

"You have a responsibility to us, Rabbi, as your supporters," said the Wolkowysk Street Rabbi, plainly irritated. "Even if you place Rabbi Koenigsberg under you, he'll still lord it over us."

Since it was a fast day, the Fast of Esther, the old rabbis all had darkened, tired faces. Yet the young Agudahniks were all lively and sprightly, with rosy cheeks and bright eyes—for they, it seemed, had not fasted. No doubt they had availed themselves of the dispensation seized on by students of the Lithuanian yeshivas who looked upon fasting as a penance meant only for the ignorant masses. The redemption of scholars, they claimed, lay in vigorous study. So the smooth faces of the well-fed young men were ablaze with passionate zeal, their eyes sparkling with anger.

Reb Moshe-Mordecai understood that these pleas were really directed toward his Rebbetzin. The whole town was saying that it was she who urged him to give in on everything. His followers believed, however, that the Rebbetzin had been overcome with grief at the loss of her child. She was not thinking clearly, and the Rav ought not to be listening to her. Rabbi Eisenstadt listened patiently to all of these complaints and then, once again, went to the bedroom to speak to his wife.

Sarah-Rivkah was sitting at the edge of her bed, as she did for hours at a time, clutching the small photograph of her daughter. This time she did not hide the photograph under her pillow when she heard her husband's footsteps. She was well aware of who was in the court chamber and the purpose of their visit. As soon as her husband entered the bedroom, she began to speak in a tone of stern determination: He should have never permitted the rabbinical judges of Horadna to harass the Graipewo Rav until he couldn't stand it and stopped coming to the court, to avoid his enemies. And those thugs who hadn't let the Graipewo Rav speak should be thrown out of the house. "Moshe-Mordecai," she said resolutely, "you ought to beg his forgiveness and help him become the Town Maggid, the Rav of Horadna—whatever he wants!"

Rabbi Eisenstadt had heard similar things from his wife many times before, and each time anger had made his mustache bristle, his nostrils quiver, his hands shake. But this time, when she added that he ought to apologize to the Graipewo Rav, he burst out laughing: he should ask forgiveness of someone who had invaded the town and stirred up strife and discord?

Sarah-Rivkah still held her daughter's picture with her fingertips. Her Blumele, she marveled, didn't look at all sickly. Look at her fresh head of hair, the sweet smile on her round lips, her long, slender neck. The Horadna Rebbetzin raised her gaunt face, and her dark eyes flashed with hatred at her husband for thinking of anything other than their lost child. She turned to the photograph again and gazed at it until her eyes became wan and glassy. Then she spoke with the drone of a leaky faucet that measures drop after heavy drop: My ancestor, the saintly Rabbi Alexander Ziskind, left a will in which he commanded his children and all his descendants not to become leaders of the Jewish community because that leads to pride and to striving for honors. And if his heirs did not obey his wishes, he wrote in his will, he would not plead for them before the Heavenly Court in the next world. He swore he would surely avenge their disobedience. So he had avenged himself on his great-great-granddaughter.

With his hands clasped behind him, the Rav looked at his wife from under his knit pointed brows and answered her with impatience. He must conduct himself according to the traditions of his family. Her great-grandfather had also instructed that he be humiliated after his death by having the four kinds of capital punishment administered to his body. But the tradition of the Eisenstadts was that a scholar is never permitted to allow himself to be humiliated—not in life and not in death. Well, now he was going to teach Horadna a lesson! Sarah-Rivkah knew how often the ultra-Orthodox community of Jerusalem had written to ask him to become their Rav and head of the Rabbinical Court. He had always turned them down, but now he was going to write them to accept their invitation.

"Then you'll have to go there alone, Moshe-Mordecai," Sarah-Rivkah said with a smile, the smile of one who knows that despite all the tears that have already been shed, there will be no end to the tears one must live with. "I will not leave Blumele's grave. All the sacred tombs of Jerusalem cannot take the place of her patch of earth here in Horadna."

The Rav gazed at his wife for a moment, and then abruptly turned and walked out of the bedroom toward the court chamber. Some of those gathered there were talking among themselves; others sat quietly, suffering from the fast-induced dryness in their mouths and pangs in their stomachs. The younger men were openly furious: Why did the Rav tremble so before his wife? True, she was a great rabbi's daughter and a great rabbi's wife, and besides, a mother who had lost her only daughter; but in religious matters, who asks a wife for her opinion? When the Rav entered, they all rose. Rabbi Eisenstadt leaned on the table with both hands.

"Gentlemen, I inherited the position of Rav of Horadna from my father-in-law, may he rest in peace, and I will not permit my wife and me to be torn apart over it. And another thing: If the Jews of Horadna want another Rav, I will not stand in their way. And if you persist in making an issue over it, then I will resign from the Horadna rabbinate altogether. Peace in my home is more important to me. So go, gentlemen, let them not have to wait for you in your synagogues to read the Megillah."

His face was drawn from anguish and strain as he spoke, and the group could see that this would be his final word on the matter. The rabbis knew that except for this one time in the matter of the Graipewo Rav, their Chief Judge had never imposed his will on them. His followers thought of him, also, as by nature a kind and gentle person, and a trusted friend to all who came within range of his concern. So none of them wanted to argue with him and cause him more grief. They all left quietly. But once outside, they did talk: The Rav had not the courage Mordecai had shown Queen Esther. When Esther claimed to have no power against the King's edict, Mordecai had rebuked her: "Think not with thyself that thou shalt escape in the King's house."

Though they received the Rav's words in silence, all the synagogues were aflame with the news that the Horadna Rav had given in to the Graipewo Rav in the interests of peace. But Horadna should bury its head in shame for having exchanged its great Sage for a maggid. Among the crowds, there would be raised every now and then a lonely voice asking: why can't Horadna have two Ravs? But the voice would be lost amid the great numbers of Jews who reacted with shock—it had never entered their minds that another Rav might join their leader in the Horadna rabbinate.

Even the members and trustees of the Stone Synagogue did not revel in their victory. "Shh!" they hissed at the children who banged their sticks and turned their noisemakers each time the Megillah reader mentioned Haman's name. In the banging they seemed to hear an accusation for their having humiliated a great Torah scholar. They had not expected Rabbi Eisenstadt to yield so easily, even to the point of warning his followers that if they didn't let his decision stand and stop the bickering, he would step down. So they congratulated the Graipewo Rav with dejected faces, as if he had made them transgress a great precept of the Torah to defend his honor. The Koenigsberg brothers didn't congratulate their father at all. All through the Megillah reading they stood next to him as silent as mourners. The new Rav of the Mizrahi came home with a reddened face, his eyes burning with tears, a choking sensation in his throat. He pointed a long, accusing finger at Perele.

"This is all your fault. You! Reb Moshe-Mordecai gave in on everything, and now I am more miserable than when his fanatics interrupted my sermon in the Grand Synagogue with their hoots. Now everyone knows that he didn't send those hecklers as you convinced me and everyone else he had."

Heartbroken, Reb Uri-Zvi cried out that now all the other rabbis would shun him. Even the trustees of the Stone Synagogue were sorry they had ever started this. And his own sons had stood next to him during services silent and downcast at the thought of the Horadna Rav having suffered such an insult.

Perele had anticipated the victory. Word had reached her that it was the Horadna Rebbetzin who had prevailed on the Rav to back down. When Perele went shopping that week, the women, their mouths piously pursed, talked of nothing but the saintliness of the Horadna Rebbetzin,

Sarah-Rivkah, and how she had never sought honors, especially since the death of her only daughter. Perele understood what they really meant: Even though the Graipewo Rebbetzin had lived to enjoy her children and grandchildren, she was still not satisfied unless people were bowing down to her. The Graipewo Rebbetzin listened with a sweet smile and returned home from the store with delicately measured Sabbath-like steps.

On the Sabbath that followed, she had come to synagogue in the long dress with the narrow waist and the bustle. Her head kerchief was intricately embroidered with pearls and she had prayed from her small, gilt-edged Siddur with such solemnity and self-assurance that she seemed to be giving an object lesson in how a rebbetzin ought to bear herself. It was with that same self-assurance that she now deigned to reply to her husband. Why, she asked him, had he come home screeching like a hysterical woman instead of greeting her with "Happy holiday" and "Happy Purim"?

"Accept the title Horadna bestows on you as your due. Get involved in community matters and invite the important townsmen to the house. Finish your book and make sure that all the scholars get it. Gradually your conflict with Reb Moshe-Mordecai will be forgotten. Say what you may, he was always very clever. He saw only too well that he had no choice, so he gave in."

16

ALL HORADNA SHUDDERED. Word had spread that at the Purim Feast Rabbi Eisenstadt had felt a pressure in his chest and sharp pain in his left arm and shoulder. He broke into a cold sweat and nearly fainted as he gasped for breath. The Rebbetzin Sarah-Rivkah cried for help, which brought the neighbors running with a doctor. He examined the Rav—listened with his stethoscope, took his pulse and blood pressure—and finally announced that Rabbi Moshe-Mordecai Eisenstadt had had a mild heart attack. He needed rest, the doctor declared, and must avoid excitement.

The townspeople, when they heard the news, shook their heads. "Is it any wonder, after all that our Rav has had to endure from the Graipewo and his bunch? Even his own Rebbetzin urged him to give in. Well, now he has given in, and it has done him in."

Rabbi Uri-Zvi Koenigsberg was terrified by the news. When he told Perele, she stood pale and motionless. Her eyes shone with the secret glow of a youthful memory, like a window at dusk that reflects the last rosy hue left in the sky.

Finally, the Graipewo Rebbetzin shook herself awake and coughed in an angry rasp. "He was sickly and nervous even as a child. He's too ambitious for a man with such a weak heart. He wants to run everything."

On the eve of Passover the fresh buds sparkled from the trees, wrapped in a transparent pink mist. Half the sky was covered with clouds while the other half revealed a deep, crystal blue. In the alleyways where the sun didn't shine, there were still patches of yellow, speckled snow. A gentle, moist spring wind caressed people's faces. The wine merchants were busy selling wine for the four cups of the Seder and the ovens were afire baking matzoh. Everywhere the people talked of the Rav's feeling better and of his launching a project he had dreamed of for a long time. He was about to establish a kollel, an academy of advanced Talmudic studies for married scholars. They would attend his lectures and be supported from the funds entrusted to him. Reb Moshe-Mordecai had always yearned to have his own yeshiva, but had been kept too busy with communal matters. Now that he had miraculously recovered, he wanted to dedicate himself to teaching Torah. Since he had no children, he might as well have students.

The first members of the Kollel were the Rav's own students, the Horadna-born young men supported by their well-to-do fathers-in-law. During the intermediate days of Passover, news of the Kollel spread to the surrounding towns, and right after the holiday more students arrived: young scholars who had not yet found a pulpit, and those who did not desire to be pulpit rabbis but did not want to embark on business careers either. They all came eager to partake of the great scholar's genius and to bask in the warm atmosphere of yeshiva camaraderie. Though they had not yet even found suitable living quarters, they sat in the Rav's beth midrash and studied with great devotion. Rabbi Eisenstadt issued an invitation to Jews all over the world to support his new academy, and no one doubted that the response from everywhere would be most generous.

The Jews of Horadna were very pleased that a kollel was being established in their city. They talked among themselves of how "out of the strong came forth sweetness"—out of controversy and strife came something good for Judaism. When the Rav saw that he received nothing but disrespect from the mob, they said, he surrounded himself with scholars. Well, let the Graipewo Rav try to establish an academy. Who would come to him to study? And who would send him money to support his students?

"Now do you see whom you're dealing with? He's already healthy again and he's thought of a new way of showing his greatness by starting a kollel," Perele said to her husband, as she bit her lower lip. "Why, even your own sons say they plan to listen to Reb Moshe-Mordecai's lectures. You must tell them that they dare not go! That's all we need, for people to say that Yankel-Dovid and Gedaliah have nothing to learn from their father!"

"I thank God that Reb Moshe-Mordecai has recovered. A great stone has been lifted from my heart," Reb Uri-Zvi answered. "And thank God Yankel-Dovid and Gedaliah are willing to tear themselves away from the business for a few hours to sit in the Kollel and study."

RABBI KOENIGSBERG SOON REALIZED what a great yoke had been placed on his shoulders when he became the Maggid of Horadna. Perele had expected such a dismal turn of events even less than her husband. For it was not the finer townspeople who were, by virtue of his new post, drawn to the Graipewo Rav's home to visit or to confer; to the contrary, those who continually crossed his threshold were brazen beggars and contentious boors.

One man with a split lip came in as if it were his own home and happily rubbed his hands. "God bless you, Rabbi. Where does one wash one's hands for eating? I haven't had a bite today." Perele recognized him immediately as an impudent beggar who tramped from home to home, but she served him some food anyway. Her husband sat at the table and asked his guest if there was anything he needed. The man, his beard sprinkled with crumbs and bits of his meal, moaned that he was in need of everything: better luck, better health, an income, and a dowry with which to marry off his eldest daughter. Perele gave him a little money, saw him to the door, and then scolded her husband for sitting and talking with such a freeloader as if he were an equal.

That same day the widow of a pious scholar, a short woman with a huge wig, came to see Rabbi Koenigsberg. Everyone in Horadna knew that she visited Rabbi Eisenstadt every few days to bewail her fate and ask him for a voucher for one or another charitable organization. And with her bundle of vouchers she would make her way to all the treasuries and plead for help. But lately, whenever she went to the Rav's home, the Rebbetzin would intercept her and ask her not to bother the Rav because he had not yet fully recovered. So the widow called on the new Maggid for one note she could give the charity trustees for food and another note for clothing. She was really starving, she insisted, and hadn't a thing to wear. Even during the heat of summer she had to go about with her heavy winter shawl on her head.

"I'll gladly give you all the letters you want, but I am not personally acquainted with the trustees of the local charities and I can't say if my request will carry much weight," Reb Uri-Zvi replied.

"We do not send people elsewhere for charity. That's not our way; we give from our own pocket," Perele interrupted and stuck a coin into the woman's hand as she hustled her out the door. Later Perele scolded her husband again, her lips snapping like shears at his naïvete, for telling the old woman that the trustees wouldn't honor his vouchers because he didn't know them personally. "When you aren't able to help, then you should rather appear heartless and refuse help, or else tell them you haven't any time for this. But you must never let the word get out that you have no authority to get things done."

The next day brought a tall, broad man, stooped like a great bent oak. His head was huge with long white frazzled hair and a thick, unkempt gray beard. One eye was clear with a darting dark iris, while the other was narrow and beclouded by a deep blood-red film. He was dressed in tattered clothes, yet he had the appearance of an exiled prophet. As he entered, he looked about anxiously as if he were carrying a great secret and feared lest he fall into the hands of enemies. Then he nearly swooned as if he had trudged across the great deserts without eating or drinking. Yet he didn't collapse into the chair, but sat down slowly, gazing at the Rav with his one clear searching eye. At the same time Reb Uri-Zvi half rose, his hands and knees quivering as if he expected the stranger at any moment to point an accusing finger at him and shout: "Thou art the man! Guilty!" But this hoary man only whispered a few words, which instilled an even greater fear in the Rav.

"Rabbi, I've come to you to obtain a rabbinical ruling," he said.

The Rav was speechless. The Rebbetzin, standing aside, gazed suspiciously at this stranger. Suddenly she screamed at him, "You drunkard! You impostor! Get out of this house this minute or I'll call the police!" The stranger did not become flustered or angry, nor did he seem the least bit afraid. He did not answer the Rebbetzin, but only looked at her with the calm, cynical, slightly perplexed smile of a thief who, though cornered, knows he will be released. He shuffled out of the room with tottering steps.

"To Rabbi Moshe-Mordecai Eisenstadt come scholars to study at his feet," shouted Perele, "and who come to you? Tramps and comedians! He has 'rascal' written all over his face, and you get up for him as if he were Sir Moses Montefiore. Couldn't you tell right away that he was a drunkard who wanted to fool you with smooth talk into giving him money for a bottle of whiskey?" Reb Uri-Zvi gaped at her with awe and reverence—she seemed to him to be the embodiment of wisdom, the very Queen of Sheba. The stranger had looked for all the world like a holy wayfarer of the wilderness, and yet his dear wife had seen through his façade and recognized him for the charlatan he really was.

On another occasion there appeared two emissaries who claimed to be collecting funds for the Etz Chaim Yeshiva in the holy city of Jerusalem. "Are you really from the Holy Land?" Perele asked suspiciously. "No, we're from Baranowicze,"* answered one of them, a tall, thin man in a long rabbinic coat. "But we have a letter from the rabbis of Jerusalem authorizing us to raise money for their yeshiva." He bore himself with great self-importance and had a strong, sincere face with the neat, squared gray beard of the sexton of a great synagogue.

His companion presented a sharp contrast: a short, fat man wearing a creased shirt, a worn tie, a coat with a frayed velvet collar. He had long hands that looked as if they had been created for grabbing and tearing, a short gray beard trimmed to a point, thick lips, and eyes in which played the smile of a man unfazed by rebuff. Perele hated him from the start for his flowery language and his smooth talk. "Don't you recognize me, Rebbetzin? I had already the honor of visiting you in Graipewo, Rebbetzin. But now you are the Horadna Rebbetzin, so it is only fitting that you should generously support so great a yeshiva as Etz Chaim of Jerusalem. The other Horadna Rebbetzin and her husband, Rabbi Moshe-Mordecai Eisenstadt, have always given us a nice contribution. Just ask him," he said, showing Perele the past year's receipt book and wearing a sexton's scrupulously honest face.

Perele, however, made only a small contribution and spoke in a deliberately acidulous tone:

"The Town Maggid doesn't receive dollars from America to dole out to charity as Rabbi Eisenstadt does. We give to charity out of our own money. You may go, gentlemen. Go, a good day to you."

When the men had left, Perele grimaced as if she had a cramp in her stomach, and told her husband to congratulate her: at last someone had called her "the Horadna Rebbetzin," even if it was a notorious bootlicker,

* "Goatsville."

a swindler, a shameless mountebank. She hadn't even the honor of welcoming to their home plain, decent people, not even impoverished townspeople with a good name. "And they don't come to you for advice or
litigation any more than they come to visit," she cried out to him in a
loud, dry voice that rattled and rasped like an iron kettle whose water has
boiled out on the fire. Reb Uri-Zvi gathered his thoughts: What did she
want of him, after all! People took their litigation to the Rabbinical Court
and she had absolutely forbidden him to sit on the Court.

"But now you're not just another judge, now you're the Town Maggid, as much the Rav of Horadna as Rabbi Moshe-Mordecai Eisenstadt.
It's time you returned to the Court and made your presence felt," Perele
screamed, beside herself, and Reb Uri-Zvi marveled once more: So small
a woman and no longer a youngster, so frail that the slightest thing made
her sick so she could only lie on the sofa groaning with headache, yet she
had more energy, thank God, than he and all their children put together,
no evil eye! And what an expert on strategy—nothing less than a general!
First she had pushed him onto the Court, then she had ordered him not to
go, and now she was sending him there again.

17

Rabbi Koenigsberg returned home from the Rabbinical Court overflowing with tales of wonder: they had treated him with the greatest
respect, they had given him the most prominent seat up front, and Rabbi
Eisenstadt had requested his opinion at every turn in the deliberations.
Perele's heart leaped with joy as she thought, "Your former betrothed is
doing this for your sake." And she believed this, even though her common sense told her that the Rav was merely being clever in not wanting to antagonize the new Town Maggid and create more troubles for
himself.

Another time Reb Uri-Zvi came home to tell excitedly how, in the
midst of a case involving two big businessmen, Reb Moshe-Mordecai had
turned to him and asked, "What does the head of the Rabbinical Court
say?" Perele again heard her heart leap and shout joyously: "Your
former betrothed is doing this all for you." But then, she looked at it all
from a different angle: her husband would never amount to anything
unless he was pushed, and now even his former adversary had to push

him. So it was in cold silence and with downcast eyes that Perele listened as her husband interpreted Rabbi Eisenstadt's intent.

"Do you understand? He is the Chief Rabbinic Judge, and he makes *me* the head of the Rabbinical Court."

On a third occasion Reb Uri-Zvi related how Reb Moshe-Mordecai had reminded him that, as Town Maggid, he must speak more often about keeping a kosher home and observing the Sabbath, and especially against the wanton ways of the young Jewish women. Soon it would be summer, and the boys and girls would be rowing down the river on the Sabbath. This time there was no joy at all in Perele's heart. She surmised that the wily Rabbi Eisenstadt was heaping honors on her husband in order to alienate him from his supporters and make him one of his own. Her victory no longer gave Perele any satisfaction. But before the townspeople she jealously guarded her station as the Town Maggid's wife. At times she would go out of her house in the middle of the week in a long, old-fashioned skirt and a small, flat hat with three faded violets. She did not carry a basket with her anymore to the shops, but had everything delivered to her home.

IT WAS PAST Lag B'Omer, well into spring. The evening sky shone a deep, dark blue and during the day the sky was ablaze with a cool, blinding brilliance. The leafy trees sparkled with fresh and moist greenery, not yet dusty and faint from the summer heat. Perele's neighbors sat in their doorways, basking in the sun, and watched her walk by with her dainty Sabbath-like steps and so lighthearted a smile that she seemed to have stepped out of an old portrait. She had already overheard the women refer to her as "the Horadna Rebbetzin" as they talked among themselves, and the more she heard it, the more she wanted to meet Sarah-Rivkah Eisenstadt. But Sarah-Rivkah was never seen in public. Perele was convinced that Reb Moshe-Mordecai had never invited her husband for dinner because he didn't want to confront her, his former fiancée. "Why shouldn't he want to see me?" she laughed to herself. "I'm a grandmother already."

A short while later, however, an opportunity unexpectedly presented itself: Reb Uri-Zvi informed her that the Schloss Street Rabbi had invited him to the Bar-Mitzvah of his youngest son and reminded him to bring the Rebbetzin. Later his wife, Bashka, came to invite her personally.

"The Rebbetzin Sarah-Rivkah will also be there and she tells me that she wants to meet you," she said to Perele, who donned a sweet smile to mask a bitter grimace. She thought that no less than her own curiosity about the bride her former fiancé had taken was Sarah-Rivkah's desire to see the woman her husband had rejected.

The Schloss Street Rabbi's celebration took place the Saturday night before Shavuoth. The men were seated in two large rooms, and the women in a third. The pug-nosed Bar-Mitzvah boy was a young scholar with a stubborn, narrow forehead, full, flushed cheeks, and his mother's pleasant, laughing eyes.

He delivered his Bar-Mitzvah discourse with fervor, his brow furrowed, and gesticulated with outstretched thumbs after the manner of an old Talmudic sage: " 'On the eve of the fourteenth of Nisan, the night before Passover, one must search the house for leaven by the light of a candle, says the Mishnah. By the same token, as one enters his fourteenth year, as one becomes an adult responsible for his actions, he, too, must search his heart for impurities by the light of the commandments. 'For the commandment is a lamp; and the law is light.' Now the question arises, on whom lies the obligation of phylacteries—on the father to place them on his son, or on the son himself? One rabbinic authority, the sage HaIttur, rules that there is absolutely no obligation on the son to put on phylacteries before the age of thirteen, according to either the Torah or the Oral Law. Yet the Talmud, Tractate *Sukkah*, says . . ." The people listened with rapt attention. One man cupped his hand at his ear to catch every word, another chewed on a strand of his beard, a third champed his lips in wonder at the boy's genius. As soon as the address was over, there was a tumult and the pealing of glasses. Everyone drank a toast with the Rabbi in honor of his son. Bashka, the Rabbi's wife, then appeared, tall and exuberant, her cheeks rosy and her eyes shining with joyful pride. She was dressed simply, in a skirt and white blouse, with just a light net over her neatly combed chestnut hair instead of a wig or a headkerchief. With several helpers, she brought platters of cold sweet-and-sour fish, stewed meat, and roasted chicken, flasks of lemonade, baskets filled with rolls and hard white pretzels, bowls of sauerkraut sprinkled with sugar, and plates filled with freshly pickled cucumbers as cold as ice. "Good people, please wash to eat," said the beautiful Bashka, and the guests rose, straightened their backs, and pushed their way toward the kitchen to wash their hands for the meal.

At the head of the table sat the Town Maggid, Rabbi Uri-Zvi Koenigsberg, wearing a square velvet yarmulka and a satin coat with wide lapels revealing a woolen tallith katan over a fresh white shirt. He sat there alone since Rabbi Eisenstadt, though he had been expected, had suddenly felt great fatigue and sent word that he could not come. He had, however, sent his Rebbetzin, Sarah-Rivkah. On either side of Reb Uri-Zvi sat two older rabbinical judges of the Horadna Court, dourly chewing, choking on their fury at how this small-town rabbi, the Graipewo Rav, had become the star of the Grand Synagogue, the head of the Court, and now the guest of honor at their colleague's feast. Still further down the table sat the students of Rabbi Eisenstadt's Kollel, in soft felt hats and black frock coats. Their beards, some wispy, some pointed, some black and others blond, still bore the fragrance of youthful and manly energy, as freshly built and unvarnished log cabins still exude the odor of the forest. Yet, while their bearded cheeks chewed and drank with the vigor of new-fledged manhood, within their creased foreheads lay engraved the great pages of the Vilna Talmud, the fine-print commentaries framing the text, and volume upon volume of codes and tractates, from the most ancient to the most recent. The young men discussed rabbinic law with the Town Maggid, coyly needling him.

They were afraid to criticize him sharply or ridicule him openly lest their mentor, the Horadna Rav, later stamp his feet angrily at them as he had done after they interrupted Rabbi Koenigsberg's sermon in the Grand Synagogue. The students knew that Rabbi Eisenstadt wanted to devote more of his time to the Kollel and less to the town; that was why he was bestowing honors on the Town Maggid—let *him* bother with the Horadna townspeople. And yet they couldn't forgive the Graipewo Rav, that fool, for accepting promotion to a place of honor at someone else's hands. So they barraged him with involved questions on Maimonides' Code, and no matter what he answered, they made derisive faces and dismissed his reasoning as pedestrian. Rabbi Koenigsberg's clear visage and white beard sweated heavily. His large, light-blue eyes became filled with astonishment. "But that is exactly what Maharam says! And those are the exact words of Kreisi U'pleisi!" But the young men wrinkled their noses, shrugged, and one after another answered, "That's just it, everyone knows how conventional Maharam can be. True, Kreisi U'pleisi is renowned as a great scholar, and yet he's not really a scholar. That is, he has a wealth of knowledge, but he treads the false path of casuistry! He gets lost in his convoluted reasoning!" Reb Uri-Zvi tried to save face by citing *P'nei Yehoshua*. But the scholars looked at one another and then at Rabbi Koenigsberg in utter amazement, as if he had delivered an insight worthy of the Bar-Mitzvah boy himself.

In the women's room, Perèle also sat up front, dressed in her Sabbath best: a dark-red gown with padded hips. On one side of her sat the

wife of the Wolkowysk Street Rabbi, with her huge bust and deep masculine voice. But now the burly Rebbetzin wasn't opening her mouth,
though her heart beat within her like a large fly caught in the web of a
tiny spider. And on Perele's other side sat the wizened, ancient wife of the
Old Marketplace Rabbi, wrapped in her faded green shawls and kerchiefs, nodding her henlike head, as always. Around the table were other
women wearing the latest-style hats with many feathers, their expressions
as pious as if they were reading the weekly Torah portion in the *Tzenah
U'renah*. And at the other end of the table, in a black dress and wearing a
black hat, sat the Rebbetzin Sarah-Rivkah Eisenstadt. In the light of the
brilliantly lit room her pale, gaunt face was much more prominent, as
were her long thin hands and tall bony neck.

Perele nonchalantly ate a chicken wing and sipped soda water from
a tall goblet of thick greenish glass. She drank from the glass by straining
her neck forward and just barely pursing her lips at the rim, like a serene
dove drinking from a spring, and with the same noble air she spoke one
word to this woman and another to that one, all the while thinking of how
Sarah-Rivkah Eisenstadt must have looked as a young girl. Could it be
that she was a withered leaf even then, and that Moshe-Mordecai Eisenstadt took her for the sake of her dowry, the Horadna Rabbinate? In her
smile and in her silence Perele saw a cleverness, a wisdom, but none of
the goodness everyone spoke of. She surely had cold, dry white limbs; a
melancholy frost wafted from her face. Her husband hadn't come—was
he really tired and not well, as she claimed, or did he want to avoid
Perele? One of the women at the table said something about present-day
fashions, and Perele seized the opportunity to pontificate loudly in a
manner befitting a maggid's wife.

"When I look at the men and women of today, it seems to me that I
am looking into a pool reflecting an upside-down world. The girls wear
their hair short and the boys have long, curly locks. Opposite us lives a
young woman, well off and pretty, but empty-headed. In one day she may
wear three outfits. In the morning she walks about, slovenly and disheveled; it's nauseating to look at her. Then during the day she appears in a
dress with a tall collar up to her chin and sleeves down over her wrists—
one would think her the paragon of modesty. But all her modesty ends
above her knees, because from there down she shamelessly parades her
legs for the whole world to see. On the evening of the same day she'll go
out in a dress down to her feet and flowing like an open umbrella. But
her top is practically naked, with a flimsy rose shawl over her shoulders.
When have you ever heard of a young woman of a good home making

herself so crazy? And she has plenty of time for all this, but talk to her about separating meat and dairy dishes, or even about having special dishes for Passover, and she'll tell you it's too much work.

"And what do you say, Horadna Rebbetzin?" Perele called across the length of the table. Sarah-Rivkah replied with a wan smile, perhaps agreeing—but she said nothing, and the luster of interest in her dark eyes slowly went out.

Since Rabbi Eisenstadt's heart attack, Sarah-Rivkah walked about gingerly, holding her breath for fear something else might happen to her husband. He now concerned himself less with communal matters, but spent long, arduous hours in heated Talmudic discourse with his students and devoted himself to the supervision of their living arrangements. He had called upon townspeople and urged them to help his students find proper quarters. People eager to rent rooms to these scholars had to appear before Rabbi Eisenstadt and satisfy him that there would be enough room, that the household was not noisy; he even inquired what his students would be served for breakfast and dinner. A few times the Rav sent for a tailor and ordered clothes for the poorer scholars. He leafed through many volumes in preparing his lectures and would often stay up working half the night.

It was serving as a Rosh Kollel, Sarah-Rivkah saw, that gave the Rav his greatest joy. He had been happy to receive the Bar-Mitzvah invitation from the Schloss Street Rabbi, because he loved children even more than the older students. He would affectionately pat and hug them as if they were his own. But on the Sabbath of the Bar-Mitzvah he had again felt a painful pressure in his chest. His face became pale and he sighed sadly, "No good, it's no good!" But when his wife wanted to run for a doctor, he said that he was in no real danger and he didn't want the doctor to violate the Sabbath on his account. After nightfall that Saturday, he told Sarah-Rivkah that he was feeling better and urged her to attend the Bar-Mitzvah. When she refused, he rose angrily from the bed and announced that then he *would* go himself. Before his heart attack Reb Moshe-Mordecai had never insisted so harshly that his wife obey him. Sarah-Rivkah went, terrified lest the patient get out of bed again. But before leaving she instructed their elderly maid to keep a watchful eye on the Rav.

Her curiosity about the Graipewo Rebbetzin had disappeared, for her mind was now totally occupied with her ailing husband. Still, she strained to smile and hear what Rebbetzin Koenigsberg was saying. When Perele had finished ridiculing the latest fashions, she turned her sardonic wit onto modern furniture. Bashka liked to dress in the latest styles—in straight-shouldered jackets with sharp lapels, in clothes without too many pleats, in coats with broad pockets and no false buttons. She had much the same taste in furniture: the tables, dressers, and sofas in the house had straight lines and sharp corners, uncluttered by pillows, covers, or ornaments. The legs were tall and sleek and the drawers not oversized, all of which made for less wood and lighter, more open furniture. There were chairs to sit on, not to sink into, and even the curtains were of light, sheer material that could not hide the goings-on in the house from the world. Perele, noting all this, wanted to ask the Schloss Street Rebbetzin why—if she believed so much in revealing everything—did she wear a net over her hair, and her husband such a huge, old-fashioned hat. But to put such a question to her hostess would have been unseemly, so instead she praised the old style of furniture: "Then a dresser was a dresser, built to be passed on to children and grandchildren. A table had wide, curved legs and could stand till the end of time. A credenza used to shine with polished glass and had ornate carvings—turrets and gates like a real castle. A chest was plated with wrought iron and rolled on casters, and you could put three brides' wardrobes in it. A house used to have high ceilings and huge rooms, the front door was big and heavy, and sometimes had an iron grate in front of it. Even before you entered such a house, you knew that a well-established family, respectable people, lived there. . . .

"Today?" Perele at last concluded her harangue. "Today both the people and their furniture are like a hastily recited prayer. One slurs a few lines from the beginning, mutters a whole chunk in the middle, and swallows the end. The important thing is to take it easy, to make life easy. Is that not so, Horadna Rebbetzin?"

Sarah-Rivkah again nodded silently and absently, and thought, "It seems the Graipewo Rebbetzin likes to boss; likes to be heard and to be seen. There's no question that the fight between Moshe-Mordecai and the Graipewo Rav was her doing." If Moshe-Mordecai had married Perele, Sarah-Rivkah reflected, he would have been happier than with her. Perele would never have demanded that he ignore the honors due him—and Sarah-Rivkah wiped her forehead as if trying to chase away these thoughts. She found it odd and even a bit annoying that the women at the table listened awe-struck to the Graipewo Rebbetzin and did not dare to contradict her.

From fashions and furniture Perele turned to berating the unlettered rabble of past and present. As a young girl she had always been puzzled because she noticed that her father, the Staropol Rav, may he rest in peace, always stood up when any scholar would enter the room. In her youthful mind she had wondered why her father, older and more learned than his guest, would rise for the rabbi just as any ordinary Jew would. But when she got older, she had realized that only a scholar can truly appreciate another scholar. "And if *he* doesn't show respect to a sage, who will, a wagon driver?" Perele sang out to the other end of the table, to the Horadna Rebbetzin, expecting her confirmation.

This time, however, Sarah-Rivkah turned her head aside and answered coldly: "I wouldn't say that: Rabbis fight among themselves more often than ordinary people. And when a Rav holds a simple Jew dear, the man will love the Rav even more and will rise from his seat ten times a day for him."

Perele was startled, and for a while she sat quietly, totally taken aback by so blunt a reply. Her expression became strained as she searched for the perfect retort to the Horadna Rebbetzin. But Sarah-Rivkah resumed her sad, placid smile. Rabbinical lineage, honor, and contention were the last things on her mind, especially now.

Suddenly, at the men's table, there fell an anxious silence. Everyone turned toward the door and Sarah-Rivkah saw the host standing stock still, his face pale; his wife, Bashka, standing beside him, even more frightened; and behind them a crowd pushing in through the front door. Bad news hung in the air and no one wanted to utter it. But Sarah-Rivkah sensed that something terrible had happened.

"Don't be frightened, Rebbetzin, your husband is alive," the Rebbetzin Bashka at last said as she embraced her. "Your maid has sent for the doctor and asked that you come," said Bashka's husband, while trying to calm Sarah-Rivkah by fanning his hands in front of her. But Sarah-Rivkah was speechless. Her face grew still paler, her eyes glazed over with the blinding darkness of overpowering fear. She had to be helped out of the room.

18

IN THE SYNAGOGUE and in their homes the townspeople talked of little else but Rabbi Eisenstadt's second heart attack. He was feeling better, they said, but the real problem was that his wife was in a state of total shock. The Rav, afraid his condition would worsen in the hospital, insisted on staying at home, where he lay in bed surrounded by constant commotion. On the one hand, the Rav wanted his Kollel students near him because, he said, they cheered him up and their presence gave him the opportunity to merit God's mercy by teaching Torah. The Rav asked whoever came to see him, however ordinary, for a blessing. But on the other hand, the doctor had ordered that all strangers be sent away. And Sarah-Rivkah, in the middle of all this, stood at times in paralyzed silence; at other times she tore at her hair and ran to the cemetery to pray for her husband's recovery at her daughter's grave and at the graves of her grandfather and great-grandfather.

It was with stiffened fingers and a quiver in her knees that Perele went about her cooking and baking in preparation for Shavuoth. She was tempted to lie down on the couch and think of the sick Rabbi Moshe-Mordecai Eisenstadt, yet, unlike her daughter, she could not tolerate a mess in her house. Three times a day—in the morning after services, in the afternoon after the court session, and in the evening from the beth midrash—she waited expectantly for her husband to return home with a report on the Rav's condition.

Rabbi Koenigsberg was no less anguished. All Perele's anxious inquiries about Rabbi Eisenstadt's progress suggested to him that she was going through the same torment as he: pangs of guilt and regret for having contended with the Horadna Rav. On the day before Shavuoth, Reb Uri-Zvi came home around noon and reported a new trouble. For years a crazy woman whose husband had left her had been coming to see Rabbi Eisenstadt. She pestered the Rav to force her husband to come back to her from wherever it was he had gone to become the head of a small yeshiva. A year ago she had left for her husband's town, intent on creating a scandal. Now this nuisance had returned and was again tormenting the sick Rav, and when anyone tried to remove her, she would start cursing in the presence of the Rav and Rebbetzin, evil oaths that scared them to death. They begged her to have mercy and stop cursing, and did not let anyone so much as touch her.

Perele stood still a long time, gaping at her husband in disbelief that anything like this could happen. Then she went to the bedroom and remained there a long time. When she emerged, she was all dressed up, wearing one of her long, flowing dresses, a half-length fur jacket with broad sleeves, and the hat with the three violets, and carried a light umbrella, even though outside there was not the slightest hint of rain. Her husband called after her: where was she going all dressed up like that, right before the holiday?

Perele looked into the mirror over the dresser and with her finger smoothed out her eyebrows and the wrinkles on her cheek. "I'm going to the Horadna Rav's house to put things in order. I see that the Rebbetzin cannot be relied on."

Reb Uri-Zvi, utterly confused, stammered to his wife that it was unseemly for her to barge into the Horadna Rav's home. But Perele just glared at him with cold eyes that told Reb Uri-Zvi, first, that she wasn't asking his opinion and, second, that he ought to be ashamed for even thinking at a time like this of her having once been engaged to Reb Moshe-Mordecai. Reb Uri-Zvi understood his wife's look and drew back quickly like one who had burned his hand. He'd meant nothing by it, he mumbled. He was only worried that she might be detained there and not get back before sundown to light the candles. And when he came back from the synagogue, he'd have no one to recite Kiddush for. And who would serve him dinner?

"I certainly hope to be back to light the candles. But if I am delayed there, you'll have to find your food yourself," replied the mistress of the house as she left, lifting her dress slightly as she stepped over the threshold, as if she were walking over a puddle of water.

In the front room of the Horadna Rav's home the Kollel students were drinking tea. When Perele entered the house, the young men all looked at her, a bit astonished by her peculiar outfit. No one asked her whom she was looking for—it was as if this were the town inn. She went into the second room, the court chamber, and came face to face with the astonished Horadna Rebbetzin. Sarah-Rivkah was sitting at the end of the long bench next to the table that took up most of the room, and was listening, with her hands lying helplessly on her lap, to a woman sitting opposite her.

Perele saw a woman in her fifties with a wrinkled face and bags under her eyes, yet with heavy rouge on her cheeks and deep red on her lips. She wore a wig—a wildly disheveled pile of hair—high-heeled black shoes and black stockings, a tight dress that accentuated her hips, and a knit jacket of brown wool. Perele guessed at once that this was the vicious agunah who cursed in the presence of the Rav and drove the whole household crazy. The gaudily painted agunah looked back at the tiny woman who had just entered, at her long dress and her flowered hat, and could barely keep from laughing. But at that very moment Perele's voice rang out, loud and clear, like a command.

"Horadna Rebbetzin, I've come to visit the Rav and help you get ready for the holiday. Would you be good enough to go to your husband and tell him the Horadna Maggid's Rebbetzin is here to see him?"

Sarah-Rivkah cast an even more forlorn look at Perele and then silently went into the sick man's room. The other woman started talking hastily to Perele. She was pleased to meet the Horadna Maggid's wife; she was just thinking of bringing her case to the Maggid. Her name was Mantcha Repnik—everyone in Horadna knew her. For years the Horadna Rav had promised to bring her husband back to her, but now it seemed he would not be able to help her. "He's got one foot in the grave," she said, winking with a vulgar laugh and motioning with her head toward the Rav's room. The woman continued to talk, one moment with a hoarse, throaty voice and the next with the shriek of a night bird. She told her story as if Perele were already familiar with half of it. In Glebokie she had discovered that her husband, after deserting her, had started a small yeshiva there. So she had gone there and found that cockroach surrounded by a gang of freeloaders, black cockroaches just like him, but much younger and even smaller. Her husband was a runt, no bigger than a fig. Only his beard was huge, and he had a cold, miserable face. But when he saw her, that ugly puss had become white as wax. They put better-looking people to rest in their graves. "That's where he belongs, and no Messiah will resurrect that scoundrel."

Sarah-Rivkah returned from the bedroom looking somewhat revived. "The place is really a mess, not at all ready for the holiday," she said apologetically. Perele made her way to the bedroom, and when she noticed Mantcha Repnik following her, she turned and said imperiously, "You can't come in, I have something to discuss with the Rav." Mantcha Repnik stood stunned. It had never happened before that she didn't get her way in the Horadna Rav's house.

The Graipewo Rebbetzin entered the bedroom, her face stiffly calm but her lips quivering and her heart beating rapidly. The Rav was sitting up in bed, propped up by pillows, the blanket drawn up to his beard, which was yet whiter than when Perele had last seen him. His cheeks were puffy, his skin grayish, his nostrils very wide, but even the wrinkles on his face radiated kindliness.

"How is the Horadna Rav?" Perele barely managed to say as she hastily sat down on a chair, feeling her knees suddenly buckle under her.

The Rav said softly, "Thank God, I'm feeling a little better." He spoke unusually quickly, his eyes cast down, fixed on the blanket. He was, it seemed, just as uncomfortable meeting his former betrothed as she was meeting him.

"The burden of the town—the Court and all the communal matters

—falls now on your husband, the Town Maggid. I understand that he hasn't had the time to come here, this being the week before Shavuoth. He has to prepare his sermons, after all. But I hope he'll come to see me after the holiday. Please tell him I would really like to discuss important communal matters with him."

Perele did not take her eyes off him. She felt he was sincere in asking her husband to take over. His words and his appearance showed that he was ill, very ill, much more than he admitted to others. She appreciated Reb Moshe-Mordecai's genius and wisdom more than anyone, and she saw it even more now that he was stepping down. Before, she thought, he had given in just to avoid a fight, yet since taking sick, he had wanted with all his heart to elevate her husband. Though he looked very old and was deathly ill, Perele could not drive out of her mind the thought that she had not been worthy of being married to so great a man. She didn't want to remember that not so long ago she had argued with her husband for allowing their sons to attend Rabbi Eisenstadt's lectures. She hadn't wanted people to think the sons had nothing left to learn from their own father. Now she felt the exact opposite: her children were not close enough to Reb Moshe-Mordecai. Yet as she was about to speak, she checked herself and uttered something very different.

"I want to thank you for being so friendly to my Yankel-Dovid and Gedaliah. Our sons attended the yeshiva for many years, but their business has forced them to neglect their Talmudic studies. But now that you've opened the Kollel, they manage to get away for a few hours to study once more."

The Rav nodded his head with sad resignation as he wondered when he'd ever again be able to teach in the Kollel. Perele turned to Sarah-Rivkah, who had been standing in a corner of the room with a sad smile, looking like a stranger in her own house.

"Horadna Rebbetzin, I've heard that your doctor is not one of the best in the city. We should ask a team of doctors to confer. Specialists will be better able to help the Rav to recover. I'll help you arrange it."

Mantcha Repnik suddenly burst into the bedroom and placed herself in front of Perele with her hands on her hips. "I really thought you had private matters to discuss with the Rav. But I've listened at the door and I see you have come here just to babble, you dolled-up mannequin. If that's the case, I'm as much a princess as you are. I've been coming here before you ever dreamed of becoming a Horadna Rebbetzin." And to prove to Perele how much at home she was, Mantcha Repnik turned to the Rav and continued her story of how she had gone to her husband's town and seized him by the ear. All Glebokie was beside itself: how could a teacher of Torah just leave his wife without giving her a divorce? Her husband, the dwarf with the long beard and stone face, claimed that he did want to give her a divorce. So she said that before she'd accept a divorce from him, God would put a pox on his skin, boils in his armpits, gout in his joints, a pain in his heart, and cramps in his bowels. She had tattled on him all over town for months until his name was as black as a burned pot. Finally, his yeshiva had tumbled like a house of cards. At first the Glebokie townspeople had sided with her, but then they'd begun to take his part. Of course, he had bought them all off. "Take the divorce," they'd told her, "the two of you are just not made for each other." "Take a divorce?" she answered them. "May the earth take them! They say that I and my husband are not a good match? But they and the angel of death are a perfect match!"

The Rav lay still, with his eyes closed, and occasionally sighing heavily. Sarah-Rivkah's face was getting paler and paler, and her hands shook. It was plain that the Rav and the Rebbetzin were well acquainted with the foul language of this harridan, but each time curses poured out of her mouth, they both shuddered.

Perele rose and said loudly, "Close that worm-infested mouth of yours! Get out of here this minute!"

Mantcha Repnik laughed out loud and again stood facing Perele, her hands provocatively on her hips. "Before they throw me out of here, they'll have to carry somebody out in a wooden box!"

The Rav tossed himself about and pleaded, "No more cursing! Have mercy! Stop that cursing!"

Sarah-Rivkah wrung her hands and said to Perele, just short of sobbing, "Please, leave her alone. We're used to suffering this and we just keep quiet."

Perele, however, tapped her foot on the floor and screamed: "Shame on you, Horadna Rebbetzin! This tramp should have her eyes gouged out! You should have called the police to kick her out. And you're afraid of her curses? She's not a widow, she's no orphan, that God should listen to her. She's a charlatan, a rogue who plays crazy to intimidate you."

Sarah-Rivkah shrank away, terrified. Perele poked her umbrella at the woman, who retreated until they were both out the door and in the court chamber. In the doorway leading to the foyer stood the students, looking on dumbfounded. Perele then raised her umbrella higher as if to poke out Mantcha Repnik's eyes and yelled at the students: "Do you call yourself men? Champions of Torah? A sly, brutish creature torments the Rav and his Rebbetzin, and you permit this to happen!" The young men looked at one another, and one of them grumbled that the Rebbetzin would not let anyone touch the woman. Mantcha Repnik suddenly called out tearfully, "Jewish children, have pity, I'm a forsaken agunah."

But Perele's voice rang out louder. "Throw her down the front stairs, I tell you. I'll answer to God and man for it! And if you won't do it, I promise you I'll split her skull right here with this umbrella!"

Mantcha Repnik ran out, a curse on her lips, and slammed the door so no one would follow her. One of the young men laughed. "The woman's a Cossack," and it wasn't altogether clear which of the two women he meant. The battle-fatigued Perele caught her breath and looked angrily at the students: She wondered if any of these so-called men had been among those rabble-rousers who hadn't let her husband speak in the Grand Synagogue. But there didn't seem to be any of the rowdy Horadna Agudahniks among them. No doubt these had come from afar to study in Rabbi Eisenstadt's Kollel because they were truly good for nothing, neither to hold a pulpit nor to run a business. . . . The young men were stunned by the harangue of this strangely dressed woman who acted as if she were Rabbi Eisenstadt's closest relative.

"Go home, all of you, and get ready for the holiday. Or go to the beth midrash and study. This isn't a tea room. The Rebbetzin and I will take care of the Rav."

She stood waiting until the group turned to leave. One of them wanted to go into the bedroom and say goodbye to the Rav. Perele said she would give the Rav regards from all his students. Then she returned to the bedroom, where she found a new scene. The Rav was consoling his wife, pleading with her to stop crying. But she just stood in a corner sobbing like a child, as if her tears were draining her years and making her once again a little girl, hurt at everyone's being against her—her father, her mother, even her doll. Rage welled up within Perele and she bit her lip so as not to start screaming that the Horadna Rebbetzin belonged in a home for the retarded or the senile. She looked at the Rav, too, with anger. The great Gaon and Rav of Horadna trembled before the curses of a scoundrel as if she were a demon. But the grudge that the Staropol Rav's daughter, his first betrothed, bore against him had never, it seemed, crossed his mind.

"Horadna Rebbetzin," Perele declared, "I've come to help you prepare for the holiday, and I must get back to my own house in time to light candles and hear my husband's Kiddush." Imperiously she ordered Sarah-Rivkah to follow her into the kitchen.

The Rav listened and looked in disbelief as his wife suddenly stopped crying and followed the Graipewo Rebbetzin out of the room with the docile obedience of a simple maid. Perele took off her fur jacket with the broad sleeves and led the way into the disorderly, dimly lit kitchen where the maid was busy washing the heaps of tea dishes that had been left in the front room.

19

So COMPLETELY did the Town Maggid's wife take charge of the Eisenstadt household that it was she who summoned a team of doctors to examine the patient. Before they entered the Rav's room, she admonished them that, whatever their finding, they should tell him he would recover. "Many of our people today," she declared in a sharp, shrill voice, "take after the Gentiles even in telling sick people the truth. But we believing Jews feel strongly that one must not rob the patient of his faith in the Almighty."

She and Sarah-Rivkah waited together outside the bedroom. When the doctors finally emerged, they were plainly reluctant to tell even the two women the whole truth; but their long faces showed clearly that they did not have much hope for the Rav. Sarah-Rivkah broke down in tears. Perele shushed her: "Stop crying, Horadna Rebbetzin. If your husband hears you, that alone could finish him, God forbid." The two of them walked into the bedroom and Sarah-Rivkah watched silently as Perele calmly and firmly spoke to Reb Moshe-Mordecai. "The Horadna Rav will yet, with God's help, deliver many more lectures to his students. For the time being, though, you must rest and talk very little. That's what the doctors ordered." The Rav listened with his head turned aside, as if he knew he was not being told the truth. Then he murmured that he had no desire to lie there like a prisoner, cut off from people. "If a scholar wants to see me," he commanded quietly, "let him in."

However, since Perele had turned the Kollel students out the day before Shavuoth, the young men had stayed away. When the townspeople learned of the doctors' findings, they all recited Psalms before an opened ark after services, in hopes of a miracle.

Just at that time, a young man, a scholar, who knew nothing of all this, happened to be passing through Horadna, and decided to call on the

Rav to engage him in Talmudic discussion. Perele met the young man in the foyer and asked him what his business was. The young man—still with a round, childlike face, curly blond sidelocks, and newly sprouted soft down on his fresh cheeks—replied that he had no special business, he just wanted to discuss Talmud with the Rav.

"The Rav is not well and must not do a lot of talking, so don't tire him out," Perele warned as she ushered him into the bedroom.

Sarah-Rivkah, standing beside her husband's bed, looked at the visitor with her great eyes as if the intended bridegroom of her departed daughter had just walked into the room. Seeing the Rav in bed seemed to disturb the young man somewhat. Reb Moshe-Mordecai asked him what his name was, where he was from, and what tractate he was studying. The young man talked about his studies and insights in a lilting voice, waving his arms and becoming more and more excited. The sick Rav listened with his eyes nearly shut, now and then raising one eyebrow, then the other, and over his yellowish face flashed a shiver like a ray of light across calm, dark waters.

Perele watched as the Rav called the young man closer to him and caressed his cheek with a trembling hand. He drew him still closer, as if the youth were a cherished child of his old age. "Those are good points you are making. But you're too daring," the Rav laughed. "Aren't you afraid to take issue with the old commentators?" He asked the young scholar why he no longer wanted to study at the Yeshiva in Radun. The young man, his blond sidelocks dangling, answered that since the old Rosh Yeshiva had passed away, the lectures were being delivered by his sons-in-law, and that was not good enough for him. "I can analyze the Talmud better than they," the young scholar concluded with a cool shrug. In Mir, he declared, he'd be able to study with older students more at his level. "So Radun is not big enough for you?" the Rav said with a smile that ran through every wrinkle on his worn face while his eyes shone with pride. "And do you have enough to cover your traveling expenses? Perhaps you need some money for some clothes?" No, the scholar answered, he had enough money and a valise full of clothes.

"Then go in good health, and good luck in your studies. In the summertime you must go for a walk every evening. The men of our generation are weak, so we must take good care of our health. And don't wait too long to get married. Give the Rosh Yeshiva of Mir my regards." The Rav kissed the young man on each temple and fell back onto his pillow exhausted. "Ask the students in the Yeshiva to pray for me, and you pray for me, too. Give me a blessing."

Tears ran from the Rav's eyes and fell into his tangled beard. The young scholar looked at the two women fearfully, struck all at once by a realization of how gravely ill the Rav in fact was. Sarah-Rivkah sat frozen, but Perele nodded and blinked at him, telling him to say his farewells and leave. "I will pray for you as I would for my own father," the young scholar stammered and softly walked out, pale and shaken.

In the room hovered a pathetic silence. The sick man lapsed into a light sleep, and Perele's eyes welled with tears as she watched him. She had never imagined that this Gaon, this cold intellect, could show such tender affection to another man's son. Only now did she understand why his followers and students were so devoted to him. As if he had heard these thoughts, the Rav suddenly awoke and groaned restlessly.

"What is to become of the Kollel? The students have all left their secure homes to study here. Without leadership the whole thing will fall apart. Almighty God!" He sighed deeply as he once again drifted off into an uneasy sleep.

Perele quietly left the bedroom and Sarah-Rivkah followed, afraid to be left alone with her sick husband. "When are you coming back?" she asked anxiously. Perele answered dryly that she'd come when she had the time. Her own husband, after all, was also getting on in years and had to be looked after, and with that she departed.

The Rebbetzin walked through the streets with a bitter smile on her face as she thought of the role she was now playing in Rabbi Moshe-Mordecai Eisenstadt's life. She stopped to watch a young boy rolling a barrel hoop through the street and then caught herself wondering why that had arrested her attention. The trees were still radiating their bright green glow, but the branches were already bowed under their heavy leafy load. The setting sun in the west seemed in Perele's eyes like the last yellow flicker of a memorial candle. "The sun will soon have set," she thought, "and tomorrow it will rise anew, as always. But a man can never become young again and rise anew." Neither could she turn back the wheel of her fate. She must guard her husband's health and see to it that he attained in Horadna the greatness that had eluded him all those years in tiny Graipewo. She was also determined not to let her sons spend the rest of their lives as shoe salesmen. The son-in-law, she knew, was a hopeless case. Serel had chosen that boor just to spite her mother, and there was nothing she could do about it.

Since Perele had been going to attend the sick Rav, her actions had bewildered her husband even more than usual. On the one hand, she watched carefully to see that he ate well and got enough sleep, didn't overwork himself at the Rabbinical Court or make his sermons too long, and didn't drink anything cold when he was perspiring. She had also taken him to one of Rabbi Eisenstadt's heart doctors for a checkup, and when he came out of the examination room with the happy look of one who has just received a clean bill of health, thank God, Perele raised her eyes to the ceiling and also thanked heaven. But, on the other hand, she carped at him more than ever for not having finished his book. "Even Reb Moshe-Mordecai," she said, "sick as he is, the minute he feels a little better, he looks through his papers and talks about having another volume of his responsa published. But my husband, the Horadna Maggid, whenever anyone comes to confer on a public matter, he stammers and asks, 'And what do you say? What's your thinking on this?' Rabbi Eisenstadt never asked for anyone's opinion. He issued his ruling and that was that."

"So what can I do? I'm not a Rabbi Moshe-Mordecai Eisenstadt. Does that mean you're sorry you married me?" His heavy hands quivered at his side. And now his dear wife had come home with a new idea.

"Why don't you go to the Kollel and conduct classes? Reb Moshe-Mordecai is concerned that the academy may fall apart."

"Are you out of your mind?" Reb Uri-Zvi looked at his wife, stunned, and fearful of this new burden she was seeking to place on his shoulders. "The scholars wouldn't attend my lectures and the Rav would never allow it. You are not to breathe a word of this to anyone! People will say I'm looking to inherit Reb Moshe-Mordecai's position while he's still alive."

"Then go visit him yourself," Perele said, "and start talking about communal matters. You'll see, he'll ask you himself to do it. He'll ask you to look after the students in the Kollel, and I'll be able to help you administer the Kollel much better than Sarah-Rivkah helped her husband. And if you're the administrator, then sooner or later you'll be giving lectures. After all, why should your life's work lie buried in print?"

Reb Uri-Zvi never ceased to wonder at his wife's indefatigable plotting, the fresh schemes she was perpetually concocting. She also advised him that when the time came for him to deliver a lecture for the scholars of the Kollel, he should ask his sons to help him. They must stand on either side of him and be ready to rebut the questions the students would throw at him to belittle his teaching and make small change of his discourse. He must insist that his sons devote themselves more to study, letting their wives and their salesmen worry about the business. In other rabbinical households, parents and children helped one another, but on her family, for some reason, all the curses of the Bible had been visited.

20

RABBI MOSHE-MORDECAI EISENSTADT slowly flickered out like a dying flame, passing away on the eve of Tishah B'Av. Exhausted by hour after hour of reciting Psalms and by day after day of waiting for a miracle, the Rav's disciples and his closest friends spread the news: "It's all over," and fell into silence. That night, as they sat on the overturned benches and recited lamentations, the gloomy darkness pressed their heads even lower. The shadows of the candles shone ghostlike as the town wept not only for the Exile and for the destruction of the Holy Temple, but also for their departed Rav.

The funeral was delayed until after Tishah B'Av to give rabbis from all over Lithuania enough time to get to Horadna, to pay their respects and to eulogize the Rav. As was the longtime custom in Horadna, on Tishah B'Av people went for walks in the tall grass of the cemetery, among the thorny bushes and the small trees laden with wild apples. This year they stood at the graves of their pious ancestors, contemplating the plot where the great Rabbi Moshe-Mordecai HaLevi Eisenstadt would soon be interred, as if the crypt of an ancient sage already stood there. People talked about his unique scholarship and wisdom, and of his reputation in the world of Talmudic learning, as if he had been dead for centuries and lived only as a memory and in his work. On their way home from the cemetery the people saw black-bordered notices, signed by the Horadna Rabbinical Court, proclaiming the great loss and announcing that only the Rav's disciples would be pallbearers. The town's grief grew with each passing hour. After the long day of Tishah B'Av, people joylessly broke the fast and went to sleep with stones on their hearts.

On the morning of the funeral Horadna was filled with rabbis, scholars and rosh yeshivas in the company of their sons, sons-in-law, and students. The black umbrellas on which the old men leaned, the broad black rabbinic hats and coats, the long beards and curled sidelocks, and the dark velvet mist of sorrow in everyone's eyes—all this black vied with the blinding sun, the bright blue of the sky, and the green of the trees.

Horadna had seldom seen so great an assemblage of rabbis and scholars in her streets. Their solemn forms and pious faces diffused an aura of godliness, an anxious hush, like the sorrow of the covered mirrors in a house of mourning.

In the office of the Kehillah, however, a storm was brewing. The sons of every visiting Rav clamored for their fathers to be given the honor of eulogizing the deceased. The students of every Rosh Yeshiva stood up for their own mentors and the members of the Horadna Kehillah argued that their Rav ought to be eulogized by the Jews of Horadna alone. Hearing this, the retinues of the visiting scholars and Rabbi Eisenstadt's disciples, members of the Agudah, gave vent to their sorrow and their rage:

"You dare to talk! All the years the giant of Torah of our generation was in Horadna, what did he get from the people in this city? You tormented him with your stupid, petty wrangling, your foolish arguments! You should be following his coffin barefoot at the end of the procession, begging his forgiveness, not pushing your way to the front!"

As soon as the news of Rabbi Eisenstadt's passing reached Perele on the eve of Tishah B'Av, she knew there would be disputes over who should deliver the eulogies—rabbis fight for the honor of delivering a eulogy at a famous rabbinical funeral no less than for the privilege of reciting the blessings at a great wedding. She lost no time in going to her sons and pressing them to insist that the honor of the first eulogy belonged to their father.

This time the sons sided with their mother. Both Yankel-Dovid and Gedaliah went to take part in the arguments that were going on in the Kehillah. The right of the first eulogy, they insisted, belonged to the Town Maggid and head of the Rabbinical Court. They were supported by the trustees of the Stone Synagogue and the Kehillah members. At last, the spokesmen for the rabbis from other towns agreed that since it was only fitting that someone from Horadna deliver a eulogy, it might as well be the Town Maggid.

Rabbi Koenigsberg was the first to eulogize, though he cried more than spoke as he stood beside the coffin in the middle of the courtyard. "The crown is fallen from our head: woe unto us, that we have sinned!" The entire town of mourners wept along with the Rabbi. But among the departed Rav's disciples and the Agudahniks drifted an angry muttering: "The Graipewo Rav has indeed plenty to weep about. He drew his share of blood from our sainted Gaon, the greatest in our generation. No doubt he thinks that now his Rebbetzin will place on his head Reb Moshe-

Mordecai's crown of Torah and anoint him the rabbinical authority of Horadna. We shall see about that!"

After the Town Maggid's address the coffin was brought inside and placed on the large board of the bima in the middle of the synagogue. Gray-haired rabbis and roshei yeshivot, one after another, ascended to speak from before the ark. Their hands and voices trembled, their backs were all bent, their eyes half blind, their foreheads creased, all aged life-long toilers in the vineyards of Torah. They spoke with much wailing and weeping, yet also with anger and reproach. One rabbi bewailed the lack of respect accorded Torah in this day and age and bemoaned the starving scholars and the desolate houses of study. Another speaker lashed out against the parties and factions that had adopted their own dogmas, having forsaken Maimonides' Thirteen Principles; they had devised their own code of conduct, fashioned after the ways of the Gentiles, in place of the laws and traditions of their ancestors. A third lamented the fate of the Jews in the Diaspora. But each speaker began and ended with the great light of the Diaspora, the luminous Sage Rabboni Moshe-Mordecai HaLevi Eisenstadt, the flame of whose life had been extinguished, plunging the world into darkness. "Torah, Torah, what will become of you?" sobbed the old rabbis and roshei yeshivot, and the people packed into the synagogue sobbed along with them. The reddish glow of the lamps blinded the tear-swollen eyes of the crowd. The gloomy faces and beards glittered like wet stones in a damp cave until the very walls broke into a steamy sweat and the light of the lamps was shrouded in a yellowish fog. When the eulogies had concluded, the Rav's disciples lifted the black-draped coffin onto their shoulders. Someone cried out with a voice that pierced the very ceiling: "And it came to pass, when the ark set forward, that Moses said, 'Rise up, O Lord . . .'" The people broke down in tears again, in wailing that welled up to the high windows above the crowded women's balcony. Not until the mourners left the confines of the synagogue could they catch their breath or wipe their drenched faces and talk to each other.

"We've always known—we knew, and yet we didn't know—who our Rav was. The great rabbis and dignitaries from afar had to come today to tell it to us, now when it's too late. Never again will Horadna have a jewel like that!"

The streets around the synagogue swayed and strained from the onrushing flood of people. When the disciples at the head of the procession with the coffin on their shoulders came to a corner, the storekeepers on either side of the street hurriedly closed their businesses. It was a long way to the cemetery, and more rabbis intended to speak there, before and after the ritual purification of the body. Yet the throng grew with every street like the rush of waters through a broken dam. The venerable old rabbis marched slowly, surrounded by their disciples, students, and children. Behind them walked great waves of townspeople, followed by the empty hearse, a simple wagon pulled by two horses. Poor shopkeepers and humble laborers trudged alongside with a silent fear in their eyes, frightened to be left in this world without their Rav. Along the sidewalks stood young men in summer hats and young women in bright summer kerchiefs. Even the non-religious covered their heads as the funeral procession passed by.

The Horadna Rebbetzin, Sarah-Rivkah, walked directly behind the pallbearers, surrounded by the wives of the judges of the Rabbinical Court. Wrapped in a black shawl, with a deathly pallor on her face, she looked otherworldly. Throughout the eulogies, not so much as a sob was heard from her and not a sound came from her frozen lips. The women around her saw it as a bad sign: she would do her crying later, alone, and God only knew when she would stop. Sarah-Rivkah was indeed waiting for the torment of the funeral with the eulogies to be over, waiting to be left alone, all alone. Then at last she could sit in her home and cry, come to the fresh grave of her husband and cry, come to cry in the tall, wild grass on the grave of her little girl. She would then fall on the graves of her father and mother, on the graves of her ancestors. Half the cemetery was already hers, she thought. And when she ran out of tears, she would be silent. While living, her husband had belonged to the world, yet he had belonged to her, too; now he belonged only to the world. All the eulogies praised her Moshe-Mordecai's greatness and scholarship and lamented for a world orphaned by his death. But no one thought it worth mentioning, or even seemed to remember, that Moshe-Mordecai himself had stood like a little orphan at the funeral of his only child. If her husband had been a carpenter as her father had secretly dreamed of being, he would have belonged only to her and their child in life, and also in death.

The wife of the Town Maggid walked in the middle of the towns-women, all of whom praised her for easing the Horadna Rav's last weeks. But Perele spoke to no one. She felt sand on her lips, a dryness in her throat, and a pain in her chest. Strange thoughts flew through her mind like blackbirds pecking at her brain. As often as she had seen and heard of the greatness of Rabbi Moshe-Mordecai HaLevi Eisenstadt through the years, never had she seen it so clearly as now amid this great assembly of rabbis and this outpouring of grief by an entire city. Even her father, the sainted Staropol Rav, had never been accorded such reverence, neither during his lifetime nor after his death. And Reb Moshe-Mordecai's reputation would grow with each passing day, Perele thought, as the legends of his greatness spread and the genius of his works was appreciated by generations to come. But her husband—her dear husband, he should live and be well to a hundred and twenty—would never achieve a third, not a fifth, of this. In spite of herself, Perele thought also of Reb Moshe-Mordecai's feelings toward her. At first she had thought it was because of her that he had relented and accepted Reb Uri-Zvi as Maggid of Horadna. But as a constant visitor these past few weeks, she had come to see clearly that it was the Rebbetzin Sarah-Rivkah who had prevailed on him to give in. And in those few moments in which Reb Moshe-Mordecai felt a little better, he had looked at his wife with love and pity. He had thanked Perele very politely, yet with nothing like a warm look, as if he had completely forgotten that she had once been his betrothed.

Perele came home from the funeral with a throbbing headache, so she lay down on the sofa with a damp cloth on her forehead. Beads of sweat dangled on the stiff hairs of her upper lip; under her downcast eyelashes welled tears that stung like needles and refused to be shed. She searched her mind for someone to blame for her bitterness and at last decided that it was all the fault of her father, of blessed memory. As a child growing up in her father's house she had heard time and time again that the world was divided into two: scholars to one side, and everyone else to the other. And scholars were also of different kinds: the ordinary scholars, the gifted ones, and the great men of genius. Nothing about a person impressed her father more than when he could exclaim about him "A gaon! A genius!" Was it any wonder, then, that she had grown up with the conviction that her husband must be a great Talmudist? So even now that she was a grandmother and Reb Moshe-Mordecai was in the next world, she could not forget that he had been intended to be her husband—and yet it was not to be.

21

THE SUMMER DAYS burned hot and suffocating. A damp heat lay on the walls and on people's faces. The skies were filled with gray clouds like billowing smoke, but it did not rain. Perele spent sleepless nights suffering from rheumatism in her knuckles and pains in her knees and back. Before dawn, she heard the feeble birds chirping hoarsely, begging for rain. During those weeks in which Perele had been visiting the ailing Reb Moshe-Mordecai, she had not attended to her own housework, and that was just not like her. She crawled out of bed and tried to do a little straightening up, but her head swam as if she had gotten up too soon after childbirth. Still, she steeled herself and got dressed, only to lie down once again on the sofa. Her husband had to bring her a glass of tea. The women in town were saying that the Town Maggid's wife had so worn herself out in caring for the Rav that she became sick herself. A neighbor from the Stone Synagogue and Bashka, the wife of the Schloss Street Rabbi, came to visit. The two women sat beside the sofa as Bashka talked about her condolence call on the Rebbetzin Sarah-Rivkah. "She sits in mourning on a low stool, without a drop of blood in her face, and says peculiar things."

"I was planning to visit her today, but when I try to walk, the whole room spins before my eyes," Perele said, heaving a tired sigh. "What kind of peculiar things?"

"Well, everyone knows," Bashka related, "how Sarah-Rivkah always hated being called the Horadna Rebbetzin. But in the past she would dismiss it with a smile; now her whole body trembles and she cries out: 'Don't call me Horadna Rebbetzin. I have paid too much for that title!' All she wants to talk about is the many happy years she had with her husband and how he told her time and again, even as he lay sick, that he could never have hoped to find a better, more suitable wife. As she says this, a fresh streak of color crosses her cheeks, yet she sounds as if she were answering the charges of some accuser."

"Well, aren't matches made in Heaven?" Perele said. "So what's the use of talking?" She kept her eyes shut as she talked, as if afraid to see in Bashka's face that she knew more than she was saying. "I'll visit her as soon as I've gotten some of my strength back."

"I'm not sure she wants anyone to visit her," Perele's neighbor from the Stone Synagogue broke in with a worried look on her face. "When I visited the Rebbetzin, she sat there cold and silent while that crazy woman, the agunah Mantcha Repnik, had the run of the house. In fact, Sarah-Rivkah was quite friendly and chummy with her."

Perele widened her eyes in astonishment and looked at the woman from the synagogue. "That foul-mouthed pest who tormented the sick Rav? The one I threw out of the house?"

The woman nodded. "Yes, that's the one. You've no idea how she was cursing. May all her curses fall into the sea."

"That agunah with the venomous mouth has certainly maligned me in that house," Perele thought. She asked in utter surprise, "The Rebbetzin, Sarah-Rivkah, tells how happy the Rav was with her. Then why does she think so little of herself as to befriend a despicable creature like that Mantcha Repnik? They say that Repnik, her husband, is a fine man, yet he had to run away from her."

Perele maintained her aloof calm until her two guests left. Then she loosened her taut nerves with a deep sigh and tapped on the windowsill next to the sofa as if playing her thoughts on the wood:

"Sarah-Rivkah must hate me, and she surely doesn't want to see me anymore, even though she could not have managed without me when her husband was ill. That must be why she clings to that crazy agunah I threw out—to make sure I don't come to visit. Even before her husband's death she looked at me with hatred when she saw how quiet and orderly I'd made her house while she didn't know how to tie a ribbon to a cat's tail. All that business about her husband having told her how happy their life had been together—she wanted it to get back to me. But she was lying . . . and then again, perhaps she was speaking the truth. Her husband might have told her this to allay any suspicions she might have had that he regretted not having married me, and now that I think about it, I never really saw any sign of regret that he had not married me. Well, then, let the former Horadna Rebbetzin stay with that wretched hussy Mantcha Repnik. I'm not going to see her."

The traffic of townspeople coming to the Maggid's house with personal or communal problems increased. But Reb Uri-Zvi couldn't analyze a problem at a glance and proffer a quick, pithy bit of advice, as the late Rabbi Eisenstadt had done. On top of that, he trembled before his Rebbetzin. Whenever he took upon himself the responsibility for a matter or decision, Perele nagged him for having once again made a fool of himself. It didn't take long for the townspeople to notice that the Maggid never made a move without first consulting his wife—so they started going directly to her.

"What does the Rebbetzin think?" asked the three trustees of the Stone Synagogue as they walked briskly into the sitting room, with the familiarity of close relatives—it was they, after all, who had made Rabbi Koenigsberg a preacher in their synagogue and put him on the Rabbinical Court of Horadna.

Meir-Michael Jaffe was the first to speak: Horadna indeed still mourned the loss of its Rav. But since this Saturday was the Sabbath of Consolation, the Rabbi ought to speak in the synagogue first and foremost about the Land of Israel, as he had at this time last year. Moshe Moskowitz did not attempt to hide his resentment at Rabbi Koenigsberg's neglect of the Stone Synagogue since his becoming Town Maggid and head of the Rabbinical Court. Now he hoped the Rabbi would return. David Ganz—chewing as he spoke, like an old man munching a hard crust of bread—complained that the Agudahniks had used the Horadna Rav's funeral and eulogies to strengthen their own position. Now the Maggid must speak about the return to Zion; let the town see that Mizrahi was, thank God, still alive and well.

"Of course I will, God willing, talk about the commandment of settling the Land of Israel. Why shouldn't I?" Rabbi Koenigsberg replied, looking uneasily at his wife, whose creased forehead now clearly betrayed her displeasure.

"The Rav will speak in the Grand Synagogue, where all the Jews of Horadna come—not in the Stone Synagogue, where only people from the neighborhood come. And he'll talk about all the precepts of the Torah, not only about settling in the Land of Israel. It's a shame the trustees want to rekindle the old arguments and pull the Rav back into the battle between Agudah and Mizrahi." Perele declared this in a shrill voice which trailed off in a sigh. "But I'm only a tired old woman and I'm not very well now."

The trustees understood that the Rebbetzin was telling them to go. They silently looked at each other, seething with anger. Meir-Michael wanted to shout: "The Rebbetzin is too quick to call her husband the Rav. He isn't the new Horadna Rav yet." Moshe Moskowitz wanted to say that it was the Stone Synagogue that had made the Graipewo Rav the Town Maggid, and the Stone Synagogue could just as easily make him the former Town Maggid, and also the former head of the Rabbinical Court! David Ganz bit his tongue to keep from saying that now he understood what was meant by the expression "a pig in a parlor." But the three trustees said nothing, they just stood there stunned and mute. They knew how to contend with a man, even the greatest Talmudist in the world like

Rabbi Moshe-Mordecai Eisenstadt. But they hadn't counted on being outwitted and outmaneuvered by a woman who moaned and groaned day and night.

That evening Perele's two sons, her daughter, Serel, and her son-in-law came to see how she felt. They asked her whether they should call a doctor, but Perele dismissed the idea with a wave of her hand; she had already seen how little the doctors really knew when they attended Reb Moshe-Mordecai. So she simply sighed and asked her husband if he had prepared his lecture for the Kollel. When the children were around, Reb Uri-Zvi felt braver, so he said that Perele shouldn't have spoken so harshly to the trustees that afternoon—they could give him a great deal of trouble. And he didn't even want to talk about conducting classes in the Kollel. Rabbi Eisenstadt's disciples would never come to hear his lectures.

Serel gave her mother a quick, angry look, ready to take her father's side. Perele saw this immediately and decided to avoid fighting with her daughter. She spoke to her husband in a kindly tone: "But the Horadna Rav, may he stay away from the living, pleaded with you to look after his Kollel."

"Reb Moshe-Mordecai, may he rest in peace, asked me to see to the Kollel's material needs, but he never meant for me to deliver lectures," Reb Uri-Zvi said, and then he complained to his children that their mother was placing a burden on him that was too big for his shoulders. He could not be the Town Maggid and the head of the Rabbinical Court and still find time to prepare lectures for so advanced a group as the scholars of Reb Moshe-Mordecai's Kollel. Besides, the young people would raise a storm against him. It had never occurred to them that he would dare to consider becoming their chief mentor, the Rosh Kollel.

Serel opened her mouth to pounce on her mother, but her husband seized her elbow with his steel-like fingers and drew her back, out of the fray. Perele cast a wounded smile at her sons and said simply, "As your father wishes. If no one will conduct classes in the Kollel, it will fall apart and the townspeople will say that the departed Rav left no worthy successor to fill his place. And this belief of your father's that the students would not accept him as their mentor—he's mistaken, you know. These scholars dread the prospect of seeing the Kollel disbanded. Do you think they want to go back to their faraway little towns to become burdens on the necks of their fathers-in-law? They'd be thrilled to accept the Horadna Maggid and head of the Horadna Rabbinical Court as their Rosh Kollel."

Perele then turned from her sons to her husband: "And why

shouldn't your sons help you conduct the business of the Horadna rabbinate and the Kollel? You're always telling me that Yankel-Dovid and Gedaliah are as learned as any pulpit rabbi. So why should they sell shoes for the rest of their lives?"

Serel glanced at her brothers, and it seemed to her that since they had sat down next to their mother their short shopkeepers' whiskers had grown into the long, flowing beards worn by the rabbis of Horadna. Suddenly a thunderstorm flashed its lightning outside. Serel clapped her hands and called to her husband. "Ezra, come, let's go home! The children will be frightened by the thunder and lightning. The girl who's looking after them isn't much more than a child herself and will be frightened, too."

Ezra immediately surmised that his wife wanted to leave because she couldn't stand her mother's talking. He also felt more than usually irritated with his mother-in-law. "If you're not afraid of getting wet, let's go," he answered. The father and her two brothers begged Serel to wait for the storm to pass, but she wouldn't hear of it. "My little chicks will be frightened. Father, give Ezra your umbrella." Perele stilled the protests of her husband and sons and said that Serel was right. She should be going home to the children. She wasn't made of sugar, she wouldn't melt in the rain.

"How could I be made of sugar when I'm your daughter? I have to thank God I'm not a hard, bitter radish like you!" Serel shouted into her mother's face and then she quickly left the house.

Outside, green bolts of lightning etched fiery trees in the sky, their roots in heaven and their branches whipping against the black earth. Clouds were split like blocks of ice, and the claps of thunder sounded like collapsing mountains. A howling wind ripped over the roofs and through the shutters, but it still hadn't started raining. Serel held her husband's arm, pulling him along and shouting at him over the wind, "The Horadna Rebbetzin sits in mourning over her husband, and my mother lies sick over not having been his wife."

Ezra stopped suddenly and looked at his wife as if he thought she might have lost her mind. As often as Serel had talked against her mother, she had never accused her of this.

Serel grabbed him and again pulled him along. "Let's go. The children are alone. You'll see—by the time she's through, Yankel-Dovid and Gedaliah will be judges on the Rabbinical Court. I could see it on their faces that they're taking a liking to the idea. My father needs this

Horadna rabbinate like a hole in the head, but she wants to become the Horadna Rebbetzin! My father didn't marry well, it's as simple as that. My God, did he not marry well!"

Ezra laughed and answered that her mother might be able to have her way with her father, but she wouldn't find the city of Horadna so easy to manipulate. "Do you think the rabbis would allow Rabbi Uri-Zvi Koenigsberg to become the Rav and the Rosh Kollel—and let his two sons, two shopkeepers, sit on the Rabbinical Court? There would be such a battle, such a blazing fire, that a flood wouldn't put it out."

"Then you don't know my dear little mother. She'll win out over everyone—every one of them!" Serel shouted, as frenzied as the winds whirling around her.

A bolt split a stretch of cloud, a few cold, heavy drops fell, and then a thick torrent of rain poured down on them. In a moment they were both soaking wet. Ezra held his father-in-law's umbrella over Serel, but she stretched her head, her hair drenched and disheveled, out from under it and let the rain cool her feverish thoughts. She felt her heart leaping out of her body from the violence of her feelings. Angrily she shouted into the night, into the wind, into the torrent of rain: "My dear little mother will win out over everyone. Everyone!"

LAYBE-
LAYZAR'S
COURTYARD

I

D URING THE LONG SUMMER AFTERNOONS, Laybe-Layzar's courtyard was abuzz with children and adults, filled with the constant creaking of doors, bathed in the blinding rays of the sun. But in the beth midrash off that courtyard, it was quiet, dark, and cool. Shadows congealed on the floor between the cramped benches and lecterns, making the aisles seem even narrower.

A single speckled patch of sunlight danced playfully on a stiff black rabbinic hat that lay on a bench against the room's eastern wall. Artfully, the patch of light sprang onto a lectern and lost itself among the large pages of an open Talmud, like a bushy-tailed squirrel disappearing into leafy branches. A moment later, it reappeared and leaped onto the shoulders of the Porush, Rabbi Yoel Weintraub, the scholar-recluse who stood in front of a bookcase, peering intently into a tract of rabbinic law.

Rabbi Weintraub was a tall, broad-shouldered, husky man with a majestic forehead that soared up to his black velvet yarmulka. His broad gray beard still showed a bit of dark brown under his chin. His back was slightly hunched as he held the book in his left hand and fed his mouth some strands of beard to chew on with his right, while his squinting eyes searched through the tiny print. Now and then he heaved a thoughtful sigh and murmured inaudibly until finally he became lost in silent thought, a knot of furrows having formed over the bridge of his nose. The fleeting sunbeam that had rested on his shoulder went off once more, this time to play in the folds of the faded velvet ark cover.

A man of Rabbi Yoel Weintraub's stature and erudition should certainly have been the Rav of a sizable town, or even of a large city. In fact, however, he hadn't even been able to hold down a pulpit in Zaskowicz, a small town near Oszmiana. He had left there in a state of utter frustration with the rabbinate. "A Rav," he said ruefully to his wife, "must be able to stand up and say that what may not be done simply may not be done! If it's not kosher, it's not kosher! But I just don't have the heart to forbid so many things."

Rabbi Weintraub's wife was his very opposite in appearance and manner: short, thin, and frail, shy and fearful in company; yet by herself, with her quiet little laugh, she was peculiarly happy. Her name was Hindele, "little hen," and she really looked like a little hen who rejoiced with every grain and every bread crumb. It was not surprising, then, that she had trembled with fear when her father brought home a bridegroom for her from the yeshiva, a tall, husky young man and a great scholar. She was even more frightened when after some years she and her husband left her father's home to become Rav and Rebbetzin in the faraway town of Zaskowicz.

At first, the women of Zaskowicz had expected to hear words of wisdom and piety from the new Rebbetzin; but it did not take very long for them to realize that this was not to be. Then Hindele went through a period of deep anguish because she was childless. Though no one knew which of them was to blame for this, Hindele believed it was her fault and so she would listen with anxious, quiet joy whenever her Yoel talked lovingly to her.

Sometimes she would give him a quizzical, wide-eyed look, wondering if he was doing the right thing when, during the cold winter, he held her by the arm so she wouldn't slip on the ice or fall in the snow as they walked to the synagogue on Sabbath mornings: Was it really proper, she asked herself, for a Rav to walk arm in arm with his wife? But never had Hindele trembled so fearfully, nor had she ever been so joyful, as when her husband told her he was giving up his position.

"And what will we live on?" she asked. He didn't know, he sighed. He only knew that he could no longer go on being a Rav, forbidding everything. Even the tiny houses of the town made him feel guilty—he was so tall, a clumsy giant, and the houses in which whole families were crowded were so low and dilapidated, with their straw roofs and crooked little windows. He sometimes imagined that even the trees around the synagogue complained because he was so tall and strong while they were bent and withered.

The Jews of Zaskowicz had no idea why their Rav wanted to leave them. He had no rivals to contend with, and he had never asked for a bigger salary—so what was wrong with Zaskowicz? It must be, they decided, that the Rav wanted a post in a bigger town. Well, they might as well console themselves in the thought that they'd have no trouble finding another young rabbi, perhaps even a stronger one than Rabbi Weintraub, one who wouldn't moan and groan like a woman in labor every time he had to declare something forbidden.

Reb Yoel and his Hindele moved to Vilna and settled in a dwelling in Laybe-Layzar's courtyard. Hindele sold fresh eggs, delivering them daily to the wealthy women of the town, while her husband shut himself up in the beth midrash to spend his days as a porush. He could possibly have earned something as one of the scholars in the beth midrash of the Gaon of Vilna. But he did not wish to attain such a position through influence, and besides, he cringed at the thought of the throng of women who perpetually descended on these scholars demanding some incantation to ward off the evil eye, or looking for someone to recite Kaddish for them. And so, Reb Yoel was content to sit alone, away from other scholars, immersed in study in the dark little beth midrash in his own courtyard. Hindele's basket of eggs would have to support them.

The Porush was still standing in front of the bookcase, delving into the work of some bygone sage in search of insight into a difficult passage in the tractate *Baba Bathra*. But his mind wandered from the intricate Talmudic problem and he thought back on his career as a rav. Had he only been a rav in a wealthy community, he probably would have had no compunctions about declaring an improperly slain or internally blemished cow not kosher, no matter how fat, or in issuing a ban on a wayward butcher. He would have chastised the wagon drivers for driving into town after sundown on Friday. But it had been his lot to serve in Zaskowicz, which had never been a wealthy town even in the best of times. Its Jews had to barter with the Polish peasants in the rural areas, exchanging soap, thread, and pots for bristle, rags, and live chickens. When the Polish government outlawed even this poor-people's enterprise, the bottom fell out for the Jews of Zaskowicz. The laborers sat all day without a stitch of work to do; the shopkeepers gazed out to the horizon, but there was not a customer in sight. The peddlers loitered around the marketplace like lost souls drifting in the netherworld; they were forbidden to enter the Polish hamlets. And it was these poor wretches who came to ask the Rav, may they or may they not, and the Rav must answer, no, they may not, it is forbidden. Rabbi Yoel Weintraub had no quarrel with the Almighty, God forbid, with His laws or His Torah; but let someone else be the one to say no, not he.

One other man besides Rabbi Yoel Weintraub sat in this beth midrash, in the rear, near the western wall between the oven and the window. This was Heskiah Teitelbaum, a master locksmith who knew the Code of Law on Daily Life from cover to cover, some said even by heart. The shopkeepers pestered him to make intricate locks for them with many tumblers, or deadlocks and strong bolts. They all wanted a good piece of work from a craftsman who would not fleece them for it. When they asked the price, Reb Heskiah made his calculations and thought a long time before answering. Slowly, he reckoned the cost of the material, how long the job would take, and how much profit he was entitled to make. Naturally his customers were very loyal to him. And yet, this locksmith appeared not the least bit eager for more work or more business. He spent the entire morning in the beth midrash, and when he returned for the afternoon services, he remained there until well past nightfall. More than once he had come from a job in some shop and wandered into the beth midrash with his tool chest and his heavy mallet under his arm. He would put his tools down on a bench and bury himself in some rabbinic tome, forgetting completely about returning to his work.

When he walked through the streets, Reb Heskiah always looked down at his own steps as if seeing to it that his feet trod the right path. His piously hunched shoulders and the white lime stain on the back of his coat bore witness to the many hours he studied while leaning against the wall of the beth midrash. People looked at his pallid face with reverence and regarded him as a saint—though also as obstinate, and as carrying his piety perhaps more than a little to excess.

Sometimes a shopkeeper would rush into the beth midrash to tell the locksmith that he had lost the keys to his store or that the deadbolt was stuck. It was a market day and he was losing business! If the locksmith would come back with him and open the door, he would shower him with gold. But Reb Heskiah, though he had finished the morning service, refused to tear himself away from study and sat firmly, not moving from his seat. No matter how much the shopkeeper cajoled and pleaded, the locksmith would not be moved. "When he says no," his partner in the shop told everyone, "he means No with a capital N."

It was because he spent more time in the beth midrash than in his workshop that Reb Heskiah had taken a partner, a workman with no shop or tools of his own, a man, in fact, who was not a master locksmith. But he stayed in the shop the entire day and worked. So Reb Heskiah paid the rent for the workshop himself and never took a larger portion of the profits for supplying the vises, saws, chisels, and all the shop's machinery, but always gave his partner an equal share.

Sometimes, however, the partner found it impossible to accomplish a given task by himself—to forge a large bolt, say—so off he would go to the beth midrash to ask Reb Heskiah to come and help. The partner was a tall man with long hands, his face and clothing usually covered with grease from the machines and soot from the smithy. When he talked, he spewed forth the smoke and ash he had breathed in from the bellows. He felt wretched about his disheveled appearance whenever he stood in the beth midrash. And he had great respect for Reb Heskiah Teitelbaum, so pious a Jew and so scholarly, a master craftsman and owner of the shop. So he would never speak harshly to Reb Heskiah, but only entreat him politely:

"I can't manage holding a glowing bar with tongs in one hand and swinging a heavy hammer with the other."

"So get someone else to help you, and let the two of you share the profit," Reb Heskiah would answer.

The partner stood motionless, his hands drooping at his sides, looking like a charred tree trunk after a forest fire. Where in the world was he going to find a helper in the middle of the day? He knew, besides, that Reb Heskiah's wife didn't earn enough from her little grocery store to run the house, and needed every little bit that came in from the shop. But such things never worried Reb Heskiah, and the soot-covered partner knew it would be a waste of time trying to convince him otherwise. So, shrugging his shoulders, he turned and walked to the door, saying, "First time in my life I saw a craftsman who hates making money."

Reb Heskiah pretended he hadn't heard, and a smile of stubborn determination appeared on his thin, drawn face. In his heart he dismissed his unlettered partner. He delved once again into his book in the western corner of the room while the Porush, Rabbi Weintraub, swayed back and forth over the broad page of an open volume of the Talmud in the eastern corner, the two of them looking lost amid the meandering aisles cluttered with heavy wooden furnishings and sacred objects.

The beams across the ceiling divided the beth midrash into three areas. In the back, along the western wall, were simple benches and tables for worshippers who could not afford to purchase a permanent place with a locked drawer. In the middle section stood the bima, with stairs leading up from north and south, right and left. Around the bima were chairs and lecterns, places inherited from fathers or paid for every Yom Kippur eve. And in the front section of the beth midrash, along the eastern wall, were the seats with finely carved armrests, in which sat only the wealthy and the trustees. Here were the reader's lectern and the ark, decorated with pillars on the sides and crowned with carved lions on either side of the Tablets of the Law, which rested on hands spread to form the sign of the priestly blessing. The clutter of benches and lecterns, the books piled high on the tables, the laver and the chandeliers virtually concealed the few worshippers who came during the week. Each one sat tucked away in a corner, straining to hear the reader standing afar off at the reader's lectern right next to the ark. When services were over and the worshippers dispersed, a secretive quietude pervaded the empty sanctuary, as if in the hard-planed and polished wooden fixtures there still resonated the mysterious silence in the depths of the dense forest.

2

IN ADDITION TO the public fast days, Heskiah Teitelbaum would fast nearly every Monday and Thursday, when the Torah scroll was read at morning services. He would sometimes fast until noon even on an ordinary weekday. All this fasting had taken its toll on his health, and the doctor who was summoned to his bedside warned him that he was surely killing himself. Yet, even lying ill in bed, he would eat only meatless dishes so as not to derive too much pleasure from this world.

Reb Heskiah's wife and daughters had brought their lament to the town's scholars, who came to reproach him for practicing the asceticism of a Gentile monk: " 'And you shall live by them,' the Torah says, 'and not die by the laws,' adds the Talmud." The locksmith nonetheless stood his ground, making his visitors so furious that instead of giving him a blessing for a speedy recovery, they left grumbling the Talmudic saw: "And the ignorant cannot be righteous."

This never bothered Reb Heskiah. He just smiled behind his beard and thought to himself that he was his own best rabbi. He, too, thank God, knew a chapter or two of the Codes. And he recovered even without the blessings of his disapproving visitors. When his wife saw that he was resuming his fasting, she spitefully started doing the same, refusing to eat before he had taken food that day. Reb Heskiah's three daughters became worried lest their mother, too, fall ill. So Malka, the eldest, would come to him in Laybe-Layzar's beth midrash and plead with him not to starve himself to death and their mother, too.

Malka was sickly, always suffering from headaches. Her black hair was tangled and matted because—so people said—when she was a young girl her father had never let her comb it. She was divorced, again because of her father. Her husband couldn't stand being told in which butcher shop he was allowed to buy his meat and when he had to stop work

Friday afternoon; nor could he tolerate being the object of his father-in-law's stern and angry gaze whenever he talked to someone during services, as if he were a schoolboy in Heder. Reb Heskiah was even brazen enough to ask Malka how careful she was in adhering to the laws governing a woman's intimacy with her husband. When Malka's husband screamed, "I can't take this anymore!" she pleaded, "Why do you let his ways bother you? Please do it for my father's sake." Very pious at first, Malka's husband became less observant with each passing day until Reb Heskiah urged his daughter to leave him. He tormented her so long that finally she and her husband divorced.

Ever since she had destroyed her marriage at her father's bidding, Malka had become even more devoted to him than her two younger sisters were. Yet she suffered too much on his account, and she had come to lose all respect for him. So when she came to the beth midrash to argue with him, she spoke harshly:

"Father, go eat," she commanded. "How can anyone get through the day without eating until one or two o'clock?"

Reb Heskiah merely shrugged: So what was new about a Jew eating cholent, what was new about his fasting! What was so special about fasting? When he fasted on those public fasts on long summer days, on the Seventeenth of Tamniuz and on Tishah B'Av, he didn't feel hungry at all, so why should a half-day of fasting bother him? What did bother him, he would cough out, is that a daughter would speak to her father with so little respect. "Go," he would say, his face suddenly very stern. "It's not proper for a woman to stay in the beth midrash."

"If you won't eat," Malka would retort, "then Mother will not eat either." But Reb Heskiah was unmoved. "Then go and tell her to eat," he would say curtly. "And what about you?" "I'm not hungry," he would mutter, and stick his nose and glasses back into his tome.

Malka felt a headache coming on, and she knew there was just no dealing with her father. But she screamed anyway; let at least Rabbi Weintraub hear, and the bookcases and the ark.

"Stubborn! If Mother won't eat, then I won't either, and you can say Kaddish for us both." Her voice trailed off in tears as she turned and ran out of the beth midrash. The Porush, Reb Yoel, knew that the locksmith was as immovable as the wall against which he was leaning. But he pitied the young woman and her mother, so he left his corner and went over to talk to Reb Heskiah. "'You shall guard your souls,' the Torah says. According to the law, a God-fearing Jew is obliged to watch his health.

Even the Prophets never tired of reminding us that the important thing in repentance is a broken heart, not pain and suffering. So how can you bring such suffering upon your wife and daughter?"

Reb Heskiah remained unimpressed. He had just that morning, he answered, taken a vow to fast the entire day. Should he break his vow because of his wife and daughter? He never told anyone how to live, so no one should tell him how to live. He knew the law quite well, praised be the Almighty!

The Porush stood silent for a minute, his hands spread out before him as he wondered, almost marveled, at how this locksmith had taken God's compassionate Torah and twisted it into a Torah of cruelty for himself, his wife, and his daughter. And yet he claimed to know the law! So one must show him that he did not know the law, and the Porush recited the clause from Maimonides' Code: "Let a man not say, 'Since jealousy and lust are the paths to evil, I will eat no meat, drink no wine, I will live in poverty and never don a splendid garment.' This, too, is the wrong path. Maimonides specifically says that one may eat meat, one may drink wine—one may!"

"I look into Maimonides to find out what is forbidden, not what is permitted," the locksmith replied.

The scholar stood still a while longer, his heavy hands outstretched and his large palms open wide. Finally, he returned to his corner, and the locksmith resumed swaying from side to side as he immersed himself once again in study. But in his heart he mocked the former Zaskowicz Rav for trying to convince him to eat. Reb Heskiah knew full well that besides the six public fasts there were the minor fasts that followed Passover and Sukkoth, which the very pious observed, and then there were the private fasts an individual took upon himself the year round. "And he's telling me that Maimonides permits eating," he chuckled to himself.

Ever since Rabbi Yoel Weintraub had begun spending his days as a porush in the beth midrash of Laybe-Layzar's courtyard, the women neighbors had been coming to him with questions about kashruth or for advice and a blessing, just as they might have gone to a great and saintly sage. Whenever he suggested that they consult the rabbis of Vilna or the scholars in the Gaon's synagogue, they would answer that they preferred to go to the rabbi of their own courtyard—he knew their problems at first hand.

One day after dark, Reb Heskiah's wife came to see the Porush to talk her heart out about her two younger daughters. Serel, her middle child, was quiet and sweet as a dove. She was her mother's right hand in her grocery store and just as perfect at keeping house. Even her father, who continually found fault with his other daughters, had nothing but praise for Serel. The only thing that disturbed him about her was her friendship, since childhood, with a young man from the neighboring Ramayles courtyard. Everyone in the neighborhood knew him and knew his parents, too. Yehiel-Michael Henes, the gilder, was a good provider, a fine young man, and an observant Jew. And yet Serel's father was against the match—a boy and girl, he declared, must not arrange their own marriage. And he objected, besides, to the gilder's attendance at the more modern synagogue of the young Zionists. "Perhaps, Rabbi, you could speak to my stubborn old husband and get him to give his blessing to the match," the locksmith's wife pleaded.

Then she spoke about her youngest daughter: "Itka is a lively, clever girl, and everyone says she is very pretty. But her father doesn't allow her to stand in front of a mirror and comb her hair—not on Sabbath, not even in the middle of the week."

The scholar had no inclination to intervene between a father and his children. He knew, however, that sooner or later the hapless woman would return to find out if he had spoken to that stubborn old husband of hers. Here indeed was a man who was hiding under the armor of his obdurate piety, like a turtle in its shell . . . "But," sighed the Porush as he walked over once again to the locksmith, "we have to try."

"Do you know, Reb Heskiah, why we have lost the younger generation? The younger generation has abandoned us because we forbid them things that are allowed; so, they say, they might as well do everything."

Reb Heskiah stopped swaying, but did not take his eyes off his book. After thinking the matter over a long time, he answered slowly, as if he were reading his reply out of the Code.

"The younger generation has left us because we've pampered them too much. If we had chastised our children more often, reminding them of what is forbidden and using a stick to make the lesson sink in, they would never have left us. Lay the blame on soft-hearted parents and leaders."

The Porush knew that the locksmith had no respect for him because his soft-heartedness had made him resign the Zaskowicz pulpit. But he wasn't looking for the locksmith's respect; he merely wanted him not to be such a stubborn, maniacal zealot, heartless toward his own children. "It used to be different," he said in a melancholy voice filled with the sweet sadness of a Sabbath eve twilight. Though outside in the street there reigned the ordinary weekday tumult, the beth midrash remained quiet and dark. "In the old days Jewish children used to get married through arranged matches. Many times the bride and groom didn't see each other until they were under the canopy. In those days it was shameful for a couple to get together without a matchmaker. But nowadays even children from the best homes get married without a matchmaker. Since there's no explicit prohibition of this in the Code and since the gilder and your daughter have known each other from childhood, you can relent in this case."

"Relent? I will not relent!" Reb Heskiah said with a loud, hoarse laugh as his head shrank into his shoulders. "And what if Serel and the boy have known each other since childhood, does that mean they have to get married? Besides, if he imitates the modern crowd by courting Serel, he'll imitate those heathens in other things as well. In fact, the gilder's friends are all among the gang that wants to build a Jewish kingdom in Israel even though the Messiah has not yet arrived."

"That's no crime," said the Porush. "On the contrary, it's a mitzvah to settle the Land of Israel and not wait for the coming of the Messiah."

At that moment it occurred to the locksmith that this Rabbi Yoel Weintraub had not merely resigned his pulpit; he must have been driven out for having supported those Zionist heretics. So he asked the Porush, "And I suppose if the gilder equates this Dr. Herzl with King Zerubavel of the Biblical Return to Zion, that's all right, too, isn't it?"

Reb Yoel replied that he did not know if one could properly compare Dr. Herzl with King Zerubavel, but it would surely be no sin to do so. And the locksmith's youngest daughter was certainly allowed to look into a mirror and comb her hair: "It's not, after all, on Sabbath that she is combing and brushing her hair. On a weekday there's nothing wrong with it at all."

"The Jewish way is that either we must or else we must not," Reb Heskiah replied hoarsely, a reddish glow in his teary eyes. And he would not discuss his daughters any further: he was their father and he knew what he was doing. He rose, his shoulders still hunched, and kissed the cover of the closed volume of the Code. It was time to go home for a bite, and on to his shop.

The Porush, having eaten earlier, after services, remained in the empty beth midrash to continue studying. "It is because of such Jews as the locksmith, zealots who have turned all of life into an either-or, that the halls of study now stand empty," murmured Rabbi Yoel Weintraub to himself as he sat down to delve once again into the Talmud.

3

PALTIEL SHKLAR belonged to a family of gardeners in Zaskowicz. After their father's death, he contended with his older brothers over the inheritance. He refused to compromise or come to a settlement—nothing less than adjudication by a rabbinical court would satisfy him. But for the then-Rav of Zaskowicz, Rabbi Yoel Weintraub, the case seemed too complex by far, what with the many transactions in which the estate and money borrowed from the town's businessmen became entwined.

The longer the case dragged on, the more clearly the Rav could see that what Paltiel Shklar really wanted was not so much the money as to get even with his brothers; he resented their higher status in the eyes of the townspeople. It was around this time that Rabbi Weintraub resigned as Rav and left the drawn-out litigation of the Shklar brothers for his successor to resolve. He moved to Vilna right after Sukkoth. Later that same year, a week before Purim, someone else moved into Laybe-Layzar's courtyard—the Zaskowicz gardener Paltiel Shklar. Rabbi Weintraub, by then a porush, had been told by his wife, Hindele, that after they had left the town a great misfortune had befallen the Shklars: their only child, a young boy, had suddenly died. Hindele had learned of it directly from Paltiel Shklar's wife, Gracia. When he heard this, the Porush's face took on so melancholy an expression that one might have thought the news had forever altered the course of his life. He asked Hindele to invite Paltiel's wife to visit them, and she came one evening when her husband was away.

Gracia was a tall woman with narrow, stooped shoulders and a high, prominent forehead covered with wrinkles. In her eyes there was always the red tinge of a reflected sunset. Her long, tender face and her smooth, delicate hands radiated a moonlike pallor. Unlike her husband, who was called Palty the Grumbler, Gracia always smiled. People marveled at how two such different types could ever have come together. And, in truth, during their betrothal Paltiel had once yelled at her, "Why are you smiling? What have you got to be so happy about?" In those days, though, she had not taken care to look deeply into his character. And even if she had known what sort of man he was, she would not have had the heart to refuse to go under the canopy with him. She did not stop smiling even after her husband's battle with his brothers, not even after the loss of their child. Now, however, it was the smile of one who had nowhere to go, nothing to live for. Her eyes became larger and redder—not the redness of the setting sun's reflection in water, but rather that of eyes continually awash with tears. And yet she still spoke with the fresh lilting voice of a child, her gentle white hands crossed on her chest, as she stood before Rabbi Yoel Weintraub and told him of all that had happened in her life since he had left Zaskowicz.

Her husband had sued his brothers in the Oszmiana circuit court and had sunk all his money into legal fees and expenses. Everyone had told him that the case would be a long one—and indeed, it was still going on. Who could predict when it would end? Their child, their only son, had fallen ill just about the time her husband had begun the court proceedings. The local Zaskowicz doctor was sure that the boy was in no danger, but close friends urged them to call in a physician from Oszmiana. Her husband's brothers wanted to help, and even sent their wives with money. But Paltiel had driven his sisters-in-law away, refusing to accept any favors from his family, especially since the doctor in Zaskowicz maintained there was nothing to worry about. Before they realized what was happening, the little boy had died, a victim of pneumonia.

After the week of mourning, Paltiel pursued the litigation against his brothers with even greater vigor. Quite suddenly, he decided to move to Vilna. His older brothers had everyone in Zaskowicz in their pockets, he said, and the whole town hated him. But in Vilna, he insisted, he had good friends who could advise him how to conduct the lawsuit in Oszmiana. Besides, he hoped to find some wealthy merchants who might become partners with him in a new orchard. At present, they were living on the money they had received from the sale of a field. Soon, however, they would also be obliged to sell their large house in Zaskowicz, with the adjoining orchard, which they had leased out until now; they were simply waiting for the lease to expire.

The Porush listened attentively and silently with head bowed. Only once did he turn to Hindele, who was stationed behind his chair as if standing guard. By the glances they exchanged, each knew the other was wondering the same thing: was it only a coincidence that the gardener from Zaskowicz had moved into their courtyard, or had he done so deliberately? A frightened Hindele took to defending her husband: "But the Rav is not to blame. If we had remained in Zaskowicz, would your Paltiel have made peace with his brothers?"

"But I'm not saying the Rav is to blame," Gracia replied defensively and retreated among the shadows that had swallowed up the bed, the floor, the ceilings, and the entire dwelling.

The Porush sat silently, smoothing out his woolen tallith katan on his knees with both hands. He was thinking of his having left the Zaskowicz rabbinate because he had not had the heart to demand that his flock live strictly according to the law. Yet it appeared there were people, like Reb Heskiah the locksmith and this Paltiel Shklar, who loved the rule of law. They seemed to like every matter balanced on the edge of a knife: it must fall on one side or another, everything or nothing at all.

The residents of Laybe-Layzar's courtyard soon came to love their new neighbor, Gracia, for her sweet, sad face and her quiet demeanor, as surely as they hated her husband. Though she never complained about him, all the neighbors were of one mind: that grouch of a gardener had ruined his wife's youth and beauty.

Paltiel Shklar was shorter than Gracia; he had a large head, a long profile, and a bulbous nose with skin that was always peeling. His protruding lower lip was as hard as leather, and his deeply set brown eyes were keen and darting. He wore a heavy pair of boots in both winter and summer, their hard heels knocking on the cobblestones wherever he went, and he always carried a thick walking stick in his hand like a wanderer. As he walked through the courtyard and the surrounding streets, he never looked at anybody, never said anything, never exchanged a "Good morning." His taut face was covered with sweat, as if he were making his way through a thick crowd, although everyone steered clear of him. When he wasn't going to Oszmiana to attend to his lawsuit, he would spend the entire day in the beth midrash in Laybe-Layzar's courtyard, not saying a word to the other worshippers, just as he would have nothing to do with his neighbors in the courtyard.

The men in the beth midrash noticed that the gardener would often remain seated during the Sh'moneh Esreh, the Silent Prayer, sometimes not rising even for the Kedushah, "Holy, holy, holy," as if he neither saw nor heard what was going on around him. He would sit absent-mindedly for hours in front of an open volume of Mishnayot, never turning a page. Knowing that he had lost his only child, the worshippers felt compassion for the father and attempted to console him. But his angry and obstinate silence discouraged anyone from offering him condolences.

Rabbi Yoel Weintraub felt worst of all, since he stayed behind after the other men left, and studied in the beth midrash alone with this morose, melancholy man. Paltiel Shklar sat in a niche near the bima, not far from the door, as if guarding against the former Zaskowicz Rav's escape from this silent Gehenna in the beth midrash. The Porush felt that the man was killing him with his silence. Sitting in a far corner near the

eastern wall, hidden behind a huge tractate of Talmud, Reb Yoel spied on
the gardener from a distance. In Zaskowicz, Paltiel Shklar had had no beard
and so had looked a great deal younger. Now his long face was covered
with sparse gray hair, as if cobwebs had fallen from a garret and settled on
his cheeks. He sat motionless, not uttering a word. But if you looked closely
at him, you would notice that the expression on his face was constantly
changing.

From behind his lectern the Porush watched Paltiel strain angrily,
furrow his brow, and stick his lower lip out even further. Was he plotting
his next move in his life-and-death struggle with his brothers? Then slowly
the anger passed and gave way to a look of wonder and disbelief as if he
could not understand how he and his brothers had become such mortal
enemies. Then the astonishment changed to a glossy red blush that covered his face—shame about the quarrel in his own family. Finally, a deep
darkness descended upon his face and he sat lamely, as if all of his
thoughts had been suddenly extinguished. The Porush felt a tremor in his
hands and in his knees: "Good God in Heaven! It's entirely possible that
with a little money and a clear head the child might have been saved."

At last, Reb Yoel could no longer endure the embittered man's silence; even being insulted would be preferable. So he walked over to
Paltiel Shklar and addressed him in an affectedly cheerful tone. "You
haven't told me anything, Reb Paltiel, about how things are in Zaskowicz."

The gardener did not so much as blink an eye.

The Porush began pleading with him in a broken voice: "Say something, Reb Paltiel. I understand quite well that you are angry with me
for not settling the dispute between you and your brothers, but the case
dragged on and I left Zaskowicz in the meantime. So why am I to blame?"

Paltiel Shklar still didn't answer, so the Rabbi had no choice but to
walk away. Another time an odd idea, about how to placate the gardener
dawned on him: he would offer to study Mishnah or Midrash with him.
But when he broached the subject, Shklar just looked at him with such
rage that the Porush quickly drew back trembling, his ears ringing with
the gardener's silent scream: "Do you think you can redeem the terrible
injustice you have done me with a chapter or two of Mishnayot?"

Thus did Paltiel Shklar become Rabbi Yoel Weintraub's terror and
torment. The more the man repelled him with his morose silence, the
more the Porush was drawn to him. A few days later Reb Yoel went over
to Paltiel Shklar once again and asked him how his litigation in Oszmiana
was going. "It's going well, very well," he answered quietly and with an

eerie smile. But his brows, his nostrils, and his lips quivered so that the Porush resolved never again to approach the gardener and open his wounds.

4

IN THE HALLWAY of the synagogue a porter stood praying every morning in a threadbare coat with patched elbows and a rope around his waist. From his pious face with its pitch-black beard looked out a pair of big, lusterless eyes filled with the fear and humility of one who felt he was only a guest in this world. The porter held a tattered prayer book in his hands as he listened through the open doors to the services going on inside the beth midrash. Each time the Porush passed the porter on his way into the beth midrash, a sickening odor hit him in the nose: the reek of rotten sauerkraut and the salty stench of empty herring barrels left out uncleaned to dry in the sun. Rabbi Yoel Weintraub once asked the porter why he prayed in the hallway and not inside.

"The people tell me they can't stand being next to me," the porter answered, and from his eyes shone the damp darkness of the cellars where he handled pots of kraut, and all but immersed himself in the brine of the herring barrels.

"Don't you have any other clothes?" the Porush then asked.

The porter shook his head—no, he had no other clothes—and hid his worn, thick prayer book in his bosom.

Once, as the Porush was passing through the hallway to the beth midrash, he saw a woman with a wrinkled face and no teeth in her mouth standing next to the porter. By her appearance she could have been his mother, but she was in fact his wife and she was complaining that she had no shoes, that he had no clothes, and that they were living in a tiny stall. She was also warning him that his boss was bound to fire him and hire somebody else to roll the herring barrels if he continued to stay all day long in the beth midrash.

The man waited with a harried expression for his wife to finish. When he saw she had no intention of stopping, he pleaded with her:

"Please, just let me say my prayers like a Jew!"

"You good-for-nothing, go inside the beth midrash," she ordered as she tried to push him through the door. "Why are you standing out here like a beggar? You're as fine a worshipper as anyone else. You make your living honestly, don't you?"

The porter, weary of his wife's sharp tongue, cried out in utter exasperation, "For Heaven's sake, what do you want of me? Haven't I told you many times that one may not stand in a holy place wearing clothes that give off an offensive odor?"

" 'You may not do this; you may not do that!' It's what you say about everything—that you may not," the porter's wife said mockingly. Then she noticed the Porush standing in the hallway behind them, waiting for the couple to step aside and allow him to enter the beth midrash. "Tell me, Rabbi," she said, "is my husband permitted to pray with the others or is he indeed not allowed to?"

"He may," the Rabbi said, glancing at the porter, who was looking at him open-mouthed. "One may not pray next to water in which flax or hemp is being soaked, since, according to the law, that would be the same as praying next to a dungheap. But as for a Jew whose clothes contain the essence of herring, there's nothing that forbids one to pray next to him."

Nevertheless, the porter continued praying in the hallway. Except once when, during morning services, the reader leading the service had a weak voice and could not be heard in the hallway, he stuck first his head through the doors into the synagogue, next his shoulders, and finally eased his entire body inside the beth midrash.

The worshippers did not notice him slip in because at that moment they were engrossed with eyes shut in the heartfelt recitation of the Shemā, "Hear, O Israel: The Lord our God, the Lord is One." Reb Heskiah, the locksmith, enunciated each word with greater care than the rest. All the worshippers accentuated and prolonged the "EHAD!"—"One" —but Reb Heskiah rose above the rest with a stubborn, chilling exultation: "And these words, which I command you this day, shall be in thine heart: And thou shalt teach them diligently unto thy children, and shalt talk of them when thou sittest in thine house, and when thou walkest by the way, and when thou liest down, and when thou risest up." Reb Heskiah struggled to clearly pronounce "VESHINANTOM"—"thou shalt teach them." He was dissatisfied with his "sh," it sounded more like an "s." And when he reached "VEDIBARTO BOM"—"and thou shalt speak of them"—he did not like his pronunciation of the "m." Reb Heskiah paused a moment and mentally leafed through the Code for a ruling on what was to be done. He repeated the phrase "VEDIBARTO BOM" so many times that he began to sound like a bell pealing: "BOM! BOM! BOM!"

Suddenly someone started screaming. Everyone turned and saw Paltiel Shklar berating the porter, who stood near the bima in the middle of the beth midrash. The usually silent gardener was yelling at the top of his voice like one possessed: "Get out of here! You stink! Out!"

The porter was also in the midst of the recitation of the Shema and knew full well that he was not permitted to interrupt the prayer for anything. But, terrified at having been discovered and dazed by the abuse heaped on him, he did halt the prayer and begged the gardener not to throw him out. He stammered and cried like a pitiful child: Reb Heskiah had recently told him that when he prayed outside the door of the synagogue, he was not to be reckoned as part of the minyan. And the reader was leading the service so quietly that from the hallway he could not hear how far the congregation had got or when to say "amen."

"I don't want to hear about it. You are stinking up the place like a skunk. Out! Get out!" Paltiel Shklar bellowed as he pushed the porter toward the door with both hands. But instead of heading for the door, the porter, in his confusion, threw himself even closer to the front of the beth midrash. He held the phylactery on his head in place with one hand as he fended off his attacker with the other.

The other worshippers were likewise unwilling to interrupt their recitation of the "Hear, O Israel," so they continued praying, standing in a circle and shrugging their shoulders. Though they, too, were revolted by the porter's stench, they were even more perturbed to see the gardener humiliate him so. An old butcher's patience ran out and he shouted at the frantic Paltiel Shklar, "Then smell your fill of the stench and be done with it! And what about me? I spend the whole day in the meat market, so perhaps you don't care to have me at services either? If the poor man has to make his livelihood soaking in the herring brine, does that make him any less of a Jew?"

"I said I wasn't interested," Shklar yelled and shook a fist at the butcher, who, though a burly man, retreated fearfully from this blustering lunatic. "I have my own burden of sorrow to shoulder, and does anyone care? So why should I care why he stinks? We're not permitted to pray with him around and that's all there is to it."

"But you *are* permitted," the porter blurted out as he pointed to the Porush. "The Rabbi told me that one is not permitted to pray near water that reeks of flax and hemp, but he specifically said you may pray next to a man who smells of herring. You definitely may."

For a moment Paltiel Shklar stood frozen, as if paralyzed. The next moment his face was aflame with rage as he whirled around and exploded at the Rabbi: "So it was you who told this idiot that he's allowed to stink up the beth midrash? Well, what can we expect? You've never had the backbone to inform anyone that there are things that are not permitted! Any more than you had the courage in Zaskowicz to tell my brothers that they're not permitted to cheat their younger brother."

The other worshippers looked on with curiosity and sympathy as the Porush sat painfully silent, his prayer shawl over his head. The gardener continued screaming at the top of his voice. "It's all your fault that I'm a pauper! And it's all your fault that my child died! You were softhearted to my brothers, those thieves, at the price of my only child's life!"

Reb Yoel's hands trembled on his knees. He groaned like a creaking beam in the ceiling of an old house, and cast a pleading look at the others, begging them with his eyes not to believe this horrible calumny. The porter, terrified by the aspersions the gardener was casting on the Porush, inched his way out the door. Paltiel Shklar walked briskly to his seat, tore off his prayer shawl and tefillin, and screamed at the Porush across the beth midrash for all to hear: "My brothers haven't won yet! There is more justice in the Gentile courts than there is in the Zaskowicz Rav. I'll show all of you yet!" With that, he stormed out of the beth midrash in the middle of services, right in the middle of the "Hear, O Israel," and hurried to catch the train to Oszmiana, where his case was coming to trial that day.

The locksmith, standing quietly in a far corner, had witnessed this whole tumultuous scene, thankful to the Lord that he had no sense of smell so that the porter's foul odor did not concern him. Reb Heskiah searched his mind for the ruling as to the precise verse with which to begin again the interrupted prayer "Hear, O Israel." But before he resumed his murmuring, he mentally summarized what he had just seen and just heard: "This is what it comes to when a Rav hasn't the heart to say no: First he hasn't the courage to insist that people follow the proper rituals of service to God. In the end, he hasn't the courage to mete out justice and see to it that brothers deal justly with one another."

5

O N THE OTHER SIDE of the bridge that spanned the Wilejka lived the Munvas brothers, fish merchants with a reputation for being honest if somewhat crude. Throughout the workweek the fish market would resound with their voices ringing out from beside tubs of live pike, carp, and tench. On Sabbath they all went quietly with their children to the Poplawy beth midrash for services. The only Munvas to grow up a "gypsy"—so the entire family called him—was the youngest brother, Moishele. Even as a youngster he displayed no interest in his studies, and later on he turned his back on learning a trade, or even becoming a fish handler. He lived with his eldest brother, slept until noon, and stayed out all night cavorting with the girls of the town.

The family, desperate to make something of Moishele, was anxious to marry him off. So, just to spite them, he brought home a young milliner, Bertha Sapir, a flashy woman with a bad name all over Bakszta Street, where she lived. When she came to their home, the Munvas family kept very quiet, but did not take their eyes off her polished bright-red fingernails, as if these were proof enough that the girl deserved her reputation. After she left, Moishele's brothers told him that if he ever married that whore, they'd twist his head off like a herring's.

Moishele feared his brothers, so with great bitterness he took to wandering from village to village. First he traveled with organ grinders and peddlers who bartered cheap goods in exchange for raw hides, eggs, and live chickens. Once news came that Moishele had been seen in Glebokie, going from house to house with a band of beggars. When he had had enough of wandering, he came home in rags so worn and filthy that the Munvas women talked among themselves of how his clothes jiggled on the floor from all the vermin in them.

The family descended on him with warnings and chastisements until Moishele promised to try to pull himself together and make something of his life. Since he was now over twenty, it was too late for him to become an apprentice and learn a good trade, so the family decided that Moishele should become an upholsterer. It didn't take long to learn how to cover sofas and chairs, and one did not require fancy tools or even a workshop —the upholstering could be done right in the customer's home. The brothers paid a master upholsterer to teach Moishele, and after he learned the trade and learned it well, the upholsterer took him on as an assistant and paid him a salary.

Once again he lived with his eldest brother and spent all his money on new, stylish clothes. He selected his clothes with such care and absorption that he seemed to be making up for the time spent wandering about the countryside in rags. Before going out for the evening he would redo the knot of his tie ten times in front of the mirror and polish his fancy black patent-leather shoes. He wouldn't come home until late at night, and it didn't take long for the family to realize that Moishele had not yet flushed his fancy girlfriend with the fiery-red fingernails out of his system. His sisters-in-law just couldn't get over it: What did he see in that sour face? And his brothers made it abundantly clear once again that a marriage was out of the question. Moishele swore that Bertha Sapir was as pure as a dove, that he was madly in love with her, and that if he couldn't marry her, he would once again become a tramp out of despair. His brothers answered that they didn't care even if he became a Christian or if he were to drop dead right then and there—he was not going to marry that hatmaker, even if he were to turn heaven and earth upside down, not unless he longed to become a heap of broken bones.

Moishele knew that his brothers, with their bearlike paws, could indeed beat him to a pulp. But when, in his mealy-mouthed fashion, he tried to explain to Bertha Sapir that the entire Munvas family was dead set against their marrying, Bertha retorted contemptuously: "And you call yourself a man? You're a dishrag, that's what you are!" These words kindled so great an anger in Moishele that he allowed his sisters-in-law to arrange a match for him with Nehamele Glass, a seamstress from Kopanica Street.

The small-framed Nehamele, with a tall wiglike hairdo, looked like a child when she smiled and like a mean old woman when she furrowed her broad brow. For her customers she sewed dresses in the latest fashion; but she herself wore long dresses with sleeves to her knuckles and around her neck a small, flat white collar with a button. Her gold earrings had been left to her by her late mother, and her brooch was a legacy from her grandmother. "And from whom," people would ask, "are the pearls, Nehamele?" "The pearls are from my grandmother Gittel, my father's mother," she would answer, as in her eyes sparkled the pearly teardrops of an orphan.

On summer Sabbath afternoons Nehamele would take a walk through Kopanica Street to the Poplawski Bridge and then return home by the same route. On one side of the street were rows of backyard gardens, and on the other side a sidewalk ran in front of the wooden gates of the peaceful courtyards along the banks of the Wilejka. And every Sabbath afternoon groups of women who gathered at the gates watched Nehamele pass by alone, clutching a small bag in her left hand. The women remarked that the seamstress earned a good living and was very likable; her customers, they had heard, all loved her dearly. Yet she didn't seem able to catch a man, nor did she have any girlfriends. It was her orphan's gloom, they decided, that turned both men and women away from her.

When the Munvas women went to the seamstress to talk about the match, they spoke to her as to a dear sister: "You don't have to be ashamed of our family. True, our husbands are fish merchants, but they are all fine men. Do you know Moishele?" Nehamele blushed and remained silent. She had seen him more than once standing in the street, leaning against a doorpost, his hands deep in his pockets and one foot crossed over the other. Moishele would always be yawning, bored to tears, and never so much as noticed Nehamele. Or if he did look at her, it was with the stare of one who was seeing her for the first time, though she had walked past him hundreds of times before. From her silence, the Munvas women could see that Nehamele would not be hard to convince. They told this to their husbands, who thereupon went to talk to their brother, that gypsy:

"You good-for-nothing boor! Would she even look at you if her parents were alive? It's your good fortune she's a poor orphan!"

Moishele couldn't even remember what this seamstress looked like, but he was curious to see a girl who would consent to an arranged marriage. When the women brought Nehamele home, he thought he was looking at a rebbetzin. Though he did not say a word, Nehamele immediately noted the sardonic smile playing in the corners of his mouth. She creased her forehead, flashed her eyes at him, and ground her pure white teeth with such anger that Moishele, in utter surprise, took his hands out of his pockets. "Now look at that! Some little scorpion!" . . . and he liked her.

That night of their first meeting Moishele sang songs and recounted his adventures as a wanderer. A mesmerized Nehamele listened with burning ears. The Munvas family was delighted by her modest blushes, and Moishele was already savoring his revenge on Bertha Sapir. Aha! When she heard that he was married, she wouldn't call him a dishrag anymore.

After the wedding the Munvas brothers found a home for the couple in Laybe-Layzar's courtyard. They seemed to want Moishele as far away from them as possible, as if burdened with a premonition that they had not yet received the full measure of disgrace he was destined to bring on them. Nehamele had not wanted to leave the neighborhood where her customers lived, but Moishele insisted that no wife of his would work; he was man enough to be able to provide for her. "Let me have your savings, Nehamele. I'll furnish our apartment and say good riddance to my boss, that slave-driver. I can work for myself and earn three times as much."

Nehamele gazed at him enraptured: He had never asked if, besides the trunk with her trousseau, she had any money; and, to make sure he wasn't marrying her for her dowry, she had refrained from telling him of the large sum she had saved. Evidently, then, he had figured out himself that she must have something set aside, and yet he had not asked for it until it was needed to set them up in their new home. Moved by his sincerity, Nehamele gave him everything she had, looking deep and trustingly into his eyes.

Congenital blabbermouth that he was, Moishele still had enough sense not to tell his wife about his former sweetheart. A few months after the wedding, however, when they were already well settled in Laybe-Layzar's courtyard, he found himself longing for Bertha once again, and went to see her with an armful of presents. But Bertha—though she knew better now than to offend him as she had before—did not fall into his arms; instead, she berated him in the sharp tones of a market woman: "You married that pipsqueak, and you want me to be your mistress? You can drop dead, just for the wanting."

Bertha Sapir liked to wear a skirt, an open blouse, and an unbuttoned, sleeveless jacket. Let everyone see her figure, she would say, and let them die of envy. A corset, a stiff bodice, and expensive clothes were for fat, ugly women—she had no need of all that. No matter how much Bertha swayed and twisted in her loose and unfastened clothing, her body remained tight and supple like a freshly wound steel spring.

As for her character, this had little of steel or iron in its composition. She was by nature a fey and languorous homebody, forever lost in romantic fantasies. Bertha's first lover had soon understood the need for ardent protestations of eternal love; but this eternal love had lasted barely three months. Her next involvement was with a married man who continually bemoaned his life with his accursed wife. From this affair Bertha gained a reputation as a seducer of married men, a reputation that caused her great suffering; and she had stayed away from men—those dogs!—until she met and got involved with Moishele Munvas. He was, after all, single and dying to marry her. Only his brothers' disapproval stood in their way.

When, out of great bitterness, Moishele had gone wandering about the world, Bertha remained true to him and waited. And when he returned, Bertha fell into his arms, hungering for him. She never doubted that when her beloved had learned a trade and was able to stand on his own, he would say goodbye to his brothers and they would be married. So what happened? He married a woman with money and of fine repute.

"I understand you very well," said Bertha, pretending to be calm as she went on with her work—though instead of sticking the threaded needle into the brim of a hat, she pricked her own finger. "You took a wife that everyone pities; a poor frightened creature who will cower when you bellow. And you want me for your mistress on the side. You should live so long!"

Moishele tried to explain: His brothers—those cutthroats—had threatened him, and swearing that he couldn't live without her had done no good. The hatmaker told him to go and not come back until he had divorced that pure dove of his, his prim little princess, that pale, dried-out lemon. Moishele's anger boiled over and he snapped back at her, "Who needs you and your sour face!" He slammed the door behind him, as if to cut off Bertha's shouting after him: "Gypsy! Scoundrel!" And yet, a few days later he felt his nose tickled by the memory of her perfume and he longed for her warm, supple body until he felt the glue seeping out of his bones.

Now Moishele, going from total silence to total confession, told his wife everything: he had married her because his brothers had badgered him to death, but it was Bertha Sapir whom he loved. Nehamele felt her blood turn to ice. She looked at him as if she suddenly saw an evil demon lurking behind his coal-black mustache. She spent the next few days in ceaseless tears. He let her cry out her shock and sadness, and then, suddenly and calmly, asked her, "Will you accept a divorce?"

"No," Nehamele hissed through tightly pressed lips, and then she threatened to tell his brothers everything. But Moishele was ready for this threat, and answered with a laugh: Since he had lost his love forever because of them, he had also lost any respect and fear he had once felt for his brothers, especially now that he wasn't dependent on them anymore. "By all means, go to my brothers. Don't dare come home until you've talked to them. Do you hear me?" he said as he pushed her out the door into the street.

6

NEHAMELE WALKED THROUGH the streets of the town with darkened, hollow eyes. Not until she crossed the bridge to the other side of the Wilejka and walked through Poplawska Street did her eyes clear, and then she became filled with a childlike joy and wonder at the thickly verdant trees. In the stone-and-wood world of Laybe-Layzar's courtyard there were no trees, not so much as a blade of grass. Living there, one could easily forget that spring had come to the world and trees had already shed their white blossoms. Nehamele, gazing at the light-green vines on the gates of Kopenica Street, reflected that she hadn't realized how happy she had been when she lived there. Every little house and every window along the banks of the Wilejka had winked at her warmly and familiarly. In the summer the tree branches had flaunted their green foliage at her, and when she went out into the street on winter mornings she had imagined that the snow-laden trees knew what she had dreamed the night before. Her clients had all loved her and never haggled with her. She wished now she had remained a spinster, so that she could have spent her life dreaming of the happiness yet to come.

LEANING ON THEIR HARD ELBOWS, the Munvas brothers sat around the table, and behind them stood their wives. They were all listening to their young sister-in-law telling them what she had to endure from her husband, their Moishele. The shadows grew thick on the wall between the stark figures, as if the shadows themselves were part of the family. No one lit a light; was it because everyone in the house was ashamed to look Nehamele in the eye? Finally, the eldest brother spoke up: "As you yourself tell it, the rascal says he's not afraid of us, so what can we do? I'd say, go home and ignore his babbling."

"His old love, the hatmaker, brags that she won't let him across her threshold until he divorces you. So don't accept a divorce from him and the foolishness will pass," said the eldest brother's wife in support of her husband. "Nehamele," the other women all intoned sympathetically, "one must be ready to suffer from a husband."

Not since her mother had passed away, leaving her alone in their little house and alone in the world, had Nehamele felt so lonely and so miserable as when the Munvas brothers told her they could not get involved. "It's a family with hearts of stone," she thought. Apparently, it was beneath the Munvases' dignity to let their youngest brother marry that notorious hatmaker, but when it came to his bilking Nehamele out of her life's savings or the way he tormented her, that they didn't care about at all. In one respect, though, the Munvases were right: She must not give in to Moishele and let him divorce her.

Now Nehamele's hell began in earnest. Moishele had for her no other name but "my dried-out lemon" or "toothpick." But as much as this pained Nehamele, she was even more fearful of the label "divorcee" which she would receive if she agreed to what he wanted. So she suffered in silence. She kept the house as neat as ever, shopped, cooked meals for her husband as before, and quietly put the food on the table, afraid to look at her tormentor's carefully groomed mustache astride his thick, full lips. It seemed to her that all his evil and coarseness resided in that mustache, which had once appealed to her so much. For his part, Moishele couldn't help regarding his wife in amazement—who would have imagined that such a small, frail, seemingly fearful woman could be so stubborn? If she had carried on, he would have laughed at her. But just because she suffered in silence, there were times when he felt pity for her; she was, after all, a lonely orphan. And at the same time his hatred for Nehamele grew as he came to realize that she was deeply committed to this marriage and that she would never consent to a divorce.

A gloom descended on Moishele, and he walked about like a man with a hangover after a night of drunken revelry. In the morning he went to work unshaven, and when he came home in the evening, he didn't wash himself or even brush off the dust and lint his clothes had accumulated through the day. He sat sullenly at the table, wolfed down his supper, tearing at the meat with his filthy fingernails and drinking beer or seltzer or downing a full quart of cold water. Then, with the same sullenness, he would go sit and gaze out the window overlooking Laybe-Layzar's courtyard. In the purple summer dusk he felt so melancholy that he could no longer bear the silence and turned to his wife, who was putting away the dishes.

"What do you expect, that a little runt of a woman like you could make me forget Bertha? She has a body like a spring and you are a toothpick!"

Nehamele stood silent and motionless, her arms raised to the shelves of the cupboard. Not until her husband turned his head and once again stared absently out the window into the courtyard did Nehamele slowly lower her hands and gingerly walk into the next room. She stood very still between the beds and pulled at the edge of a handkerchief she held fast in her teeth until it began to tear. This was how Nehamele checked her anger and pain and kept herself from weeping aloud, steeling herself to endure even more and never give in.

And then, slowly, a change took place in the ways of Moishele Munvas. He seemed to have become his old self again. When he returned from work in the evening, he was still humming the tune he had hummed leaving the house that morning. After dinner he would wash and change, groom himself carefully, and go out, usually till well past midnight. With each day he looked more satisfied, even happy. He even started talking to Nehamele with some kindness, praising her cooking and asking why she ate so little. Not another word was mentioned about the divorce or about Bertha—but neither did he offer any explanation of where he disappeared to until near dawn.

The residents of Laybe-Layzar's courtyard and the young people in the streets knew all about Moishele—about his family, his love affair with the hatmaker, and how deeply he loathed the little woman with big eyes, that spider he had married. The young men joked that when Moishele sat at home in the evening and gazed out his window into the courtyard, he looked like a condemned man who knows his days are numbered. Then later, when he started to go out in the evening all dressed up, leaving his wife alone at home, they watched him with curiosity. At first, they didn't ask any questions, but just stood in the narrow alleyways, their broad shoulders leaning against the closed shutters of the small, narrow shops, casting mischievously searching glances at the upholsterer as he passed by. "Well, Moishele," they called out to him, "you're living the life, aren't you?" "Well," answered the playboy cold-bloodedly, "when opportunity knocks, why not let it in?"

From his offhand remarks and his lascivious looks the street set surmised that, just as Moishele's marriage was over, so the affair with his former mistress was water under the bridge. After all, he worked as an upholsterer in the rich houses of the town where the husbands were away at their businesses all day, so the world was his for the asking. He surely sang songs to the housewives and won them over with those tall tales of his—and don't you worry, he had customers. Though Moishele told them nothing, the young people would speculate on where he was going and whom he was seeing. Since he wore a different outfit every night, carefully chosen from a closet filled with fancy clothes, the street-wise connoisseurs could judge his achievements by his attire.

One evening he left the courtyard wearing a dark-gray pinstripe suit and a soft shirt with a fashionable necktie. He carried a heavy overcoat and a hat in his left hand. A glance at the cloudless sky made it apparent that it was not going to rain. So why, the question presented itself, had Moishele taken a coat along? It was as clear as his face, wasn't it, that he was off to see some widow who had marriage in mind, not flirting; that's why that playboy had to look like a straight-and-narrow accountant. He surely hadn't told her of his wife, or if he had, he had convinced her that they did not live together and were on the verge of getting a divorce. Look, he had even turned down his Cossack mustache—to let everyone know how heavy his heart was and how much he needed a consoler.

Another night he was wearing broad knickers, striped socks of heavy wool, and heavy shoes with thick soles, such as sportsmen wore. His light beige jacket had two large pockets sewn on each side, and under his left lapel a smaller third pocket that looked more like a sewn patch. He carried his hat in hand and walked hurriedly, with his head tilted back. The wind blew the lapels of his jacket wide open and his necktie flapped over his shoulder and fluttered behind him. The young people poked each other with their elbows: "Where is he off to now, and who is he going to meet? He's heading for the Wilja River, to the Maccabee Stadium. There he'll sit in a restaurant with some girl who'll chatter away in Polish while he twirls his mustache. Do you think he knows how to talk to an educated young lady? She'll laugh at him, the fool; but what does she care as long as he treats her? It costs him plenty, you can be sure."

Yet another time he was seen walking in the streets in something like a squire's outfit, with the tall, narrow boots of a gentleman hunter, into which his trousers were tucked, and an embroidered silk peasant tunic with a braided silk belt around his waist. A flat cap with a hard visor was pushed back on his head, revealing a thick shock of hair that came down to his eyes. He had only one arm in the sleeve of his jacket, the rest of the jacket dangling behind him in the casual style of the local thugs. Moishele strolled along in a leisurely way, his hands deep in his pockets under the embroidered hem of his tunic, and with the bored look of a bon vivant who has imbibed his fill of the pleasures of life and has nothing left to look forward to. "Bah," chortled one of the street set, "he's going to a country hick."

But another one smacked his forehead with his palm as a light suddenly dawned on him: "Do you know what I think? I think he's not going anywhere. This is all a play he's putting on, to make us envious of him, and make his wife burst with jealousy. With him for a husband she has become black like a burned pot."

The youths devoted a bit more talk to Moishele, assuring one another that they did not begrudge him his lot in life, and then went on to chat and laugh about other things. But it wasn't long before they had exhausted all their topics of conversation, and remained standing idly about, yawning and silent.

In the alleyway of the junk-dealers the musty odor of old clothing and rags still hung thick in the air, even though the tiny shopfronts stared blindly ahead, already shut and boarded for the night. The pavement of the neighboring Ramayles courtyard was black from the pieces of coal crushed underfoot, and littered with short pieces of hemp rope from the bundles of wood sold there. The Jewish Street rang with the tumult of barefoot children playing in the dried gutter. The fruit vendors stood beside the baskets of last year's shriveled apples. Bearded Jews were walking in through the iron gates of the courtyard of the Grand Synagogue for the evening services. And neatly shaven young men were rushing to the synagogues to recite the Kaddish for a departed relative.

In Laybe-Layzar's courtyard the neighbors sat on the crooked steps, in the doorways, on the porches, and some at open windows, leaning out into the courtyard for a breath of fresh air. When they became tired of looking at the courtyard with its crooked cobblestones and flaking plaster walls, at the confused clutter of doors, stairs, and windows on top of windows, they would turn their heads toward the skies and fill their eyes with the blue stillness of the heavens. Then their eyes would wander once again over the courtyard, until they came to rest at last on the upholsterer's dwelling. There was no light in the window, and the door was shut. During the day they saw Nehamele go shopping for her husband's dinner. She walked through the courtyard with her head bowed, and when shopping in the stores she turned away from everyone's stare. She looked like an orphan coming home from the cemetery. But in the evening, after supper, when her husband, all dressed up, went out for the night, she did not appear at all. The neighbors understood that the humiliated woman must be lying down crying, her face buried in the pillow, or hiding in a lonely corner, bemoaning her fate.

"LAYBE-LAYZAR'S COURTYARD is not Sodom. We cannot allow a rake to get away with torturing his wife just because she is an orphan and has no one to defend her."

This was what the older women said as they exhorted their husbands not to stand by and permit this outrage. If that lecher scoffed at his own wife, the women argued, would he listen when neighbor women scolded him? But he would be ashamed before other men. The older men in the courtyard were laborers with wispy gray beards, fingers stiff from years of toil, their bodies crooked and lame like old, rusted metal bars. Exhausted by work and their hard lives, it was all they could do not to fall asleep at their benches in the workshops or at services in the beth midrash. Whatever they saw, they saw with beclouded eyes; whatever they heard, they heard with plugged ears. But the women were persistent, and eventually pushed their men into confronting Moishele and reproving him: Such behavior was not fitting for a Jewish young man.

"You're envious of me. Ha! You'd like to, wouldn't you, but it's already too late for you. Ha!"

The old men spat three times for letting themselves be talked into getting involved with that rascal.

Next, the younger women stepped in. They couldn't stand the thought of a sister of theirs being so mistreated by such a scoundrel. Though Nehamele was not very friendly with any of the women in the courtyard, they stopped her and started talking to her about her husband: She ought to singe his curly mustache, throw hot lye in his rotten face, and scratch out the eyes of his mistresses. Nehamele listened and kept silent, head down. When they saw they were dealing with a wife who was afraid to raise her voice to her husband, they pitied her even more and went back to incite their husbands.

Most of the middle-aged men of Laybe-Layzar's courtyard were wagon drivers in flat hats with twisted visors and with knotted beards full of the sand and dust of the unpaved highways. Two residents, however, were butchers, with flaming red faces, broad shoulders, and hands so powerful that they could seize an ox by his horns and wrestle him to the ground. And there were market vendors in tall boots, with hardy, boisterous voices—fellows who instilled fear into a market full of peasants. When they came home after a long day of hard work and headaches, all they wanted was to eat their supper in peace. Now, however, they found their strong, full-bodied wives shouting at them incessantly as they carried bowls of hot potatoes and plates of roasted meat to the table.

"Why do you keep quiet? Aren't you fathers of small children your-selves?"

Their husbands burned their lips on the steaming potatoes, caught pieces of the meat in their teeth, gagged on bread that they vainly at-tempted to swallow. They stared at their wives like oxen chewing their cud: What on earth, they were wondering, did their little children have to do with that womanizing upholsterer? But the women insisted that they had everything to do with it—small children *were* endangered by the upholsterer's evil influence. His wife was a pitiful orphan, and God did not keep silent when people looked the other way and did nothing when an orphan was wronged. And so it came to pass, one evening after supper, that the men found themselves in the street, waiting to speak to the playboy as he was leaving for his rendezvous:

"Listen, friend, we won't have to answer for your sins; your sins are your own business. But this is a respectable Jewish courtyard and we're fed up with your shameless cavorting."

Moishele saw that he was surrounded by men already in their forties with bulging stomachs, and yet with shoulders a yard wide that were not the least bit hunched. He knew all too well that when one of these fellows punched a bothersome customer or a brawling peasant in the market, he was lucky to make off with his life. Now here they were standing all around him, shoulder to shoulder so he could not squeeze through, and assessing him with cold, glassy eyes. This was one time, he realized, when he would have to be meek. So he curled his mustache and answered calmly:

"You're absolutely right. Our marriage is a disaster for both of us. That's why I'm ready to give my wife a divorce at any time; you can all be my witnesses. Now let me through."

This sounded logical and reasonable to them, so they let him pass, not wanting to insult his honor as a man. "Go fly a kite and leave us out of it," the men told their wives, washing their hands of the whole matter. "He claims he wants to set her free." The next day the women conveyed this good news to Nehamele, but this time she did not stand meekly shivering as she had the last time; instead, she covered her face with both hands and broke into a hysterical cry: She didn't want a divorce! No! No! She didn't want it!

"No is no." The neighbors backed away in confusion and gave

Nehamele new advice: "They say you're an excellent seamstress. Why not take on some work again and earn enough money so you won't have to depend on your husband and be afraid of leaving him?"

"No! No!" Nehamele cried even louder.

The women wondered: Was she so in love with him, or was she afraid of being left all alone? It suddenly occurred to one of the neighbors that the person who ought to be consulted in this case was the Porush, Rabbi Yoel Weintraub. Though he was new in Laybe-Layzar's courtyard, people had nothing but the highest respect for him. Even that filthy pig Moishele Munvas would heed him. They would ask the Rebbetzin Hindele to talk to her husband and get him to take an active interest in the matter.

No one in the courtyard could have imagined that the Rebbetzin, herself no bigger than a small hen, could fly into such a rage and scream so loudly. The baskets on her arms shook so violently that the eggs inside almost cracked. What? Her saintly husband, the great scholar, should sully himself with so sordid an affair? She had become an egg peddler just in order that her noble husband, may he live and be well, should not have to deal with boorish congregants. And now they expected him to get involved with a polygamist?

As matters turned out, however, the Porush did get involved, after all—not by choice, but through an unexpected turn of events.

BETWEEN AFTERNOON AND EVENING SERVICES, Reb Yoel conducted a class in *Ein Ya'akov*, the "Book of Talmudic Legends," for five men. With their backs humbly and studiously bent forward, they listened attentively to the beautiful teachings of the sages and piously sighed at their own sinfulness. Reb Heskiah the locksmith would remain meanwhile in his corner, engrossed in the Codes.

One day, when at last the sky had darkened and it was time for Ma'ariv, the evening service, they found that they were three men short of the ten needed for a minyan. And so, one old man hobbled out into the courtyard in search of three Jews. Two half-dressed men resting on their porches in the courtyard, still in their slippers, pulled on their jackets and came down to the beth midrash. At that moment Moishele the upholsterer happened by, sporting a broad straw hat. The old man asked him if he'd like to earn the mitzvah of being the tenth man, the one to complete the minyan. The thought of doing a mitzvah appealed to Moishele, and he liked the idea of being the tenth man to a minyan even more. So, as he

entered the beth midrash, he said to himself: "Let her wait." But now he
found himself the object of angry looks from two men at the Rabbi's table,
and one of the two recent arrivals pointed an accusing finger at him:

"A heathen like that can't be counted to a minyan, can he, Reb
Heskiah?"

But Reb Heskiah kept silent, perhaps because he did not want to
lock horns with the likes of Moishele Munvas, or else was unwilling to
render an opinion when a rabbi was sitting right there at the table; then
again, he might simply have been obeying an instinct not to mix into
other people's affairs—at any rate, he didn't answer, but continued swaying and peering into his large tome. As for Moishele, the hushed, ever-
darkening dusk in the windows, the gathering of men huddled under the
table's solitary lamp, the entire sanctuary filled with the clutter of
benches, lecterns, tables, the bima, and the ark—all somehow caused fear
and shame to descend upon him. Instead of laughing the accusation off
or becoming incensed, he sidled up to the Porush and asked plaintively,
"Is it true I cannot be counted to a minyan? Am I not a Jew?"

"Every Jew may be counted to a minyan," Rabbi Weintraub answered.

The locksmith swayed more vigorously, and recited more loudly
the passage from the Codes he was then reading, as if to shout down a
temptation welling inside him to join in the dispute. The others remained
silent out of respect for the Rabbi. But the man who had challenged
Moishele's right to be counted was not ready to concede, and he shouted
angrily at the Porush: "Is that what it says in the Torah, that it is permitted to count someone like that to a minyan? And does it also say one is
permitted to shame his wife, especially a poor, hapless orphan?"

Reb Heskiah abruptly ceased his swaying and fixed his eyes on the
Porush, anxious to see if the former Zaskowicz Rav had the courage to
say that something—anything—was not permitted.

Rabbi Weintraub leaned his hands on the table, rose from his chair,
and sighed. "To shame a wife, especially a woman with no relations to
defend her, is a wrong, a terrible wrong. But it has nothing whatever to
do with being part of a minyan. Come, let's begin Ma'ariv."

"Even chastising this footloose scoundrel comes as hard to him as
splitting the Red Sea," Reb Heskiah laughed to himself as he rose for the
service. "But saying something is allowed comes so easily to him." The
others all ambled to their regular places and corners, leaving Moishele
standing alone in his broad straw hat, as if he had been hit over the head.
He prayed without feeling or concentration, and afterwards found that he
had lost his eagerness to continue on to his rendezvous.

The Porush had yet to endure the berating of his wife. He always studied at home late at night so that she would not be alone. In the circle of light from the single kerosene lamp, he sat over the open volume of Maimonides' Code as Hindele stood over him, pointing her finger into the book as she spoke, as if to indicate that there, too, it was written that a scholar may not get involved in so foul a matter.

Her husband only smiled: "Yes, Hindele, Hindele, Maimonides always mixed in, though he, too, had forsworn the rabbinate, and his was a much greater position than I had in Zaskowicz, I assure you."

Hindele stood still in her confusion, and Rabbi Yoel Weintraub stopped smiling and sighed heavily, as he had done earlier in the beth midrash. He deeply pitied the young woman so humiliated by her husband, yet he had compassion also for the young husband whose passions were leading him astray.

8

EACH OF HESKIAH TEITELBAUM's three daughters had a distinctive appearance, even her own color of hair.

The eldest, Malka, the divorcee, looked as dour as her mother. All that was left of the thick black locks of her youth and the black flash in her eyes was a mat of tangled hair and a weary, lusterless look. The middle sister, Serel the shopkeeper, had a full head of chestnut hair parted in the middle, and a pale face, dark, sad eyes; her entire demeanor exuded a modesty as placid and as gray as a poor man's Sabbath. Only the youngest daughter, Itka, was full of life, with a robust body and full breasts that made her blouses and jackets all but burst. Because of her full hips, her clothes seemed to be too tight, which made her appear shorter than she was. Her arms were short and thick at the shoulders. Her skin was milk-white, her eyes were a bright light blue, her lips were small and fresh. Out of her every movement gushed forth a joy of life—a curiosity and a mockery. She would speak loudly and laugh even more loudly, smiling with her teeth and with her cheeks and the corners of her mouth fully creased. But what one could not help but notice most of all were the two copper-red braids that lay across the nape of her neck, blazing like the fire in her father's forge. It was these that caused everyone in Laybe-Layzar's courtyard—and in all the surrounding neighborhoods, for that matter—to call her "Itka, the locksmith's copper-braided daughter."

Her voice, her laughter, her very comings and goings, all seemed as if calculated to spite her father with his stooped back and his face blood-drained from fasting. He couldn't imagine from whom in the family his youngest daughter had inherited such red hair. What, he asked Heaven, had he done to deserve a daughter whose every move was wanton and shameless, forbidden as anything ever could be? Though Reb Heskiah had more than his share of complaints against Serel, she was in his eyes as day to night when compared to Itka.

Had Itka obeyed her father, she would have worked alongside her mother in the food store, as Serel did. But Itka wanted only to sell women's clothes in a store in the center of town. When she told her father this, Reb Heskiah almost fainted: His daughter should mingle with the rabble in the street?! But he found the entire household against him. His wife called him a crazy fanatic, and his eldest daughter, who had not yet forgiven him for causing her divorce, screamed at him, "You're trying to dam the Wilja River with a splinter." Even the quiet Serel couldn't help but get involved: "Father, she'll be selling *women's* clothes, not *men's* clothes."

"That's even worse," he answered. "All the more will Itka be influenced by today's godlessness!"

Nevertheless, Reb Heskiah relented and did not insist that his youngest stay cooped up at home or work with her mother selling groceries. He arranged for her to work in the hardware store of Sheftel Miklishansky, a God-fearing, learned Jew and a trustee of the beth midrash in Laybe-Layzar's courtyard. Besides their attending the same synagogue and Reb Heskiah being a regular customer of his, they were of one mind in regarding the new generation as all rebellious children. Allowing his daughter to work in the store of such a man, Reb Heskiah thought, was perfectly safe: Sheets of metal and iron doors, brass door-knobs, padlocks, and buckets of nails could hardly lead Itka astray. The customers were all peasants or old laborers from the neighborhood. And the salesmen were the owner's son and sons-in-law, men in their late forties, perhaps even their fifties, with grown children of their own.

As soon as Itka started earning money, however, she announced her intention of renting a room of her own: she felt too confined in her parents' house. This time Reb Heskiah did not even bother to get angry; as long as he lived and breathed, his youngest daughter would not have her way. He answered calmly that Itka would leave her parents' house and live apart from them only after she married a young man whom he, her father, would choose for her. Were he to permit her to live by herself now, how could he be sure she wouldn't be washing and combing her hair on the Sabbath?

"But you don't allow me to stand in front of the mirror and comb my hair even in the middle of the week," Itka retorted.

"It's not permitted in the middle of the week either," her father answered. "A Jewish woman should beautify herself only for her husband. Evil lurks in those braids of yours—young men see them and may succumb to impure thoughts."

"If only more young men would look at my daughters, they'd all be happily married by now," said his wife with a weary shrug. "Have you ever heard of a father praying to God that his daughters should be unattractive?" Zlata had always defended the children against her husband, although she, too, thought that Itka's plan to live alone was scatterbrained and spiteful. But with such a fanatic for a father, constantly hovering over her, watching her every step, it was no wonder that Itka wanted to escape, even if she had to run to the ends of the earth.

So Itka remained at home and worked in Miklishansky's hardware store, using her earnings to buy fancy clothes. Her laugh echoed through Laybe-Layzar's courtyard, and she befriended salesgirls and shopkeepers, as well as totally irreligious working girls from factories and shops. Reb Heskiah had to find what solace he could in the thought that at least Itka did not frequent dancing halls and theaters—about this he could be certain, because he had decreed that she must be home every night by ten o'clock. Yet the only real solution, he knew, was to marry Itka off to a pious husband. But how could he manage this for his youngest daughter, the redhead, when at the same time he had to keep a hundred eyes on Serel —Serel with the straight, modest hairdo—so she would not secretly meet with the gilder Yehiel-Michael Henes? Never would the enemies of Israel live to see him take for a son-in-law a man who arranged his own marriage!

It was a summer Sunday morning, and by Polish law all the stores and workshops were closed. Most of the courtyard's residents were sleeping late that morning, but Reb Heskiah was engaged in study as usual in the beth midrash. It was just then that Itka loved to go out on the porch and comb her long, thick red hair. The warm sunbeams drying her wet locks felt sweet and pleasant, and the wet strands caressed and tickled her neck and face. Her half-closed eyes, peering through thick lashes, watched the golden rays become blue-speckled bursts of light. Her father would surely call this joy the wiles of the evil inclination, but to Itka it was a beautiful world that was beckoning her outside. Everything was full of wonder, everything caused her to laugh, and, best of all, she loved to be looked at and admired. But all the young men of the courtyard were still asleep, with one exception—Moishele Munvas, wearing a white shirt, already shaved, and his mustache carefully curled, sitting at this early hour at a low open window and staring out into the courtyard.

Itka always laughed at the upholsterer with the curled mustache. "What do women see in him?" she would ask her friends. "It seems to me that he isn't so much a ladies' man as an effeminate man." Itka's friends would wonder how she knew so much about men. Now she called across the empty Sunday-morning courtyard to a girlfriend she could neither see nor hear.

"Yohele, are you ready yet?" she called out as she combed a dark-red lock with a brown comb and coquettishly flung it over her shoulder. Then she took a lock from the other side of her head and ran her fingers over it lightly and expertly, as a harpist touches the harp string when she is about to start playing. "Yohele, Yohele," she called again to her friend somewhere in the courtyard, aware all the while that Moishele Munvas hadn't for a moment taken his lascivious eyes off her. She began to thrash her hair about harder, with such zest and pleasure that one would think she had been bathing in a cold stream and was emerging for a few moments to warm herself in the sun's rays. Suddenly she turned anxiously toward the beth midrash, only to confirm what her heart had already told her: Her father had heard her boisterous calls and was leaning his tallith-covered head out a small window, watching her—a daughter, he knew, bears watching.

Itka disappeared into the house, while Moishele thought: "A figure like a barrel. A high bosom, soft like a pillow, and a head of red hair like a witch. From those teasing, wandering eyes and that happy laughter one would think her anything but a prude. But you never know, she might be the kind that's loose only in her fantasies. After all, isn't her father the worst fanatic in the entire courtyard, or any courtyard of the Jewish Street, for that matter?"

Ever since the challenge to his right to be counted to a minyan, Moishele had been in a sullen mood. He could not understand why his neighbors hated him so. If they were pitying Nehamele, then why shouldn't they also pity him? What could he do? He did not love her. How could anyone love a woman like that—all venom and not an ounce of pride? How many times already had he told her that he'd married her only because he feared his brothers, and to spite Bertha Sapir? "Nehamele," he would implore her, "I can't stomach you, it's as simple as that." But she was stubbornly standing her ground: Once married means married forever. Hadn't she wedded herself to him, body and soul, not to mention her life's savings? Oh, how he loathed the body and soul of that withered hag! And he loathed her even more for playing on everyone's sympathy, the poor, wretched orphan. She purposely went about with a hurt, persecuted look just to get the neighbors to hate him. Well, the devil with the neighbors—and with his brothers, and that Bertha Sapir could go to hell, too. He hadn't realized how many women would be eager to throw themselves at his feet.

Moishele yawned, clasped his hands behind his head, stretched, and twisted. He had nowhere to go so early on a summer's day. He would gladly have continued watching young Itka with the copper-red hair, but she wasn't coming out onto the porch anymore. He could hear Nehamele's silence right behind his back, but he didn't bother to turn around. What did he care if somewhere, in her hole, some mouse was eyeing him with her beady little eyes?

9

IT WAS THE EVE of Shavuoth and Reb Heskiah was feeling joy pervading his fast-worn body, as if he were reliving the ecstasy his soul had felt when it stood at the foot of Mount Sinai and received the Torah. His wife, Zlata, was preparing for the holiday by cooking the customary dairy dishes and, in honor of Shavuoth, strewing fresh green ferns, pulled out from the peasant wagons in the market, on the floors of their dwelling. Reb Heskiah, however, disapproved: "The Vilna Gaon did away with this custom because the Gentiles do the same thing on their holidays." But Zlata was not impressed. "So what if the Vilna Gaon did away with it? They say he lived here in Laybe-Layzar's courtyard over a hundred years ago. Now we have the Porush, Rabbi Yoel Weintraub, for a neighbor and he says it's all right."

The locksmith's youngest daughter prepared for the holiday with a new hat she had bought from the hatmaker Bertha Sapir down on Bakszta Street. Itka could certainly have found a hat shop closer to Laybe-Layzar's courtyard. But though she laughed at Moishele Munvas and his curly mustache, she had still wanted to get a look at his former betrothed, whom people said he could not forget, and because of whom he changed mistresses as often as he changed gloves.

The walls of Bertha Sapir's home were covered with photographs of Jewish actresses: husky women with deep, dark eyes, towering curly hair-dos, and thick white necks, their pleasant faces all looking somehow alike, as if they were loving sisters. Bertha decorated her walls with their pictures because they were all good customers of hers. She loved their theatrical productions and was able to sing by heart all the songs about Jewish girls with broken hearts. The large table near the window was piled high with pincushions laden with needles, little cardboard boxes brimming with hatpins and buttons, and, apart from the rest, a bowl filled with fringes and bows. Nearby stood a basket stuffed with velvet ribbons and another with silk flowers on twists of wire. On a tall wooden manne-quin with many hands, hats were perched: berets and bonnets, big ones and little ones; some round, some pointed; it looked like a tree whose branches were covered with all kinds of exotic birds.

Itka took her time choosing and trying on hats, looking into the mirror this way and that, sitting up close and then standing afar, ponder-ing again and again whether she preferred a hat with a long veil in the front or one with a hairnet on the back. She finally settled on a hat of dark-red felt, small and round like a little pot, barely covering her fore-head and leaving uncovered the thick braids of copper hair pinned up at her neck. Bertha Sapir had to sew a black silk ribbon around the hat, adding three fringes and an ostrich feather.

While the hatmaker worked, Itka sat idly gazing at the pictures of actresses on the wall, then leafing through a fashion magazine, finally trying on what seemed like a riding cap and giggling at her comical appearance in the mirror. But Bertha was in anything but a jovial mood and grimaced at her angrily. "You say you live in Laybe-Layzar's court-yard on the Jewish Street. That's the same courtyard where my former fiancé, Moishele Munvas, lives, that good-for-nothing gypsy, that scoundrel! How's his wife, that dried-out lemon? I know, I know, she's as good as dead, as far as he's concerned."

Bertha, a little near-sighted, became even more so when she got excited. So she lowered her eyes to the pincushion covered with needles and for a long time simply could not find the needle she needed. It took her even longer to find a small pair of scissors, and longer still to find a particular spool of thread, and all the while she was telling Itka how

Moishele Munvas had cried and pleaded at her feet that he couldn't live without her, but she'd thrown him out like a dog. Now he was giving his wife hell, and slowly but surely she was shriveling up before his eyes like last year's apple because he had other women.

"Whatever do they see in him?" Itka said casually as she reached for a large tie from the table and placed it under her chin to see how it looked with her blouse. "Everyone in the courtyard knows that your former fiancé runs around with women. But how he manages to win them over, no one understands."

The hatmaker, already half blind with rage, had her nose on the table as she looked for a small pin box. She was seething more by the minute. It seemed to her that she had been right all along: If Moishele Munvas was surrounded by a flock of women, then either he had already forgotten her or else he soon would.

"I don't know what they see in him. They probably want to have a good time and flirt, and he surely turns their empty heads with compliments and those phony stories of his adventures, that freeloader, that charlatan," Bertha said through gritted teeth as her nostrils quivered. "He acted very differently with me," she continued. "He'd crawl after me on his hands and knees until I'd let him stay near me. But take your eye off him and he'll never come home, because he's a man without character and as brazen as anyone could be." Suddenly Bertha stopped her work and looked at her customer with open suspicion. "How is it that you've never come to me before and today, here you are?"

"I wasn't working and making any money before, so I could never afford to pay what you charge," Itka answered calmly. Finally, the hat was ready and Itka tried it on again, admiring herself in the mirror. She paid for it and left with a round hatbox under her arm and a broad smile on her face. "The hatmaker doesn't have a bad figure at all," she thought, "and she certainly knows her craft. But she's a cross-eyed crow, a soaked cat dragged screeching from the water, a gossip with the foul mouth of fish-market riffraff."

On the first night of Shavuoth, the lamps in the beth midrash and the candelabra were still lit well past midnight. The benches were packed with men from the courtyard and from the neighboring streets who, as was the custom on this night, came to study until dawn.

Sitting in his usual place, Reb Heskiah was engrossed in the Tikun, the traditional text for this night of study. He had enough verses from the Scriptures and selections from Midrash to recite the whole night. At the

front table, between the bima and the ark, sat a group of men, and at
the head of the table was Rabbi Yoel Weintraub, conducting a class in the
Book of Ruth and its rabbinical commentaries.

On this night the Porush had a fresh, strong voice and clear, rested
eyes. His broad gray beard, streaked with strands of brown, shone as it
lay on the collar of his tallith katan, and his broad hands shone also as
they lay on the huge pages of the Midrash Rabbah, opened in front of
him. The Porush loved the Book of Ruth, where there are no chastisements, no prophetic doom-saying, only words of comfort, trust, and love
in every verse. Though not a great orator, he was not for a moment at a
loss for words in describing the wisdom and the noble ways of Ruth the
Moabite, of her mother-in-law, Naomi, and their relative, Boaz. It was
just these qualities that made the saintly, God-fearing convert Ruth and
her second husband, Boaz, worthy of being the ancestors of King David.
"And so it is," he explained, "that the Book of Ruth is read on the second
day of Shavuoth, the anniversary of the death of King David, of blessed
memory."

The men crowded around the table were poor retail merchants in
plain cloth hats and worn, smudged, long frock coats. There were also
artisans with thin little beards, their wrinkled, labor-swollen fingers covered with calluses and prickly hair. Today, however, even the poorest
looked their best in honor of the holiday, and their eyes reflected the
reddish flicker of the candles in their houses and the blazing lamps in the
beth midrash. Their limbs were still heavy with leaden fatigue from
the frantic, last-minute business of the afternoon before Shavuoth. And
yet they felt somewhat refreshed by the wine of the evening Kiddush
prayer that ushered in the tasty holiday dinner, and by the short nap
they had taken before going to the beth midrash for the night. They sat or
stood shoulder to shoulder around the table as they listened to the
Porush's inspired words, swaying ever so slightly, and humming to themselves the sweet cantillation of the Book of Ruth, which would be read at
morning services the day after next.

Around the bima and along the eastern wall of the beth midrash and
on the opposite bench sat middle-aged men in soft hats, their beards
fastidiously groomed and their sidelocks carefully trimmed. Each had a
locked drawer under his seat in which to keep his religious articles. They
studied for a while and then conversed in whispers until finally they just
sat still with earnest faces, already savoring the butter cakes and coffee
that would be waiting for them at home the next morning. Here and there
among this group were older men in hard black hats or tall, domed

skullcaps. Through glasses perched at the end of their noses they peered intently into the Talmud, with stern expressions on their faces and creases across their foreheads, arguing a point in the text or picking up anew some old, forgotten quarrel.

At the very front of the beth midrash, on either side of the ark, behind the heavy oak lecterns, sat the "milk-white" old men. All year long they were treated as senile and they felt superfluous in their children's homes, and guilty for taking up space. So these elders sought sanctuary in the beth midrash, where they struggled with the small print in a Talmudic volume through a magnifying glass that shook in their unsteady fingers, or through two pairs of glasses. Only at the Passover seder, at the beginning of the Yom Kippur fast, and during night-long sessions like this one, did the younger men look fondly at these patriarchs and shout into their ears: "Grandfather, may you live and be well until next year, when we'll wish it to you again."

Golden beams of light streamed out the beth-midrash windows into the darkness outside. The courtyard was bathed in a deep indigo, as if the night had spread a blanket over the rooftops, the porches and the crooked cobblestones in the street. Most of the houses had their doors and windows open to dissipate the stifling heat still lingering from the ovens and hearth plates which had, just that afternoon, been cooking the holiday meals. The older housewives, exhausted from their afternoon of cooking and housework, were fast asleep. The younger women went out into the courtyard for some fresh air. Young men were filing out of Laybe-Layzar's beth midrash, having had their fill of Torah for the night. Talking and laughing, they stood around in small groups or moved from porch to porch. No one paid any attention to Moishele Munvas and Itka Teitel-baum as together they slowly moved away from the crowd.

Itka prattled on without a stop, asking Moishele why he wasn't in the beth midrash with the other pious Jews. He answered that lately the men in the synagogue had refused to count him to a minyan because, they said, he was a devil.

"Yes, I have heard that you really are a devil." Itka smiled at him. "Tell me, what do women see in you?"

Though her tone was facetious and light-hearted, Moishele sensed her curiosity, her fear, and finally her yearning. "You shouldn't be talking to me," he whispered. He reminded her that when a sofa in her house had been in need of repair, her father had been afraid to let him, the up-holsterer from his own courtyard, pass the threshold, but had called in one from another neighborhood. Itka said nothing; she only pealed a knowing laugh, one in which Moishele could very clearly hear her answer: When she wanted something, there was nothing her father could do to stop her.

10

O N THE AFTERNOON of the second day of Shavuoth, after the midday meal, Laybe-Layzar's courtyard was empty and still, in the grip of lethargy. The residents were napping, retasting in their dreams the delicious food they had enjoyed that day. Even so, a workday dreariness was already beginning to creep into their minds. They turned and twisted, sighed and yawned with wide-open mouths, savoring their rest on soft pillows as long as it lasted.

The young people had been wandering outside the city since the crack of dawn, along the banks of the Wilja, in the Antokol forest. Or else they went on foot to Troki, with its thirteen lakes and the ruins of the castles of the Lithuanian princes of olden days. In the deserted courtyard someone opened a door, walked out onto the threshold, yawned, and looked up at the sky. Billowy gray clouds with a green luster coursed through the sky. A breeze blew a bundle of straw from an open hallway. Soon the wind gusted and tossed about a clothesline stretched between two garret windows, thrashing the red mattress covers, the blue shirts, and the white underwear. The bored neighbor in the doorway caught his breath as he wondered if the clothesline would hold. It looked as if it might yet rain today, he thought, and then he suddenly burst out laughing, his laughter echoing through the surrounding emptiness. He was delighted by the thought that the young people on the banks of the Wilja or hiking in the forest might get soaked in the rain, though he could not understand what there was to be so happy about.

Deep in the courtyard Itka sat on the porch of her home, intently reading a book. Across the courtyard Moishele Munvas was sitting near an open window, also engrossed in a book. Wearing a tight white blouse that made her bosom appear even fuller and firmer, Itka sat on a chair, her slippered feet tucked under her, bent over her book so intently that it seemed as though her neck would snap at any moment. Moishele wore a jacket, shirt, and tie, looking as if he had planned to go out, but had been waylaid by the novel, which made him forget about the rest of the world.

Every once in a while Itka would look up, glance across the courtyard, and meet Moishele's darkly flashing eyes beneath his furrowed brow. They soon returned to their books and only their secret smiles seeped through their lowered eyelids onto the pages of the novels.

At the same time Itka's older sister Serel stood near the shuttered window of her mother's food store on the Jewish Street. She wore a tailored black suit and high-heeled shoes, her smooth chestnut hair combed flat with a part in the middle, a bun in the back, and a small comb behind each ear to keep it all in place. Serel was so used to working in the store during the week that she would go there even on a holiday, when the store was closed, to meet the gilder Yehiel-Michael Henes. When she saw him coming down the street, her pale face flushed with the rosy glow of a quiet, demure happiness.

Yehiel-Michael Henes was a young man with a broad face and the eyes of a simpleton. He was wearing unpressed pants, an old-fashioned waistcoat under his overcoat, gaiters, and boots with rubber loops that made them easier to pull on. The fresh shirt he had put on in honor of the holiday was already rumpled, he really did not know how to knot a tie, and his hat was clumsily perched on top of his head. Instead of wearing it cocked to one side, with the brim turned down over one eye and a crease in the crown that would have made it look like a sleek ship, he wore it rounded, almost down to his eyes, and with the entire brim straight. Since as an observant Jew he did not shave with a razor but with a mechanical clipper, there were stubbles of hair on his upper lip just under his nostrils, on his neck, and sticking out of his ears. And his voice was just as creased and bleating as a sheep's.

And yet Yehiel-Michael was much loved by everyone on the Jewish Street because he was honest, quiet, and a reliable, skilled craftsman. When the older women came to have their old silver-coated Sabbath candlesticks replated, they took great pleasure in listening to him talk about the Land of Israel. They would be thinking all the while that if their daughters had any sense, they would seek out just such a young man for a husband. But the Jewish girls of the neighborhood looked upon him as an older brother, and some even ridiculed him as old-fashioned. Only one, Serel, the locksmith's daughter, loved him and was eager to marry him.

Serel was not the type to run around; she was never interested in going out with the other girls of her age. Her father's watchfulness over her every step had not engendered a spitefulness in her as it had in Itka. Her older sister, Malka the divorcee, was always troubled by Serel's docile acceptance of her overbearing father, and their mother would shout at her, "Why do you tremble so before your father? Listen to him and you'll stay unmarried until your hair turns gray. Go! See your Yehiel-Michael!" In this Serel obeyed her mother, not her father, and saw Yehiel-Michael every Sabbath and holiday she could.

"I heard them say a memorial prayer at services in the Grand Synagogue today for the famous Righteous Convert, Abraham son of Abraham," Yehiel-Michael told Serel. "Today, the second day of Shavuoth, is the anniversary of his death." He asked her if she had ever seen the tree that grew over the Righteous Convert's grave in the old cemetery outside Vilna. Originally a Polish nobleman, Count Potocki, he had been burned at the stake over a hundred years before for converting to Judaism.

Yes, Serel answered, she had seen the tree. It looked like a man, with a head and two outstretched arms. But what Serel was more concerned about was whether Yehiel-Michael ate on holidays at the same home as on weekdays, where he had good homemade meals, or did he have to go to a kosher restaurant? And he wanted to know whether she had had brisk business the day before Shavuoth. Serel finally demanded, not without bitterness, why he insisted on attending services at the Tiffereth-Bahurim synagogue instead of at the beth midrash in Laybe-Layzar's courtyard.

Yehiel-Michael understood why Serel was asking him this: She wanted him to attend services in Laybe-Layzar's beth midrash so he could find favor in her father's eyes. He replied that the Tiffereth-Bahurim synagogue was merrier, more cheerful. The people sang the prayers together loudly, the Rabbi expounded on the weekly Prophetic portion in a modern vein, and when a bridegroom was called up to the Torah for an aliyah, all the men rejoiced as if he were a brother.

"And besides," he said, looking down at his heavy shoes, "I do not want to deceive your father. Like many others who pray at the Tiffereth-Bahurim synagogue, I believe that we must go to the Land of Israel now, and not wait for the Messiah to lead us there." The moment Yehiel-Michael uttered these words, he was overcome with fear as if he had within him the power of a sorcerer, able to summon forth the locksmith just by talking.

Meanwhile, Reb Heskiah was jarring himself awake from his afternoon nap with but a single thought: Where were his daughters? He found Itka on the porch reading a book—most likely, one as forbidden as anything could be. But at the moment he was overcome with a greater anxiety. His heart told him that his Serel was meeting that gilder Yehiel-Michael Henes. He ran out frantically into the street, holding his yarmulka

on his head with one hand, without a robe, without a coat, his trousers held
up by suspenders stretched over his underwear.

"Impudent thing! Get home!" he yelled. Grabbing Serel by the arm,
he shouted at the gilder: "My daughter will never marry you! I don't trust
you! A bachelor who lives on his own cannot be trusted!"

Serel let her father pull her by the arm toward the courtyard as
Yehiel-Michael trudged clumsily along behind, his hands spread and eyes
wide, as if pleading for an explanation. Although he did not have the
courage to stand up to the locksmith, his heart would not permit him
simply to walk away. And so he followed, muttering incomprehensibly,
while Serel herself longed desperately to be back at last within the shelter
of her own home.

Just then, however, who should come running toward them but her
mother, in worn and crumpled slippers and without a head covering.
Zlata grabbed her daughter by her free arm and pulled her the other way,
shouting, "Why do you listen to your crazy old father? Talk to whomever
you like. See whomever you like!" Serel pleaded with both of them:
"Please, leave me alone." But her father would not let go as he pulled her
one way, and neither would her mother as she pulled her the other.

Heads appeared at all the windows and neighbors emerged from
doorways, encircling the spectacle. The locksmith, people declared indignantly, was a maniac and his wife was a little crazy, too. Look at the
shame they were causing their daughter, they were making a laughing-
stock of her! And what about Serel herself? She was, after all, a responsible young woman, a hard-working manager of her mother's business, yet
she let them drag her about like a child.

On the small porch of his home stood the Porush, Reb Yoel, looking
on the scene with eyes wide. Moishele Munvas, meanwhile, had left his
apartment and walked over to Itka's porch. He pointed to the gilder
with a look of utter contempt: "That jackass! Even if I knew I would die
for it, I would never permit my fiancée to be so humiliated!" Itka said
nothing, yet her bosom heaved as she breathed heavily and shot hateful
glances at both her parents and her sister.

At last, Serel tore herself away from her parents and ran into the
house. Itka went in after her and behind them Reb Heskiah and Zlata,
like elderly blackbirds with wings outstretched, flying behind their chicks
into the nest. It was but a moment before the neighbors heard screaming,
crying, and loud arguments coming from the locksmith's house.

Some time later, Reb Heskiah sat at his lectern in the beth midrash,
looking into a tome and swaying silently. His shoulders hunched over

even more than usual, he panted heavily and let out labored sighs. The Porush saw the locksmith's suffering, but he was not moved. He wandered about the beth midrash greatly agitated, opening and closing books, until finally he stood still near the reader's lectern, rubbing his forehead, as if uncertain that what he had seen that afternoon had really happened.

Local residents now started to file in for the afternoon service. They hurried past Reb Heskiah, their manner cold and aloof—they did not dare to scold him, but neither did they care to be friendly with him. Just as the service was about to begin, the Porush, unable to contain himself any longer, walked over to the locksmith:

"Listen to me, Reb Heskiah! If Ruth could go see Boaz at night in a barn, your daughter is allowed to speak to a fine Jewish young man in the street in broad daylight. Your piety is brutality itself. Remember what I told you: Forbid the young people what is permitted and they will, in the end, do it anyhow and also that which is prohibited. Remember!" the Porush warned, waving an accusing finger in Reb Heskiah's pale, lifeless face. And, as if to keep himself from continuing and saying something he would later regret, he turned abruptly and walked briskly to his seat, loudly reciting the opening prayer of the afternoon service, *Ashrei yoshvei veiseha*—"Blessed are they that dwell in thy house...."

11

SHEFTEL MIKLISHANSKY, the owner of the big hardware store in which Itka worked as a cashier, was known far and wide for his piety and his humility. When he entered the beth midrash, he immediately bowed to the ark across the room. Upon leaving, he gently kissed the ark cover and stepped slowly backward as if he were leaving the presence of a king. His place in the beth midrash was the first seat by the eastern wall, directly to the left of the reader's lectern. But whenever a visiting Rav or any distinguished Jew came to services, he would gladly leave his seat and insist on giving it up to the honored guest. Though he was the first trustee of the beth midrash, he flatly refused to stand on the bima during the Torah reading at Sabbath morning services and decide who was to be called up for an aliyah. He would stand at his place, intently and seriously perusing his Pentateuch without the slightest evident interest in the involved deliberations of the second trustee, the Torah reader, and the sexton over whom to honor with the more important aliyot—the third and sixth, and the concluding section, the maphtir. But should the officials on the bima find themselves in a quandary over whom to call up for the least important aliyah, Sheftel Miklishansky would signal them to give it to him. On the Sabbath when the Chapters of Reproof in Deuteronomy were read, and not a Jew in the beth midrash was willing to accept an aliyah, Reb Sheftel would tell the sexton to call him. And as the reader, hurriedly and in a hushed undertone, chanted the harsh words of condemnation, the trustee would listen with eyes downcast, bent over the Torah scroll as if convinced that Moses had meant these curses for him, and him alone. When a sage lectured at the Gaon's Beth Midrash upon his completion of a tractate, or if the Town Maggid of Vilna delivered a discourse on the "Great Sabbath," the Sabbath before Passover, other scholars would take delight in challenging and dismissing him, but Sheftel Miklishansky would say not a word, though, as everyone knew, he was a deeply learned man. Whenever the cantor waited for him to finish the Silent Prayer before commencing the reader's repetition, Sheftel would glance at him and motion him not to wait.

Was it any wonder, then, that his fellow congregants all regarded him as a saintly, humble man—even though they could not agree with him that everything about bygone times was thoroughly good and everything about the present was thoroughly bad. The only person in total agreement with Sheftel Miklishansky was Reb Heskiah, who could not thank him enough for having hired his daughter Itka to work in his hardware store.

But the Porush, Rabbi Yoel Weintraub, did not subscribe to Miklishansky's extreme views, any more than to Heskiah Teitelbaum's. And a few days after Shavuoth the Porush saw with his own eyes that the supposedly humble first trustee was in reality abominably arrogant.

It happened once that a harried Jew, a mourner, rushed into the beth midrash—a man who had to tear himself away from his shop three times a day and run to services so that he could say Kaddish. At the table behind the bima sat the Porush and a group of men studying, as usual, *Ein Ya'akov*. The mourner had sat down for a minute, hoping to hear a word of Talmudic wisdom, but since it was clear that he was anxious to get back to his meager source of livelihood, the Porush ended the class a paragraph or two sooner. The men all closed their books and, as there were ten men present, the mourner recited the Rabbis' Kaddish and then walked up to the reader's lectern to lead the evening service. At that moment, however, there emerged from behind the lectern an enraged Sheftel Miklishansky.

"Are you older than I?" he barked at the mourner. "Or perhaps you are more learned than I!"

"M-me? Older? More learned than you?" the shopkeeper echoed in fear and confusion. "I never thought any such thing, Reb Sheftel."

"Then you are probably more charitable than I!" Miklishansky bellowed mockingly. "And it must be you, not I, who are first trustee of the beth midrash!"

"God forbid!" the other man said with a shudder. "Why, you own a lot of real estate and I have to struggle to pay the rent for my shop. You and your children have a wholesale hardware store, but it's all I can do to sell a box of salt, a bag of sugar, or the head of a herring. But why do you ask me all this, Reb Sheftel?"

"Because you are a grabber. I just completed the study of Tractate *Pesahim*, and I wanted to recite the Rabbis' Kaddish, but then you come along and snatch it for yourself. Just as the Talmud says, 'The ignorant always run to the fore.'"

The trustee turned away and sullenly faced the front of the beth midrash as the mourner stood speechless at the lectern. And this is Reb Sheftel Miklishansky, whom the world considers a saintly man, the very soul of humility, said the Porush to himself as he listened to this tongue-lashing. Was this the way to treat a poor man and a mourner for having dared to say a Rabbis' Kaddish? Still, it was not the Porush's habit to reproach others, except when he deemed another's actions truly reprehensible, as in the case of the locksmith toward his wife and children. And now, he thought, that he had reprimanded the locksmith, what had he achieved? Nothing, absolutely nothing!

Rabbi Weintraub finished the Sh'moneh Esreh, the Silent Prayer, and saw that the mourner was fidgeting as if standing on hot coals. Though the Rabbi was done, the poor shopkeeper was unwilling to proceed with the recitation of the Kaddish because Sheftel Miklishansky had not signaled him to do so. But the worshippers gathered around him, coaxing him to go on and not dawdle, as they had no time to waste. The man at the lectern pointed at the trustee, with an expression that said he did not care for another tongue-lashing. One of the men remarked in response that by the time Reb Sheftel finished, they would be long gone and then he could scream to his heart's delight. Another encouraged the mourner by assuring him that the trustee never minded when the congregation did not wait for him to finish the Sh'moneh Esreh. The mourner was convinced, and continued with the service. But just as he concluded the final Mourner's Kaddish and was about to turn, anxious to leave the beth midrash as quickly as possible, the first trustee took the prescribed three steps backward upon finishing the Silent Prayer, and blocked his escape.

"Didn't you see someone was still standing for Sh'moneh Esreh? Why didn't you wait?"

"I waited for the Rabbi to finish," the shopkeeper replied lamely, pointing at the Porush.

"The Rabbi?" Miklishansky laughed derisively. "The Rabbi? What he knows, every learned Jew knows, and what every learned Jew does not know, he doesn't either."

By which Sheftel Miklishansky clearly meant that he was no less a sage and scholar than the Porush, Rabbi Yoel Weintraub. But the shopkeeper was not versed in the world of scholarship, and answered with a groan, "For heaven's sake! What am I supposed to do? Every Jew is a prince in his own eyes! Some job, waiting for everyone to finish the Sh'moneh Esreh!"

"I am to you like everyone? You consider me just another Jew?" Sheftel Miklishansky shot back with burning fury. "It is I who pay for heating the beth midrash all winter! And you still haven't paid your last year's pledges—not for your seat here, and not for your aliyot."

The shopkeeper searched his mind for a proper retort, but it was no use; he could only move his lips, vainly searching for something to say. He stood still a moment and then made his way to the door, ashamed and angry at himself for feeling so humble that he must take such abuse without saying a word. The others walked out behind him, talking indignantly among themselves: "There you are—on the Sabbath and holidays Reb Sheftel winks at the reader to go on without waiting for him, but at an ordinary weekday service he pounces on a poor shopkeeper, a mourner, for not waiting."

The first trustee remained in his corner and sat down to begin another tractate. Suddenly, he became aware of the Porush, Rabbi Weintraub, standing over him. Reb Yoel shook his head sadly and addressed him in tones of deep reproach:

"Reb Sheftel, you are a Sabbath-and-holiday Jew. On the Sabbath and holidays, when the entire congregation is looking at you, you make a show of humility for all to see, just as you put on a fine silk robe and eat cholent in honor of the additional soul a Jew receives on the Sabbath. But it appears that on an ordinary weekday there is no audience and so no reason to display your humility. It's really too bad that the poor shop-keeper didn't wait for you to finish the Sh'moneh Esreh; you might have declared this a special weekday holiday, and motioned him not to wait for you. But since he had the nerve not to wait for your signal to continue, your injured humility bounced up like a twisted poker."

The Porush returned to his seat on the other side of the ark, intend-ing to turn on the light overhead and sit down to study. But he was too shaken with anger to find the switch on the wall, and so he stood still in the dark and shouted over to the trustee:

"Berating a Jew like that before everyone for not having paid his pledges is like spilling his blood! It's no less than murder!"

"And next you'll tell me you agree with the workers who strike against the owners!" Miklishansky shouted back as he irately shut his Talmud and sprang for the door, afraid the Porush was going to chase him.

But it was someone else who chased after him: the locksmith, Reb Heskiah. In these last moments his respect for the first trustee had risen even higher, if only because he had challenged the Porush. Miklishansky, a tall man with a long, narrow beard, walked briskly with his head held high as the hunched locksmith pursued him, telling him what had hap-pened when he tried to keep his Serel from talking to the gilder Yehiel-Michael Henes, that Zionist reprobate from the Tiffereth-Bahurim crowd: The Porush had mixed in and said he had no right to tell his own daugh-ter what to do. Reb Heskiah roared through the streets like a deaf man who does not hear his own voice:

"When Reb Yoel was the Rav of Zaskowicz, he couldn't get in-volved where he should have gotten involved. But since he's become a Porush in our beth midrash, he has something to say about everything."

They walked together through the Jewish Street until they reached Gitka-Toybes' Lane. Sheftel Miklishansky was unburdening himself of his anger in deep sighs, while Reb Heskiah prattled on about how, as a young man working in the shops, he had never gone along with the striking workers. Soon, however, he began to moan that, besides his own troubles with Serel, new ones were being heaped on him by Itka, his youngest: just the night before, she had told him she wanted to enroll in a school and learn Polish and bookkeeping.

"That's a very good idea," said the trustee, standing at the gate of his house and glowering at Reb Heskiah. "Even though I take care of the records and your daughter only has to help me a little, she really ought to learn Polish and bookkeeping. My children tell me it wouldn't be hard to find a girl from an upright family who is trained and competent in handling business records, one who doesn't belong to the unions."

"But if Itka goes to a school, there's no telling whom she'll meet," the locksmith protested meekly.

"Since she won't be going to a Jewish school but a Polish one, where the teachers are all Gentiles, there is nothing to worry about. I doubt if you need concern yourself about Itka converting," Miklishansky answered, and went in.

Reb Heskiah trudged back, lost in thought and even more stooped than usual, until he reached the Jewish Street and found himself standing at the gate of his courtyard. A pale yellow light shone from the streetlights, and shadows swayed overhead on the electrical wires, leaping onto the walls and the pavement. On the far-distant Cross Mountains there glowed, as if of pure crystal, three huge crosses. In the narrow streets that led to the town garden, the leafy trees rustled in the windswept summer dusk. People crowded into the paths and alleyways, the shopkeepers lingered near their closed shops, children played, small groups of young people joked and laughed, and old men went in and out of the doors of the beth midrash. But Reb Heskiah saw and heard nothing; he still stood at the gate of Laybe-Layzar's courtyard and sighed: "Too bad. Too bad. I don't seem to have much choice. If I don't let Itka go to school and study Polish and bookkeeping, she might lose her job at Reb Sheftel Miklishansky's store and then she'll again want to become a salesgirl in a fancy women's clothing store. But as for Serel, she'll never have her way, and she will not be meeting Yehiel-Michael Henes anymore, no matter how much the Porush and the neighbors hiss through their lips."

12

I T CAME TO THE ATTENTION OF the young street crowd that the upholsterer was not changing his clothes as often as before for his evening excursions; and they saw also that he went about with a strained, preoccupied look. Either, they concluded, someone somewhere had clipped his wings, or else he was really in love.

Nehamele had noticed before anyone else that her husband seemed worried and troubled. He was no longer leaving her alone every night, but only two or three times a week; the other nights he just sat around the house, avoiding her gaze. She, too, was convinced that Moishele was deeply in love with someone, and this intensified her sadness. As long as he had been cavorting with this one one night and with that one the next night, there was still hope that her sister-in-law's prediction would come true: When he had gotten it all out of his system, he would come back to her. But if he had fallen in love, then she had no hope at all. Who, she wondered, could have captured him? Could it be Bertha Sapir again? Perhaps that was why he was so worried—he was thinking once again of marrying her, and was trying to find a way of getting his wife to accept a divorce.

Nehamele was now determined to learn the truth. Before, she had had no desire even to look at her competitors. In her determination not to accept a divorce grew the desperate conviction—like a stubble of prickly grass imbedded in a parched clod of earth—that a wife must never, before God and man, compare herself to her husband's mistresses. But now she clenched her small fists as if she were squeezing her wildly beating heart. Even if it meant she would have to poison herself when she found out, she had to know whom her husband had been seeing lately.

Nehamele devised an elaborate scheme so that neither her neighbors in the courtyard nor the people in the street should realize she was spying on her husband. She knew that on the evenings when he left the house he always came home earlier from work. On one such night, as Moishele was eating supper, Nehamele told him it was important that she see a neighbor on nearby Szklanna Street. A few minutes later she left the house carrying only a small handbag.

Nehamele hid herself not far from a corner that Moishele would have to pass by, no matter where he was going. He appeared much sooner than she had expected, as if he had wanted to steal away from the house before she returned. When she spotted him, her first thought was that he must have left the front door unlocked for her, so she must go back and close it lest they be robbed blind. But then she recalled that he must know she had an extra key in her handbag, so he must surely have locked the door when he left. Nehamele got furious with herself for thinking of protecting her home when her husband was off to see another woman.

Instead of taking Broad Street, which led to Lower Bakszta Street, where Bertha Sapir lived, Moishele turned onto Rudnicka Street and continued on it a long way. Nehamele heaved a sigh of relief—he was not going to the hatmaker. Suddenly she was afraid Moishele would turn around and see her. And then her heart pounded heavily at the thought: What if she discovered that her husband's mistress was prettier than she?

They would, Nehamele assured herself, probably meet in her house and not in the street; but her next thought was that then she would not get to see the woman who was waiting for her husband.

Moishele strode the length of Stefanska Street and bore right, past a mound of dirt from which the poor people who lived at the city line carted away wheelbarrows of clay. He passed the market where they sold old furniture, and continued on until the streets became wider and the crowds of passers-by got thinner. He turned again, this time into a quiet, elegant street, as Nehamele followed him from afar. She would dart from doorway to doorway and hide for an instant before lunging forward, as if she were seeking cover from a torrential rain in whatever shelter could be found along the way.

At last, Moishele stopped and stood in the street, looking across at a stately entrance with broad stone steps. Nehamele focused her sharp eyes on the Polish sign on the building: SZKOLA HANDLOWA—"Business School." "But whom is he waiting for here?" she wondered.

The buildings along the street were all of four or five stories, with large, square windows full of light, and trim balconies decorated with many flowering plants. It was the time of year when the days are longest, in the month of Tammuz, and the sun was still high in the western sky. The houses on one side of the street were shining with a brilliant golden hue while the houses on the other side sparkled bluish white. Nehamele ducked into the open wicket of the huge closed gate to a large courtyard. As she looked at the trees lining the sidewalk, she recalled her lonely yet peaceful maiden years in her small house on tree-lined Kopenica Street across the Poplawski Bridge. But here the freshly scrubbed sidewalks glistened, the pavement was a smoothly set array of thick, sharp-cornered slates, and the trees looked as if they had been cultivated, pruned, and manicured. An older woman in a long dress and a broad hat, carrying a silk parasol over her arm, passed through the wicket on her way out. Nehamele pressed herself against the wall of the gateway as if she had suddenly discovered she was half naked.

People started leaving the school building, one or two at a time at first, and then in groups, all of them mature, urbane-looking men or women. Some carried briefcases, others had books in their arms; they wound their way slowly and quietly down the street until it was empty once again. An older man wearing glasses appeared, with a walking stick in hand, a teacher by all appearances. He coughed loudly and wiped his mouth with a handkerchief.

Moishele Munvas remained standing on the sidewalk across the street from the business school and studied, or pretended to study, the rooftop of a building, as if wondering why smoke was not coming out of the chimneys. Now a woman came out of the school, alone, and looked across toward Moishele. He stepped eagerly from the sidewalk into the street with long strides, but halted abruptly and drew back at the woman's wink. He started to stroll in the direction of Pohulanka Street, and the woman walked slowly on the sidewalk in the same direction. Nehamele became dizzy, her vision blurred and swam before her, her heart stopped, then began beating wildly like a pounding hammer. No, it couldn't be: It was a mirage! But everything about the woman—her build, her clothes, her gait . . . it was she! She! Itka, the locksmith's copper-braided daughter.

Everyone in the courtyard knew that Itka was taking evening courses in bookkeeping, and the neighbors all said that the Messiah must surely be on his way if Reb Heskiah had allowed this. Nehamele, too, had more than once seen, through the window, Itka coming home from school, her arms laden with books. Now the girl, books in her arms, was walking towards Pohulanka Street. A minute later, Moishele crossed over and walked behind her on the sidewalk.

Nehamele would later wonder why she hadn't suffered a heart attack then and there. When the pair reached the Russian Orthodox Church, Itka slowed to a leisurely stroll as Moishele quickened his strides, and soon they were walking together. They appeared to exchange a few words and then Moishele once again lagged behind, so the passers-by wouldn't think there was any connection between them. Nehamele surmised that in their brief conversation they had made plans for meeting secretly later.

She stopped at the two stone pillars at the end of Pohulanka Street that marked the old city boundary, afraid she would see the couple walk into the Zakret Forest or disappear into a house. So she turned around and ran down Pohulanka Street and all the way home. She did not for an instant consider creating a scandal out of this or even confiding in anyone, so shaken was she by the secret affair her husband was having with the daughter of the neighborhood's most pious Jew. In anguish she shuddered: If this became known, it could destroy the world. She realized that her husband, too, shuddered lest it all become known—that was why he had been worried and restless.

When Moishele returned home that night, Nehamele was afraid even to look at him. The next day the upholsterer came straight home after work. He sat down at the table with downcast eyes and ate his supper while his wife stood behind him and looked out the window. She knew that Itka worked in the hardware store only until four o'clock, when business dropped off. But it was already six and Itka had not yet appeared. When eventually she did enter the courtyard, she was not carrying books, for she did not attend classes that day, but she had under each arm a large cardboard box.

With a frozen expression Nehamele watched Itka linger on the porch, parading, it seemed, before Moishele's eyes. The hussy wanted him to see her in a new coffee-colored jacket, in a new black skirt, pleated like an accordion, in long black gloves, and on her head a deep-red felt hat with ribbons and fringes. Then she swirled as if she wanted him to see her neck, laden with copper braids. Finally, she turned around as if in a dance, displaying a new gold-trimmed purse.

Moishele Munvas did not budge, as if petrified with fright. His wife was also terrified to look, but her eyes disobeyed her and gazed stonily across at the porch, astonished that Itka seemed not the least bit frightened. The whore even had the nerve to show off to Moishele the gifts she had bought with his money. "And who knows?" gasped Nehamele to herself. "She may even have used the money I earned as a seamstress that he cheated me out of." She scurried into the kitchen so that her husband should not see her and realize that she knew his secret.

13

URING THE DAY, the gardener's wife was never to be seen. Not until evening, when the neighbors stood at their open doors to catch a breath of fresh air, did Gracia stroll through Laybe-Layzar's courtyard. Tall, with a narrow frame, she wore a blouse with embroidered sleeves, a white silk headkerchief, and, over her full skirt, a light apron tied in a big bow in back. She looked as if, to her, every day was the eve of Sabbath right before candle-lighting. In her high-heeled summer shoes she appeared even taller and thinner. Because of those heels and because she walked around steeped in her thoughts, she would often stumble on the jagged, crooked cobblestones. She seemed, however, not to notice, but swept across the courtyard with her hands clasped across her bosom and a baffled smile on her face. Her appearance and her ways filled the neighbors with shudders and with pity. They all knew that her sorrows had left her a bit confused, that she was lost in memories of her dead child and oblivious to the world around her, like a sleepwalker. So they did not talk to her, as if a doctor or a wise man had ordered that no one wake her from her dream. But among themselves the people of the courtyard condemned her husband for spending so much time in Oszmiana suing his brothers and leaving his beautiful sick wife all alone.

In the tumult of the eve of Shavuoth and the two days of the holiday, nobody noticed that they hadn't seen Gracia. But when she did appear after Shavuoth, she looked even weaker, paler. "Dear Lord!" the women sighed. "Her husband didn't come home even for the holiday. He'll be the end of her, that miserable maniac."

The neighbors realized it was not right for them to keep silent. And yet, despite their compassion for Gracia's suffering, however moved they were by her beauty and her ways of a lost princess, they couldn't bring themselves to interfere. And so they watched, as she gradually flickered out like a candle. Some of the younger housewives approached her and asked why she cloistered herself in the house all day. Gracia smiled absentmindedly, looked up to the skies, and whispered, "My sweet little baby! I didn't see you last night. Will you be coming to me tonight?"

A shudder swept over the women. They realized that the poor woman was seeing her dead little son. They said not a word, but listened as Gracia, smiling happily, told them how her baby came to her at night in the guise of a bird. During the day her dear little Alterl slept in a dry fountain or some other secret place. But at night he darted from roof to roof until he found their house and flew in through the window. She never moved—oh, no—and did not utter a sound, lest Alterl be frightened and fly away. She lay in bed and marveled at how he found his way to their home in Vilna, all the way from Zaskowicz, and how cleverly he hid during the day so no one could catch him.

"I look and look for the nest, but I just can't find it," Gracia said, gazing at the labyrinth of crooked roofs and gables above her. "But Alterl isn't always flying around as free as a bird. On the second night of Shavuoth I had a vision of him trapped within a wall, and I saw the mice between the bricks of the wall tearing at his little body." She then broke into a gentle weeping and a mournful chant. "My baby was named Yudele, but I call him Alterl, my little 'old man,' to ward off the evil eye and to keep him with me many years. Alterl!"

The women all had small apartments and large families, but they pleaded with Gracia to stay with one of them for the night until her husband returned from Oszmiana. She could not leave her house, she replied, for Alterl would look for her at night and wouldn't know where to find her. The women dispersed tearfully and cursed the gardener: "He eats his heart out about his foolish lawsuit against his brothers, but he doesn't care what happens to his wife."

So deeply did the courtyard take the matter to heart, bemoaning Gracia's fate and condemning her husband, that they seemed to have quite forgotten about Nehamele Munvas, though she, too, was left alone by her husband for half the night. For Nehamele, it was painful and shameful enough to stand by quietly as her husband, her tormentor, carried on with Itka, the daughter of that fanatic locksmith; but now, she saw, everyone had simply lost interest in her suffering. She even heard it remarked that there was absolutely no comparison between her problems and Gracia's woes. "One can always change husbands, especially since the upholsterer is ready to give her a divorce," people said. "But losing an only child is truly a sorrow for the rest of one's life." They have more understanding and sympathy for that crazy Gracia than for me, Nehamele thought. And so she came to hate Laybe-Layzar's courtyard.

Gracia and Nehamele were next-door neighbors, with a shared wall between them. Sitting in her house at night, Nehamele more than once heard Gracia mumble, laugh, and cry to herself. When the word spread through the courtyard that Gracia Shklar was going mad from living alone, an eerie idea entered Nehamele's mind. It was so fiendish that her eyes flashed like those of a wild alley cat ready to pounce on the neck of an unsuspecting passer-by.

That night, after Moishele had gone out to meet his mistress, leaving her once again alone in the house, Nehamele went into the bedroom, took off a shoe, and started banging the heel rhythmically against the wall adjoining the Shklars' apartment. She hammered louder and louder until she heard a terrified shriek from the other side of the wall. With one shoe on her foot and the other in her hand, she sprinted to the front room and collapsed into a chair, panting heavily, her face quivering with a sly and wicked smile. Through the window she saw couples sitting on the doorsteps and on the porches, enjoying the fresh air and engaged in leisurely conversation. She alone had to sit in the house, lonely and ashamed, quivering with fear lest anyone discover that her husband was cavorting with Itka. At that very moment Itka's father sat in the beth midrash immersed in the Talmud, his rasping, pious voice echoing through the courtyard. "If he only knew!"

Nehamele returned to the bedroom and resumed knocking on the wall with the heel of her shoe. She leaped from corner to corner, frantically banging all over the wall, wanting the noise to come from all sides.

At first she pounded slowly and heavily, with the heel, then she hammered with the tip, quickly and lightly, the way she pushed the pedal of her sewing machine when driving it full tilt with her foot. Then she stood on a chair and banged high at the edge of the checkered brown wallpaper near the white limed ceiling. From the other side she heard a wild, panic-stricken screaming—Gracia was bolting for the street. But Nehamele, though herself in the grip of madness and terror, remained capable of acting with cool calculation. She returned the chair to its place, put her shoe back on and then ran outside.

Gracia was raving before a crowd of neighbors: "Demons are hitting me on the head! They're banging on my walls! Demons!"

The people looked at one another in knowing silence: the poor woman had gone completely insane. Yesterday she said her baby was coming to her as a little bird; now she was babbling about demons. In the midst of the commotion they noticed Nehamele standing off to the side, choking on her tears, her whole body shivering. "I also heard the banging on the wall!" she sobbed, "I heard it, I did!"

"When such despicable things go on in Laybe-Layzar's courtyard," said a woman in a self-righteous tone, "is it any wonder that evil spirits come to haunt us like an abandoned ruin?" Another woman prophesied that soon they'd all be hearing demons banging on the walls.

One man did attempt to make light of things: "The spirits in the empty synagogues must have found their way here." But the other neighbors were not in the mood for jokes. Some ushered Gracia back into her house, while others accompanied Nehamele back into hers. In both houses the women inspected the walls and looked up at the ceiling. "Thieves, perhaps?" one woman asked in Nehamele's bedroom. "And what were the thieves after," another asked derisively, "the good fortune she enjoys with her husband?" On the other side of the wall, in Gracia's house, a woman hit upon another idea: "Maybe it's the mice." But Gracia shouted that when the mice scampered about, their squeaking could be heard and they scratched their claws against the walls. She had heard none of this, only the hollow banging of murderous demons who had come to snatch her soul. The women calmed her down, and listened long and attentively for noises, as did the group that had gone with Nehamele. In neither house did anyone hear anything, so they left, concluding that both women had lost their minds. They had urged both to spend the night with one or another of their neighbors. But Nehamele said she was expecting her husband to return home any minute. And

Gracia said she was waiting for her little boy, Alterl; he'd be appearing soon in the guise of a bird.

"Leave me out of this," remarked one of the neighbors as he left Gracia's house, and others shook their heads in pitying agreement as they followed. They quickly dispersed to their own homes, and soon the courtyard was empty and still. Nehamele watched the lights go out in house after house as the black luster of the windows flashed up at the dark blue sky. The little houses in the courtyard were silenced, woven into the shadows of the night. The only light still shining was in the locksmith's house, and from it a shameless, frolicsome laughter emerged into the empty courtyard. Itka had just come home, and her father was still in the beth midrash. Nehamele was certain that the lecherous thing was laughing at the ghost story her mother and sister Serel had just told her. "She has a good time with my own husband and still has the nerve to laugh at me. The hussy is already home out of fear of her father, that fanatic. But my husband hasn't yet come home. He is anything but afraid of me." Nehamele ran back into her bedroom and in the darkness hit her head against the sharp corner of the dresser. For a long while she moaned through her clenched teeth. But the pain only inflamed her anger, pumping into her more courage to go on with her plan of vengeance.

Soon the neighbors heard Gracia's screams once again, like the wailing at a cemetery. Men and women ran out in their underwear or nightgowns, seething with anger. Laybe-Layzar's courtyard had become a madhouse! Gracia was shrieking, while Nehamele, standing beside her, wept silently and yet with such evident relish that the neighbors would have liked to tear her limb from limb. The women wrung their hands and the men scratched their heads: "What do we do about this?" Into the midnight courtyard leisurely strolled Moishele Munvas. Through the darkness, even at a distance, they recognized his jaunty gait, the way he kept his hands deep in his pockets, and the happy tune he always hummed. The men surrounded him, their faces stern and threatening:

"Listen, you little weasel, we're all working people and your wife isn't letting us sleep. She and Gracia Shklar are hysterical about demons banging on their walls. Now, we can't do anything about the gardener, he's a gloomy maniac and, besides, he's not in Vilna now. But we won't stand on ceremony with you: if you leave your wife alone at night one more time, you'll have to move out of the courtyard the next day or they'll carry you away in a box."

Moishele was mute with astonishment and fear before the clenched fists being shaken in his face. A neighbor grabbed Gracia by the arm and said through angrily grinding teeth that, whether she liked it or not, she was going to spend the night in their house. This time Gracia, deathly afraid as she was, let herself be led away. The neighbors again trudged back to their own homes, and only Moishele and Nehamele remained in the empty courtyard. For a moment he looked at Itka's house, but it, too, was already dark. He then turned to his wife. Nehamele was still shaking from fright, shivering with the night chill and sobbing quietly.

"Are you satisfied now? Ha! Everyone pities you, don't they? What did I do to deserve this? Come into the house!" he grumbled bitterly and Nehamele followed him trembling, but also with a secret joy. It seemed to her she had heard in his angry words a ring of kindness, a desire to make up with her. And, she thought, he must also be afraid now to continue his affair with the locksmith's daughter. He surely realized that Itka, that whore of a witch, could only bring disaster on him and on her own family. And Nehamele begged God's forgiveness for having frightened poor befuddled Gracia so badly.

14

BESIDES NOW HAVING to spend every night at home, Moishele Munvas also had to suffer the ridicule of the young people in the street, and to listen to the gardener's wife prattling the night through to her dead child. He didn't doubt for a moment that the whole episode was a fraud. Yet, although he knew his Nehamele to be a sharp-fanged little snake, she was surely too much afraid of him to dare contrive such a story herself. He was more inclined to believe that it had all been invented by the deranged Gracia, and that his witch was using it to keep him from leaving the house.

"Isn't it strange? Since I've been staying home every evening, I haven't heard a single knock on the wall," Moishele pondered as he twirled his Cossack mustache. "What do you think, Nehamele, the demons were frightened off by the fringes of the tallith katan I don't wear?"

"I wouldn't know," stammered Nehamele, ghostly pale. "Perhaps it was Gracia herself who did the knocking." She was but a hairsbreadth away from blurting out, "It was me! I did it!," so strong was the fear she felt when Moishele trained his probing, searing eyes on her. But at that moment he turned from her and gazed longingly at Itka's porch. Seeing this gave Nehamele new strength to dismiss any danger, just as long as her husband could no longer meet his mistress.

Moishele could not ever have imagined how strongly he would pine for Itka. Within the confines of the courtyard he did not dare speak to her, or even wink. From his window he watched her come home every evening, her face as fresh and happy as when they had been meeting. He couldn't bring himself to admit that he trembled lest she might be seeing someone else. He was very much upset that every morning she left the house meticulously decked out, and that when she returned she would run up onto the porch, showing off her bright copper braids pinned up on her neck, as if she were teasing him. That spiteful bitch must surely be thinking he was a weakling, a frightened mouse trembling before the courtyard ruffians' threats to give him a thrashing if he ever left his wife home alone again. In order, it seemed, to torture him more, Itka started coming home late at night, and before she went inside her house, she would look at him coldly, as if he were a total stranger. Hurt and insulted, Moishele forced himself to laugh and talk to his wife, who lurked behind him like a shadow.

"The locksmith's daughter must be really something! Just look how she wiggles her behind when she walks. Who is she trying to drive crazy, that brazen hussy?" he growled, barely containing his urge to seize his own little witch by her thin, scrawny neck. Silently, he wished a plague on her. But Nehamele was too smart to let herself utter a word to Moishele about Itka.

No less than Moishele, the courtyard's other residents were skeptical of Gracia's story of demons. Even the pious Reb Heskiah scoffed. "Unless a holy tzaddik declares that a house is haunted by evil spirits, there's nothing to worry about," the zealot pronounced, and advised his neighbors to live their lives according to the Codes and no demon would ever be able to harm them. Only Gracia believed in the demons with all her heart, which made the Rebbetzin Hindele very angry. She brought Gracia to her house so that her husband, the Porush, could convince the sick woman that it was forbidden to believe in such nonsense. It was to Reb Yoel that Gracia now confided her deepest secret: her thoughts about her neighbor on the other side of the wall.

"The upholsterer's wife lived for many years alone, with no parents, no brothers or sisters, so a demon has become her bridegroom and to this day keeps coming to bang on her wall at night when the upholsterer is away. That's why I'm afraid—the demon might by mistake wander into my bedroom instead." And Gracia raised her long, delicate fingers to her throat as if to protect it.

"Foolish woman!" Hindele scolded her. "Your next-door neighbor married a man who is worse than a hundred demons. There are no demons coming to haunt either of you." The Porush asked Gracia when her husband might be returning from Oszmiana. "I don't know," she replied wearily. "All I know is that when my husband is home, my Alterl, my sweet baby, my little bird, doesn't come to see me." The Porush shook his head and sighed, but said nothing.

When Gracia had left, Hindele angrily asked him why he hadn't rebuked her for this delusion about her child. "Even when the consolation comes from a sick fantasy," he answered, "one may not remove it until there is another consolation to take its place." All that night he tossed in his bed while heavy thoughts weighed on his mind: Perhaps he really should not have left Zaskowicz until he had made peace between Gracia's husband and his brothers. Hindele couldn't sleep either; she was thinking that perhaps she was fortunate in not having had any children: She had been spared the grief that is a mother's lot. But when her husband asked her why she was not sleeping, she blamed the heat and the dampness— and so did he. Neither drifted off until just before dawn.

They slept until the sun was high in the sky, when they were both awakened with a start by a tumult coming from the courtyard. Paltiel Shklar had returned unexpectedly and was bellowing at his neighbors standing around him in the courtyard:

"Tell it to the Porush. Go tell *him* that my wife is afraid of ghosts and spends the nights crying for our boy. Let *him* choke on my wife's tears. When he was the Rav of Zaskowicz and I brought my brothers to him for a judgment, he could have ruled honestly on the matter right then and there and I would not be suffering today. What can I do now? The trial in Oszmiana is dragging itself out, and I have to be there."

"But Gracia is your wife. Aren't you worried about her at all?" one of the men pleaded. "Shklar," another shouted, "you're a hundred times worse than that Moishele Munvas!"

Dust-covered from head to toe after his long trip, standing there in his heavy leather boots and with his knotty hiking stick, the gardener with the peeling bulbous nose looked like a strange, burly wild animal amid puny, docile house creatures. He was beating back his neighbors with his screaming and raging.

"You bastards of Sodom! You'll all rot with my brothers before I let you tell me when to come and when to go. You should be breaking that tzaddik's windows for abandoning Zaskowicz and leaving it to the dogs. Everyone's at each other's throat there, they can't agree on a rav, and let me tell you, they don't deserve any better. For my part, they can eat each other alive—they all sided with my brothers."

To the people standing around the ranting gardener, he seemed to be venting the rage that they could always sense lurking beneath his melancholy; a fight suited him as a swamp suited a bullfrog. "The devil with him!" they muttered, and went their separate ways—to workshops, to stores, to the marketplace. Paltiel Shklar looked about him with an air of victory, then turned and entered his house.

Hindele had seen and heard everything from her window. She gazed at her husband and felt the anger rise within her: more than the wild man's insults, it pained her to see her Yoel sitting on his bed with head bowed and a guilty look on his face, as if he thought he deserved the gardener's frothing censure.

Moishele Munvas had also seen everything, and as he went off to work that morning, his mustache bristled with delight. His eyes gleamed, and as he walked he could barely keep from jumping for joy. It was nothing less than a miracle! He had never dared to hope he'd be freed from his prison so soon. Now that the gardener had returned home, his wife was not likely to get hysterical about the demons, and neither would Nehamele be able to spew out that nonsense about how she, too, heard them stirring about. From this day on, he would once again be free to leave the house. Who would dare say a word to him? But one worry remained for Moishele: Would Itka still want to so much as look at him?

That same evening Moishele again dressed up to go out, as he assured his wife that at last she had nothing more to fear—even the demons were afraid of the gardener. Nehamele knew that this was the day Itka went to the Polish school after work to study bookkeeping. Yet she did nothing for a few days out of fear of the gardener, who was spending every day in his house, and also because each night Moishele came home subdued—even chastened, it seemed to her. Nehamele was overjoyed: either Itka had found another man or she had become repulsive to him.

With each passing day, however, Moishele became his old self more and more, once again humming a gay little tune as he walked, and Itka, for her part, would laugh louder and more lewdly whenever her father was not at home. Nehamele gritted her teeth to keep from screaming. But

that made her heart cry even louder, and finally one night, toward the beginning of the month of Av, she ceased to be concerned about Gracia's
husband next door, on the other side of the wall.

This time Nehamele banged on the bedroom wall not with a shoe
but with a teaspoon and tablespoon she held in her fingers. She tapped
vigorously in every corner, below near the floor and as high up the wall as
she could reach. The banging echoed through the dark bedroom and
combined with Nehamele's fear and despair to convince her that she
actually was hearing demons dancing through the air. She could see their
fiery tongues lashing out into the darkness, the horns on their heads, their
cleft feet . . . and she burst into wild screaming.

When Moishele returned home, he found a houseful of people waiting for him. His wife was lying on a bed, a damp cloth on her forehead
and a wet towel on her chest. The neighbors told him that when they
heard her screams and had rushed into the house, they had found
Nehamele unconscious on the floor. None of them reproached Moishele
or threatened him. Just for him to see his wife lying there shuddering, her
eyes shut and her lips parched, would be enough, they thought, to make
him understand that he was toying with the Angel of Death. Gracia gazed
at Nehamele in an agony of fear, and even Gracia's husband, the grizzled
gardener, stared at the half-conscious woman with dull, melancholy eyes.
His thick lower lip and his heavy chin under a thicket of gray mossy beard
quivered. This time he did not roar as he always did, but only murmured:
"It's true. It's all true. I heard the banging with my own ears. Hard, loud
thuds, like clods of earth falling on a casket in a grave."

15

AFTER THE FAST of the Seventeenth of Tammuz, commemorating the
first breach in the wall of Jerusalem by the besieging Babylonian
armies, Heskiah Teitelbaum reveled in the strictness of the mourning over
the destruction of the Holy Temple. In the following three weeks which
stretched to the day of the fall of the Temple he ate no meat and partook
of no new fruit of the season, over which he would have had to make a
Shehehiyanu, the blessing of the new season; and shouted at his wife if he
found her mending a garment. When Zlata saw that he was bent on
starving himself to death by eating only a stale piece of bread and hard

white cheese, she ran once again to the Porush to complain that her husband was killing himself and expected his family to kill themselves, too. "So don't listen to him," replied Rabbi Weintraub.

Afterward, when the two men were alone in the beth midrash, the locksmith loudly berated the Porush for so lightly dismissing laws and customs of such long standing, practices explicitly prescribed in the Siddur of Rav Amram Gaon, in Rashi's Siddur, and in many other compilations of Jewish law. The Porush answered that, first of all, the custom of not eating meat applies only to the nine days before Tishah B'Av, not to the entire "three weeks." And besides, it was not necessary to adhere to every stringency of bygone days. "We are a weaker generation and not as pious as our ancestors," he said. "It is all we can ask that Jews fast on Tishah B'Av itself."

"And that's why Jews don't fast on Tishah B'Av either, because you and your kind have declared permissible all that is forbidden," rasped Reb Heskiah, taking up the old battle anew.

"If Jews don't fast when they're supposed to, it's because you and your kind have declared forbidden even things that are allowed," the Rabbi shot back, and the two opponents parted even angrier than after their earlier disputes.

Even the summery days of late Tammuz and early Av refused to join in the mourning for the Temple. The peddlers on the Jewish Street stood with baskets brimming with fresh vegetables: white heads of cabbage and cauliflower, eggplants in satiny, dark-purple skins, lacy heads of dill, bundles of onions, and freshly dug potatoes. Beckoning from the fruit baskets on the wooden stands were meaty plums and honey-sweet yellow apricots—it seemed as if onto those wooden stands and into the woven baskets of the poor women peddlers had rolled countless small round suns, a treasure of golden ducats. The passers-by were all buying, each according to his means. Even the old men going in and out the courtyard gate, to and from services in the beth midrash, carried small paper bags in which were half- or quarter-pounds of one fruit or another. They mumbled the Shehehiyanu and slipped the sweet fruit between their beards and mustaches, forgetting, or only pretending to forget, that new fruits may not be eaten during the period just before Tishah B'Av.

On the mournful Sabbath of the Vision, when the first chapter of the Book of Isaiah is read, the sun blazed in a sparkling blue sky, and a dry subtropical heat descended on the city. The fragrance of slightly burned cholent was already wafting through the morning air, mingling with the odor of the glowing iron bars and locks of shuttered stores burning in the sun. The young people of Laybe-Layzar's courtyard and, indeed, of all the other courtyards fidgeted, eager to get to the river. Soon the narrow streets and alleyways lay empty. "O Jerusalem of Lithuania, my Jerusalem of Lithuania," Reb Heskiah groaned to himself as he sat in the afternoon heat in the empty beth midrash, swaying over a volume of the Midrash on Lamentations.

He knew the old Vilna cemetery very well, as well as the streets around the courtyard, even as well as the paragraphs and sections on the elaborately composed pages of the Code. He had wandered more than once among the gravestones of the Vilna Gaon, the Righteous Convert, and the many other holy men of the past. Now he sat alone in the silent beth midrash, thinking of the desecration that was taking place that moment on both banks of the river, right next to that very cemetery: In plain sight of the graves of these sainted sages, men and women bathed together, on the Sabbath no less, and right on the eve of Tishah B'Av. They rode in their little boats, singing and laughing. And in the nearby woods they committed the very abominations for which Jerusalem was destroyed. Before the destruction of the First Temple the Jewish people had their prophets, and before the destruction of the Second the Great Sanhedrin sat and meted out justice in accordance with the laws of the Torah. But these days the rabbis were afraid of the rabble; there was even among them a Porush who stood ready to permit anything and everything. It seemed to Reb Heskiah that the holy ark at the front of the beth midrash was mourning with him. Only he and the four walls of the beth midrash remained true to the Temple, to the ancient bereavement, to the centuries of mourners. They alone remained to console the shamed and sorrowful Divine Presence in this reckless and wanton world.

Nonetheless, on the night of Tishah B'Av many other Jews joined the locksmith in the beth midrash, squatting like mourners on overturned benches and swaying to the reader's chanting of the Book of Lamentations. Without its curtain, the ark looked half naked and ashamed, like a bride stripped of her bridal veil. None of the lights had been turned on; only a few candles that had been melted so as to adhere to the overturned benches shone on half-lit faces. Behind the stooped backs, shadows towered and swayed on the walls and onto the ceiling, as if they were observing an otherworldly Tishah B'Av of their own. Reb Heskiah was not a man given to weeping; in fact, he was often suspicious of people who wallowed in tears—he felt they could not resist temptation. "A good cry at a eulogy is just another craving given in to," he would say. So he mourned the Temple's destruction with only a groan, though with each groan he felt a piece of his heart being torn away.

To Reb Heskiah, the long summer's day of fasting was a burden light as a feather. Since tallith and tefillin could not be donned until after noon on this day, it was with a special dry exultation that he wrapped his emaciated body in his broad tallith at the afternoon service, and he bound his tefillin straps on his arm so tightly that he felt a twinge of pain. Though it was permissible to conduct business in the afternoon, the locksmith remained in the beth midrash the entire day. And when at last night fell, he went home to eat reluctantly, sorry to see the fast end. He sat quietly at the meal, afraid to ask his daughters if they had fasted; he was satisfied that Serel and Itka had at least stayed at home.

Afterward he returned to the beth midrash and tried to immerse himself in a rabbinic text, but the woeful words of Jeremiah and the dour chant of lamentations still rang in his ears. And then he could not keep from thinking about the gilder Yehiel-Michael Henes, who believed that the new Zionist settlers would rebuild Jerusalem. "I can just imagine how that bachelor observed the customs of mourning these past three weeks," Reb Heskiah thought. "And Serel wants to marry *him*? Over my dead body!"

Reb Heskiah finally managed to quell these stormy thoughts and to concentrate on his tome. Suddenly he heard wild cries from the courtyard —a woman crying, a tumult. He had never been interested in the noises and quarrels of the neighborhood; but this time, strangely, he was struck by the heart-stopping thought that something terrible might have happened to his family. He ran headlong out of the beth midrash—and found his wife and daughters in the courtyard, surrounded by a crowd and looking as if their house had burned down.

MOISHELE MUNVAS had finally caught on that there was something fishy about his wife and those demons: why was it that the demons would bang on the walls only when he was out of the house? So that night, after the fast, he had sent Nehamele to the store to buy cigarettes. When she returned, he was gone. Nehamele thought that he had just wanted to get rid of her so he could leave the house without having to listen to her whining about being afraid to stay in the house alone. Instead of leaving, however, Moishele had crawled under the bed, where he hid quietly until she returned. And there and then, in the deep-blue glow of the summer

night, he discovered that the demons who banged on the wall were none
other than his little witch! The next moment, Nehamele heard someone
leaping, panting, and growling behind her, and a hail of blows rained
down on her from all sides—now the demons were coming for her in
earnest! She ran screaming out of the house, her husband right behind her
still showering her with blows, until finally, through the beating, she saw
who her pursuer really was.

"Help! Save me!" she shrieked. "He's killing me! Help!"

Neighbors rushed into the courtyard, grabbed Moishele, and pulled
him away from his wife. Even the Porush had run out of his house.
Moishele, still struggling to wrestle free so he could continue beating
Nehamele, shouted at the men who held him fast: "What do you have to
say now, you upright, righteous people? You warned me you were going
to break every bone in my body if I ever left my wife alone with the
demons. You should have seen her prancing all around the room—just
like a devil—banging on the wall with her spoons. I knew she was a quiet,
cunning shrew, a witch, a bag of bones with poisonous fangs, but I never
imagined she was such a snake!"

Nehamele's entire body trembled, and she had to bite her fist to keep
from screaming from fright, sorrow, and shame. The neighbors surrounded her, not knowing whether to laugh or to give her what she
deserved for concocting such a devilish scheme, not letting anyone sleep
and driving the gardener's poor wife half-mad. Sensing the anger all
around her, she looked about, lost and confused. Then she saw Itka
standing calmly between her mother and sister, and her heart was scalded
by the thought: "That shameless bitch, that piece of meat with two eyes,
she must be the one who gave Moishele the idea of hiding under the bed
to see who was banging on the walls." The pain in her battered body and
the anger in her heart welled inside her until she was no longer concerned
about people finding out whom her husband was having an affair with.
In a wild voice and with complete abandon, she cried out: "I did it so he
wouldn't be able to go to *her*, that whore!" pointing at Itka. "She's the
one he's been seeing. He's been having an affair with her! With *her*!"

"I'll tear your hair out!" Zlata screeched. "I'll scratch your eyes out
for saying such things about my daughter!" But Moishele, Itka, and Serel
all stood speechless and frozen. It was at that moment that Reb Heskiah
ran out of the beth midrash and saw his wife and daughters. Nehamele,
her maniacal laugh mingled with desperate sobbing, continued to point at
Itka.

"He's been making love with her, with *her*! I followed him once and saw how he meets her when she leaves the Polish school where she goes to learn bookkeeping. Whenever she wasn't home, my husband wasn't home either. And he bought her presents with my hard-earned money, the money I sweated for when I was a seamstress. He bought her presents with it!"

Moishele lunged at Nehamele, bent on strangling, on trampling her, and the people around them did not stop him, so stunned were they by Nehamele's revelation. But in the nick of time Rabbi Weintraub managed to shield her with his broad body. Moishele dropped his hands and drew back; ever since the time the Porush had counted him as part of the minyan, Moishele had felt great respect for him.

"You'll stay with us tonight," the Porush said as he led Nehamele away by the arm. She followed docilely, though shaking spasmodically with her continued sobbing.

In the crowd stood Gracia, and she, too, suddenly broke out into a loud whining. "Quiet!" her husband roared at her, and he shouted at Nehamele as she walked away that she ought to be plucked out like nettles, and her protector, that crook, the former Zaskowicz Rav, with her. But no one in the crowd paid Paltiel Shklar any attention. They were all looking with vexed hearts at the real victim—the locksmith Heskiah Teitelbaum. He stood there bent and beaten, utterly defeated and stunned into silence. Only his lips quivered, as though he were still murmuring the prayers of Tishah B'Av, pleading for God's mercy on the mourners of Zion and Jerusalem.

16

REB HESKIAH no longer wanted to live under the same roof with his youngest daughter, and his wife feared that the neighbors would curse Itka, hiss and even throw stones at her. So Itka went to stay with her oldest sister, Malka, the divorcee. The neighbors, however, all felt sorry for the locksmith and had no intention of making sport of his misfortune. People were careful not to discuss the scandal while in the open air of the courtyard; they spoke of it only in whispers behind closed doors, in their homes. The women taxed their imaginations in condemning Itka, and the men talked of how much they were itching to tear out Moishele's walrus mustache and pull his eyebrows down to his heels. But in the end they all agreed that since Reb Heskiah was stuck in the middle of all this, it was best to keep silent. The more to-do they made, the more heartache it would make for him.

As bizarre as the entire episode appeared, no one doubted the truth of it; in fact, the neighbors could not forgive themselves for not having realized earlier that that gypsy Moishele Munvas was having a secret affair with the girl next door. But the courtyard was divided into two camps on why Itka had done it. The women said that she was simply a lascivious whore, but the men held, to the contrary, that if she were so shrewd and experienced, she would never have gotten mixed up in such a dangerous game. Probably she had never kissed a boy before out of fear of her father, so she was an easy prey for that rake who bragged how women all fell for him.

"We ought to call our neighbor the locksmith not Reb Heskiah but Reb Hoyzek—'Fool!,'" the neighbors joked among themselves, as they recalled how several Sabbaths previously he had blackened his other daughter's face in public for just standing in the street and talking to the gilder Yehiel-Michael Henes. "Hussy, brazen hussy!" he called Serel for even considering arranging her own marriage to that fine young man. So now his youngest daughter had shown him what chastity meant.

As for Nehamele, the neighbors did not judge her too harshly; none of them felt they would have been any better. She had suffered enough if she had known for so long with whom her husband was carrying on and said nothing. This view was not, however, shared by Rebbetzin Hindele, who was quite unwilling to make excuses for the upholsterer's wife and was angry at her Yoel for bringing Nehamele into their home: if this woman could devise such a devilish scheme with demons, she herself must be one of them; and besides, it was beneath the dignity of her scholarly husband to involve himself in so sordid a matter. The Porush, for his part, had never in all their years of marriage gotten angry at Hindele and he was not about to get angry at her now—he merely smiled and dismissed her childish talk:

"Hindele, my Hindele! I am no longer the Zaskowicz Rav and you are no longer the Zaskowicz Rebbetzin, but you still haven't shed the haughtiness of a Rebbetzin."

Nehamele spent several days in the Porush's home, cowering in a corner, depressed, defeated, and so fearful and hurt that she was barely able to breathe. She looked like a little hunted animal that had saved itself for the moment by ducking into a strange house, and trembled in fear of the people in the house no less than in fear of those pursuing her. She was terrified that her husband might at any moment come storming into the house, and she trembled guiltily in the face of Hindele's plainly unfriendly attitude. She understood that the Rebbetzin was giving her a nook in which to sleep and food to eat only so as not to upset her saintly husband. And Nehamele indeed regarded the Porush as so great a tzaddik that she could have kissed his hands for showing her the kindness of a father, and for not letting her tormentor cross the threshold.

Every day, through the window of Reb Yoel's house, Nehamele watched Moishele go to work. He dragged himself despondently through the courtyard, listless and only half alive, like a hung-over drunk staggering with a splitting headache after a night of revels. And coming home from work, he would loiter a long while in the courtyard staring at the Rabbi's house, but evidently didn't dare approach the door. Then he would go to his own house and stay there the rest of the night—it seemed he no longer had any taste for dressing up and going on the prowl for other women.

One evening Nehamele saw Moishele leave their house and enter the beth midrash. Later the Rabbi told her that Moishele had come to see him and begged him to let her return home, promising to mend his ways and become faithful and pious. "I told him that I wouldn't let you go back until his brothers came to see me. I want to talk to them."

Later the neighbors of Laybe-Layzar's courtyard would have much to tell about the goings-on at the Porush's, about the upholsterer, his wife, and the entire tribe of Munvases. Though Moishele had been unable to abide his brothers since they had induced him to marry Nehamele, he now, out of his need, went to see them, his tail between his legs and swearing his behavior would be exemplary from that moment on. He was fed up, he declared, with his way of life. And so, his brothers accompanied him to the Porush's house, where they parleyed late into the night. Moishele kept on insisting that he was willing to take a solemn oath in the Grand Synagogue of Vilna, before the opened ark and black candles, that he was going to become a decent human being before God and man. But Nehamele kept crying that he would break his promise, and the Porush demanded some guarantee from Moishele's older brothers. The brothers racked their brains to come up with some solution, until finally they suggested that the couple move into their courtyard on Kopanica Street, into an apartment of their own. The Porush was pleased with this plan, and Moishele and Nehamele even more so. They realized that they could not live in Laybe-Layzar's courtyard anymore; they would be ashamed to face their neighbors after all that had happened. "So, is there a God in

Heaven?" the people laughed, and none of them was sorry to see the upholsterer and his wife move out.

But the neighbors were still sorely worried about Reb Heskiah, who looked like a dying man. He had even stopped going to his shop, as he had been accustomed to do on occasion to help his partner with the more difficult jobs. Instead, he would spend the entire day sitting in the beth midrash over a tome, heaving heavy sighs. His wife was now more concerned about his suffering over his daughter than she had ever been during those insane fasts of his. Though Zlata had consoled herself with the thought that in times such as these Itka was not likely to remain an old maid, yet she understood that for her Heskiah, nothing worse could possibly have happened; for him, the world had come to an end.

As for Itka herself, with each passing day she stayed with her divorced sister she came to regret her conduct the more. Her great curiosity, her light-headed attitude, and the thrill of deceiving everyone had prevented her from seeing what a shallow man Moishele really was, how he was interested only in the playing of the game. She hadn't given a moment's thought to the possibility that her father might find out about the affair. So when her mother and Serel would come to Malka's house and tell Itka that her father looked like the living dead, she would think to herself: "They ought to behead me; that's what I deserve." But when she talked to her mother and sister, she stressed the importance of keeping the latest bad news from Father: the owner of the hardware store where she worked had been told everything, and had summarily fired her.

But there was no hiding even this from Reb Heskiah—Sheftel Miklishansky had informed him personally of his daughter's dismissal. "I didn't expect anything else," Reb Heskiah replied and continued swaying over the Talmud. In his own eyes he deserved even greater tribulations, and he was prepared to accept them from anyone—anyone except the Porush, Rabbi Yoel Weintraub.

The Porush had not expected that his warning would come true so soon: that when one forbids children what is permissible, they will resort to that which is really sinful. And he suffered not just on the locksmith's account, but on that of his foolish daughter as well. Even so, he bristled at Reb Heskiah's despair. From the locksmith's corner in the beth midrash pain-laden groans could be heard unceasingly, groans that were at times so loud one would have thought them to be coming from a man on his deathbed who desperately desired to relinquish his soul and put an end to his misery. At last, the Rabbi said to himself: "Whether he likes it or not,

I must do something!" And so, once again he found himself standing at the locksmith's lectern with outstretched hands.

"One would think your daughter converted. After all, she did not commit one of the most heinous sins of the Torah."

Reb Heskiah slowly lifted his face from his tome, and his hollow eyes, filled with a darkness like the plague of darkness in Egypt, suddenly came to life with a sardonic sparkle. He wanted to laugh, but he made do with an angry, twisted smile. "Is that so? It's permitted, is it?"

"And to be as arrogant as you, is that permitted?"

The locksmith was speechless, dumfounded—no one had ever before accused him of arrogance. But the Porush stood his ground: No matter how low to the floor Reb Heskiah kept his head, his humility was a sham; in reality, he was hopelessly arrogant. Everyone knew the story of the Patriarch Jacob's daughter Dinah and Shechem, son of Hamor, and the story of King David's children, Amnon and Tamar. But of course, such a thing couldn't possibly happen to Reb Heskiah, not even in this day and age; and if it ever should happen, why then, as far as Reb Heskiah was concerned, the world had fallen into the abyss. "So I ask you," the Porush pressed, "wouldn't it appear that Reb Heskiah is arrogant when compared to our father Jacob or to King David?"

The locksmith listened without anger or ridicule. He sighed heavily and then said in a quiet, broken voice that he had no one to blame but himself—because he had been too lenient with his daughter. The Porush looked at him in amazement and then returned silently to his seat and his Talmud. Never, he thought, shrugging his shoulders, never in his life had he seen such a stubborn, twisted old man: "And he believes he's in the right!" Even so, he couldn't let matters rest there, and so back he went to the locksmith, who seemed to be waiting for him.

"How in the world, Reb Heskiah, can you imagine that your being stricter with your daughter would have prevented all that happened? Every one of your neighbors believes the exact opposite—that if you hadn't been so strict with her, it would never have entered her mind to cavort with the married man across the way. And to a certain extent, the same could be said for the man himself."

The Porush, both hands on his knees, sat down next to the locksmith and proceeded to tell him what he had discovered in his talks with the upholsterer's older brothers, the fish handlers from the other side of the Poplawski Bridge. They told him that they had not permitted their younger brother to marry a woman who made women's hats. Moishele had cried out to them: "My soul yearns for her!" But they wouldn't hear of the marriage because they considered the match beneath them. So when he was kept from the woman he was certainly allowed to love, he had strayed onto the wrong path, to another not permitted to him.

"I didn't say anything to the Munvas brothers because they are coarse people to begin with, and besides, the matter is over and done with. But you, Reb Heskiah, as terribly obstinate as you are, still, you are a learned man. So I tell you, it's not too late: Take your daughter back into your home."

The locksmith, turning abruptly, seemed about to make a harsh retort, but apparently thought better of it and remained as before, sad and pensive. At last, after a long, thick silence, he groaned that now a new trouble had descended upon him: his middle daughter, Serel, had informed him that she was going to marry that gilder, Yehiel-Michael Henes. Serel had always been the quiet one, who never contradicted her father. Now, probably, she thought that if her sister could get away with anything, why couldn't she?

The Porush smiled in amazement, his gentle eyes radiating kindness as he asked Reb Heskiah whether he was serious, or only joking when he said his middle daughter wanted to imitate the youngest? It surely could not be that a father would go so much out of his way to misunderstand his own child's good intentions. It was just because Serel did *not* want to imitate her sister that she told him, openly and honestly, that she was going to marry Yehiel-Michael Henes. And in every courtyard and alleyway they knew the gilder to be a quiet, observant young man. So why should Reb Heskiah object? The Porush talked long and sincerely, as if the gilder were his own dear nephew. The locksmith's head sank lower toward his lectern and he said nothing, but he heard every word.

At services that Sabbath morning, the Porush watched as the first trustee, Sheftel Miklishansky, put his humility on display once again. As always, he declined the honor of standing on the bima and doling out the aliyot. When his substitute, the second trustee, leaned over the railing of the bima and, with but a wink, asked him if he'd like to be called up for the Maphtir, he winked back that someone else should be honored with the beautiful prophetic reading, "And Zion said." He would be happy just to get Hagboh, to be called upon to raise and help close the Torah scroll. But lest anyone think that Hagboh was not an exceedingly great honor, Sheftel Miklishansky took care to repeat a homily of the Chofetz Chaim,

Rabbi Yisroel-Meir HaCohen, may he live and be well, that when a Jew raises and unrolls the parchment of the Torah scroll, the worlds that are wound up in it are plainly revealed. And when the scroll is wound up and closed, whole worlds are closed off from us, for both the upper and the lower realms are within the words and letters of the Torah. "But then," Sheftel Miklishansky concluded with a shrug as he swept his broad Sabbath prayer shawl from his shoulders, "what do people know about such things today?"

Just at that moment, as the other men returned to their places and put away their prayer shawls, the Porush leaned over the trustee's lectern and whispered furtively into his ear: "The people living in the courtyard and the people who attend this beth midrash have great compassion for the locksmith, and even for his foolish daughter. But you, Reb Sheftel, you have fired the girl from her job in your store. When people find out about this, they will look upon you as a cruel man and they won't want you to be first trustee anymore."

Miklishansky felt his cheeks burn with rage, and his beard bristled. But he controlled himself and answered quietly so that others would not hear: He wasn't asking anyone for advice as to whom to employ as a cashier in his hardware store. Perhaps Rabbi Weintraub thought he was still the Zaskowicz Rav? He was nothing more than a Porush in this beth midrash. True, Reb Yoel replied, he was nothing more than a Porush here in Laybe-Layzar's beth midrash; nevertheless, he was and would remain concerned with the locksmith's daughter's case. "It was, after all, your idea, Reb Sheftel, that the girl go to the Polish school to learn bookkeeping. But when your advice turns out badly, you wash your hands of the entire matter. Her father and mother have the right to scold her for her actions, not you. . . . She didn't take a penny from your pocket, did she?"

With these last words the Porush raised his voice, as if to warn the trustee that he had a mind to speak yet louder and shame him before everyone. A shaken Sheftel Miklishansky walked quickly to the wall, and the Porush returned to his seat on the other side of the ark. He knew that this Sabbath-and-holiday tzaddik, this supposedly humble man, would give in out of fear lest his standing in the community be diminished.

That Sabbath afternoon Reb Heskiah's eldest, Malka, came to see her father and shouted at him: It wasn't enough for him to have destroyed her marriage because her husband wasn't pious enough to suit him; now he wanted to be Itka's undoing as well. But Itka was a different sort and the times were different. As long as Itka felt shame and regret for having caused everyone so much heartache, there was a chance of influencing her to act differently. But if her father insisted he would never forgive her and never let her back into the house, there was no telling what crooked path she might choose.

All the turmoil had finally bent Reb Heskiah's stubbornness, as a glowing-hot iron bar is bent on the anvil. His eldest daughter's words frightened him, especially since the Porush had similarly urged him to take his youngest daughter back into the house before it was too late. So he decided to let Itka move back home, and Sheftel Miklishansky agreed to take her back into his hardware store as well.

17

IN THE GARDENS of the city and along the river, the early fall had already singed the tips of the leaves and the edges of the plants. A bright, fiery yellow invaded the green thickness of shrubbery and trees. But in the crowded streets and courtyards of the Jewish neighborhood, where nothing green grew, the coming of fall was heralded only by the sound of the shophar at the morning services throughout the month of Elul, which preceded the High Holy Days. The shophar blasts blew a cold, raw wind through the bones and tore at the heart. Eyes looked up at the heavens brimming with the melancholy of the clouds.

The famed courtyard of the Grand Synagogue of Vilna, with its scores of smaller synagogues—just a few yards away from Laybe-Layzar's courtyard—stood empty all summer long, sparkling in the sunlight, the crystal-blue sky reflecting on the windows and the plaster shining white on the walls. But now, close to the High Holy Days, though the Grand Synagogue's courtyard looked dirt-gray from the dampness of the autumn rains, it was filled with worshippers going to and from services in the numerous synagogues, with beggars on the steps of the Grand Synagogue itself, and, in the deep round niches, the wooden stands of the vendors of sacred books and religious articles. Around the bookstands, people were gathered, leafing through and buying prayer books for the High Holy Days. A man was haggling over a blue velvet tallith bag. A hunched, wrinkled old woman leafed through the pages of a Tehinah with her long, thin fingers, as lovingly as if she were petting a grandchild's head. Nearby a boy stared in wonder at a large black spiral shophar that lay among the piles of books, like the ram caught by the horn in the thicket near the altar where Abraham had bound his son Isaac.

And in Laybe-Layzar's courtyard everyone felt the coming of autumn in the pale sunlight, no longer scorching and blinding. One morning after the neighbors had gone off to workshops, stores, or the marketplace, Gracia stood alone in the empty courtyard. Her tall, prominent, pale forehead, always lined with tiny wrinkles, was now creased even more in puzzlement: Near a window in a black, soot-covered wall there stared blindly the outline, dark and crooked, of what once must have been another window, now walled up with bricks but not yet plastered over. Gracia had never noticed it before and now asked herself why the sun shone only on the walled-up window and not on the window with glass panes. Though the demons had turned out to be only Nehamele banging on the wall, Gracia's belief in otherworldly powers remained unshaken. Surely, she thought, a cobweb-covered old man lived behind that window, and he came out only at night when everyone slept. "Who could he be, that hoary man who hides there in the darkness?" Gracia wondered. Suddenly, she was startled by weeping from the home of the former Zaskowicz Rav. For a moment Gracia stood still, then ran into her house, terrified: "The Zaskowicz Rav said that demons were fantasy. So now the insulted demons must have come to rebuke him and his Rebbetzin!"

The Porush was standing in the middle of his living room, his hands clumsily outstretched, his shoulders drawn up as if he expected the low ceiling above his head to sag even lower at any moment until he would have to support the beams with his shoulders. Rebbetzin Hindele was standing in front of him in a market smock, and near her were two baskets full of eggs. She was bemoaning her fate: having to break her feet climbing scores of flights of stairs every day to sell her merchandise. First the customer would look at an egg as if eyeing it through a microscope, until satisfied that it was fresh and as clear as the sun. Then the housewife would haggle and demand an oath that she was not being cheated. "I tell them that my husband is a Rabbi and I am a Rebbetzin; we do not take oaths, even on the truth. My word is my bond. So they answer that nobody pays for what used-to-be. 'Now you're an egg peddler, not a Rebbetzin. To us you're no different than any other peddler.'" And Hindele once again broke into bitter weeping. If only her customers really did regard her as they did the butcher's wife or the grocer's or the fruit vendor's. When *they* went to collect their bills, the customers didn't dare tell them to come next week. They knew that these women were perfectly capable of opening their mouths and attracting quite an audience. But when she went to collect and said she could not wait because her whole-salers had to be paid, the customers berated her. "According to the holy Torah," they asked sanctimoniously, "is one permitted to beat a debtor over the head, to force him to pay? You ought to know; you're a Rebbetzin who will not even be seen in public with your head uncovered." The rest of the time she was not a Rebbetzin, but when it came to getting paid, she was a Rebbetzin.

"They know, those rich women, that I cannot send a 'ruffian' hus-band to collect the money—and could I, in any case, ask you to collect my bills for me?" Hindele wept even louder as she explained to her hus-band that to spare him pain she had always kept her complaints to herself; but now she could no longer keep silent. He knew that lately she had also started selling chickens, since she could not make a living from eggs alone. So she was in the market every morning before dawn, haggling with the churlish merchants around the wagons laden with caged birds, just like all the other peddlers of chickens and geese. They all laughed at her: "Just look at our competitor!" they snickered. She kept quiet. She would not pick a fight with these women peddlers with their burly shoul-ders, their faces as red as raw meat, and the fire of hell spewing out of their mouths. She took the birds to her customers, who blew aside the tail feathers to see if the hen was fat enough. And then they didn't pay: "Next week, after Sabbath," they all said. But when she'd gone to one housewife after Sabbath to get paid, the woman called her a thief. "Thief that you are, you're cheating us all. That chicken you sold me was thin and hard as a rock. My husband threw it in my face." Hindele had felt such a sharp pain in her heart at being called a thief that she could not say a word, but just left hastily and could not even bring herself to return and demand the money owed her. Another housewife ridiculed her: From a rebbetzin named Hindele who sells hens one could not expect very much. A third woman deducted a zloty without asking her, and a fourth, a very wealthy one, paid the full amount but told her in a harsh tone never to darken her door again.

"And it's possible that my merchandise really was bad—after all, I've never sold chickens before," Hindele said, her voice trailing off in a quiet, meek tone, for now she felt ashamed of having cried and moaned like a foolish housewife. Fearful that she would continue to cry if she stayed, Hindele dashed out of the house with a basket of eggs on each arm.

And because she was carrying a basket on each arm, Hindele was unable to wipe away the tears that continued to flow from her eyes. Her lips were still quivering when Gracia Shklar, who had again come into the courtyard, stopped her:

"Rebbetzin, may you live and be well, I have a question on a matter of ritual. What is the—"

"Don't ask me any questions, I'm not a Rebbetzin anymore and neither is my husband the Zaskowicz Rav," Hindele answered bitterly, and she hurried away, her dress tangled between her legs. Though she had time and again renounced her title of Rebbetzin, she still wore a rebbetzin's long, modest dress.

A few minutes later the Porush appeared, troubled by Hindele's tears. He could not stay in the house, nor could he settle down to study in Laybe-Layzar's beth midrash. So he just stood in the courtyard looking up at the sky, half his face alight in a patch of sun, the other half in shadow as if cloven in half with a knife.

"Rabbi, should I visit the Vilna cemetery during the Ten Days of Repentance?" Gracia asked him in her lilting, melancholy voice. "As you know, my Alterl, my child, is buried in Zaskowicz. Will my going to the cemetery here in Vilna be considered as if I had gone to his little grave in Zaskowicz?" The Porush had not yet collected himself long enough to consider this question when Gracia asked him another: "Perhaps, Rabbi, you could prevail on my husband to make peace with his brothers?" She drew closer to Reb Yoel as though to entrust him with a secret. "My Paltiel says that the case in Oszmiana may drag on for years, though he is certain that he will win in the end. But meanwhile the money has all run out and he hasn't found partners here to buy orchards for him to cultivate. So could you, Rabbi, perhaps bring my husband and his brothers together?"

"How can I bring your husband and his brothers together?" the Porush stammered as he looked at the gardener's wife, fearful that she too would start crying just as Hindele had. "You may go to the Vilna cemetery during the Ten Days of Repentance. The Almighty hears prayers wherever they are uttered. You needn't go back to Zaskowicz just for that. No, you need not," and he turned quickly and went into his house.

He placed an open volume of Maimonides on the table so he would not be left alone with his disturbing, soul-rending thoughts. At first, he paced restlessly around the room and then collapsed into an easy chair with round, worn armrests—the only piece of furniture he had brought with him from Zaskowicz to Vilna. The deeper he sank into the chair and into his thoughts, the more heavily his hands drooped over the armrests, as limp as branches soaked by a heavy rain. It seemed to him that

Hindele's sobs still hung in the room and were dripping from the ceiling onto his head. This added to his thoughts a painful sharpness, like the thoughts of a man who muses over the vanity of life while wandering in a cemetery.

The news had reached him that Zaskowicz had not yet chosen his successor and that a battle was brewing, no less heated than the war the Shklar brothers were waging among themselves over their inheritance. Was he not to blame for a town of good people being torn by strife? And the greatest injustice was the one he had done his own Hindele: He had left Zaskowicz because he felt unable to continue ruling that everything in sight was forbidden. But was letting Hindele toil so hard and be subjected to such humiliation any less forbidden? Was it right for so small and frail a woman to support so strapping and healthy a husband? But how could the wrong be righted, unless he were to come out of retirement and seek another pulpit? Yet younger men, accomplished orators who could speak Polish as well, with large, untouched dowries which they were prepared to use for communal needs—even such dedicated young men had to look long and hard before they found a pulpit; his own prospects, then, were all but nonexistent. Perhaps his only chance was to inquire if his old pulpit in Zaskowicz was still vacant. And yet the factions there that couldn't agree on the appointment of a new Rav, were certain to agree on one thing—that they did not want him back. The zealots had always looked at him suspiciously for not being strict enough; and the not-so-pious, and even his former supporters, were angry with him for having left them and so created a great conflict. Besides, it would be embarrassing to go begging after having spurned all their pleas for him to stay.

Meanwhile, Zlata Teitelbaum had quietly stolen into the Porush's house. He did not notice her until she was standing directly in front of him with her weary, haggard face and her large, dark, pathetic eyes. "Today must be my day with the women," he thought as he regarded her wearily.

"I haven't any more strength to fight with my old husband," Zlata began, lifting her hands and letting them drop to her side as if to show how her strength had been drained. She was already accustomed to her Heskiah's redoubled piety and crazy observances during the month of Elul, in anticipation of the High Holy Days. But she had hoped that after the disaster with Itka he would at least not say another word against the marriage of Serel and the gilder Henes. Even the Rabbi had been confident that her husband would at last relent. Now, from out of the blue, he had changed his mind and announced: "Serel can marry anyone she

chooses, even Yehiel-Michael Henes, but I will not attend the wedding."
So now what was she to do?

"Then let the wedding go on without him. It's perfectly permissible,"
the Porush answered, but then recoiled from his words with the thought:
"What am I saying? A wedding without the father of the bride?" His
quick "It's permitted" had finally led him as far astray as the fanatic
locksmith's incessant "It's forbidden." Zlata looked at Rabbi Weintraub
suspiciously, wondering if he might be laughing at her. He tried to reassure her that since the wedding could not take place before the winter,
there was still time for her husband to soften. Didn't he always, as she
herself had said, become even more wildly fanatical, a frenzied penitent,
just before the New Year?

Zlata departed as stealthily as she had come, leaving the Porush in a
more painful and anguished state of mind than before. Why had he resigned the Zaskowicz rabbinate—was it not to relieve himself of the responsibility for solving everybody's problems? And yet now, as a porush,
he still found himself embroiled in other people's problems, in the affair
of the upholsterer and his wife and now in that of the locksmith and his
daughters. As long as one lived among people, it seemed, one could not
help but get involved. All he had accomplished was to leave a town to
seethe in its acrimony and recriminations, and to make a worn-out peddler of his Rebbetzin.

In the afternoon the Porush locked his house and went to the Gaon's
beth midrash in the courtyard of the Grand Synagogue. He did not return
until evening, when he found Hindele in the kitchen preparing dinner.
She cast a knowing sidelong glance at him, her eyes sparkling like faceted,
polished jewels: it was most unusual for her husband to be neither at
home nor in Laybe-Layzar's beth midrash; yet she did not ask him where
he had been. But he told her anyway, in the cheerless voice and hollow
tone of an old wall clock.

"I was in the Gaon's Beth Midrash today, talking to the p'rushim
about the possibility of joining them and receiving a stipend. They told
me that their allowance is not a third of what they need to live, and that
the trustees would never agree to take on another porush." He stood
quietly for a while, filling the narrow room with his tall-framed body.
Then he sat down on a little bench and sighed. "It's too late for me to
learn a trade, but maybe I can earn some money selling something. Why
don't I sell fish in the market on Friday, just as you sell eggs and chickens? What do you think, Hindele?"

At first, Hindele could not believe these words were not uttered in jest. But when she realized from his despondent expression and hollow voice that he was in earnest, she wailed even louder than she had earlier that day in complaining of her shabby treatment at the hands of her customers. She was deeply hurt at the thought that her husband felt she wanted him to be a breadwinner. But, beyond that, his plan struck her as so absurd that she found herself laughing in the middle of her weeping, and asked him why he had particularly chosen to sell fish. Was it because he had had to deal with fish handlers recently, with Moishele Munvas' brothers? "Rabbi Yoel Weintraub and the Brothers Munvas are surely from the same mold, aren't they?" Hindele laughed until her laughter turned into tears; finally she composed herself and became silent as she set the table. All during the meal she stole furtive glances at her husband, as if they were newlyweds. She watched how careful he was not to let crumbs fall on his beard, and how gingerly he ate his chicken so his fingers would not get greasy. Hindele suppressed a smile as she thought that she was ready to work harder and endure even more humiliation for the honor of having so refined and fastidious a Talmudic scholar for a husband.

Later, in the evening darkness, Hindele heard her husband sighing through the stillness of the bedroom. He had not been able to sleep, and neither could Hindele, although she had labored the entire day, running all over and trudging up and down countless stairs to peddle her merchandise. In the moonlight shining through the window she could see her husband's beard, its weave of copper and silver, and his arm in the rolled-up sleeve of his white nightshirt. He usually lay in bed on his back facing the ceiling, his head on a high pillow and his arms folded behind his head. On such nights, when sleep eluded her, she could not stop marveling at her good fortune at having so tall and splendid a man for a husband, and she delighted in him like a little girl who has her father all to herself. But as the night took on a blue-black hue, thick as the swirls in a full ink bottle, she could no longer see him. She could only sense that he was still not asleep, and she wanted to hear his voice. After crying away the morning and the evening, Hindele longed, in her bed, in the dead of night, to be pampered and soothed by her husband's sweet voice.

"Yoel, you're not sleeping? Tell me, Yoel, when a wife has no children for ten years, the law demands she be sent away, divorced. So tell me, why haven't you divorced me?"

The Porush's heart was heavy for his Rebbetzin—thirty-five years now they had been married, and still she thought of this. In the same affectedly playful tone he replied: "But we don't know which of us is at fault, so, according to the law, I don't have to divorce you."

"But you were allowed to find out," Hindele jested, and then teased: "You should have left me and married another woman and then you'd know."

The Porush didn't answer as he felt sleep overtaking him. But in one corner of his mind a thought twitched: If he had had children, he would not have been able to leave Zaskowicz; he would have had to bear the burden of providing for a family. And he was, moreover, not at all certain that children would have given him joy. Young people were by nature hot-blooded and did not believe in treading the middle path, especially not these days. His children would either have been fanatics, like the yeshiva students who despised all things secular, or else would have forsworn Torah study altogether and renounced the authority of the rabbis. Their mother, perhaps, would have enjoyed them.

His eyelids drooped and his thoughts congealed in his dimming mind, like a film over still waters. But from the other bed words still poked at him like rays of light, and a joyful, almost childlike voice was arousing him once again from sleep.

"Do you know, Yoel, when I fell in love with you? At first, when Father, may his soul rest in peace, brought you to the house, I was frightened; you were so tall, broad and handsome, and I was so small. But the first time we went for a walk, before our betrothal, you told me the story of the pillows and I fell in love with you immediately."

As Hindele prattled on, Reb Yoel lay on his bed like a giant boulder sunk in moss, listening to her chatter that sounded like running water. She was to this day still moved by a story of her husband's childhood: While a student in a small town, he had given one of his two pillows to two old women who were putting together a dowry for a poor bride. Since he always liked to sleep with his head high, he sorely missed his other pillow. True, since he had told her the story before they were married, she could not then know how much he liked to sleep on high pillows. She was just moved by the idea of a pious youngster, a budding scholar, studying in a strange town, giving up one of his two pillows for a poor bride.

The Rebbetzin curled herself under the covers and soon fell asleep. But on the next bed her husband remained wide awake—exhausted, yet far removed from sleep. He lay as still and rigid as a wooden beam; only his tall, vaulted forehead wrinkled above his closed eyes. After intense and prolonged deliberation, he came at last to a decision: he would go to Zaskowicz and perhaps, with the Almighty's help, he could convince the people to take him back as their Rav.

Slowly the thick darkness became thinner, grayer. Doors, windows, and roofs began slowly to creep out of the night. The gray ran off like murky water down a drainpipe. A green dawn sky spread cold and gloomy. In the turbid light of dawn the damp nakedness of Laybe-Layzar's courtyard rose up into the day like a golem from a lagoon. All things seemed lonely, permeated with the sadness of fall. Only the fowls in their cages, held in readiness for the upcoming holidays and for kapporoth, crowed, cackled, quacked, and gobbled. In the Porush's home the iron latch creaked hoarsely and Hindele appeared with two empty baskets. She had hurried to the market for her merchandise that morning and met a neighbor from the courtyard, another peddler, who was on her way to the market ahead of her. And when Hindele walked out of the courtyard into the narrow, winding Jewish Street, she saw a long line ahead of her, women with empty baskets, peddlers and suppliers who, like her, were running to the market for their merchandise.

18

As THINGS TURNED OUT, before the Porush had time to plan his return to Zaskowicz, a delegation from the town came to Vilna, two days after Rosh Hashanah, to see their former Rav. The first one to notice the visitors was Gracia, who had been wandering through the courtyard as usual. She recognized one of the three men in the delegation as her husband's older brother, but instead of greeting the people from her home town, she ran frantically to the beth midrash to give the Porush the news.

"Rabbi, three men from Zaskowicz are here, and one of them is a brother-in-law of mine," she gasped out, clutching at her chest as if to keep her heart from leaping out of her.

The Porush rose from his seat wide-eyed, but before he could ask Gracia for details, the three men were suddenly standing before him, like the three angels who had appeared before Abraham. They shook hands with the Rav and proceeded at once to the reason for their visit.

"Good day, Rabbi. Zaskowicz has sent us to you with a mission: to bring you back with us. As we hear it, you haven't made a fortune in Vilna and neither have you attained any great position—you haven't even the tranquillity and peace of mind you so longed for. But things are even worse with us in Zaskowicz. Since you left, the town has been torn apart by a flaming controversy.

"Such a bitter quarrel has never happened before, in all of Zaskowicz's history as a Jewish town, and especially not at this time of year, in the days between Rosh Hashanah and Yom Kippur—and just because we can't agree on a new rav. The two sides have become nothing short of mortal enemies."

"If you return, Rabbi, perhaps peace will also return to our family," said the elder Shklar brother, glancing at his sister-in-law Gracia.

The surprise and poignancy of his old flock's loyalty moved the Porush to the brink of tears, and it was some time before he was able to collect himself. If he had believed in magic, he would have said that he had somehow summoned these men of Zaskowicz by his concentrated thinking about returning there. He saw in this the hand of Divine Providence, the "Finger of the Lord." It was all he could do to stammer out, "My friends . . . ," before he had to pause again to regain his composure. But the delegation, having no idea of the Rabbi's thoughts and emotions, looked at him fearfully, as if they expected that he would, God forbid, turn them down.

"Come to my house, gentlemen. My Rebbetzin is not in and, alas, I do not know how to go about serving guests. But we will be able to discuss the matter more comfortably there."

As he spoke, the Porush realized that he must not exhibit too much joy or jump at their offer too quickly, lest he undermine the respect a town should feel for its Rav.

The Zaskowicz representatives waited for him to lead the way. He paused an instant beside Gracia who still stood as if entranced in the middle of the beth midrash. "See if you can persuade your husband to join us," he whispered to her and then made for the door, followed by the visitors.

Reb Heskiah, meanwhile, had stood up in his nook in the beth midrash and was watching the scene in utter amazement. He had heard, across the empty room, the conversation between the Rav and the delegation, but could hardly believe what he had heard. All this time he had been convinced that Rabbi Weintraub was hated by the townspeople of Zaskowicz for being so liberal, a man of compromise. And here the town had actually sent emissaries to beg him to return and be their Rav again.

A dazed Gracia now stood beside the locksmith, talking, as it seemed, to him and yet not talking to him at all. She looked out the window off into the distance and chanted plaintively, as if reciting a Yiddish prayer from the Tehinah.

"Yes, I can arrange for my husband to make peace with his brothers. He himself wants it. But my child, my little Alterl, will not come to life through that. Only one good thing will come of that: We will once again live in Zaskowicz, so my Alterl will not have to look for us in strange places. In Zaskowicz he knows just where our little home is and I know just where his little grave is."

Gracia left the beth midrash with her hands folded across her chest, looking like a pious young housewife on Friday night after candle-lighting who has already put her children to sleep and awaits her husband's return from the synagogue to make Kiddush.

About two o'clock that afternoon, Hindele hurriedly entered the house to gather together a few dozen eggs for her customers—but then stumbled backward to the door as if she had seen an apparition from the netherworld. At the table sat her husband and around him sat four men: Three whom she knew from Zaskowicz, and the fourth, their neighbor Paltiel Shklar, her husband's bitter enemy, who had never before set foot in their house. The guests from Zaskowicz rose and sang out merrily: "Well now, here is our Rebbetzin!" But the merriment was short-lived. They had, of course, long since heard that the Rebbetzin had become a peddler running from house to house. Now, however, when they saw her burst in, evidently in great haste, with two empty baskets, bent and darkened, with a worn, crumpled shawl around her shoulders and a market woman's apron around her waist, they became confused, ashamed, saddened, and finally angry. They could not understand how the Rav could have given up the large house the town had provided for him to settle in this squalid little apartment in a forgotten corner of one of the poorest courtyards in Vilna, nor could they comprehend his having made a common peddler of his Rebbetzin.

Paltiel Shklar's older brother was a full head taller than his two companions. His face was clear and placid, his round white beard neatly trimmed, his broad mustache carefully combed. His slow, deliberately measured movements and his calm gaze attested to his status, his awareness of being the head of the entire Shklar clan. In him, there was not a trace of charity or compassion. In fact, he exuded the very opposite: Here was a man who would clearly stop at nothing to have his way. Nonetheless, when he saw that he could not have his way, he was prepared to compromise—unlike his younger brother, that cantankerous loner with a tuft of thin, prickly hair on his chin and the thick, mossy brows over his eyes. The older Shklar brother said little so as not to incite the younger, and indeed, whenever the older brother did speak, Paltiel did not fail to become agitated. He looked at his brother with jealousy and awe—how did he manage to win everyone over with his glib tongue and even with his appearance?

On the other two men from Zaskowicz lay the wretchedness of their poor town. The representative of the more observant faction had a tall, round cap with a hard visor and a worn gray frock coat with patches here and there. His tall, thin frame and the thistled beard on his wrinkled face gave him the appearance of a desiccated and shriveled pine tree thickly covered with clusters of withered brown needles that never fell off the branches. Around him was an aura of grated radish, onion, and sauerkraut, all from his own little backyard garden, and the odor as well of herbs, sour milk, and the dung of his one half-starved cow.

From the other man's crumpled hat and from the fact that he wore a shirt and tie, it was clear that he represented the "enlightened" faction of the townspeople. Such a Jew would never go about with his fringes flying out of his shirt; instead he would be wearing a small tallith katan with the fringes neatly tucked into his pants. He read the Warsaw Yiddish paper every Friday night, and at services the next morning he would be prepared to do battle if a memorial prayer was not said for Dr. Herzl on the anniversary of his death. In an argument, he was capable of flying into a deadly rage. But whenever he was not locked in combat over spiritual matters, his eyes looked about with the sad weariness of a merchant waiting, as if for the Prophet Elijah himself, for a customer to come in and buy a few ounces of salt, a few pounds of groats, a herring, or a can of kerosene. Since, however, bands of Polish ruffians kept the peasants from walking into a Jewish store, the merchant's only customer was a Jewish housewife who came in on Friday to take—on credit—a quarter-pound of yeast, a pouch of tea, and a few candles for the Sabbath candle-lighting.

The visitors told the Porush about the turmoil in the town over the selection of a new Rav. The longer they talked, the more he felt the same old heartaches he had known day in and day out in Zaskowicz whenever the poor townspeople would ask him for a ruling and he would have to answer that, according to the law, this or that was forbidden, prohibited, unfit . . . "You may not! You may not!" But he had no doubts or misgivings now; he knew that, come what may, he must return to Zaskowicz as

Rav. In his heart he even accepted the community's grievance against him—left unsaid but clearly visible on the emissaries' faces—for having left Zaskowicz in the first place and thrown it into turmoil and decline. And opposite him stood Hindele, beaming with joy, though trembling at the thought that he might yet refuse. So the Porush did not want to delay answering any longer.

"My friends, I am prepared to return to Zaskowicz and assume once again, with God's help, the yoke of the rabbinate."

"And what about me? What about the injustice done me?" Paltiel Shklar said sharply as he rose from the bench and stood at the table, turning his head to all sides, with mistrust, fear, and rage.

"That's why I came along," said the elder Shklar, "to urge you to agree to take the matter to a rabbinical court over which the Rabbi will preside. Or else he can arbitrate the case himself, and we can dispense with the suit in the Gentile court in Oszmiana—a suit that's eating us up alive. Well, Paltiel, do you agree?"

Paltiel stood silent, and when such a stubborn, ill-tempered man hangs his head in silence, it means he agrees. Rebbetzin Hindele clapped her hands and called out: "Such distinguished and dear guests! And sitting at a table with no tablecloth and not a crumb of food to eat!" Hindele forgot about delivering eggs to housewives. She scurried about, spreading the Sabbath tablecloth on the table, rushing to the kitchen to prepare food for her guests, yet all the while listening to the conversation of the men around the table in the next room.

The delegation wanted the Rabbi to return with them to Zaskowicz immediately. Of course they understood perfectly well that it was impossible to move from Vilna to Zaskowicz in a day. And Zaskowicz, too, had to prepare the Rav's house, and arrange a fitting reception for him and the Rebbetzin. So let the Rav come just for the rest of the High Holy Days, for the Sabbath of Repentance and Yom Kippur. In fact, if the Rav were to deliver the traditional discourse on the Sabbath of Repentance, surely the warring factions would be inspired to make peace with each other as befits Jews before the Day of Atonement. With the Rav present, the solemn day of fasting and prayer would be entirely different.

"Our guests are right," Hindele intruded—something she had never done in all the years she had been the Zaskowicz Rebbetzin.

"I will have to think about that," the Porush answered and then invited his guests to partake of the food his wife had served. Paltiel rose again, this time to leave, for he felt unwelcome and alien. But the Rav seized his arm. "Why are you hurrying off, Reb Paltiel? You too are a dear guest here, a very dear one."

"In this world we are all nothing but guests," the elder Shklar said with something of the piety of Yom Kippur eve.

When the Zaskowicz delegation finally left and Hindele went out into the courtyard, her neighbors were already waiting for her: "Is it true, Rebbetzin, that your husband is going to be the Rav of Zaskowicz again?"

Hindele answered harshly: "Of course it's true! Did you think we were going to stay with you here forever?" The neighbors understood Hindele's anger as clearly as if she had plainly added, "And what do you expect, after what my husband has had to put up with from all of you?"

Yom Kippur was already knocking on everyone's door and it looked as if the entire courtyard would soon be buried in chicken feathers. Frantic housewives noisily scurried about until late at night, and the crowing of chickens in their cages, waiting for the kapporoth ceremony, echoed from one end of the courtyard to the other. But as busy as everyone was with the preparations for Yom Kippur, the people of the courtyard still found time to get together in little groups and look for someone to blame for losing the Porush whom they had all come to regard as their Rav.

"It's all the fault of the trustee, Sheftel Miklishansky. It never occurred to him that a Rabbi, too, has to eat. A plague on such a trustee!" howled the market peddlers. The women had their own scapegoat: The fault really lay with the outsiders who had moved into the courtyard. Everyone had been busy, day and night, with that gypsy Moishele Munvas and his venomous Nehamele, not to mention the sick Gracia and her miserable husband, the gardener. So the courtyard simply had forgotten, in all this confusion, that in its midst lived a great tzaddik. Now Laybe-Layzar's courtyard would once again become a den of churls and boors. "It's lucky we still have the locksmith, Reb Heskiah, for a neighbor. He may be a fanatic, Lord help us, but even so he's a very learned man."

The next day the Zaskowicz representatives came to the beth midrash in Laybe-Layzar's courtyard for morning services and afterward stood around their Rav. A few men of the courtyard came to plead with the Zaskowicz emissaries: it was certainly their fault, they knew, that the Rav was leaving them and it was too late to set things right. And they wished the Rav a happy return to Zaskowicz, in good health. They asked only that he stay in Vilna for Yom Kippur and Sukkoth and pray with them in the beth midrash where he had prayed and studied the entire year. The Zaskowicz men, well practiced in argument, immediately took them to task: "By what right do you ask that our Rav stay here with you for Yom Kippur and Sukkoth? Is it for the large salary, the splendid home, and the great honor you offered him?" The people of the courtyard were not about to keep silent at this, but the Rav waved his hands, indicating that he wished to speak.

"My neighbors are right. I myself was thinking that I ought to spend Yom Kippur and Sukkoth among the people I have lived with all year. Go, gentlemen, in good health and good speed, and tell the people of Zaskowicz that I wish them a happy and healthy New Year, and that after the holidays, with God's help, I will be returning to become once again their Rav."

19

THE MORNING OF Yom Kippur cast a golden autumn hue over the empty streets and in the courtyards along the Jewish Street in Vilna. The sun peeked into the cellar windows, through the crooked panes of the garret windows, and along the cold, narrow alleyways, but hardly anyone was to be found there—for everyone was in the synagogues. Bands of light and shadow played on the shutters and bolted doors of the closed shops, which looked as if they, too, were immersed in prayer in the thick, hazy quietude, wrapped in prayer shawls woven from sunbeams. In every overflowing beth midrash, large electric bulbs burned all day beneath the lampshades and tiny bulbs sparkled in the chandeliers. Tall memorial candles stood in wooden boxes filled with sand to prevent fire.

It was the middle of the morning service. The harmonious chorus of the chanting worshippers, not yet fatigued by prayer or fasting, echoed through the stony emptiness of the winding streets outside the courtyard, reaching all the way to Zamkowa Street, where greenery still gleamed behind the iron fences surrounding the houses and gardens of the Polish gentry. And farther down in the city gardens, and along the banks of the Wilja, strolled the young Jewish men and women who were estranged from the beth midrash. But on Yom Kippur these young people felt no less strange in those tree-lined avenues among the strolling and laughing Gentiles. Women were sitting on benches, bathing their faces in the cool sunlight. Autumn had come early, and the leaves were already ablaze in shades of orange, deep wine-red, fiery red, brown, and yellow, as though the gardens themselves were a giant beth midrash with lamps burning in the daylight, interwoven with the waxen flickering of the memorial candles.

The packed women's section of Laybe-Layzar's beth midrash was all abuzz. In the front row, right next to the curtain that overlooked the ark in the men's section, stood three women: Gracia Shklar, the Rebbetzin Hindele, and Zlata, the wife of the locksmith Heskiah Teitelbaum.

Gracia, wearing a long white dress and a pale-blue silk kerchief over her hair, overshadowed the other women. From her tall, slightly bent figure and round, narrow shoulders there radiated a beauty that her garments could not conceal. She folded her hands on her chest under her heart and a wan smile played on her lips—the sorrowful resignation of motherhood denied and shamed. As she listened to the pious murmuring and sighing around her, Gracia felt glad to be among her friendly neighbors, simple and kind, who were praying so devoutly on this Day of Awe. She herself, however, neither prayed nor wept. She only smiled and every now and then raised her brows, creasing her high forehead as she recalled how happy Yom Kippur used to be when her little boy was alive and she had prayed to the Almighty to grant him a good year. The smile on her lips quivered like a trapped bird struggling to escape from a net. Gracia wanted to escape from her thoughts and from the women around her, all of whom still had their children. So she closed her eyes and thought back to her maiden days when she used to walk alone through the vast forests around Zaskowicz.

On the edge of the forests the leaden gray clouds hung, as if barricading the sky to prevent the birds from flying to warmer lands for the winter. Under the thick tangle of branches, the late-blooming sage was already in full flower, sparkling with cool violet blossoms amid the luscious green of the leafy ferns. Deeper into the thicket lay a clearing covered with dry silver moss. And still farther into the pine forest the damp, deep-red rust of the overgrown ivy adorned the rotted tree stumps.

Suddenly, darkness descended upon everything as if the daytime sky had in a trice become a starry night. Deep in the thicket was hidden the secret world of the poisonous mushrooms, speckled with a rainbow of color. The forest lay still, steeped in quietude; only an occasional beam of light managed to pierce the vault of the branches, quivering like a torn violin string. Through the beams shone the hanging clusters of gold-green needles, and on the thick autumn spiderwebs draped over the bushes the raindrops flickered in the sunlight like radiant jewels. Gracia did not want to open her eyes and look out onto the barren earth of Laybe-Layzar's courtyard, where, she knew, the only greenery was the mold on the plastered walls.

Rebbetzin Hindele stood next to her, in a dark-red velvet dress with long, narrow sleeves. Her deep, round little hat looked surprisingly fashionable, worn stylishly back on her head, perhaps even a bit too far back. Peering into her Mahzor, she luxuriated in the prayers, pronouncing each word with diligence and care, as if to make up for all the days, weeks, and months she had neglected prayer for the sake of her eggs and chickens.

Standing beside Hindele was Reb Heskiah's wife, Zlata. Tears were flowing not just from her eyes but even from her tall wig onto her prayer book. She bemoaned the bitter lot of her eldest daughter, Malka, the divorcee; she prayed for the good fortune of her middle daughter, Serel, who would soon be marrying Yehiel-Michael Henes; and she pleaded for her youngest, Itka, who had nearly driven her poor old father to the grave with her pranks. Zlata's three daughters all stood behind her as if bearing witness to her prayers and pleading.

The eldest daughter, Malka, wore a dark-gray dress of knitted wool and a kerchief on her hair. She held no prayer book in her hands, not even a simple Yiddish tehinah, nor did she utter any prayer; she only sighed incessantly, as if she thought her sighs would help her mother to pray. Itka also had no prayer book. Stylishly clad in a broad, brown-flecked suit, she stood still and erect, her face cool and aloof. Though it was not yet noon, the fast had already given her a headache. But she was suffering greater pain from the way the women around her gossiped with their eyes even while they piously muttered prayers with their lips. Not wanting to upset her mother, she did not leave the women's section even for a minute. To the piercing glances of the busybodies she replied wordlessly with her heavy braids of copper hair tucked up on her neck. Over the multifarious coiffures of the married women in their lavish wigs and silken shawls, over the small, round caps and broad felt hats laden with ostrich feathers, adorned with flowers, studded with sparkling sequins and trembling golden tendrils, with dangling ribbons, hairnets, and veils—over all and over everything there triumphed the copper braids of Itka, the locksmith's daughter.

Of Zlata's three daughters, only Serel prayed, from a small, thick Mahzor with hard covers, silvered edges, and a golden clasp. She was wearing her black suit over a white cambric blouse. Her straight, smooth, chestnut hair, plainly combed to either side of a straight part in the middle, glowed with a soft aura of chastity. Her gaunt face shone with a silent happiness. She had convinced her Yehiel-Michael not to spend Yom Kippur in his regular synagogue, the Tiffereth-Bahurim, but to pray instead in the beth midrash of Laybe-Layzar's courtyard to show her father his uprightness and piety. From time to time Serel would steal up to the curtain in front of the women's section and peek into the men's section. Her usually pale face, today even paler from the fast, suddenly flushed a warm and rosy color. Unable to locate Yehiel-Michael in the crowded throng, she grew nervous, worried that he might be talking to someone during the services and that her father, God forbid, would notice it.

In the packed beth midrash, behind all the heads covered with yarmulkas and hats, stood the locksmith, Reb Heskiah, enfolded in his prayer shawl. Since the Kol Nidre at the beginning of Yom Kippur the evening before, through the entire night and through the morning, he had not ceased studying and praying for even the briefest moment. From time to time he would sit down for a second to catch his breath, then at once leap to his feet again. Reb Heskiah paid no attention to the bristly pieces of straw underfoot that pricked the soles of the worshippers' shoeless feet as a Yom Kippur penance, nor did he mind that his shirt, his white kittel, and even his prayer shawl were drenched with sweat. He could feel only the rock-hard anguish in his heart, the heavy, tear-laden sorrow that he would have liked to cry out like a raincloud so that his soul could become clean and pure once more, fit to serve his Creator.

As he knelt on his weary knees during the cantor's recitation of the Temple Service for the Day of Atonement; as he shut his eyes tight and clenched his teeth during the "Hear O Israel"; as he stood long and frozen during the Silent Prayer, moving only to bow at the appropriate blessing and to beat his chest solemnly during the confessional, the "Al Hayt"—Reb Heskiah kept praying over and over for but one thing: "Lord of the Universe, give me the strength to remain stubborn!" This generation was strange to him. His own children and even the supposedly pious Jews were strange to him. Everyone was looking for dispensations, interested only in finding out that they were permitted to do whatever they wished, desiring nothing more than to get by with the minimum of precepts in service to the Creator of the Universe and His Torah. Even a rabbi, the Porush, believed in bargaining with God. And that's what the people wanted—witness the fact that the people of Zaskowicz had come to the Porush, Rabbi Yoel Weintraub, and begged him to return and become their Rav once again. It was a new world, a world of cutting corners, of bargaining and compromise: half for the Almighty and half for . . . But this was the Day of Judgment—he did not want to accuse his fellow Jews on this day. He spoke only for himself, and all he asked was that the Lord help him to live only for Him. He did not want to just get by, he wanted to accept stricter laws, to bend under a still heavier yoke of ritual and custom. Let his daughters marry whomever they wished and let their mother side with them. He sought no friends among the members of the congregation and no accolades from the scholars for his conduct; the words of the Sages were his only friends, the Code of Law his only mentor. It mattered not to him that everyone looked upon him as a figure out of the past. In fact, he did not even care whether or not a place was being prepared for him in Paradise. He prayed only for his corner in Laybe-Layzar's beth midrash where he could serve his Creator. "*Oy, Ribono-shel-olam*, Lord of the Universe, give me the strength to stay stubborn!" Reb Heskiah groaned into the prayer shawl which was drawn over his head and eyes, making him look like a sheeted ghost that had risen from the grave to pray among the living.

In a corner near the bima stood Paltiel Shklar, wearing a weekday hat and his weekday prayer shawl hung low over his shoulders so that the fringes dragged on the floor. Who could say whether he was even praying? He did not move his lips, yet he did not take his eyes off the Mahzor he was holding with both hands as if it were a heavy stone. He realized that the suit he was bringing against his brothers in the Oszmiana court was bound to drag on forever and would cost a fortune, and he had barely enough to get through the next day. He saw no choice but to return to Zaskowicz and reach a settlement with his brothers through the Rav; let him at least get some part of his inheritance. But when he had seen the respect his brother enjoyed when he arrived with the Zaskowicz delegation, bitterness and melancholy had overtaken him anew.

Even as a child in his father's house, Paltiel had felt unwanted and unloved. Instead of loving him all the more for being the child of his old age who might have brightened his later years, his father had hated him for having come so late and unexpected. And just as his brothers were very different from him in appearance, so were they completely different in character. They were strong and boisterous men, tall, with handsome, manly faces. But their hearts were as false and black as the night. For all the refinement they could put on display, there was not a drop of human kindness in their veins. After their father died, they had begrudgingly allowed Paltiel his portion of the inheritance and taken him in as a partner in the orchards. But he was the only one who worked, and like a horse; yet not even to humor him did they ask his opinion about running the business. So he had decided to leave them, rather than remain a hired hand whom his brothers could rob blind. But when the arguing broke out over how to divide the business, all Zaskowicz sided with his brothers— because everyone was counting on favors from them. They were all seduced by the brothers' silver-coated tongues and their sweet words, or else they simply sided with strength and success, as people are always disposed to do.

Paltiel Shklar gazed into the Mahzor with the cold, bulging eyes of a fish cast out onto dry land. Instead of paying attention to the prayers, he became lost in his own thoughts: "It's a world of thieves and swindlers! These nice people would trample to death anyone who tried to cheat them out of a barleycorn. But when it's someone else who's been wronged, they very sweetly advise him not to fight back. Let anyone besmirch their honor in the slightest and they would never forgive, let alone forget. But when another demands justice for his suffering and humiliation, they admonish: 'For shame! You're nothing but a grouch; a vindictive man.' They're all alike, the people of Zaskowicz and the neighbors in Laybe-Layzar's courtyard. They demand righteousness of others, not of themselves. Everyone's out for his own good. They swindle each other the year through, stealing the bread right out of each other's mouths, but on Yom Kippur they all ask each other's forgiveness, put on their prayer shawls over their white kittels, and continue to fool one another from head to toe. See how they sway, the way they shake their heads and cry and moan. . . ." These were the thoughts that boiled inside Paltiel Shklar as he stood with tightly pressed lips, not saying a word or batting an eyelash; his eyes, laden with darkness, fixed intently on his Mahzor.

The air in the beth midrash grew musty from the fumes of the burned-out candles on the reader's lectern and the tall memorial candles still burning in their wooden boxes. Random beams of sunlight mingled with the dark-red light of the electric lamps. The bands of light were blinding to the eye and cut across faces like knives. The sheaves of sunlight swarmed with sparkling specks of dust, which hovered like lost souls from the primordial chaos entering the beth midrash through the windows in search of succor on this Yom Kippur. Bodies and faces radiated heat, beads of sweat settled on brows and beards. A steamy white mist hovered around the copper laver and polished the brass balls atop the iron railing around the bima. The men took their prayer shawls off their heads and wiped the sweat from their necks and foreheads. Some stole outside for a breath of cool air and waited for the bang on a lectern that would signal the beginning of the Yizkor Service.

Even the Porush, Rabbi Yoel Weintraub, took the prayer shawl off his head for a short respite from the heat, though he did not turn his face away from the wall in the front of the beth midrash where he had been standing throughout the service. Before his eyes hung a mist of light and tears, and in that mist hovered a small, poor cottage in the village of Utian. That was where he had been born, had gone to heder and studied in the beth midrash. His father had been a distiller in a pitch factory all his life, and from his eyes had shone the gleaming darkness of the deep Lithuanian forests. His father's veined hands with their crooked fingers had looked like the trees from which he drew pitch. And his tiny mother had looked very much like his own Rebbetzin, Hindele. But Hindele was by nature as joyous and sensitive as a child, though at times not above shouting a bit in order to get her way; whereas his mother had been a quiet, humble, hard-working woman, a maid in rich households, who worked to help her husband support the family and to allow her little boy to sit over the Talmud in the beth midrash.

When he had turned fifteen, he had fulfilled the injunction of the sages: "Exile yourself to a place of Torah." He wandered from one yeshiva to another—a year in Lachowicze, another in Kobryn—until he settled down to some years of serious study in Slonim. A few years passed without his seeing his parents, although from time to time he would send them a letter. It was in these years that he had become fanatically religious, and the more he missed his home, eating in the houses of strangers who took in yeshiva students and sleeping on the hard bench in the beth midrash, the more zealous was his piety and the more intense his devotion to learning, as he sought consolation in the study and observance of Torah.

One day in Slonim, while he was observing the fast of the minor Yom Kippur on the eve of the month of Shevat, along with some old men, one of his friends, another student, came to him during the Torah reading of the afternoon service and said, "Yoel—you from Utian—your mother is waiting to see you out in the hallway." At first he did not believe him. It was a long way from Utian to Slonim, and his father had not written him that his mother was coming. Not until his friend had repeated this several times did he believe that his mother was really waiting to see him. But his crusty, clotted piety kept him from leaving the beth midrash to see his mother while they were reading from the Torah. For, he reasoned, he was the tenth man of the minyan who was fasting that day and if he left, there would then be lacking a quorum of fasters for the reading of the Torah portion read on fast days: "And Moses besought the Lord his God, and said, Lord, why doth Thy wrath wax hot against Thy people . . ." How could he leave then, in the middle of the Torah reading? So he stayed and listened to the chanting of the reader and strained not to miss a single word, even though his heart was imploring him, screaming, "Your mother waits! Your mother!" But this only made him more determined to quell his evil inclination and not go out even after the Torah reading, so he stayed for the Silent Prayer. He stayed as well for the cantor's repetition of the Prayer, the recitation of the invocations, hymns, and psalms associated with the fast, and finally the Prayer of Confession of Rabboni Nissim. Not until every last part of the service was over and the last mourner's Kaddish recited did he go out to see her.

Throughout the service, the student who had told him about his mother sauntered around the beth midrash, looking at him with a mischievous sneer. Young Yoel, knowing that the student was a scoffer and did not fast on the minor Yom Kippur, began now to suspect that the story about his mother was a fabrication, designed to distract him from his precious prayers. And so, after all the prayers were over, he left his place near the western wall of the beth midrash and went into the hallway, but he did not find his mother. Two old men who always sat there to warm themselves near the oven told him that a small, frail woman had appeared in the hallway while he was praying and had asked for him. The woman had said she was his mother and had come all the way from Utian. But when a student told her that her son did not want to interrupt his prayers, she had stood at the door and watched him awhile and then gone away. One of the men sitting near the oven had asked the woman why she didn't wait longer. But she had said only, "My son is a saint"— and then she had left.

Yoel ran out into the courtyard and then through the snowy streets, shouting, "Mother! Mother!" He asked after her in the inns of Slonim, in the town hostel, he approached strangers in the street—no one had seen or heard of her anywhere. At last, exhausted and desperate, he returned to the beth midrash. There he was approached by a man who told him that he had been in the community hall of the beth midrash when Yoel's mother had come in and put down her bundle; she had then walked back into the hallway and toward the door of the main beth midrash. Some time later, she had returned to the community hall, picked up the bundle, and left.

Yoel felt at that moment ready to kill himself from grief and shame. He could not afford to travel home in the middle of the term, and besides, he would be ashamed before his Rav and before the other students if he did so. They all regarded him as a diligent student and a God-fearing young man; how could he just tear himself away from his studies that way? But more than the people of Slonim, he would be ashamed to face his mother: Wasn't it she who had said, "My son is a saint"? It would distress her to know that he had interrupted his studies. And so, he remained in Slonim and resolved to leave the yeshiva at the beginning of the month of Nisan for the Passover recess. Then, in the third week of the month of Adar, only a week before he was to leave for home, he received a letter from his father telling him that he must say Kaddish for his mother.

When Yoel returned home for Passover, it was with a long mourner's rent in his coat. His father told him how his mother had made her way from Utian to Slonim, halfway on foot with a band of beggars, halfway in the back of a wagon, and she had not been ashamed to beg in order to continue. She had traveled in the wagon until her last groschen was gone and then had continued on foot. And she had returned from Slonim to Utian in the same way. Yoel fell into his father's arms and begged him to tell him if his mother had forgiven him for not going out to see her in the middle of the service. But either his father did not know or he did not wish to tell him. He would only say that upon returning from her long wintry trek, his mother had contracted pneumonia and in the throes of her fever she had repeated over and over, "My son is a saint! My son is a saint!"

20

THE PORUSH HEARD a stifled groan behind him and a loud wailing coming from the women's section. All those who had gone out earlier to cool off were coming back inside for Yizkor. Rabbi Yoel Weintraub prayed facing the wall. His hands clutched the silver-brocaded collar of the prayer shawl draped over his head as the tears ran down his cheeks into his beard. Though now a man of sixty, he had still not forgiven himself for his failure to leave his prayers to see his mother some forty-three years before. Since then, on each solemn Day of Atonement, he would recall the minor Yom Kippur he had taken upon himself in the yeshiva of Slonim when he was a boy of seventeen. He could see his mother standing before him in her tattered winter cloth, her feet bound in rags, trudging along with a band of beggars through the deep drifts of snow and the frost of the blizzard. The beggars were going from town to town collecting alms, but his mother was traveling with them only as far as Slonim to see her son, the pious scholar who could not leave the yeshiva to come home, not even for the holiday. And when she had finally reached the hallway outside the beth midrash, this son, this righteous fool, refused to interrupt his prayers to see her. Though his heart fluttered and thrashed about with his longing to see his mother, he had quelled the temptation, because "fear of God" came before honoring one's father and mother. So she had turned and gone out once more into the blizzard, disappearing into the freezing cold and the driving snow, and leaving him but one utterance, one keepsake that had become for him an eternal mystery. "My son is a saint!" Had his mother sincerely and joyfully called him a saint, and was that why she hadn't dared disturb him in the middle of his prayers? Or had she said it with heartache and bitterness because he was more devoted to his prayers than to his own mother, and perhaps even felt so poor a mother was beneath him? For over forty years he had sought to divine his mother's true meaning, and for over forty years that truth had eluded him.

Someone had banged the bima, calling for silence as the cantor cleared his throat in preparation for chanting aloud the repetition of the Silent Prayer of the Additional Service. The Porush felt a nudge at his shoulder; it was the sexton, who was bestowing upon him the honor of opening the ark. He raised the curtain and then the door of the ark and gazed with misty eyes at the Torah scrolls in their white satin mantles with gold embroidery. He knew that the scrolls were not to blame. They had commanded him to fast and atone only on the tenth day of the month of Tishrei, on Yom Kippur. The minor Day of Atonement which some observed on the eve of every New Moon was a later tradition, handed down from the mystics who wanted to assume more hardships than were demanded by the Codes. He need not have, nor should he have, let his mother wait in the hallway, especially when they had not seen each other for so long a time. And his punishment was that he was never to see her again.

The Porush closed the ark and returned to his seat. He sobbed with the rest of the congregation at the reading of "U-Netanneh Tokeph," the Prayer of Rabbi Amnon. The congregation chanted the Kedushah with fervent exaltation, and the Porush's voice pealed out each word of "Holy . . . Holy . . . Holy." He knelt when the cantor recited the order of the Temple Service on the Day of Atonement. Like an onrushing flood whose waters rise until the waves tower over the trees and the houses, so did the tears and the wailing swell over the heads of the worshippers when they reached the liturgical poem in memory of the Ten Martyred Rabbis executed by the Romans. The tears melted from the pale faces of the people, faint from fasting, like the wax of the burning memorial candles. Beards hung limp like dead carcasses. Outstretched hands with wrenched fingers groped blindly in the air, searching for something to hold onto. Together with the rest of the congregation, the Porush labored under the heavy yoke of the Yom Kippur services. But above all the prayers of contrition and confession the Porush's heart cried over the shamed image of his mother ever present before him. Bedraggled, huddled in her rags, weary and humiliated, she had disappeared into a winter blizzard because she did not want to disturb her son in his observance of a minor Yom Kippur.

But his mother's death had changed him. He continued to study and observe the laws, but came to hate fanatics and avoided zealots like the plague. As a young man, in the yeshiva's environment of students and scholars, he did not fully realize how strong his aversion was, not until after his marriage he left the yeshiva and became the Rav of Zaskowicz. Only then, when he encountered the new generation of rebellious youth, did he fully understand that the fanatic observance of the endless minor Days of Atonement was responsible for the desecration and abandonment of the real Sabbath of Sabbaths. So he stayed away from any manner of extreme, refusing to build fence upon fence. The Torah, he believed, must not look like a town of battling neighbors, each carefully marking the boundary of his property with a picket fence or a high, thick wall topped with barbed wire so that no one can pass through.

The young people of Zaskowicz had expected they would have to do battle with the new Rav. But he only said to them: "You'd like to use the community hall for meetings or to stage debates? Why not? By all means! You'd like to have a library? Fine, let there be a library, then. You say you'd like to prepare to settle in the Land of Israel? That is surely no sin." He was a constant source of wonder to everyone. The implacable zealots persecuted the free-thinkers, warning them that if they continued in their ways, they would find themselves cast out of the community and their parents would rend their clothes over them as if they had converted. Nonetheless, the young free-thinkers did not mend their ways, and neither did they break away from the Jewish community. Many times, so many times, it happened that the fathers disowned the children but the children did not disown the fathers. True, the Rav had in time become *too* lenient, and had reached the point where he could not bring himself to forbid something that was clearly and expressly forbidden in the Codes. It was because of this that he had resigned; let some other Rav sit and imperiously shake his head "no." But now he saw the hand of Providence compelling him to return to Zaskowicz.

The congregation, exhausted by the long Additional Service, chanted the Afternoon Service quietly with almost the calm indifference of an ordinary weekday. The Porush also felt unburdened after having poured out all his tears and memories. But when he was called upon to read the Book of Jonah, he held the rollers of the parchment scroll tightly and wept as he read the prayer of the Prophet Jonah from the belly of the fish, crying so loudly that everyone in the beth midrash held his breath. Rebbetzin Hindele, in the women's section, also heard her husband's weeping. She stood on her toes and looked with frightened eyes through the curtains into the men's section. After the Afternoon Service the congregation recessed for an hour to rest and prepare for the Concluding Service, the Neilah. The Porush was the last to leave the beth midrash for the recess, but on his way out he noticed that among those who had decided not to go out into the courtyard for fresh air were his old adversaries. In one corner, with his back to the congregation, stood the gardener from Zaskowicz, Paltiel Shklar, and in another, swaying over a holy tome, was the locksmith, Reb Heskiah. He was using even the break in the Yom Kippur services to study the Codes.

Laybe-Layzar's courtyard now bustled with the thick crowd in their holiday finery. The older women were wearing long black or white shawls, or tall wigs, while the younger ones wore intricately styled small or big hats, all of them together creating the effect of a bed of flowers. A golden late-afternoon glow lit the faces of the mothers as the residents of the courtyard and the people from the Jewish Street chatted pleasantly and coddled their children. On this day, little boys and girls did not pull their hands away from their mother's warm fingers, but let themselves be coddled, looking around with big, quiet eyes, as if they understood that this day was different from all the other days of the year and they must be on their best behavior.

In a corner of the courtyard the gilder Yehiel-Michael Henes was talking to Serel Teitelbaum for all to see. Though they had not formally announced their betrothal and Serel's stubborn father had not yet given them his blessing, everyone knew that their wedding was inevitable and so they had no need to hide from anyone or be ashamed to be seen together. Serel asked Yehiel-Michael how he liked the services in his new beth midrash. He grunted and said that he would have felt much happier, much more at home, with his friends at Tiffereth-Bahurim. There the services were brighter, more cheerful. In Tiffereth-Bahurim there was more chanting and in Laybe-Layzar's beth midrash there was more weeping. "And how is your fast going, Serel? If you feel faint, I have some valerian drops you can sniff." But Serel replied with a wan smile and dry lips that the fast was going well. In fact, she almost didn't feel that she was fasting at all—she must be getting to be like her father.

Yehiel-Michael, no longer wearing the rumpled clothes of a bachelor, had bought a new suit. Serel noticed this, and noticed as well that he did not take his eyes off the now-empty apartment where Moishele Munvas had lived. He must be considering, she surmised, whether that place would be good for them. But she had other plans, so she asked him softly whether he had heard that the Porush was returning to Zaskowicz after the holidays and his house would be vacant. Yehiel-Michael had not heard, and as he was somewhat slow anyway, it took him a moment to realize what Serel was driving at. "Is that so?" he finally said, and he turned from house to house, trying to determine which would be more suited for them. Serel's mind, however, was already made up: The Rav's apartment was roomier and more comfortable. Her decision, furthermore, had nothing whatever to do with any fears of suffering the upholsterer's wife's bad luck if she were to choose that apartment; even so, she felt it would be more dignified to live in the former home of the Porush than in the former home of that gypsy Moishele Munvas.

Rebbetzin Hindele waited for her husband near the door to the men's section of the beth midrash, and the two of them stood there together for a time. He, broad-shouldered, wearing a black rabbinic frock, his velvet yarmulka perched atop his tall, wrinkled, sagacious forehead; and she, a frail woman in an old-fashioned, long velvet dress. She asked him why he had wept so during his recitation of the Book of Jonah. He answered that he had always found it overwhelming to read the story of the Prophet who refused to carry out his mission and tried to run away from the Almighty Himself; Divine Providence had caught up with him and brought him back to fulfil his mission, just as every man was put on earth to fulfil a mission. Still, he could never understand a prophet suffering over the fact that a city was not destroyed—even so sinful a city as Nineveh.

The Porush took his Rebbetzin by the arm and led her to their home. In Laybe-Layzar's courtyard there remained a throng of people, men in their prayer shawls and neighbors breathing in the cool air of the early evening. Hindele was a bit embarrassed that her husband, the Rav, was grasping her arm and she tried to pull away. But he held on to her and, with a good-natured frown, grumbled, "Nu, nu," as he led his wife through the courtyard to their home, just as he had held her on those winter Sabbath mornings in Zaskowicz when they walked together on the ice-covered streets to the synagogue to bless the coming of the New Moon.

THE
OATH

1

A WEEK BEFORE HIS DEATH, the wheat merchant Shlomo-Zalman Rappaport summoned Rabbi Avraham-Abba Seligman, the shopkeeper from the corner of Straszuna and Zawalna Streets, and kept him at his bedside a long time, longer than any other visitor. They spoke in private; Shlomo-Zalman had asked that no one be allowed in while they talked. As the visitor was about to leave, he was met in the living room by the sick man's wife, Bathsheva, who asked him what he and her husband had discussed. He replied that her husband would tell her himself. Bathsheva wrung her hands and whispered that Shlomo-Zalman was speaking to everyone about his last days. She hoped they were all consoling him, easing his mind.

"One mustn't," Reb Avraham-Abba said in a deep, sad tone, "one mustn't lie to a dying man and tell him he will recover. He knows quite well what we are thinking and only suffers more when we try to deceive him. Even if the words of comfort lighten his heart for the moment, later his pain will be even greater."

"Then what do I say when he starts talking about not lasting very much longer?" Bathsheva asked.

"Nothing at all!" was the visitor's emphatic answer as he put on his coat, and departed.

Reb Avraham-Abba, who was known as "the Divorced Rabbi," had the reputation of a pious and righteous man. But his advice to Bathsheva Rappaport struck her as extremely odd—she had never heard before that one must not encourage a sick man concerning his health. All of her husband's other visitors had, as they left, heartily expressed the wish that God would grant him a speedy recovery.

The next day the sick man called his wife, son, and daughter to his bedside. His face looked like wrinkled parchment, and the whites of his eyes had a yellowish cast. Only a magnificent white beard, divided into two pointed halves, still shone with a regal glow, as if he were conducting the family's Passover Seder. Though he talked to his son, Shlomo-Zalman never took his eyes, welling with fatherly concern, off his wife:

"Gavriel, I want you to take an oath that you will leave the University and study with the shopkeeper Rabbi Avraham-Abba Seligman. He will teach you Talmud and the Codes."

Even Bathsheva, who had always heeded her husband and looked up to him, was petrified, wondering if he was not already speaking from a beclouded mind.

"But . . . but I study every night at home," Gavriel stammered.

"There is not much one can accomplish in only two hours a day and without a rabbi," his father replied. "You must leave the University and immerse yourself day and night in Talmud study with Rabbi Seligman."

Gavriel barely knew the Divorced Rabbi by sight, and had never heard him described as a renowned scholar. But even had he been as great a sage as the Vilna Gaon, Gavriel Rappaport would never have left the University to study with him. He had taken up agriculture and dreamed of becoming a landowner and cultivator, as his father had once been. Now, therefore, all he could do was look anxiously first at his mother, then his sister, at a loss as to what to say.

"The Almighty will help you and you will get well. Then you'll make plans for Gabik's future," Bathsheva said as she stepped closer to her husband's bed, her hands clasped as if in prayer.

"Don't try to console me. I can feel my heart giving way and your words distract me from preparing myself, from setting my house and soul in order," the sick man said with such a groan that his wife quickly drew back, recalling the words of Rabbi Avraham-Abba Seligman.

After Shlomo-Zalman Rappaport had suffered his heart attack, the doctors had warned him not to exert himself, not even to utter an unnecessary word. But when his family barred visitors from seeing him, he became angry and excited: Convinced that he would never rise again from his sickbed, he wanted to bid his friends farewell and make a final disposition of his affairs.

"Are you going to take an oath, Gavriel, that you will do as I ask?" The father focused on the son a pair of severe and piercing eyes.

"But wasn't it you who sent me to study at the gymnasium and then to the University? You used to tell me that if you were younger, you'd become a land cultivator again yourself," Gavriel cried, and he shuddered, breaking out in a cold sweat when he realized he was shouting at his mortally ill father.

"I regret many things now that I have done and said," the sick man muttered as he shook his head. Then, propping himself up with difficulty on his elbows he said, "Well, will you give your word, or will you deny my last request?"

"I give you my word, Father. I give you my word," the son answered, his lips quivering, all the while gripped with fear lest the excitement give his father another heart attack.

Shlomo-Zalman turned his head toward his daughter and a warm smile spread over his face. He winked at her, and she put her long, thin hand into his palm. His weak, trembling fingers stroked her soft skin and he heaved long, pained sighs to clear his voice of the tears welling up inside him.

"Asna, promise me that you will marry an observant young man, a yeshiva student."

Asna, tall and supple like a young sapling in spring, felt her entire body tremble quietly and her large eyes became twice their size. She did not realize that she had drawn her hands away from her father's, just as she was unaware of the huge teardrops rolling slowly down her cheeks.

"I haven't given any thought to marrying," she stammered.

"I would really need a few more years to set my house in order," said Shlomo-Zalman. "I see I can't rely very much on my children. Go, let me have some rest." His head fell back onto the pillow and his daughter was the first to run out of the room, weeping loudly.

The dying man lived about another week. When he was not feeling pain, a soft, amazed smile played on his lips, as if he was listening to himself and marveling at how a dying heart could run down so sweetly and peacefully. But when he felt the stones pressing on his chest and could not catch his breath, he lay on his back, staring with wide eyes filled with the primordial void. His eyes rolled as if they were struggling to free themselves from suffering. In such moments his wife would lean over him and hear him gasp, "Perhaps God will take pity on me and take my soul today." When the doctor arrived, Shlomo-Zalman would admonish him not to prescribe anything that would prolong his suffering by so much as a day. Later, when the spasms passed, his son and daughter stood on either side of the bed as he lay still, his eyes closed, his face dry and worn, steeped in a thick silence as if warning his children that he would never forgive them, not even in the next world, if they disobeyed his last wishes.

On his last afternoon, Shlomo-Zalman Rappaport felt unusually well. He swallowed a few spoonfuls of broth, ate a little boiled chicken, and afterward drifted off into a light, dreamy sleep, his breathing soft and regular. In the parlor, his exhausted wife and children collapsed into

deep slumber. When Bathsheva awoke, it was already dark. By the pale
light of the snow outside, she could see her son and daughter asleep on
the sofa, their heads awkwardly leaning against its back. Certain that her
husband was also still asleep, she quietly opened his door just a crack, and
peered in.

He was lying with his head thrown back, his mouth wide open; his
beard hung down as if slaughtered.

THE LARGE THRONG that attended the wheat merchant's funeral came from
many quarters. Since he had been born to Lithuanian Hassidim and attended a Hassidic beth midrash every Sabbath, a large contingent came
from the small Hassidic shtibls in the courtyard—from the Kaidanovo, the
Stolin, the Lachowicze, and, of course, the Slonim. But just because they
lived in Lithuania, and so were constantly surrounded by Misnagdim,
these Hassidim had grown less fervent in their devotion to the Rebbe, and
no longer journeyed to see him, but waited instead for his emissaries to
come to them for financial support. On joyous occasions or at funerals the
sea of billowing black frocks, the wind-swept beards, and the fire that
burned in their upturned eyes reminded the world that these Jews were
yet Hassidim.

Standing apart in a circle of their own were the Lubavitcher Hassidim from White Russia, their every movement betraying their fiery zeal,
their stubborn determination, their fanatical loyalty to the Rebbe, their
arrogance, and their contempt for the world. And in another group stood
the affluent congregants of the Grand Synagogue of Vilna, surrounding
the town's rabbis: sedate Talmudic scholars in long black overcoats and
stiff black hats, their sidelocks neatly twirled and tucked behind their
ears, their broad, neatly trimmed beards covering their chests. The sharp
scholarly glances from behind their glasses and the lines on their
parchment-white faces told of cloistered lives lived within the four cubits
of the Torah, of the endless cycle of handing down legal rulings by day
and writing responsa by night as thick shadows crept across the beth-
midrash walls.

Shlomo-Zalman Rappaport had dealt with many a Jew, befriended
many others, and, though a Hassid, had been on friendly terms even with
the free-thinking Maskilim. Members of the Choral Synagogue also came
—pharmacists, building managers, self-styled legal consultants, a crowd
wearing rubber shirt collars and yellowed cuffs, their wrinkled faces clean-
shaven to the point of being blue. From Shawelska and Rudnicka streets

came the cloth manufacturers, with their short, pointed little beards and elegant coats, long and wide, made of the finest cloth.

And finally, from the small streets around the courtyard of the Grand Synagogue came the common folk: poor peddlers in their short sheepskin coats and tall winter hats; workers with toil-worn hands and prickly beards, permeated with iron rust and powdered with sawdust from the workshops. Among the mourners the tall, broad-shouldered grain merchants stood out, their faces hard and sharp-featured, their boots up to their knees. These merchants—men who, trusting no one, never bought a sack without first inspecting a handful of its contents—had always dealt with Shlomo-Zalman Rappaport on credit with total confidence.

Also attending the funeral were representatives of the wealthy yeshivas in Landwarow and Niemenczyn. The deceased had sometimes visited these yeshivas not so much to do business with them as to observe how they conducted their affairs out in the country. He had never given up his dream of working the land. And, since Shlomo-Zalman had on weekdays attended the beth midrash of the old-age home on Portowa Street, and had always supported it, the home sent a minyan of old men especially designated to attend funerals. They would precede the casket in the procession, wearing black capes and broad, stiff hats, carrying canes, solemnly murmuring psalms.

The very last in the procession were those who, one would think, should have been first: the residents of the large and stately courtyard on Portowa Street where Shlomo-Zalman Rappaport had lived. The neighbors knew better than anyone of the strict kashruth maintained in his home, and of his devout observance of the Sabbath and all the holidays. On the eve of the Gentile New Year, the first of January, when most Jewish homes were filled with celebration and revelers drinking, dancing, and singing, the windows of the Rappaport home were dark and quiet. Shlomo-Zalman could be seen every morning going to the beth midrash, his prayer-shawl bag under his arm, and on the Sabbath he would never walk in the street with his cane. Nevertheless, his wealthy, assimilated, half-Christian neighbors respected him for his dignified bearing and his upright way of life. Even his wife and children commanded their neighbors' respect.

Bathsheva Rappaport was a full twenty-five years younger than her husband, and looked like an older sister to her two children. She was a woman with a pale complexion, and a bit too thin. Her face was still clear and unwrinkled, and not a single gray strand glimmered in her hair. Though her husband had been old enough to be her father, it had been apparent to all how much she loved him and how much faith she had in him, especially when she walked at his side, gazing with delight and pride at his parted white beard. Both children had their mother's eyes, deep-set over dark-blue circles. And just as her father had kept aloof from his neighbors, so had Asna not befriended any of the young ladies of the courtyard. She would walk through the courtyard with quick and quiet steps, as if she were constantly hurrying somewhere. Gavriel, however, would be seen coming and going jauntily from his house, still in his student's frock and sometimes in the company of a friend, though he never shouted up to his family through an open window as the other boys frequently did.

"An aristocratic family," the neighbors all said of the Rappaports. And yet they couldn't help wondering what so pious a Jew was doing living in a courtyard with mostly irreligious neighbors, why he insisted on giving his children a secular education, and why his wife always dressed in the latest fashions. It was this paradox that made his rich neighbors feel uneasy, like strangers, at the funeral, and they looked nervously about for someone who would explain what sort of person the deceased had really been. But even his closest friends and associates were no less perplexed by his conduct and character.

"He was a strange man," the people in the procession said to one another. "An honorable man, it seems, in the eyes of God and in the eyes of men, every bit as much at ease in the wheat exchange as in the beth midrash. But he always sought to live distant from his own kind. He was even odd in money matters. On the one hand, he was a tough business-man, hard as a rock, and on the other hand, as softhearted and charitable a soul as you'll ever find."

The funeral procession pressed onward, long, yet subdued—partly because the deceased had been ill a long time before succumbing, partly because the mourners were so motley an assemblage of Vilna Jews. And then, also, because Shlomo-Zalman had instructed that no eulogy be de-livered. A thick black veil over her head, the widow followed the casket through the streets, her son and daughter holding her by the arms on either side.

The day had the mild after-Purim glow of early spring. Through the smoky gray clouds shone a high vault of sky. The last remaining patches of yellowish snow shriveled and cowered in the alleyways. The mourners looked hopefully up at the trees, whose naked branches seemed to be straining and writhing in preparation for the coming buds.

When the procession went over the bridge that crossed the Wilejka, the crowd thinned out—the old people did not have the strength to trudge up the hilly countryside, and the shopkeepers remembered they had businesses to attend to. The farther they went, the more people dropped out of the procession, until almost the only ones left were the Hassidim from the Kaidanovo shtibl. As they followed the funeral cortege, they remarked among themselves that Reb Shlomo-Zalman's children in Russia, by his late first wife, would certainly not be saying Kaddish for him—the Bolsheviks had taken away Rappaport's children along with his estate, and they had renounced their Judaism. And yet he had sent the boy born to his old age by his second wife to the Polish school, and his daughter to the Hebrew gymnasium. He had always believed that piety and enlightenment could live under the same roof. Not until his last years had he begun to say that the wisdom of Torah and worldly knowledge were like fire and water, and that he regretted having sent his son to the Polish school.

At the very end of the procession followed the shopkeeper Rabbi Avraham-Abba Seligman, walking on the sidewalk with straight, measured steps, his head bowed. When the wagon hearse drove ahead, he lagged behind, and when it slowed down to climb the hill, he gradually caught up. Young Gavriel Rappaport turned around several times, searching for the Divorced Rabbi, and spotted him on the sidewalk far behind. He quickly turned away, wiped his eyes, and let his father's casket move a bit further ahead of him. His mother, too, slowed down and turned her heavily veiled head toward her son until he once again drew nearer and walked just behind the casket.

At the cemetery a plot in an honored row had been prepared, amid stately tombstones surrounded by chains or enclosed by iron fences. The covered casket stood at the edge of the open grave, surrounded by the deceased's closest friends. The men sobbed quietly and their tears rolled into their beards. Pre-dusk shadows trembled on the sparkling white snow, which, at the cemetery, still stood tall in stiff, fresh drifts. Behind the hill, thickly covered with row after row of sunken monuments, could be seen the half-ball of the fiery setting sun. Asna buried her head in her mother's shoulder so as not to stare at her father in the now opened casket.

Her mother looked through the thick black veil at Rabbi Avraham-Abba Seligman, standing quiet, tense, and sorrowful on the other side of the gaping grave. Bathsheva felt her heart turning to stone and the tears freezing in her throat. She knew that more tears would be coming, and that she would be crying long after the children would have forgotten. But now she must be sure to obey her husband's last wishes. She raised her veil over her eyes and whispered to her son, "You promised your

father you would leave the University. You promised you would study
with Rabbi Avraham-Abba Seligman. Will you remember your oath to
your father?"

"I will remember," Gavriel muttered, watching in terror as his father,
clad in pure white shrouds, was taken from the black bier. At that very
moment the fiery sunball disappeared behind the cemetery hill, thickly
studded with old, sunken tombstones.

2

RABBI AVRAHAM-ABBA SELIGMAN was born in Kelem, studied in the
"Talmud Torah," as the yeshiva there was called, and married in
Kibart, a small Lithuanian city near the Russo-Prussian border. He had
not been married a year when the war broke out and Czar Nicholas ex-
pelled all the Jews from the border towns near Prussia. Reb Avraham-
Abba's in-laws, with whom he and his wife Hodel had lived, were detained
in the Lithuanian heartland, but he and Hodel managed to get to Vilna,
where many other rabbis had sought refuge. The fleeing scholars organized themselves into a community which was supported by the Jews of
Vilna, and Reb Avraham-Abba studied in the beth midrash of these ex-
patriated rabbis, supporting himself and his wife on the allowance they
doled out to him. When the German army occupied Vilna, however,
famine held the city in an iron grip and the Jewish community could no
longer afford to give support to scholars. Hodel, therefore, now went to
work and became their breadwinner. Even as a girl in Kibart, she had
worked in a shop and shown a sharp head for business.

When the war ended, the Lithuanian rabbis returned to their towns,
and Hodel expected that her husband would also assume a pulpit in one
town or another. But Reb Avraham-Abba insisted that he could not, he
was not fit and did not want to become a rav; he suggested to Hodel that
she open a store of some kind in Vilna. Hodel argued that her parents had
wanted a scholar for a son-in-law who eventually would become a rav
and she a rebbetzin, not a shopkeeper. And if a shop it was to be, then
why in a foreign city like Vilna and not back home in Kibart, to which
her parents had by then returned from their wandering? But her husband
persisted: He had not studied Torah in order to make a living by it, and
since that left nothing for him to do but be a shopkeeper, then he wanted

to be a shopkeeper in Vilna, where no one knew him. In Kelem and in Kibart, where they regarded him as something of a scholar, they would be forever showering him with undeserved honors and he would have to get involved in communal matters. No, the only thing to do was to open a shop in Vilna.

Hodel was a screamer with a flaming red face and a ball of chestnut hair which was always falling out from under her headkerchief. But she had come from a very pious home and was a clever woman with a generous amount of common sense, so she knew that her husband was not merely "something of a scholar," as he referred to himself, but an exceptionally great Talmudist. So she agreed to stay in Vilna and found a vacant store on the corner of Straszuna and Zawalna Streets. She had saved a little money, knew quite a few people in the city, and, as the store was located in a commercial area at the intersection of several busy streets, she stocked up on groceries and was soon doing a brisk business.

Though the war was over, peace had not yet truly come to the city of Vilna; it seemed that as soon as one crisis passed, another arose to take its place. The government kept changing. When the German occupation ended, the city was taken over by the Polish Legions, who were soon ousted by the Bolsheviks. The Red Commissars had not yet had time to set up a government before they were driven out in turn by the Poles. With each new regime, the currency changed, as did the prices of goods. Bullets were constantly flying overhead. But when the shooting abated, the people scurried to the stores to buy food. And despite the danger from all sides, the shopkeepers all kept their stores open. They knew that this was a time to sell and make their profits—customers paid whatever price was demanded. Hodel conducted her business with great zeal from the early morning till late at night, though she never knew under what government she would be waking up next morning and if all her hard-earned money would not be worth a groschen. Her husband, however, instead of helping her to attend to customers, stood over her, watching her with a thousand eyes to make certain that she did not, God forbid, give someone in error too small an amount or too little change. He set the price on each item, charging only slightly more than the merchandise cost them, just enough to cover expenses and to permit a daily profit that could be counted in groschen. And he would extend credit to people he did not know, proclaiming that in such times it was a sin to turn anyone away. After all, when a man was denied a bag of grain on credit, his family starved along with him. And when the suffering of his family became unbearable, he would go out into the gunfire looking for food. So, should he, Rabbi Avraham-Abba Seligman, be responsible for the life of a Jew who went out into a hail of bullets in search of food? May it never come to pass!

Hodel soon realized that her husband was no less stubborn than learned, and an odd, unpredictable man. Was it permissible, she demanded, for her to risk her life in order to support the two of them? She began to quarrel with him, by day in the store, by night at home. She would even follow him to the beth midrash, demanding but one thing— that he should stay away from the store. Reb Avraham-Abba said not a word in response to his wife's protests, but made a point of coming to the store still more often, always arriving just when his wife was surrounded by customers. And he watched her even more closely than before.

The Bolsheviks again drove out the Poles, and occupied Vilna, letting the Lithuanians in from Kovno. Hodel began thinking of bringing her parents from Kibart to Vilna. It was just about this time that she found herself unable to endure her husband's crazy ways any longer. As if it weren't bad enough that he had made it his mission in life to ensure her scrupulous honesty in her business dealings, he also objected to her investing so much time and energy in the business to begin with: one must never forget that it was the Almighty who provided, not the store and its merchandise. He insisted furthermore that she not compete too fiercely with the other shopkeepers—the customers would shop where Divine Providence sent them. For Hodel, this was the last straw, and she demanded a divorce. But instead of feeling chastened, as she had expected, he agreed immediately: "When you are no longer my wife, I will be free of the responsibility for your actions."

After the divorce, Hodel remained with the store, and Reb Avraham-Abba went from synagogue to synagogue asking if anyone needed a tutor for their children. Hodel knew that he was struggling and her heart sank out of pity for him, but also out of anger that she still worried about him at all. She had never imagined that she would miss the stubborn maniac so. After the Bolsheviks took over Vilna, all business soured. The Soviet authorities shot several Jewish shopkeepers for speculating in goods and for refusing to accept Russian currency. Commerce dwindled to nothing as the farmers became afraid to bring their produce into town. To Hodel, the decline of her business seemed a punishment from Heaven for leaving her husband, and she decided to return to her parents in Kibart. She would have a free hand to conduct business in Lithuania, and perhaps she would even marry again, this time more wisely and with better luck.

Before Hodel had a chance to sell out her merchandise, however, the

Polish army once again marched into Vilna, forcing the Red army to retreat into White Russia, and their allies, the Lithuanians, to withdraw deeper into Lithuania. The city was in chaos as whole groups of Jews left with the Lithuanian army for Kovno so as not to remain under the Poles.

Hodel sought out her former husband and found him in a small beth midrash. She handed him the key to her half-empty store: "I don't want to be cut off from my parents, so I am leaving with the Lithuanians," she announced. She took a roll of paper money from her bosom and placed it on the lectern before him. "Here, this should be enough to get you started. You said you wanted to be a shopkeeper, so be a shopkeeper, and wear yourself out being honest in business!" and she ran out of the beth midrash before she would no longer be able to contain her tears. Hodel knew the pious Reb Avraham-Abba would never shake her hand in saying goodbye; after the divorce she was, after all, a strange woman to him. But she knew as well that if he would just live long enough, he would return every last groschen of the money she had given him.

And so it was that Rabbi Avraham-Abba Seligman became the proprietor of his ex-wife's grocery store, and acquired the sobriquet of "The Divorced Rabbi." It took some time for his customers to get used to the Divorced Rabbi's habit of closing the store in the middle of the day when business was heaviest, to spend several hours in the beth midrash. They had to accustom themselves as well to rummaging through the merchandise and doing their own weighing and measuring while the proprietor stood behind the counter immersed in some rabbinic tract. He would not take his eyes out of the book even to give a price, take money, or count change. And if an uninitiated customer would start to haggle with him, the other women would berate her: "What, you have the nerve to haggle with him, with Rabbi Avraham-Abba Seligman?"

The widowed Bathsheva Rappaport also knew of him. And from all she had heard, she had decided that he was a whole man, a man of uncompromising principles. In the last year of his life, her husband had more than once said that he envied such a whole man, by which he meant one who wholeheartedly pursues a particular path in life; whereas he, Shlomo-Zalman Rappaport, had tried to yoke together many things which did not belong with one another. He had wanted to be a Hassid and a worldly man as well. He believed that God sends every mortal his bread, yet he thought about business day and night. He wanted to live humbly, but he could not forswear the luxuries of life. He had done all he could to ensure that his children would be pious Jews, and yet he sent them to be educated among children from irreligious homes. Bathsheva

had continually reassured him that their son and daughter would follow
in his footsteps, but Shlomo-Zalman would only shake his head sadly.
And she knew, also, that in his last year her husband had often visited the
Divorced Rabbi in his store. So she understood why he had, before his
death, bade his son become the student of Rabbi Avraham-Abba Seligman.

3

A GREAT SHADOW fell from the chandelier over the bima, all the way to
the door. The shadow swayed to and fro, as if unable to decide
whether to forsake the empty beth midrash for the summery dry weather
outside or stay within its dark, musty walls. The beth midrash was as dark
as a cave; but in a corner of the east wall burned a lone electric lamp,
casting a pale red glow on the heads of Gavriel Rappaport and Rabbi
Avraham-Abba Seligman. For three months now they had been studying
Talmud and the Codes together.

Gavriel had a brilliant mind; after his first lesson in *Yoreh De'ah*,
the volume of the Codes on Kashruth, he could easily recite the eight
characteristics of a non-kosher animal by heart. With the same facility he
was now studying the laws of keeping milk and meat separate, like an
oversized mischievous boy chewing on a white roll, yelling and laughing
with each swallow. The Rabbi was determined, however, to master thoroughly each particular point of law and so he buried his head in the huge
tome, in the columns of the minuscule cramped Rashi script framing the
text, as though in a forest of tall straight trees he had chosen to crawl
through the thick, thorny underbrush.

While the Rabbi thrashed through the text, creasing his brow and
mumbling, the student sat quietly, bored to death. His uncanny ability to
master the laws of the Code and recite them chapter and verse gave him
pleasure in the heat of the moment; but soon a thought would gnaw at
him: What on earth was he doing studying Tractate *Hullin* or *Yoreh
De'ah*? Was he planning to become a rav or a ritual slaughterer? It had
been a totally different matter when his father was alive and he used to
study two hours a day at home. He had been only too pleased to do it for
his father, and he had rather liked the respect he earned from his friends
for his knowledge of the Talmud. But now he had put away his student's
cap, losing one semester already, and hadn't registered for the new school

year. He spent his mornings studying in the beth midrash of the Old Age Home of Portowa Street, where he led the morning services and recited Kaddish for his father. And in the evenings he came to study with the Divorced Rabbi. He had become a yeshiva student, a recluse scholar, a "bench-warmer," and all because of his father's whim as he lay on his deathbed.

Reb Avraham-Abba finished analyzing the point in the text and started explaining the matter to his student, his face so earnest and taut that he might just as easily have been reciting the Shema, enunciating every letter and stressing every word. He began with the original controversy in the Talmud and went on to the dispute among Rashi and the Tosaphists, each of whom had his own interpretation of the text. Then he introduced Maimonides, and later the objections of the Tur. Finally, he discussed the *Beth Yosef,* which measured and weighed all previous opinions and then issued a ruling. And then the discourse first began: commentaries to the *Beth Yosef* arguing bitterly over his conclusions and details of the case and considering further applications and ramifications.

Finally, Gavriel could restrain himself no longer, and burst out in desperate laughter. "You're teaching me as if a housewife—no, ten housewives—were standing here, each with her own question about having accidentally poured milk into a pot used for meat, all of them anxiously waiting for our pronouncement."

The Rabbi's taut face softened, and in his warm and gentle voice there rang deep, sad echoes: "The Torah is a link with ancient times. It is like a path that runs from primeval forests through deep canyons and caverns and over tall mountains; and because the path is so long, so narrow and winding, it is easy to lose one's way in the wilderness—in those enticing, so very subtle hypotheses and fine points of logic. At first, these flights of thought may seem to be rewarded by untold treasures, by ever-joyful surprises. Such sharp and arcane reasoning sears the mind. But in the end, nothing remains but chaos and a void.

"The Torah was given to us to show us how to live. We must insist that its precepts stand before our eyes straight and clear. Not just the laws in the Code, but even the stories of the Humash, the words of the Prophets, the parables of the Midrash, the mysteries of the Kabbalah—everything was given with but one purpose, to teach us how to live, how to act, from morning till night, day in and day out, every day of our lives."

"I've already heard all this," Gavriel said, turning away impatiently.

Instead of rebuking his student for his lack of respect, the Rabbi rose from his seat and paced through the beth midrash. In the darkness the tall

Reb Avraham-Abba seemed yet taller and his arms, folded in his sleeves in front of him as if he were cold on this hot summer day, gave his drawn-up shoulders a sharp angularity. His hard and stubby beard, abruptly cut short as if with an ax, was as black as coal in the middle and sparkling white around the edges. When he was silently listening, the dusk of the distant heavens glowed in his eyes. And when he smiled, one could see in the long wrinkles that spilled down his cheeks that he was a gentle soul. And yet every time Reb Avraham-Abba spoke, Gavriel was overcome with a feeling of having been thrown into a dungeon with the iron door slammed shut and bolted with yet another bar, another lock.

"Those who study in order to observe see new wonders daily in the same old precepts, like one who rejoices each time he sees the cherished face of his beloved. It is precisely the same with people with an eye and a heart to appreciate the wonders of creation, the manifestation of the Creator in nature. Every day he marvels anew at how the sun rises and how it sets, at the storm's thunder and lightning, at the beautiful shape and sweet taste of the fruits he has eaten so many, many times before. And if he doesn't feel this way, then his prayers and his blessings on these fruits are nothing more than habit."

"Yet you yourself did not become a rav," Gavriel blurted out with a boyish impetuousness.

The Rabbi refrained from replying that his not becoming a rav had nothing to do with this. He just smiled and sat down again in front of his open volume. "Neither the Patriarch Abraham nor even Moses was anything more than a shepherd, not a rav. A rav can very easily lose his humility, but a shepherd learns to love Creation."

"Since our Patriarchs were shepherds and farmers, my father should not have interfered with my study of agronomy at the University," Gavriel retorted with even more impatience and resentment, as if the Rabbi were to blame for this. "That God created reason and knowledge in man is the best proof that they are indispensable."

"Once the fields and the forests and the Seven Wisdoms brought man closer to the Almighty, but today's wisdom and the city life of the worldly-wise man have done nothing but separate him from his Creator. Your father understood this, and that was why he insisted that you devote yourself only to the study of Torah," Reb Avraham-Abba answered, whereupon he dived once again into the *Yoreh De'ah* to continue the analysis of the matter they had started discussing, even if only for himself.

His silence and the red glow of the light overhead were interwoven with the nocturnal shadows of the empty beth midrash. But the young man stood leaning with both elbows on his volume of *Yoreh De'ah* and swayed ever more excitedly along with the lectern and the large open tome on it, as if struggling to free himself from the stony silence and the dense shadows that encircled him more and more tightly. Finally, he told his teacher that he could not study any more that day—for some reason he was not grasping the subject matter very well—and the Rabbi nodded that he was free to go. Just as eagerly as Gavriel sought to escape from the beth midrash did Reb Avraham-Abba wish to stay with his sacred tomes, whose words shone on the pages like stars in the heavens. The stars seemed so small in the sky and yet, if a man could only come close to them, he would be able to behold their glory, their magnificence. The same was true of the letters and words of the Torah, but to Gavriel Rappaport they were distant and strange because his heart was far from them. The Rabbi pondered as he had many times before, as to whether he had done the right thing in promising the dying Shlomo-Zalman Rappaport that he would become his son's teacher. But since he had given his word, he would be patient as long as the young man did not refuse to continue studying with him.

Gavriel walked from the long, narrow Straszuna Street onto the broad Zawalna Street. He imagined the passers-by taking notice that he walked with no friend at his side or girl on his arm. This Tammuz summer day had been hot and humid, but now a cool evening breeze rustled through the leaf-laden branches of the trees that lined the boulevard. Never before had Gavriel looked so amazed at the dark-blue sky or at the golden-yellow shine of the electric streetlights; never had he noticed that the houses had so many windows, doors, balconies, and steps, all leading to the street, where the people were hurrying off to one place or another, some to the summer theater, others to meet people in a cafe. They were hurrying just to be in a hurry, for no other purpose. Everyone does it because . . . everyone does it; everyone laughs when everyone laughs. Of course he was still in mourning and he remembered all too well that he led the services every day at the reader's lectern where he said Kaddish for his father. So he could not now in any case be frolicking with his friends, even if he were still at the University. But he had no one to talk to or to visit anymore. He was embarrassed before his old friends, who would surely ridicule him for leaving the University in order to sit all day in a beth midrash. And he did not want to become friends with the yeshiva students from the synagogue courtyard; they were simply not for him.

Suddenly, through the dusk of the summer evening Gavriel saw a group of young men in broad scout hats and jackets, wearing short pants with tall woolen socks up to their bare knees, carrying full knapsacks on their backs and hiking sticks in their hands. The group was returning from a long hike in the forests beyond the city, their faces bronzed and burned by the sun. Gavriel looked at them with envy. This summer he was to have traveled to a large estate outside the city and begun his practice of agronomy. He had long dreamed of how he would go swimming every day, how he would climb trees and go horseback riding. Then his father had taken ill and sentenced him to the cloistered life of a bethmidrash Jew.

When Gavriel arrived home, he found his mother and sister in a small room which contained a bookcase filled with volumes, shelves of books on the wall, a closet of dark mahogany, a couch, and some chairs with frayed, faded covers. This was the room where his father had spent the evenings looking over his business ledgers and where he had sometimes rested on the couch during the day. Every day, when darkness fell, Bathsheva and Asna stayed out of the other rooms in order to avoid the mirrors on the walls, as if afraid that the ghost of Shlomo-Zalman would emerge from them at any moment.

The widow had in a short time become thin and pale, and her hair had begun to gray as a hard sorrow seeped into her face. All she had to rely on to support herself and her two children was the small amount of money her husband had left her, and the much greater amount that people still owed him. Shlomo-Zalman Rappaport had been an orderly man, and so everything was very neatly and exactly recorded. But his wife, never having concerned herself with his business dealings, now found it difficult to see her way through these records and accounts. And even Shlomo-Zalman's best friends were not hurrying to pay their debts. Even when they paid, moreover, she could not be sure whether they were giving her the full amount that was owed. So Bathsheva would every night ensconce herself behind piles of paper and ledgers, and by day seek out the merchants with whom her husband had done business.

On this particular night, however, the widow did not look as worried as usual. For the first time since her husband had passed away, she had ceased to feel that she and her children had been left alone in the world: a letter had arrived from Shlomo-Zalman's younger brother in Latvia. Her brother-in-law remained a landowner near Libau, while her husband's estate near Witebsk had fallen into the hands of the Bolsheviks. "We've received a letter from your uncle, Baruch-Issar," she announced, as she handed Gavriel the few handwritten pages. "He is coming to visit us."

His uncle wrote of how broken he was over his older brother's death. Then he spoke of the hardships of running an estate and working the land. Even so, he had no thoughts of giving it up, because he remembered how his brother Shlomo-Zalman had suffered when he had had to move to the city and become a merchant. And, as busy and swamped with work as he was, he was still determined to visit his brother's family. Shlomo-Zalman had always written him how he hoped he would live to be proud of his son and daughter, and that Gabik had a brilliant mind for both Talmud and his agronomic studies at the University. Uncle Baruch-Issar then went on to boast that he, too, was a proud father—of three fine daughters—and when he came, he would be bringing photographs of them. He hoped he could visit at the end of the summer or the beginning of fall—it was a complicated matter to obtain a visa in Riga to go abroad, and the trek to Vilna was long and involved. He would not be able to take the direct route through Kovno because Lithuania and Poland were still at war over Vilna. Before ending his letter, Uncle Baruch-Issar once again made mention of his lovely daughters. Gavriel's face lit up with joy, his hands trembled, as if in these few handwritten pages lay his salvation.

4

BEFORE THE RUSSIAN REVOLUTION, Shlomo-Zalman Rappaport had lived on his estate in Witebsk, with Bathsheva's father as his partner in the wheat business. The two men attended the same small Hassidic shtibl, and they were often guests in each other's home. Shlomo-Zalman's first wife was then still living, and their grown children observed the precepts of Judaism and led their lives in accordance with the Torah. Bathsheva had always looked upon her father's partner with respect, and he had always treated her like a dear, cherished niece. They would talk long and frequently, and Shlomo-Zalman never ceased to be amazed at how pale this young girl always was, as if constantly terrified of something. Her parents worried a great deal about their daughter becoming an old maid. Instead of befriending the other girls of the town, she was always hiding in some corner of the house.

After the death of his first wife, Shlomo-Zalman visited his partner's home much more often, with one new business proposition after another.

And he would talk as well about how hard it was to keep house by himself, all the while not taking his eyes off Bathsheva for a moment. Her parents had never expected the widower to ask for their daughter's hand in marriage, or that she would agree, but when it happened, they did not stand in their daughter's way. Shlomo-Zalman Rappaport was then still a wealthy landowner and merchant, a very charitable man, respected by his fellow Jews and the Russian authorities alike. Although now in his fifties and the father of grown children, he bristled with good health and vigor, while the much younger Bathsheva looked like a half-withered flower. She needed a worldly-wise man for a husband, one who would be like a father to her.

After the wedding, however, Bathsheva blossomed in the shelter of her husband's love and protection. When, soon thereafter, his children by his first wife became revolutionaries, she became his chief comfort and support in his conflicts with them. And she showed him even more loyalty and trust when they were obliged to flee Witebsk and go to Vilna, where he had to make a new start in business. It took some time, but eventually he became a merchant of high standing, though he never again attained his former wealth. In every venture, in every crisis, his wife stood faithfully at his side. She strictly followed his instructions—in conducting the household, in raising the children, even in buying her clothes. Shlomo-Zalman often had to tell her to buy a new coat or have a dress made or get a new hat, since she never bought any clothes on her own, fearing they could not afford it.

And the children obeyed only their father. Even as a child Asna had been unruly and peevish with her mother. When she grew up, she became disdainfully cold and hard. She could not stand her mother's being so fearful, so blindly pious, so old-fashioned in all her ways. Father even had to tell her how to dress! For her part, Bathsheva had never ceased to be amazed at how little her husband understood their daughter: He thought her gentle and shy, when in fact she was bitter and stubborn. Her refusal to have anything to do with the neighborhood girls was out of sheer haughtiness, and not, as her father believed, because she was a pious Jewish child. When, however, her husband took ill, Bathsheva showed greater strength and fortitude than Asna. At first, the fearful months of mourning following his death had brought mother and daughter somewhat closer. But then Asna had become, as before, more stubborn and less patient with her mother, and Bathsheva refused to put up with it any longer. When Asna announced her intention to go to work as a salesgirl or cashier, Bathsheva replied that if she was so eager to work in someone else's business, then why didn't she help oversee her father's unsettled accounts?

"You can do that by yourself," the daughter retorted angrily, though so quietly that the walls themselves could not hear any quarreling in the house. "Maybe you would like me to walk around like you, with a purse stuffed with receipts, and go begging the merchants to pay their old debts?"

"It would not hurt your chances of finding a pious scholar for a husband, as was your father's last wish," was her mother's curt reply.

Asna bit her lip and said no more.

Bathsheva spent the next day trudging from one debtor to another. The heat had frazzled her hair and caused her to perspire. The clatter of the street still rang in her ears, she could feel the dust on her lips, and her throat was parched from her day-long arguments with the merchants. The wheat dealers who had shown her husband such respect now had no time for her, and claimed that Shlomo-Zalman had written them down for more than they actually owed him. She was even more frustrated by those who did not bother to deny their debts, but calmly dismissed her by saying that they simply did not have the money to pay her at the moment. If the widow Rappaport did not care to wait, she was free to fetch the bailiff and take them to court. Upon hearing such an answer, Bathsheva would stagger into the street, the world swimming before her eyes, and she felt as if she were a crumbling pillar of dry dust.

At the same time she could not help thinking about the children. She knew that Asna was seeing a young man, a friend of Gavriel's. No doubt it was he who had put the thought of getting a job into Asna's head, so that she could be free of her mother at last. And what would become of Gabik? With each day an anger seethed in the boy toward his father for having forced him into becoming a Talmud student. She wondered whether all her sacrifices were to any purpose: Was he or wasn't he learning something? Perhaps she ought to speak to his teacher.

THE CORNER OF STRASZUNA and Zawalna streets was a commotion of passers-by and business throughout the hot summer day. But in the store of Rabbi Avraham-Abba Seligman a stillness reigned amid the soft shadows of the half-closed shutters. When Bathsheva entered, she found no customers within, only the Divorced Rabbi himself standing behind the counter, peering into a rabbinic tract. When he did not raise his eyes from the book, she came closer, said good morning, and reminded him that she

was Gavriel Rappaport's mother. Reb Avraham-Abba gave her a warm
nod of recognition. Abruptly, Bathsheva's quiet voice took on a note of
anxious maternal concern:

"I came, Rabbi, to find out how my son's studies are progressing. Is
my son learning anything? Because if he isn't, then why waste time? He
has to think of his future, after all!"

"Your son has a brilliant mind; he is exceptional, in fact, and his
time is not being wasted even if he does not devote his life to the Talmud.
Every day he studies is a day won." Though one was not permitted to
gaze directly at a woman other than his wife, the pious shopkeeper looked
straight into Bathsheva's eyes, and in the wrinkles of his face lay kindness
and compassion for the lot of a widow. Suddenly he noticed how tired she
was, and brought a chair out from behind the counter and stood over
her for so long that she finally sat down. He then returned to his place,
took out a ledger from a low drawer under the counter, and opened it.
When at last he found what he was looking for, he chanted the same way
scholars chant passages of Talmud: He owed her late husband, may his
soul rest in peace, seventy-four zlotys and forty groschen. The debt was
not due until the twenty-fifth of Tammuz, but since he had the money
now and she had happened to come by the store, he might as well pay
her.

"That can't be!" Bathsheva shouted, and then drew back as if her
own voice had frightened her. Embarrassed at having spoken to the
Rabbi as if he were not telling the truth, she stammered that her husband
had always written everything down, and she had not found in any ledger
or on a single piece of paper that the Rabbi was one of her late husband's
debtors.

"Reb Shlomo-Zalman did not write it down because he knew that
I wrote it down and that was enough," Reb Avraham-Abba said with a
smile, and then he explained that he had purchased goods from her husband nearly a year before. "I paid half the amount then and arranged not
to pay the other half for a year because I was afraid I might not be able to
do so sooner. You can see for yourself what I've written here in my
ledger."

Disconcerted if not astonished, Bathsheva rose from the chair as
Reb Avraham-Abba came around to the front of the counter so she could
go behind it and inspect the ledger. Just at that moment a short, dumpy
woman walked in, and then stood dumbfounded at the door to see, behind the counter, a woman in a black dress and a hat with a widow's veil,

looking into a ledger as if she were an owner. The customer could hardly believe her eyes: a woman behind the counter of the Divorced Rabbi's store?! Being obviously a widow, was she perhaps a bereaved relative of his, or someone he intended to marry?

To show that she was no stranger in the store, the customer briskly poured various grains from the large, full linen sacks on the wooden stands into small paper bags, as casually as if she were in her own pantry. She took some sour cucumbers from a glass jar with a wooden spoon, chose a pack of dried fish from a woven basket, cut off a piece of hard cheese, and took all of it over to the scale to weigh. All the while she talked incessantly, scolding the shopkeeper: His shelves, thank God, were laden with a great deal of merchandise, but in no kind of order—candles, tobacco, matches, and cigarette boxes were all mixed together on the same shelf with crockery, dairy products, and loaves of bread. What if the tobacco spilled out onto the food or the glasses of the naphtha lamps fell and broke? A fine thing it would be to sell food covered with slivers of glass!

"Are you a niece of the Rabbi's, or perhaps a closer relative?" she suddenly called out to the woman behind the counter. She did not wait for an answer, but kept on talking, telling Bathsheba that it was plain to see that the customers watched over the Rabbi's business better than he did himself. The Rabbi, after all, was always immersed in his holy tomes. But sometimes a strange woman, some wild, slovenly goose, would burst in like a whirlwind and leave the place a mess, and then the steady customers could not find a thing. And what did the Rabbi do about it? Why, nothing! He sat behind half-closed shutters in the middle of the day, so how were people even to know that there was a store here in which they could buy things?

"The Almighty sees even in the thickest darkness, and he leads the customers who are supposed to come in here by the arm." Reb Avraham-Abba smiled as he stood in the middle of the store while the woman weighed her purchases on the scale.

Reb Avraham-Abba was accustomed to suffering patiently the banter of his too loyal customers. But now he could hardly wait for this customer to leave so he could resume his interrupted conversation with his student's mother: Well, she could surely see in his ledger that he was indeed a debtor of her late husband's, and he would like to settle the debt immediately. Besides that, he added, she could take food items and any other household goods she needed on credit.

"Fine," answered Bathsheva in a flustered tone. "I will take things against the amount of the debt the Rabbi owed my husband. I'll do my shopping here, then." She was so confused that for a long time she forgot to walk out from behind the counter so that the storekeeper could resume his place.

5

BATHSHEVA BEGAN COMING to Rabbi Seligman's store more often to buy her groceries, and to ask how her son's studies were progressing. In the Rabbi—as a man of great faith and one who, though a stranger, was so loyal to her family—she saw someone she and her children could depend on. He offered her advice on how to deal with each debtor in accordance with his financial situation, yet without releasing him from the debt. If she could not settle with a debtor, she must, he said, take him to the Rabbinical Court, and even to the Polish courts if necessary. "After all, we do not live in a jungle." Reb Avraham-Abba also wanted to know more about the widow's daughter. Bathsheva told him that Asna had taken a job in a store and was seeing a young man, educated but irreligious. Her father would never have permitted it—on his deathbed he had demanded that she promise to marry a Torah scholar.

Reb Avraham-Abba listened attentively, his elbows resting on the counter and his eyes focused intently on a book. He answered her in a deep, strained voice: "Don't say anything to your daughter. She will not obey you anyway, and you'll only cause her to transgress the commandment 'Honor thy father and mother.' "

Once, Bathsheva had occasion to see that her son's teacher could be as hard as stone. A customer asked to buy some groceries on credit, and Reb Avraham-Abba refused, demanding that she first repay what she already owed. The woman swore that she would pay it all back, but now she had fallen on hard times—her husband and son were not working. When she saw that the storekeeper was unmoved and was staring at her, watching her every move to make sure she did not take anything in spite of him, the woman began cursing all the "self-righteous, religious Jews with their cold, pitiless hearts." And as she left the store, she spat out, "Tfu! A pox on you all! No wonder your wife left you!" Bathsheva desperately looked for a corner in which to hide from embarrassment, but

Reb Avraham-Abba did not even wince, which was the least one would have expected from any man in such a situation. He merely spoke to himself, his face solemn and earnest as if he were reviewing a point of law or the logic of a Talmudic argument:

"I know that she can pay. But since she knows that I am an observant Jew, she thinks that she needn't pay me because the good deed ought to be enough for me. But it is forbidden to lend to a person who borrows with no thought of repaying."

One Monday afternoon, Bathsheva found him outside the store, propping the open doors against the wall. A strong wind soon blew the door shut, so he came outside the store and struggled with the door until he secured it to a hook in the wall with a piece of string. Never before had Reb Avraham-Abba been so concerned that the door be so wide open. When he saw Bathsheva looking at him curiously, he explained that on Monday all the beggars make the rounds, so the door must be wide open for them.

It did not take long for some beggars to appear, dressed in rags, their shoes tattered, their faces benumbed and contorted, their hands and feet twisted like the withered roots of an unearthed tree stump. The paupers marched in silently and left each with the few groschen Reb Avraham-Abba gave them. But one beggar, a lame and blind man who tapped his way through the street with a stick he held in his right hand, felt the coins Reb Avraham-Abba had placed in his left hand and started to shout: "Groschen? You dare to give me groschen? What am I, a schnorrer?! Before I became blind, I was every bit as upstanding a merchant as you, and I gave my share of charity!"

"I can't give you any more than that; I have to save something for the others," Reb Avraham-Abba replied.

Enraged at being treated like any other beggar, the blind man flung the coins onto the floor and stalked out of the store, looking as though he were walking on wooden legs. Reb Avraham-Abba came out from behind the counter and knelt down to pick up the scattered coins, but they were lost in the clutter of goods on the floor. Rising, he turned to the widow Rappaport and said, with a sigh and a look of concern on his face, "When a man is blind and, to make things worse, also lacks imagination, he cannot comprehend that other people are, no less than he, created in the image of God. And when we cannot see that the next person is also created in God's image, we have no pity for him—like that blind beggar who does not want to know that others have the right to live, too."

Afterward, Bathsheva reflected that both her father and her husband had liked to live well, and when they could afford it they had not minded giving to charity. But if they had trembled over every groschen and gotten down on their knees to find a few of them as Rabbi Avraham-Abba Seligman had done that morning, they might never have given to charity at all. Her father had been a Hassid and so had been her husband, yet they had dealt with all sorts of people and conducted business like everyone else. But Rabbi Avraham-Abba Seligman was a different sort: When he spoke to people, even when he was selling his merchandise and talking to his customers, his demeanor was that of a man engrossed in the performance of a mitzvah. It was hard for her to see any chance of her Gabik growing up to be the same kind of man as his teacher.

Gavriel had missed a few sessions with the Rabbi. When he did come by, making a pretense of eagerness to resume studying, Reb Avraham-Abba did not ask him where he had been, lest the boy blurt out that he had no desire to study Talmud. As long as he made the effort and kept up appearances, there was hope that he would come to study sincerely. So whenever Bathsheva would ask if her son was diligent in his studies, Reb Avraham-Abba would simply mutter "Mhm" without raising his eyes from the tome in which he was immersed. As long as Gavriel did not tell his mother of his absences, the Rabbi reckoned, he would have to come to the beth midrash sooner or later, lest his mother discover the truth. When, however, the young man failed to appear for four days in a row, Reb Avraham-Abba felt he could no longer hide the truth from Bathsheva; and so it was that that Thursday evening, when she came in to shop for the Sabbath, he told her that Gavriel hadn't been coming to his lessons.

Bathsheva stood stunned and speechless, and Reb Avraham-Abba said nothing further. When some customers walked into the store, she left, still not having uttered a word. As she walked home, the groceries she was carrying became as heavy as stones. A vision of the Divorced Rabbi's face, despairing as the day he walked out of her husband's sickroom, hovered before her eyes.

At home, she found her son, her daughter, and her daughter's suitor, all in a lively mood, sitting in the brightly lit parlor and laughing loudly—in the same parlor, where, not very long before, the head of the family had lain on the floor covered with a black cloth, that parlor which it was still a struggle for her to enter in the evening. Now the glaring electric lights chased the shadows from every corner of the room and the robust laughter of youth rang out the open windows and into the streets. Even the curtains on the windows fluttered in the evening breeze, as if elated that at long last the room was free of all shadows and sorrows.

The first to see Bathsheva enter, and to cease laughing, was Asna's suitor, Mulik Durmashkin, followed by Asna and then Gavriel. The son and daughter gazed fearfully at their mother: she looked very pale and dejected, as if some tragedy had just befallen her, and they were afraid to ask what had happened. Finally, she composed herself and turned to Gavriel: "Why did you deceive me by pretending you were going every day to study with the Rabbi? It's already a week since you last met with him." She sat down on a chair and looked at him with lusterless eyes.

Gavriel was confused and embarrassed before his friend. Mulik Durmashkin had long, pale, delicate fingers, and when he thought intently about something, he would open and close them as if testing his ability to make a fist. He was the spoiled favorite son of a rich family, a young man with a knowing smile, narrow shoulders, and a thin, long face. The hard, taut muscles in his gaunt cheeks and the stiff, thick hair that topped a creased forehead bore witness to a strong character, and to a stubbornness even greater than Asna's. Now he looked silently at his supple fingers, and Gavriel understood that Mulik, no less than his sister, disapproved of him for not having had the courage to face up to his mother and tell her the truth.

"Do you at least attend services somewhere?" Bathsheva asked. "Do you say Kaddish every day for your father?"

Springing out of his chair, Gavriel began to rant: Of course he prayed every day and recited Kaddish. She could ask the men or the sexton in the beth midrash in the Old Age Home. And he *had* been going to study with the Rabbi every day; it was just in the last week that he hadn't done so, because the heat made him yearn for a little fresh air, for the forest and the green fields. He hadn't looked at a meadow all summer. So he'd spent a few days bathing in the Wilja and lying on its banks. Gavriel started to laugh: Was it his fault if his mother didn't even notice that his face was tanned from the sun?

Bathsheva looked at her son's sunburned face and wondered why, indeed, she hadn't noticed it before. The dark-blue rings under his eyes were gone. Shlomo-Zalman's heir had a small, moist mouth, a soft, almost childlike chin, and the nervous and sometimes brazen laugh of a weak, overgrown boy. Only his large, dark, restless eyes, and his tall forehead with its prominent temples, bespoke his rare abilities.

"And now that you've gone bathing and gotten yourself a suntan, will you return to your studies?" his mother asked.

"Gabik received a letter from Uncle in Latvia that he is visiting us for Sukkoth," Asna interjected, as if that answered her mother's question.

Astonishment was written all over Bathsheva's face—she was amazed that her brother-in-law should have written to Gavriel and not to her. Asna explained that Gavriel had written to Uncle asking him to come as soon as possible, and Uncle had answered that he could not make the trip before Sukkoth.

Gavriel sat down again, agitated and ashamed, as his sister glared at him angrily for being afraid to tell their mother the truth. Mulik Durmashkin continued to open and close his long white fingers as if to show that, in spite of their stubbornness, they were doing just what he wanted. Bathsheva also sat quietly, but with tears in her eyes. She saw that her son did not intend to keep the oath he had made to his father, not even until the end of the year of mourning.

Nonetheless, Gavriel began going to the Rabbi for lessons once again, and even visited him in his store. By the store's doorway, during the summer, there stood baskets of fruit, at which Gavriel gazed with sad longing. The fruit seemed to him like a joyous greeting from the fields and forests, and he could gauge the time of the season by the kinds of fruit in the baskets. The blackberry season was long since past, and so was the season for red raspberries and the hard green gooseberries. The transparent white currants had also disappeared, and the yellow honey-sweet cherries and the soft, mirror-smooth black cherries became rare visitors. Now juicy ripe plums beckoned him with their dark-purple skins and deep-red fleshy bodies. The vegetable gardens were having their say, too: the first young potatoes with their cherubic rosy skins were soon followed by the large, bulbous potatoes; radishes with notched heads as tough as bark; sparkling white heads of cabbage; and green cucumbers—thin and twisted, some wide and swollen. Next to last year's wreaths of onions, lying on the wooden stands in their thin brown skins, this year's fresh green ones winked with their long white heads crowned by their stubby roots. Each time Reb Avraham-Abba raised his eyes from his book and looked out the open door at the fruits and vegetables outside, he would once again reflect that only he who makes a blessing over the fruit and knows that nothing grows by itself has the double joy of the blessing as well as the fruit.

Though tree branches were still creaking under the weight of their thick green leaves and the days were still as blindingly brilliant as polished brass, customers were now entering the store with beclouded faces. "There goes the summer!" they sighed. "When you hear the first shofar blasts on the first of Elul, it makes your heart sink."

To Rabbi Avraham-Abba Seligman, the sounds of the shofar brought sweet musings and thoughts of repentance—if it were not so contrary to the way of the world, and if he had had no bills to pay, he would have closed the store until after the High Holy Days to devote himself entirely to the service of the Almighty. His student, by contrast, became with the approach of the Days of Awe even more restless and impatient, aware as he was that he would now have still more time for praying and studying, studying and praying. He would have to recite the endless penitential prayers and beat his breast: "We have transgressed; we have been treacherous; we have stolen . . . ," confessing to sins he had not committed.

Far more despondent even than her son was Bathsheva, for as the holidays drew near, she felt the pangs of her loneliness and sorrow ever more strongly. Just a year before, during the Rosh Hashanah and Yom Kippur services, when she had looked out from the women's section into the men's, she had been able to see her husband enfolded in his prayer shawl. Just a year before, she had been in the sukkah with him as he recited the Kiddush over a goblet of deep-red wine, her son and daughter standing beside her, listening solemnly—as solemnly and piously as befitted the children of Shlomo-Zalman Rappaport.

6

Uncle Baruch-Issar arrived on schedule, just before Sukkoth. He was taller than his late brother, narrower in the shoulders, with a protruding belly and a long, wispy gray beard. From his jocular manner and boisterous talk, one would have thought he had come for a wedding, not to console his departed brother's family in their year of mourning. Gavriel attached himself at once to his uncle, and Baruch-Issar took his nephew by the arm with a gesture of great solemnity, as if the young man were already his son-in-law-to-be. He had shown Gavriel photographs of his three daughters—girls with thick eyebrows and fleshy lips, wearing long dresses with short sleeves, designed to conceal their thick legs and reveal their beautiful round arms. A country vigor radiated from their faces, though they posed with dreamy expressions. The youngest was petting a kitten that lay on her lap, with one hand, resting her chin on the other, and looking off into the far, far distance. The middle daughter sat engrossed in a book, while the eldest was playing a violin. "She's the musician in the family," said Baruch-Issar. Gavriel, however, was not looking at the violin, but staring at the girl's low décolleté, her full breasts and her broad thighs. He knew that this was the intended one, though he suspected that he could just as well choose the middle daughter with the book or the youngest with her kitten. The clever uncle showed them the pictures without a word about marriage, and when his sister-in-law, Bathsheva, asked whether any of the girls was already engaged, Baruch-Issar waved his hands:

"That should be my biggest worry! The young men stand in line for them like horses at a water trough."

Asna, for her part, did not show her uncle any particular affection or trust. She disliked the commonness of his manners, his boisterousness, the way he would pinch her cheeks as if she were a little girl, and the way he bragged about his daughters. She even found fault with his appearance, especially his thin, long, frazzled beard. Her father had always walked and talked calmly with an aristocratic bearing, his white beard resting placidly on his chest, neatly combed into two evenly rounded halves. She asked her mother how her father could have a brother so different in character and appearance. But Bathsheva said nothing, careful not to reveal her own qualms. She had noted only too well how Gavriel quivered with joy when he looked at his uncle, as if Baruch-Issar had come to free him from prison.

Gavriel had built the Sukkah, as in years past, on the balcony of their third-floor apartment. Their guest recited Kiddush with a robust cheerfulness, and Gavriel, enraptured by his uncle, sang the blessings with him. But his mother stood pale and silent, her head bowed, and his sister, too, stood silent with sorrowful eyes.

During the meal, Baruch-Issar talked to his nephew about farming: The weeds in the wheatfields and the gardens were sapping his strength, he complained. And what about the University, had they found a solution to this problem yet?

Gavriel replied with the same brilliant ease as when reciting section after section of the Codes for his teacher, Rabbi Seligman: If the weeds had already smothered the oats, barley, and wheat, then it was too late. You had to weed the fields when the wheat was still young and it was still not damaging to tread on the freshly planted earth. Worst of all were the dandelions. They had no fear of frost or heat, or of drought or dampness. You had to tear them out of the garden before they had a chance to release their seeds. The best time to pull them out was after a rain; they came out most easily then, along with their roots.

"Why don't you ask me, Uncle, how to plant cabbage, cucumbers, or potatoes?" Gavriel asked, speaking rapidly and animatedly, breathlessly eager to demonstrate to his uncle his university training in agronomy. But then, suddenly, he leaped over all the planted fields and gardens and began to talk about the Talmud. "Test me, Uncle, on Tractate *Hullin* and on *Yoreh De'ah*, especially the laws of slaughtering, of unfit animals, and the prohibitions of mixing meat and milk. And if you like, you can test me on the three 'Babas'—*Baba Kama, Baba Metzia, Baba Bathra.*"

"Not me, not me!" Baruch-Issar said as he withdrew his greasy fingers from the fish head on his plate and spoke half jokingly and half in earnest. "I can test you only in caring for the land. But when it comes to Talmud, my little brother, you'll have to go to the Rav of Dwinsk, the Sage of Rogotchev, or to your own Vilna rabbis for a testing, not to me."

Bathsheva smiled with both pride and sadness. She would have preferred that her son display his brilliance in Torah alone. Asna was also smiling, but with contempt. She was ashamed of her brother, who, though already twenty-one years of age and older than she, was acting like a child. Her Mulik was much more mature and would never brag like this. Through the light mist wafting from the bowls of hot soup Baruch-Issar gazed at his nephew's high, sagacious forehead, at his small, fresh lips and childlike chin, as if he, too, were wondering whether such a boy would be a fitting husband for his daughter or a competent cultivator of land. A cool breeze blew through the walls of the Sukkah and a dark sky peeked through the roof of fir branches. In the glow of the lamp and the candles the uncle's eyes sparkled with the imbibed wine of Kiddush, and a glossy flush played on his fat cheeks. He ate with relish, leaning forward over the plate, talking continuously to his nephew, all the while stealing glances at his sister-in-law to measure the impression his words were making on her.

"A land cultivator, a university-trained agronomist with a diploma —that's no small matter. But practical experience is no less essential, especially for an agronomist who is city-born and knows everything only from books. It just isn't possible to learn the smell of the earth or the fragrance of all the various plants from books. Take such simple things as harnessing and unharnessing horses, or spreading dung on an open field, or assigning the chores to the farmhands and then overseeing them— there are no courses in any university for that, my little brother. To learn these things you have to plow the earth with your nose; you have to be there to raise the calves, foals, and chicks, to prune the trees in the orchards, and you must nurse the garden yourself, with your own hands."

"But that's what I've been saying all along," Gavriel replied, and told his uncle how Jewish agronomy students had appealed to the Jewish landowners of Poland to offer them practical experience because the Polish gentry would not let them work on their land. So if a Jewish agronomy student had a relative who was a landowner, it was indeed a stroke of good fortune.

"Well, Gabik, too bad you have to depend on such good fortune," Bathsheva joked sarcastically as she cleared the dishes from the table. "Now, if you wanted to be a rav and get experience answering practical questions from congregants who came to you for a ruling, the doors of every rabbinical court would be wide open to you. You won't find any Poles grabbing those positions."

Gavriel was about to reply, but he caught Baruch-Issar's wink and said nothing. He felt a warmth coursing through his veins and happiness in his heart, as if his uncle's secret nod to him had skillfully sawed through the bars of his prison cell.

To raise everyone's spirits, Baruch-Issar started joking with his bored, unfriendly niece and asked her whether she would introduce him to her young man. But Asna remained silent, and her mother also had nothing more to say. Bathsheva was thinking of her late husband, and how he had sought from Asna a promise that she would marry only a Talmudic scholar. But Asna, at least, had never really promised anything, while Gavriel had taken a solemn oath, and here was his own uncle helping him to break it. The widow brought another course to the table and sat down with the others to eat the holiday meal, but her lips felt dry as if she were in the midst of a fast.

On the morning of the first day of Sukkoth, uncle and nephew attended services in the shtibl of the Kaidanovo Hassidim. When the congregants learned that their visitor was the younger brother of the late Shlomo-Zalman Rappaport, they welcomed him with open arms, just as they scolded Gavriel: "So where has the shaygetz been hiding?" His father had always been a wise man; it was only in his last days that he had acted foolishly: If it was his intention to take his son out of the University and make him study with a rabbi, why couldn't he have chosen a Hassidic rabbi instead of a Misnaged? And why, of all people, that shopkeeper-rabbi Seligman?

The Kaidanovo Shtibl was already aglow on the first day of Sukkoth with the festive spirit of the holiday's climax, Simhat Torah. Patriarchs with long, thick, curly sidelocks were facing the wall, ecstatically engrossed in prayer. Their sons, men in their forties and fifties, stood at their lecterns, their faces turned toward each other as they swayed, shifting from one foot to another. In between prayers mumbled at top speed, they would pause to exchange witticisms and clever homilies; abruptly, they would stop, turning their gazes piously toward the ceiling: they were, after all, engaged in prayer.

In these Lithuanian Hassidim who no longer made pilgrimages to the Rebbe, all that remained was an outward liveliness without the Hassidic fire—the melody without the Rebbe's words and insights. And yet, Hassidim are still Hassidim. So, before services they still immersed themselves in a warm mikvah, and their beards sparkled yet with beads of water, and their washed faces shone. The reader at his lectern, his prayer shawl over his head, did not indulge in cantorial embellishments; he would fervently but hastily call out the concluding verse of each psalm of the preliminary morning service, and the worshippers would then loudly go on to the next psalm. All the while, fathers would be watching their sons—short lads with pudgy, round, clean-shaven faces who were bouncing from one end of the shtibl to the other. On an ordinary weekday these Hassidic young men could be found in a restaurant, or walking with a girl down a wooded lane, or on a secret date behind some backstairs, no different from all the other boys of the town. But on the Sabbath and holidays they still kept up appearances. Their clothes were custom made by tailors who charged a hundred zlotys for cutting and fitting a jacket. They wore soft shirts with stiff, rounded collars, ties held in place with diamond pins, and golden cufflinks. Girding their fashionable short jackets were silken Hassidic gartels, into which they stuck their thumbs as they strutted the length of the shtibl. During the Silent Prayer, they stood solemnly at attention as if riveted to the floor, swaying from side to side and, at times, to and fro like a pendulum. They then resumed their pacing until the congregation reached the Kedushah, "Holy . . . Holy . . . Holy!" Suddenly one of them would kick a friend in his pants from behind and then stand innocently staring off to the side so that his friend could not guess who had done it. The victim, not wanting to be a debtor but not knowing which one of his friends to repay, would stroll calmly behind the nearest one, give him a slap on the back that resounded throughout the shtibl, and quickly dart away. Their fathers would give them angry looks and wave a threatening finger. But by the twinkle in their eyes and the smile that played at the corners of their mouths, one could tell that the fathers only wished they could join in the fun.

Gavriel Rappaport looked on at this sport with glee; but a thought gnawed at his heart: Why couldn't he have continued at the University and come to the Kaidanovo Shtibl on Sabbath and holidays just like the other young men? Why weren't their fathers forcing them to study Talmud? And as Gavriel looked at Baruch-Issar, his sense of grievance against his late father grew, for his uncle was the kind of man in whom pious words and not-so-pious deeds blended as easily as clouds passing through one another. When the congregation shook their palm branches and citrons in unison during the Service of Praise, and the Kaidanovo Shtibl looked for a moment like a palm grove, Baruch-Issar stood in a corner, calm and unconcerned. Since he had no palm branch and citron of his own, he simply borrowed someone else's and recited the blessings stiffly and coldly. Not until after the service, when the others surrounded him and eagerly asked him how Jews lived in faraway lands, did Baruch-Issar turn the conversation to the Lithuanian Hassidic communities and show the depth of his knowledge of the great Karliner Hassidic family with all its branches and dynasties.

"About Reb Mordcale of Lachowicze and of Reb Osherel, the first Stoliner Rebbe, nothing more can be said; by now they are both legendary," he said as he piously swayed along with the lectern on which he leaned, tugging at his wispy beard with all the fingers of his right hand. "But our grandfathers still knew Reb Shlomo-Chaim of Kaidanovo. Ah, now there was a saint, Reb Shlomo-Chaim Kaidanover! His Siddur, the *Ohr Hayashar*, contains a section on his customs, along with the Sabbath song of the Great Reb Aharon Karliner. The old Kaidanovo Rav, may his soul reside in Paradise, had four grandsons: the Rebbe of Novominsk, the Rebbe of Horodyszcze, the Rebbe of Puchowicze and the Rebbe Reb Baruch-Mordecai of Kaidanovo, may his soul reside in Paradise. What a saint that Reb Baruch-Mordecai was..."

Gavriel was amazed not only at his uncle's incredible memory but at his reverence for these rabbis, a reverence that seemed completely out of character for him. The Hassidim invited Baruch-Issar to Kiddush in their sukkah in the Grand Synagogue courtyard. But he declined, asking Gavriel instead to take him to his Rabbi, the shopkeeper Avraham-Abba Seligman.

7

I T WAS A WINDY, sunny day. People walked with their backs turned to the wind to keep the flying dust out of their eyes. Women held their billowing dresses down with their hands, looking plainly annoyed at the dishevelment the wind was causing to their hair. Gavriel's hungry eyes devoured the exposed women's knees in sheer stockings. He felt himself drawn to every slim female with long legs, and inwardly he groaned at the thought of his youth going to waste. Even so he was, thanks to his uncle's company, in a holiday mood. The sky was high and blue, and the passers-by they encountered were elegantly dressed. As soon, however, as they turned into the narrow, winding Straszuna Street, where but a beam of sky fell as if into a cellar, Gavriel's spirits also fell. In the middle of a courtyard stood a large sukkah into which women were bringing food for their husbands.

In a corner of this same courtyard lived the shopkeeper-rabbi Avraham-Abba Seligman. Close by stood his own private sukkah, with walls of unplaned wood, patched here and there with pieces of plywood, and a roof of fir branches. He cooked for himself, served himself, and ate alone in this ramshackle structure, where he also slept for the duration of Sukkoth. Two copper candlesticks covered with drops of melted wax stood in the center of the sukkah's table, which also bore a woven basket containing sliced hallah, a plate of cold noodle pudding, and some left-over prune compote in a saucer.

In honor of the holiday, Reb Avraham-Abba was wearing what had once been his wedding attire: a soft, broad hat and a coat now frayed at the elbows. He sat at the table with his eyes closed, his hand resting on the thick cover of a large tome as he concluded the Grace After Meals. When Gavriel and his uncle walked in and said "Good Yom Tov," Avraham-Abba's gaze seemed to have just returned from misty distances.

Gavriel introduced his uncle, and the Rabbi quietly shook his hand and motioned with a finger for him to sit down. Baruch-Issar waited politely for his host to ask him how Jews were faring in old Courland and Latgalia, or to offer a homily on the holiday Torah portion or even a simple witticism, and he expected him to put a little food on the table, as was customary for anyone welcoming guests to his sukkah. But Rabbi Seligman remained silent—not out of anger or spite, but simply because he felt no need to spend time in idle chatter. Gavriel also kept still; he had run out of excuses for having missed his Talmud lessons these last weeks, and he felt that even his teacher was no longer expecting him.

Baruch-Issar was the first to break the silence, speaking, with many pious sighs, of the waning of Judaism in his homeland, Latvia, even though in Dwinsk there still reigned such great lions as the Sage of Rogotchev and the Gaon, Reb Meir-Simha. Imagine being able to boast of two such great names!

"One must never say that Judaism is waning anywhere," Reb Avraham-Abba interjected. "That borders on blasphemy. And," he continued, looking intently at Gavriel, "if it is as you say, then a young man ought not to be traveling there."

Baruch-Issar was momentarily nonplussed. To him, it was no more than the custom for any gathering of pious Jews to produce a chorus of sighs, reciprocal lamentations of the sorry state of Jewish life as a proper punishment for their sins. And what had caught him even more by surprise was his host's getting so abruptly as he had to the heart of the matter. But since he had started, Baruch-Issar decided that he, too, would speak straight to the point. He leaned forward over the table as he addressed Reb Avraham-Abba: According to what he had heard, his brother had asked Gavriel on his deathbed to leave the University and become a Talmudic scholar. But what would the Talmud say, since Gavriel still wanted to become a farmer? Haven't we had great Jews, even sages of the Talmud, who worked the land? So what would the Rabbi say, would it really be a crime against his deceased brother for him, Baruch-Issar, to take his son back with him to Latvia? "We have a true Jewish home on my estate near Libau," he concluded. "No worse than my sister-in-law's."

"I cannot speak for the deceased," said Reb Avraham-Abba, "but, for my part, there is no objection. If your nephew wants to go with you and his mother approves, let him go."

"Could I ask the Rabbi to talk to my sister-in-law and get her to agree to this?" Baruch-Issar asked, softening his tone and donning an innocent expression. To Gavriel, his uncle's tactics—the brazenness of a hardened businessman who carefully probes to see how far he can go— were terrifying. But Reb Avraham-Abba calmly gazed at the closed tome for a while and at last replied: "I really don't see why I should be the one to persuade the boy's mother to let him go. And how can I be sure she'll listen?"; and he suddenly smiled cheerfully at his student as if Gavriel were a mischievous little boy.

Baruch-Issar was by now convinced that he would not be getting anything more out of this strange rabbi, and that he was not, in any event, especially welcome here—or was it just that this solitary man disliked visitors? Whatever the case, he bade the Rabbi a hearty farewell and, with his nephew, took his leave. Gavriel, for his part, had been deeply pained by his teacher's apparent coldness and aloofness toward him.

As they walked home, Baruch-Issar muttered reflectively, half to himself, "I don't know . . . If you go by his appearance and manner, he doesn't seem like the great gaon and tzaddik everyone says he is. And from the way he lives, the unfriendly way he acts, I can see why everybody calls him the Divorced Rabbi . . . I just don't know. Anything is possible with these Misnagdim; only a Misnaged could reconcile such opposites. And yet, on the other hand, my brother was an excellent judge of character and would not have entrusted the welfare of his household to just anyone. Your Rabbi is certainly a very clever man, you can see that by his eyes and his measured words . . . Do you know what I think, nephew?" he said, stopping suddenly in mid-stride, in the middle of the street. "Your Rabbi doesn't believe for a moment that you'll make a Talmudic scholar; he's just not telling you that in so many words. Now your leaving depends entirely on your mother."

THE FIRST TWO DAYS of Sukkoth were unhappy ones for the Rappaport family. Gavriel argued vehemently with his mother, stamping his feet and shouting that he had never taken a solemn oath, he had merely said something reassuring to his father, and even that was done out of fear that his father might suffer another heart attack if he were upset. The usually quiet and docile Bathsheva retorted, with a strong show of authority, that it did not matter whether he had indeed taken an oath or had merely nodded his head; it was still his duty to obey his father's last wishes.

Baruch-Issar, shrugging his shoulders, took his nephew's part: "My brother Shlomo-Zalman always wrote me that he was very proud that his son was studying at the University. Even though it wasn't easy paying the tuition and there were many anti-Semitic rowdies who taunted Gavriel at the lectures, it was all worth it just to see him get his degree. 'And then,' Shlomo-Zalman wrote me, 'I'll send Gabik to you to get practical experience in running an estate.' So what happened all of a sudden?" Baruch-Issar asked as he stood in the middle of the room with his hands outstretched, facing the wall so as to avoid facing his sister-in-law. Asna, too, sided with her brother, finally becoming so furious with her stubborn mother that she stormed out of the house.

But the more sense Baruch-Issar made, the more Bathsheva hated him. She saw all too clearly that he was only out for his own good, and wanted to have Gabik become his assistant on his estate and marry one of his daughters.

"Even the Hassidim in the Kaidanovo Shtibl," shouted Gavriel, "said that it was wrong of Father to have made me study with a Misnaged rabbi. Ask Uncle, he heard it himself."

"But you must not repeat it; your Rabbi is a great scholar and a saintly Jew," Baruch-Issar scolded his nephew, and then he urged his sister-in-law to speak to the Rabbi during the intermediate days of the holiday: since he had said he had no objections to Gavriel's leaving, he must have a definite opinion on the matter.

RABBI AVRAHAM-ABBA SELIGMAN did not open his store on the intermediate days, but sat in his sukkah all day long. Bathsheva was now standing before him, on the verge of tears: he had spoken to her as he had never done before—as if entirely disregarding her feelings. It was not important, he told her, whether or not Gavriel had given his dying father his word that he would devote himself to the study of Talmud. His father would take no joy in the next world from the few hours of study forced upon his son. And the Torah did not need a student to whom the study of Talmud was a torment and whose mind was closed to the pages of the Codes. With each passing day Gavriel was learning less and less and his resentment becoming greater. Perhaps there was more to be gained if he were to live with his uncle.

"But he would not study at all in his uncle's house," Bathsheva protested angrily, tears in her eyes. "My brother-in-law wants him to marry his eldest daughter."

"Fine, then, that's fine," Reb Avraham-Abba replied. "If his uncle wants to become his father-in-law too, he will watch over him and guide him onto the right path. I think Gavriel will fear him more than you or me. He will obey his father-in-law."

Bathsheva saw things quite differently: As little as Gavriel respected his mother and his teacher, he would still be more faithful to his father's dying wishes while living near them than in the home of an uncle who considered those wishes foolish to begin with. Besides, she did not want to be separated from her only son, and she was amazed that the Rabbi did not seem to understand this.

On her way back home, a shaken and distressed Bathsheva reflected that Gavriel might not even ask for her approval of his marriage to his uncle's daughter. He could even let himself be talked into marrying a girl he did not care for. He was a light-headed and spoiled child, a free-spirited, irresponsible boy. Even Asna's young man had more character than her Gavriel. . . . The poor Rabbi, poor man, had a hard life, he ate only dry, cold food. How could a person live all alone like that? Why hasn't he remarried? Bathsheva was startled to find herself suddenly thinking of the Divorced Rabbi in this way, and she started to run as if her feet were racing against her confused thoughts. When she got home, she found her son and his uncle sitting in the dimly lit parlor, conversing amicably.

Baruch-Issar was speaking: "Dung must never be spread on a field when it is still fresh. Before you use it, it has to remain in the stalls under the cows for at least three months. That's why you have to have a well-built barn with lots of straw on the ground. Of course, it would be easier to keep the dung in heaps outside, but that creates other problems. Lying in the wind and under the sun and rain, it tends either to crumble away or else to become rock-hard. Then the only thing you can do is bury it in a big ditch . . ."

"If you want to go, you can go." His mother's voice startled Gavriel. "But I will not answer your letters, and if you get married, I will not come to the wedding."

Gavriel quickly rose and then just as quickly sat down, his eyes glued to his uncle, who was slowly scratching his beard. Baruch-Issar had decided that there was little to be gained from arguing with his late brother's widow—he would never be able to get Gavriel to come away with him against her will, either to help him run the estate or to become his son-in-law.

"After all, Gabik, your mother is right. You should not leave home before the year of mourning for your father is over. Besides, there really isn't very much work in the fields in winter. And later? Later we'll see." Baruch-Issar winked at his nephew and loudly informed his sister-in-law that since she no longer had anything to worry about, there was no reason for them not to enjoy the rest of the holiday.

8

AUTUMN CHANGED ITS FACE several times. At first, it set the town ablaze with the dazzling colors of the foliage: flaming red, wine red and bright red copper, with all shades of orange, gold and yellow. And when the leaves fell, the sky became a cold, glistening mirror; the air was dry, hard and as clear as glass. On the stark-naked trees each branch, each little twig, stood out thin and solitary, as if drawn with a slate pencil on a tablet. Soon the gray clouds began to descend, and a milky-white mist drifted upward. A thick, driving rain fell ceaselessly, pummeling the pavement and drenching passers-by in the streets. Everything was saturated with dampness, and with the rotting odor of waterlogged wood.

At last, the clouds exhausted themselves and the sun shone once again. The dry, pale, brassy days passed in such astonished quietude that they seemed to have lost their way in time, not knowing whether it was the onset of winter or the beginning of spring. Unexpectedly, people in the street felt an icy slipperiness underfoot and saw the walls sparkle with a coat of white frost. At first, the snow came silent and thick, as if it had been lurking in wait for the right moment to fall. Soon, however, a storm developed that whipped down flurries of frozen pellets. Well-bundled-up passers-by wrestled with the wind and with the fiendish howling in their ears.

Gavriel's mood followed a course much like the weather's. Baruch-Issar had returned home just after Sukkoth, but not before assuring his nephew that the forthcoming Passover would see him living on his estate near Libau. Gavriel's great joy and hope now inspired him to return to his Talmudic studies with renewed zeal—a demonstration to his mother and his teacher of his willingness, after all, to fulfill his father's last request.

But then, as time passed with no further word from Baruch-Issar, he began to grow uneasy; steadily, the fear deepened in him that his uncle might be reneging on his promise. Soon Gavriel's interest in Talmudic study flagged once again, and he ceased to pay attention to the Rabbi's instruction as they sat together in the beth midrash. At home, he shouted at his mother that she had been his undoing: Uncle would easily find ten agronomists to take his place, especially since he had never even finished his studies. Out of his great boredom—and, just as often, simply out of spite—Gavriel would sleep very late, no matter how often his mother would wake him and remind him that if he didn't get up soon he would miss the last morning service, and so miss saying Kaddish for his father.

Evenings he would spend with his only friend, Asna's suitor, Mulik Durmashkin—who was trying to take advantage of Gavriel's low spirits to turn him into a communist.

Mulik Durmashkin's parents owned a furniture business in which his two older brothers also worked. He, however, was studying at the University to be a radio engineer. No one in his family suspected his involvement in leftist politics, and neither did Gavriel, who had met and befriended him at the Jewish Students Union at the University, and invited him to his home.

At first, Shlomo-Zalman, who was still then in health, had nothing against this young man with the clever, smiling eyes. But as Mulik started coming to the house more often to see Asna, Shlomo-Zalman began to have reservations about him; and yet, he could find no definite grounds for this feeling, especially since Mulik behaved with perfect propriety and came calling on Asna only when the entire family was at home.

Bathsheva, for her part, had nothing against Asna's young man, except for her astonishment and disappointment at his failure to pay a visit when Asna's father was lying ill. He had not even attended the funeral. When she asked Asna about this, her daughter replied, as she usually did, with teeth clenched in anger: "Perhaps you would have also liked him to rend his clothing and mourn with us all seven days?" To Bathsheva it seemed that when Shlomo-Zalman had tried to make Asna promise to take a Talmudic scholar for a husband, he must have been thinking that she must not marry this Mulik Durmashkin. But Asna, to the contrary, became even closer to Mulik out of dread of her father's last request.

Not until Asna became a frequent guest in the Durmashkin home, and she began to be looked upon as a future daughter-in-law, did Mulik tell her about his sympathies for the Soviet Union. Asna listened to him with amazement and horror. She had been raised in a middle-class family and had attended a gymnasium, first a Hebrew and later a Polish one. Since childhood, she had heard from her father nothing but evil about the Bolsheviks—they had confiscated his entire fortune and torn his children by his first wife away from him. Asna had more than once reflected, with curiosity and wonder, that somewhere she had brothers of the same father, Red commissars who did not even want to know her. She could well imagine what her father would say, were he alive, about her having a suitor who was a leftist. But she was already deeply in love with Mulik, with all the stubborn determination and loyalty she had inherited from

her mother. She trembled with fright each time he confided in her about
the secret work he was doing "for the cause" at the city's radio factory
where he trained. Asna could not even make him promise not to reveal
his secret to her brother.

One evening, as the three of them sat together in the parlor, Mulik
began to speak at length about capitalism and the exploitation of the
working class; about the advance of the proletariat and the backwardness
of the reactionary bourgeoisie—and just look at him, Gabik Rappaport,
hanging in the air like a spider, between the Talmud and the clergy on
one side and his exploiter uncle in Latvia on the other. No matter how
much Asna signaled to Mulik with her eyes to stop, he would only smile
knowingly and continue, as if it pleased him to see how his love's beautiful gray-green eyes with their long dark eyelashes became even more
beautiful when filled with fear and anger. Mulik demanded to know why
he, Gabik Rappaport, as a member of the Jewish Students Union, had
never shown any interest in the ideological battles that raged between the
union's political factions. Why had he never been curious enough to learn
about the poverty and oppression under which the White Russian peasants lived around Vilna, in Disna and Glebokie? What did he think about
the workers at the radio factory who had recently been sentenced to long
prison terms for their political activities? Was he aware that the same
Polish sugar the poor Polish worker and peasant could not afford was
exported and sold for groschen abroad? Had he at least heard about the
peasant uprisings in the villages of western White Russia and the western
Ukraine, and their bloody suppression by the Polish Army? "I'm sure you
haven't heard. You're too busy going to the beth midrash every day,
where I wouldn't set foot even on Yom Kippur!" Mulik snapped the long
fingers of his delicate white hands. "Do you at least understand why the
president of Poland has come to Vilna now?"

"Why?" Gavriel asked as he glanced at his sister, who was sitting
with head bowed.

"The president has come to Vilna to incite the Poles and to mobilize
nationalistic feelings. The Polish regime is preparing an offensive against
the Soviet Union in order to justify annexing Soviet East Ukraine and
East White Russia and uniting them with West Ukraine and West White
Russia, which are groaning under the Polish yoke. The Polish overlords
cannot bear to see the Soviet republics of Ukraine and White Russia
living free and happy when the same people on the Polish side of the
border are oppressed and know nothing but want," Mulik declared, and
then, half joking and half serious, he asked Gavriel if he would care to

join in an illegal demonstration during the military parade the city was planning in honor of the visiting president.

Asna remained dejected and silent, and the dumfounded Gavriel also said not a word. He felt his very temples harden with terror at the thought that his sister had gotten herself involved with a communist; he knew full well that the Communist Party advocated the violent overthrow of the government, and was outlawed. Mulik could see on both the others' faces how frightened they were, and he smiled contemptuously at their petty-bourgeois cowardice. Then, with a dry laugh, he told them he was only joking—he understood all too well that they were not fighters for the revolutionary proletariat. And he quickly departed into the darkness of the night.

A wet snow fell against the windows as brother and sister sat speechless together, in a state of shock. They were both thinking of their mother, who had not yet returned from her rounds of collecting loan repayments. In the quiet of the large, dark room they imagined that even the old furniture around them was having restless thoughts.

"You can see and marry whomever you wish, but not him. Not if you have any pity for Mother," Gavriel murmured, so gravely that he seemed suddenly to have aged twenty years.

Asna answered in a tearful voice that she loved Mulik and would marry no one else. She despised the "golden" young men—God help us!—those bags of wind, those big-bellied fops who stared with bovine eyes at any female that came along. Mulik was a principled person, very well read and loyal to himself and his convictions. She believed he would yet change his political opinions; he did not, after all, actually belong to the Communist Party, he was only an active sympathizer. If he really believed everything he said, he would have sought out a girl who was a party member.

To Gavriel, as he listened carefully, there were evident contradictions in what Asna was saying. Nonetheless, they both agreed on one thing: Mother must not find out about this, just as Mulik's own parents were unaware that their son was an illegal leftist and activist. After that night, Gavriel felt as if he was aging with worry about his sister, and he ceased to be angry with his mother.

The income from the repayment of Shlomo-Zalman's loans was no longer enough to support the Rappaports, so Bathsheva started to deal in new and used canvas sacks. Her customers were the same grain merchants who had done business with her late husband, and a hired laborer delivered the sacks. She had told her children several times that they

might have to leave their luxurious apartment in the courtyard on Portowa Street, and move into a smaller dwelling in a poorer section, where
the rent would be half as much. Her children both agreed, but Bathsheva,
eager to hold on to everything that reminded her of the many happy years
with her husband, did not hurry the move.

Every evening, Bathsheva returned home either rain-soaked or snow-
covered and frozen. It broke Gavriel's heart just to look at his mother,
who only a year earlier had looked like his older sister. Now her face was
haggard and pale, her hair had grayed, the sparkle in her eyes had been
extinguished. Gavriel had wanted to help her in the business, in buying
and selling the sacks, but she replied sternly that she would give him no
excuse to abandon his studies. And she would smile at him lovingly and
sufferingly, the way she had years before during the long fast of Yom
Kippur, when, as a little boy, he would be at her side in the women's section of the synagogue and would interrupt her prayers.

One morning, Asna, still in her nightgown and robe, woke her
brother and, with lips trembling, whispered to him to go quickly into
Mother's room.

Bathsheva was sitting on the bed in which Shlomo-Zalman had lain
ill and died. As a widow, she had at first refused so much as to touch any
of his things, and would not even walk on that part of the floor where he
had lain before the funeral, covered by a black cloth. Lately, however,
she had begun using his things and sleeping in his bed, as if she thought
she could in this way be reunited with him. Now, as she sat on the
bed—her face so pale she seemed like someone just emerging, after a
long, hard struggle, from an illness in which she had hung suspended
between life and death—she told her children of the nightmare from
which she had just awakened:

She saw her Shlomo-Zalman coming down from the cemetery hill in
his shrouds. It was winter and a deep snow covered everything. He was
walking briskly toward the city, but the faster he walked, the longer grew
the tree-lined path between the tombstones. At first, she followed him, but
then she saw that the cemetery stretched on without end, and he was
getting weary and beginning to falter, bent forward and barely trudging
on. So she started to run after him and shouted, "Shlomo-Zalman! Where
are you going? Stop and you'll see that the cemetery will end!" She had
no idea what she had meant by this, and could not remember whether she
had really shouted it or merely thought it. But he—may he stay away
from the living—did not turn around to her, but continued walking
through the cemetery, over the unending paths through the tombstones,

as if all the buildings of the city had been transformed into gravestones. Terror-stricken, she ran after him, breathless, with her last ounce of strength, until at last she fell, and awoke. . . .

"Don't miss a Kaddish, and study diligently, Gavriel, and Father will rest peacefully in the next world and not have to wander about restlessly in his shrouds," Bathsheva told her son, in a voice pained and drawn, as if the eerie pathways of the cemetery still stretched out before her eyes.

Gavriel returned to the beth midrash of the Old Age Home near his home on Portowa Street and studied on his own from morning till night, and then would go to the beth midrash on Straszuna Street for his lesson with Rabbi Seligman. Gone were the dazzling displays of devouring a page of Talmud and immediately reciting it by heart, or of anticipating the Rabbi's every distinction and question concerning the text and brilliantly answering them. Gone, too, were the idle chatter, the stories and the childish laughter; Gavriel now studied slowly, patiently, methodically, and with great concentration, and without so much embellishment as the traditional chanting of the text. Only, from time to time, his mind would wander and he would think about his uncle, who did not write to him; about his mother, who was working even harder; about his sister, who was becoming more involved with Mulik. Every day after work Asna ran off to see her Mulik. And in the evening, when brother and sister sat quietly in the parlor, they looked knowingly at each other, their somber eyes mirroring their fears over Mulik Durmashkin's secret activities. But they breathed not a word about it, not to their mother, not even to each other.

9

PURIM MARKED THE END of the year of mourning for Shlomo-Zalman Rappaport. Although his widow continued to wear black, his son felt the gloom that had seeped into his bones melt away and disappear like the snow outside. The ice on the Wilja had cracked and cold, dark rivulets gushed and rattled between the large split blocks of ice. With a tremor, the leafless trees raised their bare branches brimming with sap, in anticipation of their first yellow and pink buds.

The mild and vaporous weather and the deep blue sky towering overhead intoxicated Gavriel. As for Asna, with the onset of spring and the advent of the political demonstrations of the first of May, she was in a fever of mingled love and fear for Mulik. But Gavriel refused to worry about his mother or his sister—or about his teacher, who waited for him every evening in the beth midrash. He stopped thinking as well about his uncle Baruch-Issar, who had not invited him to his estate in Latvia. One morning, instead, Gavriel went to the horticultural gardens in Soltaniszki on the outskirts of Vilna.

The owner of the hothouses, Godl Wilenczek—a middle-aged man with shrewd eyes, a narrow forehead under his disheveled stubby cowlick, and a mouth habituated to coarseness and profanity—had done business with Gavriel's father, and so greeted him as if he were a member of the family. When Gavriel told him that he would like to learn farm work, Godl took him to the greenhouses, where the peasant girls were removing tiny cucumber plants from small clay pots and planting them in the soil of the greenhouse. Wilenczek, as usual, prodded the girls to work faster, and complained to Gavriel:

"Vilna is Siberia! You have to knock yourself out to get cucumbers here early in the season . . . Your father, now, there was an honest man. If he told you the seeds were a few years old, you could be absolutely certain they would not produce just a bunch of leaves. The other seed merchants are all thieves. Their word isn't worth a dog's bark."

He then began yelling at the girls—at one for potting the roots of a plant too deeply; at another for drowning a plant with an entire can of water instead of a light sprinkle; and he snatched the pot from a third for re-potting a plant that was too shriveled.

"What are you bitches good for, besides rolling in the grass with boys and having bastards?" he roared as he stalked out in his tall boots to another field, where workers were sawing boards, building wooden boxes, and installing glass panes in the new greenhouses.

The girls working on Wilenczek's estate came from the outskirts of Vilna or the nearby villages. They all cast furtive glances at the well-dressed young master, then winked at each other and giggled. As for Gavriel, he didn't know what to look at first: at the bent-over forms of the peasant girls—their breasts like pumpkins, their broad behinds bobbing in the air, their fleshy feet set firmly on the ground and far apart—or at the transplanting work they were doing. He trod on heaps of steamy dung, on piles of cut lumber and over spools of wire. He slipped on the leaves of last year's plants, which had been thrown out to make room for new ones. The air was filled with the odor of rotting vegetation, but Gavriel drew it in greedily through his widened nostrils. His eyes could not imbibe enough sunbeams as the light flickered and flashed on the hundreds of panes of the open greenhouse windows.

Suddenly he felt something soft and slippery slap his cheek and heard resounding laughter behind him. A girl had pulled a broad, rotten lettuce leaf out of a pot, but instead of casting it aside, she had thrown it, ostensibly by accident, into the young master's face. She turned toward him her own dirt-covered, freckled face, with its short, slightly upturned nose, and stared at him with impudent eyes that darted blue flames. She raised her elbows over her head, as if merely to stretch and straighten her heavy body, but in the process giving the young man a better look at her firm, broad, fleshy figure through her short and flimsy dress. Gavriel, confused and ashamed, yet delighted, smiled good-naturedly; his blood was boiling, and he had to make a special effort to recall anything of what he had learned about horticulture during his few semesters at the University. He sought out Godl Wilenczek and asked him if he could come there every day to learn and to help.

"It would be my pleasure." Godl Wilenczek spread his arms wide. "But the way I heard it, you were studying with the Divorced Rabbi—the shopkeeper across the lumber yard—and you were thinking of becoming a rabbi yourself."

"I only studied with him during the year of mourning for my father. But what I want is to work the land, not to be a rabbi."

As Gavriel walked home, he was thinking that he must remember not to dress like a city fool when he went to the fields. The first thing he would do when he got home, he decided, would be to look for his boots, his hat, and the jacket he wore when he would go with his father to the landowner in Landwarow. He walked with a feeling of excitement and renewed vigor. Every so often he would stop to feel the bark of the trees that lined the road and to listen to the hum of the telegraph wires. His mind too was humming, with happy thoughts, as if the veins in his temples had themselves become telegraph wires.

Gavriel did not conceal where he had been from his mother. He told her that he planned to go there every day to work . . . and would she please let him live. It was because of her stubbornness that he had fallen a year behind in his studies. Now he wanted some practical farming experience and then he would look for a way to re-matriculate at the University. He was surely not going to be a yeshiva student! Bathsheva knew the gardener from Soltaniszki, and knew only too well that he was anything but a refined man. But she also remembered Reb Avraham-Abba's recent warning:

"Though your son has spent the entire winter studying Talmud, he has studied without joy. With each day he has sunk deeper and deeper into despair, as if sinking into a black stream. And when a young man studies without joy, it's no good—no, it's absolutely no good!"

It pleased Godl Wilenczek to have so learned a young man following him around the estate like a pet calf. They would both crawl in a field where cabbage was about to be planted and pat with their bare hands the dung that had been spread, to see if it was thick enough or if still more was needed. After the field was plowed, harrowed, and flattened with a smooth wooden roller, Gavriel displayed his intelligence by determining how best to checker the field and set up the rows so that the cabbage heads would have enough room to grow. Wilenczek, absolutely delighted, slapped Gavriel on the back and shouted, "Where there's Torah, there's wisdom." When the girls saw that their boss was treating the young master like a younger brother, they began to sidle up to him and smile mysterious yet meaningful smiles.

When the time came to transfer the cabbages from the hothouse pots into the fields, great care had to be taken not to transplant the blackened stems along with the rest of the plant. Gavriel would feel the plants, smelling their leaves and gazing out onto the furrowed fields with as much pleasure as he did at the healthy peasant girls. He became more and more drunk with the air and the sunshine; he wanted to run and shout for joy. Even when clouds filled the sky and only long, pointed sunbeams could pierce through the cloud cover, they seared his heart and ignited within him a desire, a fever. To conceal the yearning that caused beads of sweat to form on his face and neck, he would look up at the sky and talk to Wilenczek in such deep and solemn tones that one might have thought the sedate young man to be his partner of many years.

"If it rains hard, the stems will rot."

"Yes, we still have plenty to worry about," said Wilenczek. "When the white butterflies begin to appear, you have to crawl between the beds and crush the little yellow eggs like this," clicking his fingers together in demonstration. He then launched into complaints about the customers who bought the early cabbages: "If you give them hard round heads, they want only the flat ones. Yellow fever! Yellow fever with a kosher shroud, that's what I'll give them! ...

"Tell me, Gavriel, are your mother and your Rabbi happy that you are working here for me? People say that the Divorced Rabbi is a tzaddik. In the summertime I bring my produce to his store, so I wouldn't want him to have anything against me."

"What are you talking about? My mother and the Rabbi are very happy," Gavriel replied anxiously, hoping Godl Wilenczek would not discover that he hadn't even asked his Rabbi if he could work on his fields.

His reverence for so holy a Jew as Rabbi Avraham-Abba Seligman did not deter Godl Wilenczek from eating non-kosher food. When he and Gavriel sat on overturned wooden boxes in the middle of the field to eat, and Gavriel would ask him if the salami was kosher, Wilenczek, his mouth stuffed with food, would dismiss the question with a wave of the hand. "Don't ask! The main thing is to be a good chum, to have a good shot of vodka and to enjoy what you eat, and leave the rest of the mumbo-jumbo to the Divorced Rabbi. Let *him* observe it all. L'chaim!" And after downing his drink, he rolled up a few slices of his non-kosher salami and placed them gleefully on his outstretched tongue.

More than any other girl working in the fields, the one who had jokingly thrown a lettuce leaf in his face that first day continually hovered around Gavriel. She would look brazenly at him with a teasing blue sparkle in her eyes, as if she felt that this refined, urbane young man with the childlike face and the honey-sweet lips yearned only for her—for her, the coarse and shameless, the daring and shapely. And she would deliberately work near him, stopping with a heavy earth-filled wooden box in her hands to show him how well the plants took to the ground with hard, short roots. As she set the wooden boxes on the ground and unashamedly bent her broad body over the furrows, she jostled him as if accidentally, first with an elbow, then with her knee. Gavriel glanced about to make sure no one was looking and grabbed the peasant girl by her broad, muscular shoulders. The girl, purring with delight, gazed at him calmly with a knowing, experienced look, waiting for him to tell her where and when they would meet. But then fear suddenly overtook him, and he stammered like a lost little boy, babbling something about not planting potato buds too early, they could freeze in the late frost of spring. He was relieved when Godl Wilenczek called him from the other side of the field, giving him an excuse to leave the peasant girl, who was still throwing sly, mischievous glances at him. After he had stepped away from her, he turned and saw the girl still looking after him with a curious and earnest expression. Gavriel sensed that had he asked her, she would tell no one about any secret meetings they might have. But he was upset at himself for being so shy, for allowing the Talmud and his upbringing to prevent him from doing what all the other boys in the field did without a second thought.

More than anyone else Gavriel admired Godl Wilenczek—for his knowledge of agriculture, for his robust way of life, and even for his big mouth. In the evening he liked to recount for his mother and sister the outrageous things Godl had said during the course of the day, and he always concluded that he liked this raucous gardener from Soltaniszki better than his uncle in Latvia, who was more businessman than agronomist. Asna, as usual, was furious with her brother, for being so weak in character that anyone could win him over. But his mother's heart ached even more over her brilliant son's associating with such a boorish rogue.

"And is this wonderful boss of yours a good Jew, too?" she asked. "Does he at least pray every morning and eat kosher?"

"He's not a bad man, and the important thing is, he's a healthy fellow who knows how to enjoy life," answered Gavriel. "Who cares if he prays every day or eats kosher?"

One day in May, Godl Wilenczek had to go into town to attend to some business, so he left Gavriel in charge of the fields. On the way back home, the gardener stopped his wagon in front of Rabbi Avraham-Abba Seligman's grocery store. Whip in hand, he strode into the store with an expansive "Good morning," confidently expecting the Divorced Rabbi to give him a basketful of praise for his good deeds.

"It's me, the potato man! Did you know that your student is studying with me to be a gardener? You may not be able to make a rabbinic hat from a sow's tail, but out of a page of Talmud you can make anything. Why, in just a short time Gavrielka has grasped the essentials of gardening better than all the peasants who have ever worked for me put together. This summer, Rabbi, you will have the satisfaction of knowing that the vegetables you buy from me were grown with the help of the student you sent to my estate."

"And how is he conducting himself?" Reb Avraham-Abba asked quietly, as if he had indeed sent Gavriel to Godl Wilenczek.

"He is living the life," Wilenczek laughed. "The shiksas swoon over him, and the peasant boys chew last year's straw because they're all jealous of him." Suddenly he stopped, realizing he had babbled too much. "What difference does it make how he's acting? I am making good use of him, and he's making good use of me, too. I'll make him a wealthy man yet, don't you worry."

Seeing the storekeeper, this pious fanatic, standing cold and silent, Wilenczek too fell silent, fidgeting with the whip in his hands. Was this how he was repaid for his kindness? Then, just to spite the Divorced Rabbi, he laughed even more boisterously. "And what if Gavrielka is the son of the Hassid Shlomo-Zalman Rappaport—does that mean he has to put his teeth in a glass every night? Must he run from a girl like a demon from incense? Ha, ha, ha!"

Reb Avraham-Abba recoiled from these words as if someone had hung a side of non-kosher beef in his store. He said nothing until Wilenczek—and the stench of his hutzpah—had gone. Then the Rabbi hastily closed the store, as though he had suddenly remembered that this was a minor fast day and he had to return to the synagogue for the penitential prayers. As long as he had had nothing more than a suspicion, he had not wanted to put the widow Rappaport through the ordeal of having to ask Gavriel do something he would very likely refuse to do. But now that he knew definitely with whom Gavriel was associating, he was greatly alarmed: he had no choice but to go to her and warn her to take her son away from that ungodly place. And if he should not find her home, he thought, he would leave a note on her door telling her not to fail to come to see him.

As it happened, Bathsheva and Asna were both home when Reb Avraham-Abba arrived—both of them looking extremely dejected. But the Rabbi took no notice, and spoke with an almost otherworldly voice, shrouded in piety, as if emerging from a deep well. Bathsheva, he declared urgently, must get her son away from the Soltaniszki estate immediately, there was not a moment to lose. He had just found out that her son was mixed up with very bad company there. The issue was no longer whether Gavriel was going to be a Talmudic scholar, but whether among those loose peasants he wouldn't abandon the right path entirely. Gavriel was young and naïve, so the danger was great, very great, that he might go astray and do things that would shame him and bring dishonor to his family. There was only one thing to do: Bathsheva must write to her brother-in-law in Latvia and ask him to invite his nephew there as soon as possible. And then Avraham-Abba, having already spoken longer than was his custom, concluded, "It is my responsibility to your late husband, and my responsibility to you, that I warn you before it's too late."

Bathsheva didn't know what to worry about first: what Reb Avraham-Abba had just told her, or the news she was about to give him. That morning, after Gavriel had left for Soltaniszki, Asna's future mother-in-law had come running to her, weeping because Mulik had been arrested.

Until that moment, Mulik's parents had had no idea that their son was an active communist, and neither had Asna until recently, Bathsheva told him as she wrung her hands.

"But my Shlomo-Zalman knew better than anyone that if Gavriel were to study to be an agronomist and work with the peasants in the fields, he would become like them. And he also saw long before any of us what kind of boy Asna was getting involved with. That's why he wanted her to promise she would marry a Talmudic scholar. He knew how far our children might stray without his guidance."

Asna sat in a corner, looking pale, disheveled, utterly defeated; she kept silent, but she was furious with Mulik for ruining their happiness. Suddenly, she sprang out of her chair, screeching "Mother!," and ran out of the room. Bathsheva sat heartbroken and speechless, shaking her head as if she were once again in mourning for her Shlomo-Zalman. And Reb Avraham-Abba also stood sternly silent—his arms folded just as they had been a year earlier when he had visited her sick husband and, standing in that very same room, had told her that since Shlomo-Zalman was fully aware of his condition, she must not try to deceive him into believing that he would recover.

10

THE WIDOW RAPPAPORT became still grayer after her son left to join his uncle in Latvia and her daughter, once his wealthy parents had gotten Mulik Durmashkin out of jail, went off with him to Paris.

Bathsheva had followed all of Rabbi Seligman's advice, so convinced was she that every word his lips uttered would inevitably come to pass. Had she only listened to him before, and allowed Gavriel to leave with his uncle earlier, she would not have had to move heaven and earth to get Baruch-Issar to invite his nephew in the first place, and to get Gavriel to agree to go, in the second. As regarded her brother-in-law, she could not be certain whether he was simply putting on an act or had indeed changed his mind about Gavriel. And Gavriel, for his part, had become so attached to Godl Wilenczek and his peasant workers that it seemed for a while impossible to tear him away from them. It was only his curiosity about his uncle's estate and his daughters—and perhaps, too, his mother's tears—that had finally persuaded Gavriel to go.

Matters had been quite different, however, with Asna. She had never for a moment considered breaking off with Mulik or not leaving with him, and she refused to listen to a single word her mother spoke to her. Bathsheva ran again and again to Reb Avraham-Abba, weeping and groaning: "For heaven's sake, the boy is a communist! Asna's father would sooner have disowned his daughter than consent to her marrying such a boy, let alone leaving the country with him! Shlomo-Zalman always carried a wound in his heart over his children by his first wife—they were torn away from him and they remained in Russia. So what would he have thought of Asna's behavior?"

To this Reb Avraham-Abba replied that it did not matter what her late husband would have thought—he would never have changed Asna's mind. Besides, it stood to reason that if Mulik had really been a communist, his parents would never have been able to buy his way out of prison, even by bribing the police; even the greatest lawyer could not have gotten him out if he had truly been an important red agitator. So it was clear, then, that he had never actually done anything, except to associate with leftists—or at least hadn't yet had the chance to do anything. And since his parents felt he should leave the country so he wouldn't end up in prison again, and they had even promised to support the couple, Bathsheva ought to give them her blessing and just make sure they were properly married before they left. It also stood to reason that the boy's parents would feel the same way.

Afterward, Bathsheva was amazed to consider how Reb Avraham-Abba should have been able to figure things out so accurately from behind the counter of his grocery store, bent over his tomes. Mulik's parents insisted along with Bathsheva that the couple marry before leaving Poland, so a canopy was quickly put up and the ceremony hastily performed. Seeing them off at the railway station, Mulik's mother, a broad-beamed woman with a large head and short-cropped hair, hugged her new daughter-in-law in her fleshy arms so tightly that Asna nearly snapped like a thin, dry twig. "Take care of him, your husband, and don't let him jump into the fire again," the mother-in-law cried.

As for Bathsheva, when she looked at her son-in-law, with his long, delicate fingers and his dry, angular face, she could not believe that Asna would have much control over such a man. The thought that her daughter would not be happy filled Bathsheva's pain-darkened eyes with tears, and abruptly she astonished herself by quietly asking something she knew she should not have asked: "Asna, how can you leave me here alone?" The question visibly perturbed Asna, but instead of following her feelings, she screwed up her face and in her usual way shot back a sarcastic remark—one that her mother would never forget:

"But you're not being left alone; you have your friend, the shop-keeper—Rabbi Avraham-Abba Seligman."

THE HIGH HOLY DAYS were once again approaching. How time flies, Bathsheva thought: Gavriel had left before Shavuoth and Asna right after Tishah B'Av, yet it all seemed like only yesterday. She could not under-stand how she had managed without the children—may they live and be well—for so long. The year before, around this time, just before Sukkoth, her brother-in-law, Baruch-Issar, had come to visit. His plan to take Gabik back with him to Latvia was heaven-sent, Rabbi Seligman had said, and, as usual, he was right.

True, it appeared from Gavriel's early letters that he was not es-pecially happy in his new home. But just recently he had asked his mother to come to see him as soon as possible, for things had developed between him and his uncle's eldest daughter, Ettele, for which congratulations would soon be in order. He also wrote that he was informing Rabbi Seligman in a separate letter. In his early letters the "good" student had not even sent his teacher his regards, so angry was he at Reb Avraham-Abba for having instigated his leaving Godl Wilenczek and the Sol-taniszki fields. But now Bathsheva went to see the shopkeeper to ask him if he thought she should go to her son's engagement.

When Bathsheva arrived at Rabbi Seligman's grocery, however, she found it closed. She stood still, gazing at the bar across the storefront with its padlock as if she had nowhere else to go. The heels and the points of her shoes were crooked, and she had on the same black hat and coat she had worn through the year of mourning, though she had closets filled with clothes and shoes. The gray, overcast day became even darker in her eyes as a raindrop or two fell onto her face. She remained standing motionless in front of the big locked door, wondering where she would be able to find the Rabbi now. A large, cold drop struck her temple—and suddenly she remembered that there was a beth midrash in this courtyard where he lived and worked, that very same little beth midrash where he had taught Gavriel. Lately, he had been closing the store earlier and earlier to go to the beth midrash.

Since she had known him, she reflected, he had not changed: the same stubby gray beard that did not get either longer or shorter, or even grayer; the same attire; and, if she was not mistaken, it was always the same book into which he would be squinting as he stood in his store. He never seemed sad when he was alone with his tomes—only when he was among people. So why, she pondered, did she bring every little problem to him and disturb his studies?

Nonetheless, off Bathsheva went to the little beth midrash and, sure enough, she found Reb Avraham-Abba, bent over a large tract of Talmud. Vexed by his none-too-friendly expression and his furrowed brow, she barely managed to stammer that she was deserving of a mazal tov: Gavriel was marrying his uncle's eldest daughter and wanted his mother to be there for the engagement. Should she go?

"Yes, I know. Gavriel wrote to me too about it. Of course you should go," Reb Avraham-Abba murmured, and Bathsheva felt a pain in her heart at the impatient way he spoke to her, without the slightest regret or concern, as if her leaving meant nothing to him. But, she argued, perhaps she ought not to go. Her son, after all, had not asked for her blessing to the marriage, his letter hadn't even said anything about the sort of girl the bride was. Wouldn't it be enough for her to be at the wedding? Was there any law that a mother must attend the engagement? Besides, it was so complicated to go abroad, it wasn't easy to get a passport to leave the country. Bathsheva pleaded with Reb Avraham-Abba to change his verdict, but he only answered in a more forceful, even angry, tone—very much out of character for him, she thought—that she must do everything she can to be present for her son's engagement and she should stay there until after the wedding.

As Bathsheva made her way home, a bitter, defeated smile played on her pale face. She thought of her daughter's latest letter from Paris, in which she wrote that so far Mulik had neither work nor a position. "Yet life is merry in Paris," she wrote, "and I am certain, Mother, that things aren't too gloomy for you either." No doubt Asna had in mind her own remark at the railway station about her mother's having a friend in Rabbi Seligman. And yet, he had never before acted so unfriendly to her as he had that day. Could it be that he was afraid people might talk, that she was visiting his store too frequently?

A neighbor of Bathsheva's came out of the gate, an open umbrella in her hand, and stared in amazement, uncertain whether this was indeed Madame Rappaport or only a poor woman who looked like Madame Rappaport. Bathsheva entered the courtyard gates and gazed up at her windows on the third floor as if wondering whether she still lived there. She imagined that behind all the other curtained windows lived happy families, that only from her windows emanated the mute sorrow of empty rooms. Why did she have to live in a house with such a stately entrance? A woman as small and thin as she was could slide into a house with a low, narrow door. And why a home with such large rooms, high ceilings, and a mirror that ran the entire length of the parlor? She could tuck her hair under her hat before going out and look at her aging face in a small mirror just as well. And now that the children had gone, she still wasn't selling any of her furniture and housewares because . . . she thought she might yet need some of it for a new household. Rabbi Avraham-Abba Seligman must have guessed what she was dreaming, and that was why he became so irritated with her.

Bathsheva opened her door and was greeted by an eerie silence. For the first time she could remember, she had a grievance against her late husband: How had he failed to understand that when children were raised in a richly appointed house and attended the gymnasium, even their own father could not overturn everything in one day—not even on his deathbed—and make a rabbi out of his son and make his daughter marry one? And, it would seem, a widow from such a rich house was also unfit for a rabbi.

11

IT HAD BEEN over sixteen years since his wife, Hodel, had left him, and in all that time Reb Avraham-Abba had given no thought to remarrying. Since he had found it in accordance with Jewish law that he remain without a wife, the notion was no longer a part of his world—a world that consisted solely of the beth midrash, his home, and his grocery store, all within the confines of the same courtyard on Straszuna Street. When a customer would ask him if he had seen the latest news in the newspaper, he would answer that a person did not have to know everything. And when a woman neighbor would good-naturedly scold him for not taking walks and getting some fresh air on Friday evenings during the summer, as did all the other fine Jews of the courtyard, he would reply that, much as he would like to, he had no time. The woman would laugh: the wholesalers and the market dealers bring his merchandise right into the store; the customers take what they need and weigh everything themselves, and he never raises his eyes from his Talmud . . . and still he says he has no time to take a little walk on Friday evening. How much Torah is there to learn, after all? He never went to a neighbor for the Sabbath Kiddush Saturday morning, and he never invited anyone to his own home. He would not even allow a neighbor to cook a meal for him. They would look at him and marvel: So robust a man, no evil eye!—and he's never sick. May the Almighty protect him.

Reb Avraham-Abba was indifferent to his neighbors' attentions. Nor did the widow Rappaport stir up any special thoughts or feelings within him: He had taught her son Talmud, but only because it was her dying husband's request. She also sought his advice concerning her daughter. After the children had gone, however, and Bathsheva continued to come to him with her problems, he slowly came to understand that the widow had become attached to him. Not until then did he begin to see the woman in her, and he recalled what the Sages of the Talmud had to say on the subject of women, both the good and the bad. He also began to think about his divorced wife, Hodel. He had, some years before, repaid the money she had given him to run the store when she left for Kovno. But he had never been able to learn if she had found the right husband— her *zivug*, her true life-partner. Now the thought weighed heavily on his mind: if Hodel had not yet remarried and then heard that he was about to stand again beneath the canopy with someone else, she would curse him for having ruined her life.

As he was turning the matter over in his mind, a letter from his student arrived unexpectedly, informing him that he was about to marry and that he was asking his mother to attend the engagement. Reb Avraham-Abba read the letter with rejoicing. While the widow Rappaport was away at her son's engagement, she would have a chance to sort out her situation more clearly and decide if she was really ready to marry such an old-fashioned Jew, and he would be able to ascertain the fate of his first wife. It was for this reason that he had spoken to Bathsheva so harshly when she had come and told him of her reluctance to go to Gavriel's engagement—in no way did he wish to come between a mother and her only son.

A month later, Bathsheva visited him once again, to tell him that she had all the necessary papers and would soon be leaving for Latvia. Reb Avraham-Abba understood that she had stayed away from him an entire month because of the angry tone he had used to her; this time, therefore, he spoke with all the kindness and warmth he could muster:

"Go in good health, and have faith in the Almighty that He knows what He is doing. If you should want to—and be able to—remain with your son in Libau, then regard it as a matter of Providence. And if you should want to return, then that too will be God's will."

Bathsheva smiled uncertainly and was about to ask him what he meant, when—perhaps also by the intercession of Divine Providence—a customer came in, ending their conversation for the moment. While the customer rummaged through the shelves, Reb Avraham-Abba took note that Bathsheva was dressed well, warmly and even fashionably: she was wearing a gray winter coat with a broad fur collar, tall boots, a deep round hat, and woolen gloves, and was carrying a large black handbag. He was pleased to see that she understood the importance of dressing well for her in-laws. What he could not understand was how he, an older man, a divorced rabbi, had found favor in her eyes.

After Bathsheva left for Latvia, Reb Avraham-Abba wrote to an old friend from his yeshiva days, now living in Kelem, and to the Rav of Kibart where he had married Hodel, asking them if they knew whether his former wife had remarried. Throughout his years of solitude, Reb Avraham-Abba had never noticed the passage of time, so engrossed was he in prayer and study, his days passed in the store and his evenings in the beth midrash, in more prayer and more study. But that winter he counted the days and the weeks until he received a letter—not from his friend in Kelem or the Rav of Kibart, but from his student, Gavriel, informing him that the engagement had taken place and that the wedding was set for the third night of Hanukah. Gavriel wrote also that he spent several hours every evening studying Talmud, and sometimes the entire day, since in the winter there was little work to be done in the fields. He said nothing, however, about his mother's plans or how long she would be staying. "Well, it really isn't so important for me to know," Reb Avraham-Abba shrugged. Yet he was upset in spite of himself, and annoyed with Gavriel for not having written more about his mother; he was also disturbed at not having heard from Lithuania whether his divorced wife had remarried.

On the third night of Hanukah, Reb Avraham-Abba was persistently mindful, even as he lit the menorah candles, that this was the night of Gavriel Rappaport's wedding in distant Libau, and that at that very moment his widowed mother, tears in her eyes, might well be leading him down the aisle to the canopy. In an old, worn coat and a flat cloth hat, the recluse shopkeeper stood in the flickering light of the menorah and sang in a low voice the *Ma'oz Tzur Y'shu'ati*—"Rock of Ages, My Salvation."

He had lately, to his own bemusement, found himself overcome by a strong desire to have someone standing next to him to answer "amen" when he recited the Friday-night Kiddush, or to have another singing with him on Hanukah when he lit the menorah. Through the double windows, sealed for the winter except for the one small pane that could be opened for ventilation, he saw the lights of other menorahs flickering through the frosted panes. The stars in the sky twinkled a pale green, shimmering with a quiet, holy reverence. Across the empty courtyard was cast the long shadow of a neighbor trying to open the door of a snow-covered bin of firewood. Reb Avraham-Abba walked away from the window, shivering: cold! He should have lit the oven, but lately he had found it difficult to do the housework that would ordinarily be the task of a wife.

Gavriel's mother was truly to be admired, he thought. When her husband was alive, she had a maid to do all the housework, but now that he was gone, she did everything herself with not a word of complaint. And so? . . . Reb Avraham-Abba stood in the middle of the room with a furrowed brow and a perplexed look, as if he had lost the thread of an argument in the Talmud, and then he recalled once again that this was the night of Gavriel's wedding. . . . Would his mother be staying on with him or would she be returning? His mind dwelt persistently on this subject. And again he grumbled in spite of himself, upset to find himself preoccupied with these strange thoughts instead of delighting in the miracle of Hanukah. And with a grunt, he trudged into the kitchen to fix himself some dinner.

At the beginning of the mid-winter month of Teveth, Reb Avraham-Abba received two letters on the same day: one from the Rav of Kibart and the other from his old friend in Kelem. The Rav's letter said simply that Hodel had left Kibart some time ago, and that he did not know where she was or if she had remarried. But his old yeshiva friend wrote that, after many inquiries, he had found out that Hodel had long since remarried and was now living in Anikst. Good friend that he was, the classmate went on to say that he understood Reb Avraham-Abba's intent in asking after Hodel: to see if he might yet be able to remarry his former wife; but, sad to say, Reb Avraham-Abba had come to this decision too late. And to console him, his friend concluded the letter with a few homiletic remarks on the Talmudic discussion concerning one who takes back the wife he had previously divorced.

Reb Avraham-Abba, however, was, to the contrary, elated to learn that Hodel had remarried and found happiness as he had hoped. Now he became even more restless with thinking about the widow Rappaport; such thoughts even disrupted his strict daily routine. Instead of immersing himself in a rabbinic tract, as he had always done while standing behind the counter in his store, he now leafed through a notebook of his in which he had written moral thoughts and commitments which he had resolved to carry out in life.

The women who came to the store to shop rummaged as usual through the cluttered shelves, talking loudly and arguing incessantly. All the while Reb Avraham-Abba stood quietly behind the counter and did not lift his eyes from the book in which he had for these many years inscribed his life's moral accounting and taken stock of his soul:

"Put on tefillin every day." Blessed be the Lord, he had fulfilled that pledge. "Not speaking ill of others or otherwise taking time from Torah study." He had been careful and successful in fulfilling the first half of that resolution, he thought, but as for the second half, he only wished he had as many intercessors in heaven as there had been times he had needlessly interrupted his study. "Not to laugh at anyone, even good-naturedly; to keep a distance from people and to love solitude." And at the top of every page Reb Avraham-Abba had written, in the elaborate sacred script of the Torah scroll, one particular principle of the Sages: "What is man's end in this world? Only to make himself dumb. Only to make himself into a deaf-mute." These words illuminated every page of his diary like lanterns shining through the darkness from every corner of benighted streets.

Reb Avraham-Abba sighed deeply: this teaching had always been a source of torment for him. He had indeed always yearned to journey through life like a deaf-mute. That was why he had not become a rav—a rav must listen to all that the world has to say, and he must say a great deal himself; but a storekeeper need not say anything. True, a merchant cannot be a complete recluse or keep completely silent, yet he need not be embroiled in the affairs and politics of a townful of congregants.

Even so, one thing was clear: one cannot be a deaf-mute to one's wife. That was why Hodel had been unable to live with him and had always complained that he did not care that there was a war going on, that governments were being toppled, that the value of the currency kept falling. The only thing he knew, she would shout, was to stand over her like a watchman and make sure she wasn't overcharging for the merchandise. Bathsheva Rappaport was certainly a different sort of a woman, but she would never be able to accept so silent and withdrawn a man as he, any more than Hodel could, especially now that the children had left and she was all alone. He would have to be close to her and become more communicative. And yet, even if he desired this, was it in his nature to do it?

Reb Avraham-Abba closed the notebook and shrugged his shoulders. What had become of him? he asked himself. His life had become a dream within a dream. She probably wasn't planning on returning; she would stay with her son. So what sense did it make for him to wonder how he would act as her husband?

A customer asked Reb Avraham-Abba if he had any buckwheat and he said yes, a whole sackful, but he could not remember exactly where in the store the sack was. Another woman asked him how much he would charge her for an eighth of a pound of yeast and a dozen eggs. He creased his forehead and then creased it again, but he simply could not recall how much the merchandise had cost him. The women looked at each other in amazement: it had never before occurred that the Divorced Rabbi could not point from behind the counter to a corner of the store where the sought-for goods could be found, or that he could not remember the cost of an item to the groschen.

One day, a frail little Jew came into the store, wearing a woman's kerchief under his hat and over his ears, a light summer coat though it was deep winter, and big, heavy army boots as if he had bought them from some deserter. The man rubbed his frozen hands and hopped near the oven to warm himself. "It's cold, Reb Avraham-Abba. What do you say, Reb Avraham-Abba, cold, eh?" The Rabbi just mumbled, "Yes, it's cold," and once again opened his notebook, which looked on the outside like a printed volume. The man, curious, tried to look into the book, but Rabbi Seligman quickly closed it and leaned his elbows on the cover as if to prevent the man from opening it and leafing through the pages. Reb Avraham-Abba knew that nearly anyone who would read his book either would not understand or would laugh at his spiritual comments: his resolutions; gems he had culled from his study of the rabbinic literature; interesting laws from the Codes and simple reminders concerning daily ritual, like the one about putting on tefillin every day. And no one would have laughed harder than his student, Gavriel Rappaport, who had wanted to hear only clever new insights; he had often complained that there was nothing remarkable about his teacher's analysis, he was doing no more than repeating the very words of the Talmud or the Tosaphist commentaries. How foolish people could be! They could understand perfectly well why a rich man carefully counted his money in the bank over and over, but they couldn't understand that through copying down laws and words of wisdom, they become part and parcel of one's character, one's private trove of the spirit.

"Life is bitter without a wife, Reb Avraham-Abba. Believe me, it's bitter!" The man was searching with his frozen hands for a piece of paper in which to wrap a slippery piece of schmaltz herring. "And I'm not even talking about me. First of all, I'm a widower just two years now and, second, who would want me? But you—you've been without a wife for so many years now. Tell me, is it really permitted?"

"If life without a wife does not lead into temptation and does not interfere with one's study of Torah, then it is permitted," the Rabbi said with a smile. He may have wanted to wander through the world like a deaf-mute, oblivious to the folly of life—the vanity of vanities—around him, but he could still listen and still answer patiently, especially when he saw he was doing a good deed by letting another human being unburden himself, and it was clear to him that this widower had a strong need to pour out his heart to someone.

Some time passed without Reb Avraham-Abba hearing again from the Rappaports, either mother or son, and finally he was able to fall once again into his pious daily regimen. Purim was quickly approaching; one day the snow began to melt and the icicles hanging from the eaves became soft and glistened in the sunlight. A day later, a fresh snow fell and the wind blew the thick snowflakes onto trees and roofs.

In Rabbi Seligman's trampled and muddied grocery store, women were buying food for the upcoming Purim feast and talking among themselves about cooking and baking. Reb Avraham-Abba was behind the counter, though this time not looking into any book. He was standing at attention and swaying, absorbed in the Silent Prayer of the afternoon service, not throwing so much as a glance at the women searching through the merchandise and the basket filled with noisemakers for the Purim Megillah reading. He knew that none of them would take more than a fair weight or put less than the actual price down on the counter, especially not with everyone watching everyone else. But since mistakes did happen, and perhaps there was a customer or two who was not especially careful even with all eyes watching, in his heart he relinquished his claim to any merchandise improperly taken, so that no one would bear the sin of having stolen from him.

Then, at the very moment he was concluding the Silent Prayer and took the prescribed three steps backward, he heard a familiar voice ring out: "Good morning, Rabbi." Never had he turned his head so quickly to see the one speaking to him: there in the middle of the store stood Bathsheva Rappaport, wearing the same clothes as on the day she had left Vilna. Her face looked younger, fresher. In each hand she held a large woven straw basket filled with fruit.

"My son, your student, and my brother-in-law have sent you Purim gifts—apples from their orchard," Bathsheva explained, a bit embarrassed by the stares she was receiving from all around her. The regular customers all recognized her and gazed at her meaningfully. "The day after Purim," she continued, "is my husband's yohrzeit, the second anniversary of his death. So I've returned to set a stone over his grave, since I didn't have a chance to do it before I left for my son's wedding."

It could have been that Bathsheva had nothing more in mind than what she said; then again, she might have said it for the benefit of the women around her in the store. But in her words Avraham-Abba heard the good news that now for her, as for her children, the time of mourning for her Shlomo-Zalman had come to an end. He wanted to ask her how his student was doing and into what sort of family he had married, but to pose such questions in front of all his customers was more than he could bring himself to do. So he simply came out from behind the counter to inspect Bathsheva's baskets of apples. The women in the store also looked into the baskets. "Antonówki," said one woman as she tossed back an apple she had taken out. "Papierówki," said another as she eyed an apple from the other basket.

With radiant eyes, her face flushed, Bathsheva explained that in the beginning of the winter the Antonówki apples had a pale yellow skin and the Papierówki apples had pale green skins and were fresh and shiny. Even now, when the skins were somewhat shriveled and browning, the apples' flesh under the skin was still sweet and tart. Bathsheva doled out an apple to each customer as a Purim gift, and told them with a sprightly laugh that while staying on her brother-in-law's estate she had become an expert on fruit and produce, on everything from dairy products to honey.

The Rabbi merely listened and said nothing. He did not know what to say. Nor could he rid himself of the unseemly thought that Bathsheva's laughter was still the laughter of a very young woman.

12

WITH EACH DAY Bathsheva had spent on her brother-in-law's estate near Libau, it had become clearer to her that her son had not achieved much through his marriage. His wife was an ordinary woman, and not even very pretty. His father-in-law was hardly a great landowner, and his mother-in-law a rather plain woman who busied herself with running the household, worried about little else but marrying off her other two daughters, and was continually irritated by her husband's inveterate optimism. Surprisingly, though Bathsheva hadn't cared much for Baruch-Issar when he had visited her in Vilna, now he was the one she liked best of all his family. His expansive and generous manner, his love of the good life, his cleverness, and the desire to find favor in the eyes of God and men—all reminded her of the character of her late husband in his younger years. She finally came to understand that Gavriel had married more for the sake of his uncle than for the sake of his uncle's daughter.

When Bathsheva told the family that she was returning to Vilna, Baruch-Issar only pretended to be upset. She sensed this, but was not distressed by it, for she understood her brother-in-law's embarrassment at not being as successful in reality as he had led everyone to believe on his visit to Vilna. He also must have realized that the two mothers-in-law would not be able to live together in peace for very long, and he feared that Bathsheva's presence might cause Gavriel to lose his affection for his bride.

Gavriel, however, could not bear to see his mother leave. "Don't go! Don't go!" he implored, and he would speak about his sister in Paris with such longing that Bathsheva trembled, and privately reproached him: "Have you gone completely mad? You've just gotten married and you're crying that you can't live without me and your sister! What will your wife say? What will your mother-in-law say?"

Gavriel acted even more foolishly when he saw her off. He kept kissing her and saying to his wife, "Ettele, just look what a beautiful young mother I have!" Her daughter-in-law looked at Bathsheva, confused and guilty. Baruch-Issar had tears in his eyes, and his wife sighed with a worried look on her face.

As hard as her departure had been for Bathsheva herself, she had been happy to leave at a time when she could still part from everyone as a friend. And yet, on her second visit to the grocery store after her return to Vilna, when Reb Avraham-Abba asked her about the family into which her son had married, she replied with bitterness in her voice that Gavriel had jumped from one empty ditch into another. With his brilliant mind, he could have grown up to be the greatest of rabbis. But he had broken his oath to his father, and for what? To become the son-in-law of a small landowner. The longer Bathsheva went on in this vein, the more astonished Reb Avraham-Abba became. He kept shrugging his shoulders until at last he interrupted her angrily:

"I don't understand you! Had your son entered into a family of great wealth, he might have strayed entirely from the right path, as he was about to do when he was working in the fields at Soltaniszki. It's truly a miracle that he took your niece for a wife and his uncle for a father-in-law, even if they aren't such wealthy people."

Bathsheva's response was a happy smile at Reb Avraham-Abba's good-natured anger, and at his being so much more clever than she. "I really have nothing against my brother-in-law's family. It's my spoiled only son's good fortune that he didn't marry a girl as hot-blooded as his sister. I just say that a mother must not live with her children if she can make a life for herself."

Bathsheva's heart pounded as she awaited Reb Avraham-Abba's reply. And yet she had not expected him to answer so quickly and to the point, with not a trace of cunning or reserve: If she was ready to stand with him under the canopy, she must already be fully aware of what sort of man he was. But he wanted to warn her that all her friends and her late husband's friends would feel she was making a big mistake. And he asked her, before anything else, to inform her children.

"I don't understand! My children didn't ask for my approval of whom they married. Why must I ask theirs?"

"But you are older," Reb Avraham-Abba said with a warm laugh. "Today people think nothing of it when young people marry without their parents' blessing, but they still don't expect parents to remarry against the wishes of their children. I think you ought at least to let them know." And so, Bathsheva wrote to her children, and began to sell her furniture.

The news that the widow Rappaport was marrying the Divorced Rabbi made such a sensation in the city that she could not help marveling at how right Reb Avraham-Abba had been. She had never before realized how many self-appointed friends she had, all with her best interests at heart. It was not long after she had sold almost all the furniture, and an emptiness had settled over the denuded rooms, that she received a visit from Asna's mother-in-law, that broad-beamed woman with the large head and short-cropped hair. Ordinarily, Bathsheva would see the Durmashkins only when either of them received a letter from the children in Paris. But now her in-law stalked into the apartment with a distinctly haughty air, and made the solemn pronouncement that—though she did not want to meddle in another person's life, God forbid—yet she had to say in all honesty that the Divorced Rabbi was not the right match for a woman of the widow Rappaport's station.

Bathsheva's cheeks flushed with anger, and she would have liked to tell Mulik Durmashkin's mother that she had no right to talk of anyone's station in life, and that her son was a communist in Paris as he had been in Vilna, or at least so it seemed from Asna's letters. But, taking a lesson from Reb Avraham-Abba, Bathsheva held her peace. She remembered how he once had told her: It is not always necessary to prove to others that one is right; it is sometimes enough to know it ourselves.

"My husband, may he rest in peace, did not hold anyone in higher esteem than Rabbi Avraham-Abba Seligman," she replied calmly but firmly. "I am a poor widow and no longer a young woman, yet he is willing to marry me. I wish only that I were worthy of him; that I were only able to truly appreciate his learning and righteousness." Her in-law, silenced, backed slowly toward the door.

As for the merchants to whom Bathsheva had so often gone to collect debts owed her husband, and to whom she had later sold canvas sacks, they suddenly noticed that she had an attractive face and the high cheekbones of an aristocrat. If she would only dress well, she would have the thin and shapely figure of a young girl. Her white teeth still sparkled between her lips when she smiled. In her every gesture it was clear that her late husband had doted on her. So why should she marry a crusty old-fashioned Jew whose only fortune was a small grocery store?

Since Bathsheva was still selling canvas bags, customers and merchants had ample opportunity to tell her that she did not know her own worth. A woman like her could always find a finer suitor than a poor Talmudic scholar who was wasting away in a little beth midrash. A woman peddler who in good times had used to deliver dairy and chickens to the Rappaport home once confronted her: "They say the first wife of the Divorced Rabbi barely escaped with her life. They say he is so bitter a grouch he can kill people with his looks. So who is pushing you to marry him?" Out of respect for Reb Avraham-Abba, Bathsheva did not even bother to answer the gossip. But finally, when she could no longer stand all this advice, she asked him: "How is it that people know so little about you?"

"To please people, you have to flatter them by acting like them and being like them," he said, standing as always, with his hands folded into his sleeves. After a moment of silent thought he spoke again, more emphatically: "That is why the man of faith is so fortunate. Since he seeks to please no one except the Almighty, he is not disappointed when people do not understand him."

Such words only made him greater in Bathsheva's eyes. At the same time, her admiration for her late husband also grew because he had understood Reb Avraham-Abba so well. She decided, therefore, that anyone who insulted Rabbi Avraham-Abba Seligman was also insulting her late husband, no matter how much they might praise the memory of Shlomo-Zalman Rappaport. On the other hand, if her own son had not been able to see the greatness of his teacher, what could one expect from simple, uneducated strangers? She had even had to beg Gavriel, during her stay at Baruch-Issar's estate, to write to his teacher to tell him about the wedding and that he spent several hours a day studying Talmud. It seemed that Gavriel missed everyone in Vilna except his Rabbi; and Bathsheva saw that Reb Avraham-Abba knew this. Nonetheless, he delayed their wedding until her children answered.

First came a telegram from Paris in which Asna said she was happy that Bathsheva would no longer be alone. Then a letter arrived from Latvia. It was Baruch-Issar writing that the entire family was in seventh heaven from joy. After his signature he added a short, dry postscript that Gavriel would write to her separately, and then concluded cryptically: "It is only now that I begin to understand how exceptionally wise was my late brother, Shlomo-Zalman, may he rest in peace, and how correctly he foresaw and provided for everything."

"Gavriel hasn't written to me because he is angry that I am going to remarry. He's still a child," Bathsheva thought, and she took Baruch-Issar's letter to Reb Avraham-Abba. On the way to the grocery store a thought she often had nowadays recurred to her: "God in Heaven, how time flies!" She had returned to Vilna on the eve of Purim in early spring and here it was, deep into the summer month of Tammuz and she was still a widow. The people walking in the streets sweated from the heat and choked on the dust. The closer one got to the center of the city, the louder and more tumultuous the clatter of the wagons and the thicker the crowds of passers-by. The sun shone blindingly in the eyes, burning the metal roofs and baking the bricks of walls and the cobblestones.

The dust-laden wind whipped at Bathsheva's face with straw and dry grass it had swept off a farm wagon stationed there. She was overcome by an almost nauseating impatience at the thought that here she was, trudging along once again on the same sidewalk of Zawalna Street, across from the lumber yard. Now the heat was drying her out while she soaked in a

summer sweat. And yet, before she knew it, the leaves of autumn would
be falling. The grass on her late husband's grave would be growing high
and thick. A deep and holy silence always reigned over the hallowed
ground of the cemetery, where no one dared touch the bushes or the
trees. Nothing ever changed there. But in her life, everything kept changing. First she had left Vilna for Libau, then left Libau for Vilna. Lately
she had taken to changing her clothes often. On this day she was wearing
a printed dress with small summery birds flying among large flowers—too
ostentatious, perhaps, for a woman who wanted to marry a rabbi. True,
Rabbi Seligman was not a rav, but even so she would have to conduct
herself more like a rebbetzin. Did they really suit each other? she wondered. Perhaps her friends—whether true friends or pretended ones—
were right: perhaps, after all, she and the Divorced Rabbi were not a
proper match.

As Reb Avraham-Abba read Baruch-Issar's letter, slowly and with
great concentration, Bathsheva stood by silently, quite angry at him for
having convinced her to write to her son about their coming marriage.
Soon, however, she realized that her anger at Reb Avraham-Abba was
as childish as Gavriel's anger at her.

"Don't be upset, there's nothing to worry about," he said as he
returned the folded sheets of paper to her, and she noticed that with those
simple words he spoke to her for the first time with the familiarity of a
husband. "You had to let your son know that you are getting married, but
you do not need his approval. And he'll change his mind yet."

"What did Baruch-Issar mean by saying that only now did he understand how wise his brother was, may he rest in peace, and how correctly
he had figured everything out?" Bathsheva asked, once again worrying
that perhaps Baruch-Issar regretted his daughter's match with Gavriel,
that Gavriel should have become a Talmudic scholar as his father had
wished, since he was fit for little else.

"I think I know what your brother-in-law meant, though I'm not
sure that he is right," Reb Avraham-Abba murmured and then stood in
silence for a while, turning Baruch-Issar's postscript over and over in his
mind, pondering its meaning and wondering if he should explain it to
Bathsheva. At last he spoke: "Your brother-in-law believes that when
your husband, may he rest in peace, asked me to teach Gavriel Talmud,
he was also thinking that I should look after you."

Bathsheva trembled in every fiber of her being. Though Reb
Avraham-Abba professed to be uncertain whether her brother-in-law
was right, she could see in his face that he too divined a conscious plan on

Shlomo-Zalman's part to keep her from being left alone and friendless after his death. And, indeed, the thought had occurred to her more than once that through her marriage to Reb Avraham-Abba she herself was fulfilling her husband's last wishes—the wishes both her son and her daughter had disregarded.

13

A<small>T THE SAME PLACE</small> behind the counter where the Divorced Rabbi had used to stand, his second wife was now poised, and, just like him, she allowed the customers to select and weigh the merchandise for themselves. The customers sensed her stare fixed on them, however, and so did not feel the goods too much with their poking fingers, so that another customer should not wish to pass by this piece of smoked fish or that block of cheese or butter. Bathsheva enlarged the business. If a customer asked for an item that was sold out or had not been carried before, it would be but a few days before that item appeared on the shelves. The entire atmosphere of the store brightened as white paper now lined the shelves and the sacks of flour meal and groats were neatly arranged so as to provide broad aisles through which to pass. When Bathsheva told a customer the price of an item, the customer did not dare to haggle. She still had the bearing of a wealthy woman, not of a small grocery owner; the customers who came in could not stop wondering why she had married this old-fashioned man whose place she gladly took in the store so he could study in the beth midrash. And once outside, the customers would talk among themselves about the shopkeeper.

"He is not wealthy, and as a man he's certainly no Samson. So there must be a very special reason if such a woman has married him."

Bathsheva could see the puzzlement in the faces of her friends and neighbors. And yet, none of them was as puzzled as she was by *their* attitude: They had been Reb Avraham-Abba's neighbors and customers for so many years, and all they had to say about him was that he was an honest man. Didn't they understand that he was a higher sort of human being? With each passing day he grew yet greater in Bathsheva's eyes. She had always known him as a quiet man, but since the wedding he had begun to talk to her more often, and she understood that just for her sake he was acting against the grain of his temperament. The matters he would speak to her about were often the most mundane; and yet, his ways of thinking and acting were so unique, so distinctive in character, that she would be left with much to ponder from even the most incidental conversation.

Shlomo-Zalman, may he rest in peace, had had a more generous nature than Reb Avraham-Abba, she thought, and would never stint when giving charity. But then, he would never pause to think exactly how best to help people; if anyone asked him for a donation and he could afford it, he would give immediately and promptly forget it. Reb Avraham-Abba, may he live and be well, was not nearly so generous; he was even stingy to himself. He was always wondering if they could get along without something or other, and he was no more eager to give his money away to others. And one had to admit that his carefulness was not due simply to a lack of funds—sometimes the charity doled out was a matter of mere groschen—but he knew that money was precious and he insisted on doing everything with a strict accounting. Still, she had never in her life seen anyone weigh matters so carefully when it came to helping a neighbor.

Once, on a Friday, a delivery man from the market came to the store with a plea. "Do me a favor, Reb Avraham-Abba, lend me five zlotys for the Sabbath. It is easier for me to carry a wagon with grain than to ask for a favor, believe me, but I have no choice."

Rabbi Seligman at once handed the delivery man the five zlotys and laughed with surprise, shrugging his shoulders. "What kind of favor am I doing you by lending you these five zlotys? What difference is it to me whether the five zlotys spend the Sabbath with me and lie about doing nothing, or spend the Sabbath with you doing a mitzvah?" Reb Avraham-Abba spoke so long, contrary to his nature, insisting that he was deserving of no special thanks from the delivery man, that when the man left with the money, he was encouraged and beaming. Bathsheva looked after him and thought, "Such a simple man, and yet proud, too proud to ask favors."

On another occasion a man in a black felt hat and a long frock coat walked into the store. If Reb Avraham-Abba had not told her later that the man was a shopkeeper from Zawalna Street, Bathsheva would have sworn that the man was a rav. His learning and his piety shone from his pale face, from his silken beard, from his soft, creamy hands and his every turn and gesture. Before he managed to stammer out that he had come to ask for a small loan, he looked about the store apologetically and excused himself ten times. It was clear just from looking at him that having to beg for money in this way was agonizing for him. Rabbi Seligman lent him exactly what he asked for without uttering a single word. Bathsheva thought that her husband had not been very cordial to this fine, pious Jew, so she asked him later why the scholarly-looking merchant was any worse than the humble delivery man. His answer seared its way into her memory:

"When I told the delivery man that I was not doing him a favor, he believed me. But had I tried to convince the shopkeeper of this, he would never believe it and it would only cause him greater anguish. He is a Talmudic scholar and knows perfectly well that he is not doing me any favor by borrowing money from me. So he would think that either I am mocking him, God forbid, or that I am happy he has to come to me begging instead of I to him. In a situation like this, it is best to say nothing."

Bathsheva smiled to herself, reflecting that she had found a treasure that lay before everyone's eyes but which she alone appreciated. "It is a world of busy and blinded people," she thought. "What do their eyes see if they do not see the greatness of the shopkeeper from Straszuna Street?"

That evening, while she prepared dinner and busied herself with the pots on the stove, he stood between the dining-room table and the entrance to the kitchen and spoke to her:

"I have often wondered why it is that the person you help can become your bitterest enemy. We think that he must be jealous of us, or is it that he is simply a wretched soul who likes to repay kindness with evil? It never occurs to us that perhaps we helped him in such a way that his blood boiled in his veins. And then we wonder why he doesn't want to know us anymore. Even the Almighty does not want to know such a collector of good deeds—one who does a mitzvah and in the same motion loses his portion in the World to Come."

Since their marriage, Bathsheva had become more and more curious as to why Reb Avraham-Abba's first wife had left him. But he never mentioned her—and Bathsheva, for her part, soon stopped talking about her late husband. She should not speak of her Shlomo-Zalman anymore, she felt, nor should she ask her present husband about his first wife.

Matters did not, however, rest there: One day, Reb Avraham-Abba received a letter that seemed to leave him very pleased, and he told her that it was from an old friend from the yeshiva in Kelem. His friend had learned of his remarriage, and was sending him his congratulations.

"While you were visiting your family in Latvia," he told Bathsheva,

"I inquired of my friend in Lithuania if my former wife had already remarried so that I could do the same. It was this very friend of mine who wrote me that Hodel had found a husband long ago." Reb Avraham-Abba was hoping that this explanation would make clear to Bathsheva why he had delayed the wedding for so long.

"But is there any law that a divorced man cannot remarry until his former wife has remarried?" Bathsheva asked.

"There is no such law, but since I had been a source of suffering to her, I did not want to remarry until she had found her happiness." For a while he stood motionless in the middle of the room, his head bowed as if he were gazing down into a deep, brush-covered well—into his soul's own darkness. "She, my first wife, was still young then, and she was very devoted, even though she was hot-tempered, embittered, and overworked —and a war was going on. So instead of gently and skillfully teaching her how to run the business in accordance with the values of the Torah, I was stubborn and unyielding—even fanatically strict. I, too, was but a young man then."

After this discussion, Bathsheva understood that Reb Avraham-Abba complied so easily with her wishes because he wanted to make up for his harsh treatment of his first wife. When she told him that they needed a bigger apartment, he grimaced and groaned. But then he himself found an apartment on the very same street with three rooms and a kitchen; he brought in painters to do the walls and hired some men off the street to move what was left of the furniture from the Rappaports' old apartment on Portowa Street.

At first, he protested when Bathsheva insisted that he should have new clothes made. "What's wrong with my old clothes?" he asked as he arched his back and awkwardly danced about as if suddenly finding himself on an icy sidewalk. But soon enough he agreed, and even asked her if he should order a new pair of trousers with a short jacket or with a frock coat, or with a full, long, old-fashioned rabbinic coat. Bathsheva told him that he ought to have one pair of trousers with a short jacket for week-days, and another pair of trousers with a long frock coat for the Sabbath and holidays. He agreed to this, but only on the condition that she would get a new dress and coat made for herself as well.

Sometimes they would argue because Bathsheva wanted to stay longer in the store so that he could spend more time studying Talmud in the beth midrash. She knew that before they were married, when he had been alone in the store, he had often closed it for the afternoon to spend a few hours in the beth midrash. But now that they had become man and wife, he would return to the store after a short while to relieve her behind the counter.

There was, however, one concession he remained unwilling to make. On the Sabbath of the Blessing of the New Moon, Bathsheva looked out from the women's section and saw how Avraham-Abba was praying, stationed in a far corner of the beth midrash near the bima, and looking so poor and insignificant in a worn prayer shawl and a plain cap, instead of a proper rabbinic hat. He did not lift his eyes even for an instant from the tattered pages of his thick Siddur, as if he knew no part of the prayers by heart, and he seemed so withdrawn that one might have thought his sole desire was to take up as little space as possible. Later at home, Bathsheva voiced her complaint: If he refused to conduct himself with greater dignity, he should at least not make himself smaller than the men who sat up front. He was too anxious to run away from honor; he was simply too humble.

"You are wrong; I'm not at all humble. I feel that wherever I sit is the front of the beth midrash," he joked. But then he became very serious and began to share with her the innermost thoughts that had been simmering within him these many years: A person who runs after honor is one who does not believe in himself at all. His heart is restless and empty, like an old, dried-out wooden barrel whose metal hoops have rusted and whose staves have rotted. This barrel wants to be mended and filled with the liquid of honor, with glory and admiration. But the seeker of glory cannot escape his true self; wherever he will go and whatever he will do or say—everywhere and always his pride pulls violently at every fiber of his being, as if he were lying in a Bed of Sodom. Whereas one who learns Torah in earnest and with pure motives considers himself small, very small, but also great in his own eyes—very great. Whenever one looks at the sea or at the tall mountains, he always feels small because he feels dwarfed by the grandeur of nature. But when a man lives with the Torah, which is greater, more majestic, than the greatest sea and the tallest mountains, he cannot help feeling small. Man is as great as he is able to understand the Torah and the ways of the Almighty.

Bathsheva did not understand everything Reb Avraham-Abba said, but then she hadn't really been listening to every word. She was plainly happy to hear his deep, solemn voice and to think that she alone was privileged to hear the thoughts he had carried inside himself for so long. For some time thereafter, his voice and his words still echoed peacefully and secretly within her, like the secret flutter and buzzing of life brimming in the tall grass of a meadow that lies sleeping in the midday sun.

The sun was shining into the grocery store—a lovingly warm and golden sun whose beams frolicked like musical strings with the melancholy of early autumn. There were no customers, so Bathsheva had a chance to think about her children. She had not received a letter from Asna for weeks. In her last letter she had written that she was still very happy living in Paris. But why wasn't she saying anything about how happy she was with her husband? To be happy with a husband, it was not enough just to love him. Sooner or later a wife had to take an interest in those things that were especially important to her husband. Asna had never had any friends that were beneath her station. So how could she possibly fit into the company of Mulik's friends when all of them believed that everyone was equal?

Gavriel was luckier in this respect. He liked the work in the fields, and his uncle's entire family concerned themselves with just that. The only problem was that he did not love his wife. What a foolish boy! At first, he was angry with her for remarrying, and wrote not a word. Later he made peace with her, just as Reb Avraham-Abba had predicted, and since then had continued to write such long, loving letters that she trembled lest Gavriel's wife and in-laws become hurt and jealous.

Bathsheva felt that she still could not understand her son. She might be a woman and not very well educated, and yet she considered herself so very fortunate to be able to hear Reb Avraham-Abba's thoughts on Torah. Yet Gavriel, with his fiery, brilliant mind, had refused to be the student of such a scholar and tzaddik.

May God help my children to be no less happy with their spouses than I am with Reb Avraham-Abba, Bathsheva thought, as she piously tucked a lock of her still youthful, shining hair under her headkerchief. Was she not sinning against her first husband for being so happy with Reb Avraham-Abba and for telling everyone so? No, she was doing him no wrong and neither was she shaming his memory, may his repose be in Paradise. Since her Shlomo-Zalman, of blessed memory, had demanded before his death that the shopkeeper from Straszuna Street should become their son's rabbi, it was impossible that he, in the next world, could have anything against her for having married that same rabbi.

Bathsheva stood still facing the door, leaning her hands on the counter, for a long time. Her eyes welled with tears, as sunbeams shone on those tears, the very same sunbeams which at that very same moment shimmered and played on the grave of Shlomo-Zalman Rappaport.

GLOSSARY

Agudah: Ultra-Orthodox faction in Jewish communal life. Before World War II the Agudah was vehemently opposed to Zionism, which in their view represented an impious refusal to wait for the coming of the Messiah, who alone was the proper, divinely ordained instrument of the people's redemption and restoration to the Land of Israel. In modern Israel, the Agudah fights against the separation of religion and state. See also *Mizrahi*.

Agudahnik: Member of the Agudah.

Al Hayt: "On the sin . . ."; penitential prayer recited on Yom Kippur, a litany of sins and transgressions for which forgiveness is implored. It is accompanied by the symbolic gesture of beating the breast as each form of transgression is named.

Aliyah: Lit., "an ascension" or "going up." A section of the Torah portion assigned to be read aloud in the synagogue on a given Sabbath or Festival. Each aliyah is bestowed upon an individual worshipper who ascends the bima (pulpit), in principle to read the section himself; the more usual practice, however, is for the section to be read by the Torah reader, with the worshipper reciting the appropriate blessings before and after the reading.

Amud: Reader's lectern, placed directly in front of the ark containing the Torah scrolls. On some occasions the reader leads services from the amud.

Baba: Aramaic for "gate"; used to indicate a section of a work.

Baba Kamma, Baba Metzia, Baba Bathra: First, middle, and last book, respectively, of discussions on the Law in the Talmud.

Beth midrash: House of study, or synagogue, where worshippers come both to pray and to study the law. See *Midrash*.

Beth Yosef (or Beth Joseph): Lit., "House of Joseph," title of a classic commentary on Jewish law by Rabbi Joseph Caro (1488–1575), who also edited and compiled the *Shulhan Aruh* ("The Prepared Table"), the most popular and authoritative code of law, used by Orthodox Jews throughout the world.

Bima: Synagogue pulpit, on which the Torah scroll is placed for public reading and from which the reader sometimes leads the service. In Eastern European synagogues, the bima was normally located in the center of the sanctuary.

Blessing of the Cohanim: See HaCohen.

Brith: Lit., "covenant"; in Jewish religious practice, the rite of circumcision (*brith milah*) —the sign of the covenant between God and the Children of Israel. The rite is performed on the eighth day after the birth of a male child.

Bund: Lit., "union" or "federation" in Yiddish; the familiar short form of the name of the Jewish socialist party in Eastern Europe—in full, the Algemeiner Yiddisher Arbeterbund in Li'te, Poilen un Russland ("General Federation of Jewish Workers in Lithuania, Poland and Russia"). The Bund belonged to the Socialist International. In addition, however, to the general economic program it held in common with non-Jewish socialist parties, the Bund was strongly committed to the promotion and preservation of a secular Yiddish-language culture in Europe, and in the Diaspora generally. It therefore vigorously opposed the Orthodox rabbinical establishment, on the one hand, and, on the other, the Zionists, who advocated instead a return to the Land of Israel and the primacy of Hebrew over Yiddish.

Chofetz Chaim: Lit., *The Will to Live*, famous Talmudic work by Rabbi Israel Meir HaCohen of Radun (1835–1933), great Talmudist and legal authority, usually referred to by the title of his work, in accordance with rabbinic custom.

Cohen (Cohanim): See HaCohen.

Courtyard: In the Jewish ghettoes of Eastern Europe, a large structure containing apartments, stores, and synagogues, all built around an open central area, usually with one gated exit to the street that was closed for the night.

Ehad: "One," as in the prayer "Hear O Israel! The Lord is our God, the Lord is One."

Ein Ya'akov: An annotated compilation of the aggadic (tales and parables) sections of both the Palestinian and the Babylonian Talmud, by Rabbi Ibn Habib (or Haviv) (1460–1516). Forcibly baptized in Portugal in 1497, he reverted to Judaism in Salonica. Only the first two parts of *Ein Ya'akov* were published during his lifetime, the remaining four parts being completed and published by his son Rabbi Levi Ibn Habib (1480–1545), Chief Rabbi of Jersusalem.

Esrog: Citron; used together with a lulav, or palm branch, during services on the Festival of Sukkoth.

Gabbay: A trustee; a lay congregant charged with assigning duties and honors to other worshippers and overseeing the general functioning of a synagogue. A position of respect.

Gaon: Title of spiritual/intellectual leaders and legal authorities in the Babylonian Jewish community in the post-Talmudic period, from the sixth to eleventh centuries. In later times, "gaon" became an honorific title for a leading Talmudic scholar of great authority and distinction.

Gaon of Vilna: Rabbi Elijah ben Solomon Zalman (1720–1797), one of the greatest Talmudic scholars of the Diaspora. As was not unusual among the rabbis in Lithuania, the Gaon of Vilna refused to assume an official rabbinical position. He led a vigorous, even ruthless battle against Hassidism, and also against the Haskalah ("enlightenment"), even though he wrote not only famous commentaries on the Talmud, Midrash, and Zohar (see below), but also treatises on mathematics and the geography of Palestine; he was also the author of a Hebrew grammar. The religious Jews of Lithuania (the Misnagdim) regard him to this day as their spiritual leader and authority.

Gehinnom (Ge-Hinnom, also Gehenna): The "Valley of Hinnom" (Jeremiah 32:35), valley southwest of Jerusalem where children were sacrificed to the god Moloch at a site called Tophet (Isaiah 30:33). In later times, Gehinnom (or Gehenna) became the Hebrew (and therefore Yiddish) term for Hell.

Gelilah: The ritual of rolling up and binding the Torah scroll, after a public reading.

Gemara: Same as *Talmud*; the vast body of elaboration, interpretation, and commentary on the Mishnah (*q.v.*), the codification of the Oral Law. While the language of the Mishnah is Hebrew, that of the Gemara is Aramaic. (*Gemara* means "teaching" in Aramaic, *Talmud* the same in Hebrew.)

Get: Divorce; also, the bill of divorcement which the husband, in the presence of witnesses, places into the hands of the wife whom he is divorcing.

HaCohen: "The Cohen" (pl., "Cohanim"), "the priest"—a descendant of the priests who officiated in the Temple in ancient times. In Jewish religious practice, the Cohanim retain certain residual ceremonial functions, such as bestowing the Blessing of the Cohanim on the congregation on the Sabbath and holy days.

Hagboh: The ritual of raising the Torah scroll in the synagogue for all the congregation to see, following a public reading.

Halttur: A sobriquet for the twelfth-century scholar Rabbi Isaac ben Abba Mari, taken from his best-known work, the *Sepher Halttur*, a classic compilation of Jewish civil and religious law.

HaLevi: "The Levite," a descendant of the tribe of Levi, to which the priests—the descendants, according to the Bible, of Moses's brother, Aaron—belonged. In ancient times, all male Levites (i.e., those not of priestly descent) assisted the priests in the Temple.

Halahic: pertaining to the Halahah, the Law.

Hallel: Lit., "praises"; a group of psalms of praise added to the liturgy on the New Moon and the three pilgrimage festivals of Sukkoth, Passover, and Shavuoth.

Halutz (pl., halutzim): A "pioneer." One of the pioneering settlers in the Holy Land during the late nineteenth and early twentieth centuries, before the establishment of the State of Israel. Most (though not all) halutzim were of secular orientation, and held socialist or communitarian convictions that found their most notable embodiment in the kibbutzim, the collective agricultural settlements.

Hanukah: Lit., "dedication" or "consecration"; a holiday of eight days, also called the Feast of Lights. It commemorates the rededication of the Holy Temple to the service of God in the second century B.C.E., after the recapture of Jerusalem from the Syrian Greeks by Jewish forces under Judah the Maccabee. See also *Menorah*.

Haphtorah: extract from the Prophetic books of the Bible, read during morning services on the Sabbath and Festivals, after the reading from the Torah. See *Maphtir*.

Haskalah: See *Maskil*.

Hassid: Lit., "pious one," an adherent of a rabbinical spiritual leader, or rebbe, genealogically or spiritually descended from Rabbi Israel ben Eleazar, the Baal Shem Tov (1700–1760), who stressed joy and spontaneity in prayer, faith in God, and faith in a tzaddik —a "righteous" or "holy man," the Rebbe—as the three cardinal principles of Jewish life. A Hassid subordinates his will to the will of his rebbe.

Havdalah: Lit., "distinction" or "distinguishing"; ceremony that marks the end of the Sabbath and so distinguishes it from the rest of the week, which the ceremony ushers in.

Heder: Lit., "room"; an elementary Hebrew school, most often conducted in a room in the teacher's (melamed's) house, where reading Hebrew, prayers, the Pentateuch, and the rudiments of Jewish law were taught.

Hetman: The chief or general of a Cossack army; in czarist times, such quasi-autonomous forces were notorious for periodically engaging in brutal and murderous attacks on defenseless Jewish and Catholic Christian populations.

Hullin: Lit., "profane (i.e., as distinct from sacred) matters," a tractate in the Mishnah (see below), dealing primarily with the laws of shehitah (ritual slaughtering) and of the preparation of animal food.

Josippon (or Josephon): A popular general history of the Jews, in Hebrew, believed to have been written in the eighth century. It was based on the work of the first-century Jewish historian Josephus Flavius.

Kaddish: Prayer recited by mourners at daily services for a period of eleven months after the death of a family member, and thereafter on the anniversary of the death (see *Yohrzeit*).

Kapporoth: Lit., "atonement"; a ceremony that takes place on the morning of the day before Yom Kippur, in which a chicken is waved overhead and symbolically assigned to bear the punishment that might otherwise be in store for the supplicant. The chicken is generally eaten at the meal just prior to the onset of the Yom Kippur fast. The ceremony evolved after the destruction of the Temple, where the lamb was the sacrificial animal.

Karaites: A Jewish sect that rejects the Oral Law, accepting only the Bible. It is believed to have originated in the eighth century B.C.E., in and around Persia. It is noteworthy, however, that in the course of time the Karaites developed their own oral law which in some points coincided with rabbinic law.

Kashruth: The process of making (or keeping) utensils, food, and a home kosher, that is, in conformance with the Jewish dietary laws.

Kedushah: responsive reading during the reader's synagogue recitation of the Shemoneh Esreh prayer (see below) built around the prophetic vision of ministering angels praising the Lord. "Holy, holy, holy . . ." (Isaiah 6:3).

Kehillah: An organized Jewish community, with its own governing body or council.

Kiddush: Lit., "sanctification"; a brief ceremony that ushers in the Sabbath (on Friday evenings) and holidays, and is also performed prior to Sabbath and holiday meals. The Kiddush is recited over a glass of wine, which is drunk at its conclusion.

Kittel: White floor-length gown worn during services on the High Holy Days and at the Passover Seder, as a symbol of purity.

Kollel: An academy of advanced Talmudic studies for married men (as opposed to a yeshiva, which was exclusively for unmarried men).

Kreisy U'Pleisy: Lit., "The Cherethites and Pelethites" (2 Samuel 8:18). Title of a famous Talmudic commentary by Rabbi Jonathan Eibeschütz (1690–1764), after which he is frequently called, in accordance with the widespread rabbinic custom of designating an author by the title of his work. The Biblical Cherethites and Pelethites were mighty men of war; Rabbi Eibeschütz employs them as a metaphor for mighty men of the spirit, that is, Talmudic scholars.

Lag B'Omer: The 33rd day of the seven-week period of the "counting of the omer" (the seven weeks between the beginning of Passover and the festival of Shavuoth—see below). Lag B'Omer falls on the 18th day of the month of Iyar, in late spring. Legend has it that on this day an outbreak of plague stopped among the pupils of Rabbi Akiba in the second century C.E., and Lag B'Omer is therefore also known as the scholars' holiday. On this day is suspended the state of half-mourning that prevails overall during the seven weeks.

Lulav: Young palm branch, which is used together with the esrog (citron) and willow and myrtle branches, waved during Sukkoth services as part of the Festival.

Maariv: Evening service.

Maggid (pl., maggidim): Preacher, or deliverer of inspirational sermons, who might be an ordained rabbi, though often was not. Maggidim were frequently itinerants, traveling from town to town, although a maggid might receive a formal appointment as the preacher in one town or synagogue.

Maharam: Rabbi Meir ben Gedalia of Lublin, called Maharam of Lublin (1558–1616), one of the greatest and most authoritative commentators on the Talmud.

Mahzor: A special prayer book for festivals or the High Holidays, as distinct from a siddur, the daily and Sabbath prayer book—though a siddur, being more comprehensive, might be used on all occasions.

Malbim: Rabbi Meir Leibush (1809–1879), a great Talmudic scholar whose most famous work was a commentary on the Bible written to demonstrate the unity and harmony of Biblical precepts and statutes with the Oral Law.

Maphtir: Lit., "one who concludes"; the person called up for the concluding section (aliyah) of the Torah portion read on a given Sabbath or holiday. It is the Maphtir who, after the Torah reading, chants the Haphtorah, the Prophetic reading for the given occasion (see above). To "receive Maphtir" is considered an especially great honor.

Maskil (pl., maskilim): Lit., "one who enlightens"; a proponent or advocate of the Haskalah ("enlightenment"), the movement for modern, secular education and learning among European Jews beginning in the late eighteenth century and continuing into the twentieth. The Maskilim pioneered in the revival of Hebrew as a secular and literary language—as opposed to the traditional view of it as a purely sacred tongue, a medium exclusively of religious and philosophical expression. The Haskalah was strongly opposed by the rabbinical establishment and by devout Orthodox Jews generally.

Megillah: Lit., "scroll"; in popular usage, the term is most often applied to the Book of Esther, which is read from a scroll on the holiday of Purim (*q.v.*)

Menorah: Candelabrum; in Jewish religious practice, the menorah (of eight branches) is most prominently associated with the festival of Hanukah, being used to hold the candles whose lighting is the central ritual of the holiday (from one candle on the first night to eight on the eighth night). The candle-lighting symbolically commemorates the miracle that, according to the traditional account, occurred at the time of the rededication of the Temple to the service of God: a small cruse of holy oil which was all that was found to rekindle the Temple menorah, apparently sufficient only for one day, lasted instead for eight days, until new oil could be prepared.

Midrash: Scriptural interpretation or exegesis; a rabbinic homiletic commentary on the Scriptures containing historical and, often, legendary material, with a strong moral bent.

Midrash Rabbah: Collection of midrashim (plural of midrash) to the five books of the Pentateuch and to the "five scrolls"; it consists of Genesis Rabbah, Exodus Rabbah, Leviticus Rabbah, Numbers Rabbah, Deuteronomy Rabbah, Song of Songs Rabbah, Ruth Rabbah, Lamentations Rabbah, Ecclesiastes Rabbah, and Esther Rabbah.

Mikvah (or Mikveh): A ritual bathhouse.

Minhah: Afternoon service.

Minyan: The quorum of ten adult males required for public worship, at the thrice-daily services; also used to refer to a service itself (thus, the "morning," "afternoon," or "evening minyan").

Mishnah: Legal codification which contains the core of the Oral Law, as compiled by Rabbi Judah HaNasi (135–220 c.e.) on the basis of previous collections; the Gemara, or Talmud, is the body of commentary, elaboration, and interpretation of the laws of the Mishnah.

Misnaged (also transliterated as "misnagged"; pl., misnagdim): Lit., "an opponent"; an Orthodox Jew in Central or Eastern Europe, especially Lithuania, with an intellectual or legalistic approach to religious life and practice, in opposition to the mystical, emotional approach of the Hassidim.

Mitzvah: Hebrew for "commandment" or "precept"; in Yiddish parlance, most often used in the sense of a good deed or praiseworthy act.

Mizrahi: The Orthodox religious wing of the Zionist movement. Within the ranks of Orthodox Jews in Eastern Europe there was an ongoing and bitter conflict between the Mizrahi and the strongly anti-Zionist Agudah (*q.v.*).

Musaf: The "additional" service, added after Shaharis (morning service), on the Sabbath and the major holidays.

Neilah: The concluding, and holiest, service on Yom Kippur, the Day of Atonement.

Phylacteries: See *Tefillin*.

P'nei Yehoshua: "The Face of Joshua," a compilation of commentaries on the Talmud by Rabbi Jacob Joshua Ben Zvi Hirsch (1680–1756), a great and renowned rabbinical authority often referred to by the title of his work.

Porush (pl., p'rushim): A recluse Talmudic scholar who would spend his days in study in a beth midrash; homeless p'rushim slept in the community hall of the beth midrash and would be given board at the homes of charitable congregants.

Purim: Festival commemorating the rescue of the Jewish community of Persia, by Mordecai and Queen Esther, from the evil designs of Haman, chief counselor to King Ahasuerus, as recounted in the Book of Esther. The holiday is marked by merrymaking, the exchange of gifts, and feasting. See also *Megillah*.

Rabbi: In Hebrew, *rav*, a "master" or "preceptor"; a person who has successfully completed the required course of study and received rabbinical ordination. A rabbi does not necessarily exercise a clerical function, as the spiritual leader of a congregation or community; he may devote himself entirely to scholarship and study, or even be engaged in some other trade, business, or profession. See also *Rav*.

Rabiener: German term for Rabbi; in Eastern Europe—most notably, Lithuania and Poland —"Rabiener" was the term for a "modern" rabbi, that is, one who had both a secular and a rabbinical education. Among the ultra-Orthodox, the title "rabiener" was often used contemptuously.

Rashi: Rabbi Solomon Itzhak ben Isaac (1040–1105), French rabbinical scholar, one of the greatest commentators and exegetes of the Bible and the Talmud.

Rashi script: Semi-cursive form of Hebrew letters, used mainly for the writing and printing of rabbinical commentaries, especially of Rashi.

Rav: Rabbi; for the purposes of this translation, the title of "Rav" has been used primarily to indicate the formally appointed spiritual leader of a community—e.g., "the Graipewo Rav" or "Zaskowicz Rav." (See also *Rabbi*.) A "Rav" among the Misnagdim should be distinguished from a Hassidic "Rebbe" (*q.v.*).

Reb: Honorific title of address for a man of learning or scholar, used with either the given name alone or the full name (rather similarly to the English use of the honorific "Sir" for the holder of a knighthood).

Rebbe: A Hassidic rabbi, a spiritual leader and guide whose will is law for his followers. The position of Rebbe among the Hassidim (in contrast to that of Rav among the Misnagdim) is hereditary. See also *Hassid*.

Rebbetzin: The wife of a Rav (that is, of a rabbi acting as the spiritual leader of a congregation or community).

Responsum (pl., responsa): A written reply to a question on Jewish law or practice, by a qualified rabbinical authority.

Righteous Convert: A gentile who converts to Judaism; in Eastern Europe, the most famous Righteous Convert was Count Potocki, who lived in the eighteenth century.

Rosh Kollel: Head of a kollel (*q.v.*).

Rosh Yeshiva: Head of a yeshiva (*q.v.*).

Sadducees (Hebrew, *tzedukim*): An exclusive aristocratic sect of the time of the Second Temple. They did not accept the immortality of the soul or, more importantly, the validity of the Oral Law. Their faith and practices were centered around the Temple cult, and they disappeared after the destruction of the Temple, in 70 c.e.

Sandak (derived from the Greek *synteknos*, "godfather"): At a circumcision ceremony, the man who holds the infant while the circumcision is performed.

Sanhedrin: The assembly of seventy-one leading rabbis who in ancient times (until about the end of the fourth century) constituted the supreme religious governing body of the Jewish people, the final authority on all matters of law, doctrine, and religious practice.

Seder: The ritual, accompanied by a festive meal, observed in Jewish homes on the first and second evenings of Passover (in Israel only the first Seder is observed).

Selihot: Penitential prayers recited at special midnight services during the weeks preceding the New Year, Rosh Hashanah.

Seventeenth of Tammuz: Date of the first breaching of the walls of the besieged city of Jerusalem, presaging the destruction of both the First and Second Temples, in 586 B.C.E. and 70 C.E., respectively. Observed as a fast day by the devout. See also *Tishah B'Av*.

Shabbos: Sabbath.

Shabbas Hazon: The "Sabbath of the Vision," the sabbath before Tishah B'Av, on which is read the prophetic lament of Isaiah.

Shabbas HaGadol: "The Great Sabbath," the one before Passover, on which, traditionally, the rabbi gives a lengthy discourse on the laws of Passover.

Shabbas Nahamu: The "Sabbath of Consolation," the one following Tishah B'Av, when the consoling prophecy of Isaiah is read.

Shabbas Shuva: The "Sabbath of Return," the Sabbath between Rosh Hashanah (New Year) and Yom Kippur (Day of Atonement), marked by a lengthy inspirational address by the rabbi and by the reading of the call for repentance by the Prophet Hosea.

Shaharis: Morning service.

Shalah monoth (or Shalah monos): Lit., "sending of portions"; the custom of exchanging gifts of cakes, sweets, and fruit on the eve of the feast of Purim.

Shavuoth: The Feast of Shavuoth (Weeks), which occurs seven weeks after the beginning of Passover. Originally, Shavuoth was a celebration of the harvesting of the first fruits; after the destruction of the Temple, tradition added to it the commemoration of the Giving of the Law on Mount Sinai.

Shaygetz: A contemptuous term for a Gentile man or boy, especially a peasant; may also be applied, sometimes humorously, to a non-observant Jew.

Shehehiyanu: Blessing that expresses thanks to the Almighty for having permitted one to live long enough to have enjoyed a festival, a new fruit, or any personal occasion of joy and happiness.

Shehinah: The Divine Presence.

Shema: Lit., "Hear"; the first word, and Hebrew name, of the prayer "Hear O Israel, the Lord is our God, the Lord is One"—the central and fundamental expression of faith among Jews, recited in the morning and evening with fervor and deep concentration.

Sh'moneh Esreh: Lit., "eighteen"; the central prayer of the Jewish service, consisting of eighteen blessings, recited silently and while standing; often referred to as the Silent Prayer. In the presence of a minyan (quorum of ten), the reader repeats the prayer aloud, reading the Kedushah ("Holy, holy, holy") responsively with the congregation after the second blessing.

Shiksa: Contemptuous term for a Gentile girl or woman, especially of peasant origin.

Shophar: Horn of a ram, or of any other kosher animal except an ox. It produces a resonant piercing blast. The shophar is blown on Rosh Hashanah (and at services during the preceding month), as a symbolic call to repentance and spiritual reawakening.

Shtetl: Yiddish for "village," "small town"; a substantial part of Eastern European Jewry lived in such small towns until World War II. The Holocaust wiped out the shtetl, and the word itself has become a symbol of the annihilated Jewish culture of Eastern Europe.

Shtibl: Lit., "small room"; a small place of worship, usually a room in the house of a Hassidic rebbe. Even larger hassidic synagogues, however, came to be called shtibl.

Shulhan Aruh: Lit., "The Prepared Table," the most popular and authoritative Code of Jewish Law, used by the Orthodox all over the world, compiled by Rabbi Joseph Caro (1488–1575). See also *Beth Joseph*.

Siddur: The daily and Sabbath prayer book, which can be used also for all religious services, including Festivals and High Holy Days.

Sidelocks (payes): Locks of hair at the temples that may not be shaved with a razor and are not even trimmed with scissors by the very pious, especially Hassidim.

Silent Prayer: See *Shemoneh Esreh*.

Simhat Torah: Lit., "rejoicing in the Law"; the holiday that marks the annual completion of the reading of the Torah, or Pentateuch.

Sukkah (pl., *sukkoth*): A temporary dwelling, a booth, with a thatched roof (in northern countries of fir branches) in which Jews eat and sometimes also sleep during the Festival of Sukkoth.

Sukkoth: The Feast of Tabernacles, festival of eight days commencing five days after Yom Kippur. Sukkoth originated as a harvest festival, but later came to serve as a commemoration of the Israelites' wandering in the desert, when, according to tradition, they lived in booths, or sukkoth.

Tallith: Prayer shawl worn by adult males, usually after marriage, generally covering the head during the more important sections of the service.

Tallith katan: Small tallith, also called "the Four Corners," poncho-like garment worn under the shirt or in lieu of a shirt, on the corners of which are knotted fringes or tzitzit as commanded by Moses (Numbers 15:37).

Talmud: The same as Gemara (*q.v.*).

Tehinah: Prayer book in Yiddish, mostly for women.

Tefillin: Phylacteries; worn on weekdays by adult males, usually during morning prayer.

Tiffereth-Bahurim: Lit., "the beauty of young men," from the proverb "The beauty of young men is in their strength" (Proverbs 20:29) Tiffereth-Bahurim was a popular young people's congregation in Vilna, with Mizrahi (Zionist) leanings.

Tikkun: Compilation of Biblical and Talmudic passages for the all-night session of study observed on the first night of the Festival of Shavuoth (*q.v.*)

Tishah B'Av: The Ninth of Av (Hebrew month around July–August); the anniversary of the destruction of both the First and the Second Temple, a fast day and an occasion of deep mourning. The Book of Lamentations (traditionally ascribed to Jeremiah) is read at services on this day.

Torah: In the stricter sense, the Pentateuch, the Five Books of Moses, the foundation stone of Jewish law and tradition; more broadly, "Torah" means learning in general, the entire corpus of Jewish law and tradition.

Tosaphists: See *Tosaphot*.

Tosaphot: Commentaries on the Talmud, critical and explanatory, by scholars in France and Germany in the twelfth to fourteenth centuries, collectively known as the Tosaphists.

Tosaphtah: A supplement to the Mishnah (*q.v.*).

Tzaddik: Holy man, saintly person. Hassidim treat their rebbe as a tzaddik and believe in the sublime power of his will, of the blessings he bestows upon them.

Tzenah U'renah: A compilation of rabbinical commentaries and legends on the Pentateuch written in Yiddish by Rabbi Jacob Ashkenazi (1550–1626). *Tzenah U'renah* literally means "Go forth and see [ye daughters of Jerusalem]" (Song of Songs 3:11).

Vilna Gaon: See *Gaon of Vilna*.

Yarmulka: Skullcap worn by Orthodox men and boys so as to have their head always covered, as a sign of piety and humility before the ever-present and all-seeing God.

Yecky(ies): Among Eastern European Jews, an abusive slang term for German and Austrian Jews, or sometimes any Jew from Western Europe.

Yeshiva: An academy of Talmudic studies.

Yizkor: Memorial service for the dead, recited on Yom Kippur and on major festivals; "Yizkor"—"May (God) remember (the soul of . . .)"—is actually the first word of the central invocation of the service.

Yohrzeit: Anniversary of a person's death, when the nearest relative or relatives recite the Kaddish for him.

Yom Tov: Lit., "good day"; general term for a holiday.

Yoreh De'ah: Famous work on the dietary laws by Rabbi Jacob ben Asher (1270–1343), who is often referred to by the title of this work.

Zivug: The true, predestined spouse intended, according to a Jewish mystical doctrine, for every given man and woman; the person one must meet and marry in order to fulfill one's destiny in this life.

Zohar: Lit., "brightness" or "splendor"; major work of the Kabbalah, that is, of the doctrine and practice of Jewish mysticism. Authorship of the *Zohar* is traditionally attributed to Rabbi Shimon bar Yohai, who lived in the second-century c.e. It is one of the holiest works of Judaism.

A Note About the Author

CHAIM GRADE, who died in 1982, was the author of numerous works of prose and poetry in Yiddish. His first prose work to be translated into English was the philosophical dialogue *My Quarrel with Hersh Rasseyner*, and among his other writings to appear in English have been the novels *The Yeshiva*, *The Agunah*, and *The Well*, and a memoir of the Holocaust, *The Seven Little Lanes*. Born in Vilna, Lithuania, in 1910, Mr. Grade came to the United States in 1948 and lived in New York City with his wife, Inna. He received many prizes and awards, including the B'nai B'rith Jewish Heritage Award for Excellence, the Morris Adler Prize of the American Academy of Jewish Research, and the Remembrance Award of the World Federation of Bergen-Belsen Associations.